FROM A HIGH PLACE

"Edward Mathis achieves a strong sense of Texas place, character, and regional speech."
The Washington Post Book World

"Mathis has a fine sense of plotting."
The Pittsburgh Press

"WONDERFUL!"
The Houston Post

"The scenery and setting details are what set this novel apart from the mainstream and will make readers await further Dan Roman mysteries."
The Miami Herald

FROM A HIGH PLACE

Edward Mathis

BALLANTINE BOOKS • NEW YORK

Library of Congress Catalog Card Number: 85-14533

ISBN 0-345-33370-5

This edition published by arrangement with Charles Scribner's Sons

Manufactured in the United States of America

First Ballantine Books Edition: July 1987

To my wife, Bonnie

1

NOBODY LIVES FOREVER. IT'S AN OLD DOG-EARED CLICHÉ, but unlike a lot of other old clichés, it springs from irrefutable truth, a specific rule of nature: we're born and we die, everything in between is simple heedless happenstance, a flick of the wand of capricious fate.

Not a popular concept, perhaps, but quite possibly an acceptable one, since each of us has at some time or other endured the buffeting winds of an indifferent fate, confronted ubiquitous death in one of its many devious fashions.

In thirty-six years of living I had made the grim encounter more times than I wanted to remember, more times than any man should. And each time I had lost something of myself, had grown incrementally more vulnerable. The icy-breathed gray specter is a plunderer without conscience, a sneak thief and a cheat.

And now, once again, death had reached out its clammy fingers and touched me, made me a loser in a race I hadn't known I was running.

"Is it her, Mr. Roman?" He had a remarkably deep voice for such a small man. Standing no more than five-

1

six in high-heeled western boots, thin as a ballpoint pen, Sheriff Leon Tolkin would never have made the height/weight requirements of his own department had he not been elected.

Silently, I handed him the photograph and stepped away from the gurney. He took my place and tilted the picture to the light, his small, quick eyes darting back and forth from the snapshot to the bloodless face with the softly curved lips that still retained a faint synthetic color. His head dipped perfunctorily, then bobbed up and down.

"Yessir, I'd say that's your girl all right." He turned back to me, his pointed features bunched. "You agree with that?"

"Yes," I said. "But if you want to confirm it there's a small banana-shaped scar on the heel of her left palm."

He grunted and gave me the photo. He turned to the girl, folded back the sheet from the naked torso, and lifted the slim left arm. The small hand drooped limply at the wrist. He took the hand in both of his and turned it carefully, almost tenderly.

"There it is," he said quietly. "That what you mean?"

I nodded without looking. I had been sure from the first moment I saw the young, impish face, the pug nose, and the sprinkle of freckles that lay now like faded spots of rust across an alabaster canvas. I had stared at that unsmiling face too many times during the three days it had taken me to find her. A seventeen-year-old face that should have been smiling, and wasn't. I couldn't help wondering why, couldn't stop the raw mixture of empathy and anger shivering through me like the echo of a sad and ancient dirge.

Tolkin placed the slender arm beneath the sheet and re-covered the body, smoothing the fabric, his thin, gnarled hand lingering for a moment on the outline of the dead girl's shoulder. He nodded at the cadaverous, bald-headed man hovering a few feet away. "Thanks, Lou. I'll get back with you in a day or two." He turned to me and sighed.

"Well, at least that's something. At least we know who she is."

"Janalle Louise Cottle," I said, speaking around the knot in my throat. "Parents divorced. She lived with her mother in Dallas. She was on her way to visit her father in Chattanooga. She had been spending some time with her grandparents in a small town called Butler Wells in southeast Texas. They put her on a bus for Chattanooga, and they're the ones who hired me when she didn't show up on time."

He nodded and led the way back through the waiting room of the funeral home. An open casket, banked with flowers, backlighted in a soft, unearthly glow, sat on a raised platform inside a room aptly called the Slumber Room. A knot of people stood looking down at what I presumed to be the remains of a loved one. But maybe not, nobody was crying.

Outside it was still a bright, windless day, late October cool, the small, wooded park at the end of the street a shimmering tapestry of yellows and browns and reds, the last blush of life before the final icy edge of winter.

A sour taste welled into my throat; death was everywhere, all you had to do was look.

"What do you think of our little town?" Sheriff Tolkin and I angled across the street toward his office, a rectangular one-storied building made out of concrete blocks painted yellow that was a half-block away.

"Seems like a nice place," I said. "It's quiet enough."

"Weekday. Wait'll Friday night and Saturday. Boys

3

from The Brick Factory get their pay. Wouldn't know the place. It gets right hectic.'' We reached the sidewalk and strolled past a pizza parlor, a men's clothing store, and a bicycle shop. At each place Sheriff Tolkin rapped on the window and waved. An old lady crossing the street down at the corner shrilled a greeting and waved wildly. Sheriff Tolkin waved back. From the other corner a yellow and tan hound loped lazily into the park where stoic old-timers in faded overalls survived the empty days, chewing tobacco and killing grass with their amber discharges.

I lit a cigarette to help fight the bad taste in my mouth. We passed a nondescript building with a faded sign naming it the Bricksburg Courier. Sheriff Tolkin picked up a thin paper from a rack by the door and tapped on the window. He waved and held up the paper and made a writing motion. I assumed he was adding it to his tab. He tucked the folded paper under his arm.

We came to a stop beside my pickup. I took the data sheet that Mrs. Beatrice Cottle had given me out of my inside jacket pocket and gave it to him.

"You'll find both parents' addresses and telephone numbers on there," I said. "I suspect her mother will want the body returned to Dallas. She had custody of the girl."

He nodded slowly, folded the paper again with his thin fingers, and stuffed it into his pants pocket. He took a small step forward and held out his hand.

"Appreciate your help, Mr. Roman. Probably never would have found out who she was if you hadn't come along. Sent her prints off to the FBI, but I didn't expect much. She's too young to have much of a record, I reckon."

I released his hand and opened the door of my pickup. "I doubt it. She was pretty steady according to her grand-

4

parents. A little wild at times, impulsive, but then, who isn't?''

I climbed into the truck, and he stepped off the curb and stood near the open window. "You'll be heading back to Big D, I expect."

"Back to Butler Wells," I said, "I own some land near there. But I won't be leaving until morning. I haven't slept in over thirty-six hours. I noticed a motel coming into town. I think I'll sack out for a few hours and hit it early tomorrow."

He frowned slightly and glanced at his watch. "Almost supper time. You're welcome to spend the night at my place. The old lady can always add another plate, dump another slice of ham in the frying pan."

"Thanks," I said. "I appreciate the offer, but I had a hamburger out on the highway. What I need more than anything is sleep. I'm afraid I wouldn't be very good company."

"You're more than welcome," he said heartily, backing a step away as I started the motor.

"I know. Thanks again."

He stepped back to the curb and watched while I backed out into the street and drove off. A tough old coot past his prime. A grown man locked for all his days inside the body of a teen-ager. I wondered how he pictured himself, if the badge and the hat and the big gun strapped to the slender waist made him feel as big as the next man. Probably. Maybe size, like beauty, is only in the mind of the beholder.

I was up and out on the highway before daylight the next morning. A few miles out of Memphis I picked up a small convoy of eighteen-wheelers heading for Dallas and points west. I tucked my pickup into their slipstream, driving the speed limit when they did, easing up when they deemed it safe to do so. A hundred miles or so east of Dallas I had to peel off for gas and a pit stop, but we had made good time, and it was still light enough to drive without lights when I pulled into the driveway of Ben and Beatrice Cottle's small frame house in Butler Wells.

As I had halfway expected, they were gone. A hunchbacked old man I didn't know tottered to the edge of the porch next door and told me there had been a death in the family, that they would be gone for a few days.

I thanked him, feeling a small rush of relief along with a twinge of guilt. I went back to my pickup and wrote out a check for the two hundred dollars they had forced on me the day I began looking for their granddaughter. I ripped a page out of my notebook and left a note of condolence, then folded it around the check and dropped both through the mail slot in the door.

Like most Social Security pensioners they weren't exactly living the high life, and while I had in a sense discharged my obligation to them, it wasn't the kind of case I wanted to accept their money for. I had offered my services gratis in the beginning, pathetically grateful for something to do after a week alone in my cabin, faced with the eternity of another week stretching before me.

But they would have none of that, and so I had lied like a trooper, told them I charged fifty dollars a day, carefully avoiding the skeptical glint in Ben Cottle's sharp old eyes. He clearly hadn't believed me, but sometimes pride is forced to bend to the exigencies of reality, and he had settled for insisting that I accept a four-day advance.

Maybe they would cash the check and maybe they wouldn't. I had long ago quit trying to second-guess people when there was money involved, even a small amount such as this. The cynic in me automatically assumed they would; some ragged remnant of long-lost naiveté hoped they wouldn't. But maybe to judge them wouldn't be fair. Two hundred dollars didn't mean a lot to me, to them it might well represent the difference between dog food and hamburger meat for the coming winter.

Feeling defeated again I drove through the deepening twilight toward my cabin. The sky was torn with ragged clouds stained crimson, and light fell from house windows in butter-yellow slabs, the night itself a penumbral glow, swelling and darkening like a living, growing organism. I felt drained, and the dread of one more lonely night haunted me like a bad memory.

2

It was completely dark by the time I reached the cabin. I sat for a moment and let the car headlights wash across the sturdy, rustic structure. I stared at the peeled spruce logs from Colorado and hand-worked, East Texas cedar shakes. It had taken my father and me the better part of one summer to build it, sweating through the long summer days, working sometimes into the night by the light of Coleman lanterns. It had been hard work, manhandling the logs, driving number-ten spikes, striking the heavy rafter beams, work replete with blisters and mashed thumbs, an occasional oath that slipped out and drew only a companionable grin instead of a rebuke. Men doing men's work. There was something satisfying about building one's own shelter, something basic and primeval.

It was the first time my father sought my advice, the first time I learned that he was a secret drinker. Despite that, despite the grueling hours and hard labor, it was the finest summer vacation of my life.

Two moderate-sized rooms and a bath, furnished for the most part with giveaway furniture, it was neither elegant nor pretentious. Instead, it was solid and weathertight, homey and comfortable, exactly suited for its intended function as a vacation/hunting cabin.

Inside, I found one lonely can of beer in the refrigerator. No bacon, no eggs for breakfast, nothing at all to eat except one curling piece of brown bologna and a tattered slice of cheese. No milk, and one stale heel in the breadbox.

I opened the can of beer and sat down on the couch. I ate the slab of cheese and just sat there for a while drinking and dreading the drive back to town. I thought of all the stores I had blithely passed on my way home and wondered if life was much easier for people who were organized— and smart.

I finished my beer and was ripping the cellophane from my last pack of cigarettes when I saw the car lights flash across the small picture window at the front of the cabin.

From where I sat I could see the last thirty or forty feet of the gravel driveway, and I put away my wallet and rose reluctantly to my feet. I lit a cigarette and watched a small foreign-made car drift to a stop beside my pickup, its lone occupant sitting rigidly erect in the shadow cast by the dusk-to-dawn light.

I caught a silhouette glimpse of a thin, sharp nose, fist-sized lump at the back of the head, and decided my visitor was a woman. An old woman.

I got up and went to the door. I opened it and stood sideways in the doorway, a welcoming gesture recognized by country folk everywhere.

"Come on in," I said in my most cordial tone.

The car door snapped open. "Why, thank you, Daniel, I do believe I will." It was a high-pitched nasal voice with a lot of carrying power. I recognized it right off the bat.

"Well, doggone if it ain't—isn't Mrs. Boggs!" I gingerly squeezed her thin, long-fingered hand, my voice sickening with the false cheerfulness we all seem to exude when encountering one of the ancient ones, particularly one who has had some influence on our lives, whether good or bad.

Mrs. Ethel Boggs had been my English teacher for four, interminable years, an ancient one even then by our youthful yardstick, stern and dedicated, unyielding in her lonely battle against sloth, boorishness, and bad grammar. But never unfair.

"I'm pleased to see that you are still so articulate, Daniel," she said, smiling faintly, shyly, the artificial perfection of her teeth startling against the sun-browned maze of a time-ravaged face. I got her seated in my best chair before I answered.

"It just comes natural," I said. "I ain't been working on it none."

She laughed, a high, dry cackle. She nervously fingered the single strand of pearls that she had always worn in class on Mondays, Wednesdays, and Fridays for as long as I could remember. On Tuesdays and Thursdays she had worn an Indian necklace of brilliant turquoise with an icicle-shaped pendant designed to define cleavage. On Mrs. Boggs it had swung unimpeded, lain forlornly on the narrow expanse of her flat bosom.

I wondered why I remembered that, wondered why, after all these years, she had come to see me.

"Could I get you something, Mrs. Boggs? A Coke, maybe—sorry, I don't drink coffee so I don't think I have any. But I have Cokes, orange juice, and I think some grape juice if it hasn't gone bad."

Her birdlike gray eyes flicked around the room, came to

rest on the chest that did double duty as a bar. She pursed her mouth and frowned.

"Is that whiskey I see there on the chest, Daniel?"

"Yes, ma'am, it is. You see, sometimes I have visitors—"

"Well, then just a touch, if you don't mind. I find that spirits are an excellent antidote for insomnia. You'll find that out, young man, when you get older."

"I already have," I said, going into the kitchen for ice cubes and glasses.

"No more than two fingers, please."

"Fine. The only mixes I have are the orange juice and Cokes I told you about—"

"Oh, on the rocks will be fine, thank you." I heard a heavy sigh. "I like your cabin, Daniel. Didn't you and your father build this while you were still in school?"

"Yes, ma'am, we did."

"My, this is nice enough to live in all the time. Up here on the hill I'll bet you can see the entire valley. Are those the lights of downtown Butler Wells I see through the window?"

"Most of them." I handed her the drink. "The ones to the south are the lake shore developments." I sat down on the sofa across from her. I tasted my bourbon. She drank half of hers, then sighed again.

"It's certainly not the same little city we used to know, Daniel. I don't for the life of me know where they all come from, but we have almost doubled our population in the last twenty years." She sampled her drink again and either smiled briefly or grimaced, it was hard to tell which. "We have so many . . . riffraff, I suppose you could call them."

"Damyankees," I said solemnly. "They've just opened

the doors in Dallas. Just letting them come in willy-nilly, letting them live anywhere.''

She gave me a sharp look, then wagged her finger and smiled—a little coyly, I thought. ''You're teasing me, Daniel. I'd almost forgotten what a tease you were.''

''Cutup,'' I said, ''and roustabout. And, oh, sometimes you put ''disturbing influence'' on my note when you sent me to the principal's office.''

She giggled, a tinkling girlish sound as incongruous coming out of that seamed face as a fog horn in Arizona. She wagged her head ruefully and finished her drink.

''Those were the good old days,'' she said wistfully, gently swishing her ice cubes around in her glass, running her free hand across her temple and onto the sleek cap of white hair that ended in a tight chignon at the nape of her neck. Her eyes moistened, and she smiled warmly. ''Do you ever feel the urge to come back to Butler Wells to live, Daniel?''

''No, can't say I do.''

''You'd be surprised at how many of my old students have,'' she said. ''The ones from around your time. Nostalgia, I suppose. They come home to visit and then they leave. And the first thing you know they're back to stay.'' She swished her ice cubes again. ''They seem so lost, somehow, disillusioned, cynical.'' The ice cubes rattled.

''A little more bourbon, Mrs. Boggs?''

''Oh, my, no—well, just a tad. Not nearly so much as you gave me before.''

I nodded and poured two fingers. ''How's your husband doing, Mrs. Boggs?''

She made a muffled sound and I turned to look at her.

Her face had changed color, the smile a frozen carica-
ture. One hand clutched spasmodically at her pearls, the
other trembled at her cheek.

"Mrs. Boggs?" I took a step forward, alarmed.

"You don't know," she said, her voice muted and
somehow plaintive. Then she shook her head. "No, of
course you don't. You've been in Tennessee. Bea Cottle
told me she had hired you to find Janelle. I talked to her
just before she left for Dallas for the funeral. She advised
me to come and see you about Mr. Boggs—"

"Mr. Boggs?" I cut into the flow of her words. "What
about him?"

"Mr. Boggs is dead, son," she said, her tone kindly,
the way she might have told me about the death of my
father. I dredged around in my memory and came up with
a short, gray-haired, distinguished-looking man who had
had something to do with city government.

"I'm very sorry to hear that." I took another step, wondering if she still wanted the drink. She leaned forward and
took it out of my hand. She nodded her thanks, tasted it,
then looked up at me, her eyes moist again, dark and remote.

"You must think I'm terrible, sitting here chatting and
laughing, having spirits, and poor Mr. Boggs just into the
ground."

"No, of course not. We all handle death in different—"

"They say it was an accident, but that just isn't possible
and that's why Bea Cottle advised me to come up here and
see you, Daniel."

"What kind of accident, Mrs. Boggs?"

She took a drink and shuddered, whether from memory
or the whiskey I couldn't tell. "A fall, of all things. Of all
the ways there are for people to get killed, a fall from a
high place is the one thing that would never in this world

13

have happened to Ardell P. Boggs.'' She punctuated her declaration with an emphatic nod. Then she looked at me and smiled slyly. ''But they wouldn't know that, would they?''

''They?''

''Well . . . perhaps he, or she. Whoever pushed or threw poor Mr. Boggs over Scales Bluff. It would have been easy, you know. He only weighed a hundred and twenty-five pounds.'' Her eyes sought mine again. ''You remember Scales Bluff, Daniel? It's only a quarter of a mile from our house.''

I nodded and sat down. I recalled Scales Bluff, but I didn't remember where she lived in relation to it.

''Let's go back a little. Why do you feel it would be so unlikely for him to fall from the bluff?''

''Not unlikely, Daniel. Impossible. Mr. Boggs suffers— suffered from acrophobia. He was afflicted even before we were married. It was such a nuisance at times. If there was a ladder to be climbed to prune a tree or paint an eave, it was I who always had to do it. Standing on a chair and changing a light bulb was all the poor dear could manage. And at times, not even that. Looking suddenly over the railing on our porch sometimes brought on an attack of vertigo. He hated the new library because the front entrance was so high. He made arrangements with Mrs. Jalesco to go in and out by the rear entrance. He would never in this life have gone anywhere near Scales Bluff of his own accord. The very thought would have made him ill, and he would have fainted before he came anywhere near the edge.''

''I didn't know that,'' I said, a light going off in my head. Ardell Boggs had been the assistant librarian.

''Not many people did. He went to great lengths to keep people from finding out. He was ashamed. As silly as that may seem to us, he felt it made him less a man." She was silent for a moment, her ravaged face thoughtful. "And perhaps it did. We are seldom more than we consider ourselves to be." Having delivered that philosophical gem, she tossed off the rest of her drink, placed the glass firmly on the table beside her chair.

"How about the police? Have you talked to them?"

"Yes. On several occasions. I went directly to the Chief himself, Chief Chandler—"

"Chandler? Not Webb Chandler?"

"Yes. I'm sure you remember—of course you do. He was in your class if memory serves."

"Yes. We went through all twelve grades together. I didn't know he was back in Butler Wells, though. The last I heard he was a cop somewhere in California."

"He's been our chief of police for three years, Daniel." She shook her head and clucked. "You should get into town more often, stay abreast of things"

I nodded agreement. "What did Webb have to say?"

She squinted up at me, her eyes slightly out of kilter. "About what?"

"About your theory that Mr. Boggs couldn't possibly have fallen."

"It isn't a theory, young man. It's a fact. And that's what I told Chief Chandler."

"And what did he say?"

"Oh, he listened politely and nodded a few times and told me how sorry he was, and then he asked me who in the world would want to harm poor Mr. Boggs and for what reason? I couldn't answer him, of course, not with any degree of certainty, but I did remind him that there are people in this world who don't need a reason to kill. People who are crazy, people who are driven. My goodness, I read it in the papers all the time. People who kill other people just for fun, or because they hear voices.'' She drew her crossed ankles back beneath her chair and smoothed the duncolored fabric of the simple nylon dress. ''And then I told him the other reason Mr. Boggs would never in this world have walked out to that bluff. Not even if his acrophobia had suddenly been miraculously cured.'' Hands folded neatly in her lap, she cocked her sleek head at me, a ghost of a smile and eyes like splinters of gray ice.

''What?''

''Snakes,'' she said succinctly. ''That strip of ground between the road and the edge of the cliff is full of snakes. The city is supposed to keep it mowed and cleaned out, but they don't do it by any means. There's rocks and blackberry vines and tangles of brambles all along there. Mr. Boggs was scared to death of snakes. Not as much as he was of heights, but almost. And so am I. That's why when we took our walks we always went south toward the marina. We never walked north up the hill to the bluff. Nobody lives up that way anymore since that bunch of hippies burned down the old Bowart place. I heard the kids were bickering over the land and had it tied up in the courts. No telling how—''

''What did Webb say to the snakes?''

''He was sympathetic, I reckon. He said he'd see that the city got out there and cleaned out that strip. But I'll have to see it first before—''

''No, ma'am. I mean what did Webb say about the snakes with regard to Mr. Boggs walking over to the cliff?''

''He never said anything at all that I recall. I saw him up there on the bluff the next day wearing boots and kicking around in the blackberry vines. I don't know if he saw any snakes or not. And that's not really the point. Mr. Boggs and I *believed* there were snakes there whether

16

they were or not. And that was enough to keep us on our side of the road where people keep the weeds mowed out behind their fences. We have a right pretty view of the lake from our back porch. We didn't need to get any closer than that.'' She reached out and idly ran a finger around the rim of her glass, flicked it gently with a long shiny nail.

I ignored this. It was either that or end up driving her home. I wasn't all that sure I wouldn't have to anyway. But maybe not. She obviously had more than a nodding acquaintance with the hard stuff and, except for that one unfocused second, was handling it pretty well.

I watched the gray-green eyes for a moment, opened wide and staring past me into decades of vanished time, scores of failed chances. It was hard to visualize her as a dewy-eyed young innocent burning with a holy zeal to cure the ignorance of the world. By the time I had come into her tender mercies she was already old and bitter and disillusioned, settling for discipline instead of perfection, demanding compliance with the twin furies of scorn and ridicule.

I hadn't much liked her as a teacher, but I had respected the hell out of her.

"When did it happen, Mrs. Boggs, what time of day?"

She blinked and looked at me with suddenly vacant eyes. She nodded. "In the evening. At dusk or shortly after dark. He was taking his nightly walk."

"You said a while ago that you took your walks together. You weren't with him that night?"

She made a negative movement with her hand. "No, I was . . . indisposed. I suffer from arthritis and sometimes—" She bit it off and shook her head suddenly, the blankness gone out of her eyes. "I won't lie to you, Daniel. I was . . . I was smashed. I occasionally drink a little

17

too much. It just seems easier to drink sometimes than to think . . . to remember . . .'' Her voice, dry and husky-harsh, trailed off fitfully.

"I can buy that," I said.

"I woke up sometime during the night—the early morning hours, actually. He was not in the bed, not in the house at all. I went outside and looked, even walked a short distance down the road toward the marina. Then I became frightened, panicky. I called my son in Buffalo. He came and brought his two boys. I called Chief Chandler. He came with one of his officers. They found him along about daybreak. My two grandsons saw him from the top of the bluff. He was lying among the rocks in the shallow water.'' Her voice was dry and dispassionate, in control as always, but the long slender fingers were clenched white in her lap, pressed tightly between her thighs to keep them from trembling.

I suddenly had a visceral feeling of empathy, an unsettling premonition of how it must be to be old and afraid and alone.

I cleared my throat. I was trying to think of something compassionate to say when she dropped the second shoe.

"Poor Chief Chandler. He looked so distraught, so genuinely upset over Mr. Boggs's death. But perhaps it was just that having two deaths in such a short time, and one of them his best friend—'' She broke off and gave me a quick glance. "But I don't suppose you know about that, either. About Clay Garland.''

"Clay Garland?'' I echoed mechanically as a creeping chill ran down between my shoulder blades. "What about him?''

"He shot himself,'' she said quietly, sadly. "And I must say I'm not terribly surprised. He never did adjust to being in that wheelchair. He was always such an active boy, so physical—''

"Wheelchair? I didn't know he was sick. I saw him maybe five or six years ago down at the courthouse. He certainly looked fit then, brown as a nut and hard as hickory."

"It wasn't sickness. He was in an automobile accident three—no, almost four years ago. His spinal cord was injured—severed some said—although I never did hear the straight of it from anyone in the family. Melissa is about the only one who comes into Butler Wells nowadays. She's such a sweet girl, but I never had the opportunity to discuss Clay's accident with her." She clucked her tongue, her eyes drifting toward my makeshift bar. She sighed. "Poor Melissa. With all her good fortune I somehow feel she has had an unhappy life. A rich, handsome husband, all that money, and a beautiful young daughter. You'd think that would be enough to make anyone happy."

"Not necessarily," I said.

"If you ask me, I don't think she ever fully recovered from that terrible accident. It was a terrible, terrible thing to experience."

"She was injured?"

"Oh, no, not Melissa herself. It was the other car, the Schumachers'. That poor woman and her two children." She paused and looked at me, waiting.

"What happened?"

"They were killed. Burned to death. It was out on Stanton Road where it runs along beside that little creek. You know, where—"

"I know where you mean. Was it Melissa's fault?"

"Oh, no, Clay was driving their car, and as it turned out it was April Schumacher's fault. But just being involved, seeing those poor people burn—" She broke off and shuddered. "I'm sure it would have marked me for life. Poor Melissa."

Melissa Arenson, now Melissa Garland. The mismatch of the century, I thought. First me, then Webb Chandler, then Clay Garland. A poor third choice. But maybe not so surprising after all. Clay Garland was *the* rich man's son, Walter Garland being by far the wealthiest man in Butler Wells, if not in Tulliver County. The first day of our freshman year Clay Garland had driven to school in a spanking new apple-red convertible Buick. I hated his guts. It wasn't until our junior year, when he became one of the Infallible Four, that I began to tolerate him at all.

"Mr. Boggs was a British Commando, you know." Her voice knifed into my thoughts like a wind-driven bough scratching a window.

"I never knew that," I said.

"Few people did. He didn't like to talk about it, to remember those terrible days."

I tried to filter the picture of the man I remembered through the framework of the British forces I had seen in Vietnam. Well, maybe things had changed some since WW II.

"Will you take my case, Daniel?" Her voice had regained its nasal crispness, some of its volume. "Bea Cottle told me you charged fifty dollars a day." She paused and seemed to wince. "I can assure you that I am capable of meeting your fee."

"Mrs. Boggs," I said, then stopped, fumbling for a cigarette, stalling to find the right words. I got the cigarette going, avoiding her eyes. "I honestly don't think I can do any—look, Webb Chandler is a fair and honest man. I'm sure of that. I haven't seen him for sixteen or seventeen years, but people don't change, not really. He's in a position to help you. He must have known your husband—"

"No," she interrupted quietly. "He didn't know my husband. No one in this town really knew him. They saw him as a little man in a little job. Assistant Librarian. He never even made Head Librarian. People knew his name, yes. They called him by name when they met him on the street. Always Mr. Boggs. Never Ardell or Ardie. Not more than a handful of people knew that he could quote the Bible from cover to cover, that he could recite verbatim the entire works of Keats and Shelley and Longfellow and Shakespeare—"

"Mrs. Boggs," I said. "I'll tell you what I will do. I'll talk to Webb in the morning. I may have to leave tomorrow, but that much I'll promise. We won't talk about money because I'd like to see Webb anyway, and I wouldn't feel right accepting your money for just talking to an old friend. Okay?"

She nodded primly, her wrinkled lips in a tight, austere line. "I'd be much obliged, Daniel. And don't think I'm needing charity. Mr. Boggs was a canny man. He left me with more than enough for my needs." She rose to her feet, as thin as a reed, but square-shouldered beneath the cloth of her short poplin jacket.

"No charity involved," I said. "If I'd have known Webb was back, I'd have been to see him long before this." I walked her to the door. "Are you sure you feel up to driving home? I mean that lane of mine is pretty rutted—"

Her ghostly smile came back, a hint of humor or maybe cynicism in the gray-green eyes.

"Don't fret, young man. It takes more than a couple of shots to put me under the table."

21

"Okay," I said, watching her walk a straight, if slightly unsteady, line to her car.

Truly one of the ancient ones.

She opened the car door and turned toward me again, her face in shadow. "I didn't have a chance to tell you back then, but I was sorry about your father, Daniel."

"It was a long time ago," I said, wondering what her version would be. I had been a Viet Cong prisoner of war at the time, and when I finally returned I had heard a half-dozen different accounts of his death. However, all the stories had agreed in two aspects; he had frozen to death not thirty feet from where I stood, and he had been drunk at the time. Which blows the old aphorism that God takes care of fools, little children, and drunks; by that time he was more than a little of all three.

"At the time I couldn't understand how a man could so hate life that he would just lie down and die. I believe I can understand it now."

"It wasn't only that," I said. "He was drunk."

"That's what I mean."

She lowered herself carefully into the little car and bounced down the dusty hill, taillights flitting like fireflies in a fog. She reached the blacktop in record time, made the turn and accelerated, the small motor singing like an angry hornet.

No one could have done it better.

I sat for a while digesting what she had told me, thinking about her meek and self-effacing husband, the town, old classmates, the early life and times of stalwart Dan Roman, defender of freedom and truth, honor, and the right to pursue relentlessly, if ineptly and unsuccessfully, unwary members of the opposite sex.

After a time my stomach rumbled in protest and I snorted the furry smell of sweet nostalgia out of my nostrils, climbed into my pickup, and followed Mrs. Boggs's tracks into downtown Butler Wells.

3

Like most small Texas towns that also happen to be the seat of county government, Butler Wells had its very own courthouse. Slightly less than a hundred years old, its original off-white quarry stone had mellowed over the years to a melancholy gray.

Studded with gnarled post oak, pine, and towering elm, the courthouse square had once been the heart of the city's downtown business district. It was still there, but the businesses had for the most part moved west to the mall on the Interstate. Even the stolid, dependable old Roxy Theater advertised CLOSED on its marquee and invited erstwhile customers to the new Roxy Twin at the mall.

Same old urban flight, I thought, slowly making the square, counting an even dozen vacant store fronts, glassy-eyed and glumly reflecting the lights of my pickup. At least four more than the last time I had taken the downtown tour. A few of the older, established businesses still hung on grimly, either too tired or too stubborn to follow the trend to the highway.

And yet, here and there, attempts at refurbishment had been made: a jewelry store with a bright facade of glass

24

brick and tinted plate glass; a music and computer store with a new stone false front; a brightly lit restaurant featuring home-style cooking that sported a gleaming new face of tan brick and redwood; and a detached clothing store that had obviously been torn down and rebuilt along modern lines.

All of my old hangouts were gone. Clyde Beatty's drugstore and Ice Cream Parlor at the corner of Main and Crescent had succumbed a long time ago, outgunned by the twin forces of the Mall Pharmacy and the shiny new Dairy Queen with its soft ice cream and expanse of black-top parking where the younger set could show off their latest four-wheeled acquisitions. Gino's Pool Emporium was now a bicycle and lawnmower repair shop, and old Paul Whistler's ENCO station on the northeast corner of the square had been converted into a prosperous-looking real estate agency.

To my adolescent mind the square had been the essence of sophistication, a place for Friday night cruising, a place for seeing and being seen, a place of furtive assignations with wet sticky kisses and warm submissive flesh the ultimate goal. Except for one memorable night, it had never paid off for me. But, like most teenagers, I had been blessed with boundless energy and the many failures did little to dampen my enthusiasm.

Changes. As city dwellers we learn to accept them in our daily lives, are only vaguely aware of the shifting shapes around us as the metropolitan giants fill up the holes, creep endlessly outward, absorbing the countryside. But, for some reason, those of us who come from small towns expect to find things the way we left them, and find change, good or bad, strangely disquieting.

At the southwest corner of the square I turned right, moving west again along a narrow curving street that doubled as a farm-to-market road and would eventually take me within a half mile of my cabin.

Traffic ran from thin to nonexistent. It was bedtime in Butler Wells. What night life there was would be concentrated around the mall, the movie theaters, the fast food restaurants, the dimly lit honky-tonks huddled along the service road just outside the city limits.

The town slipped by around me, hallmarks of my youth leaping out of the uncertain darkness into the swath cut by my headlights, disappearing, leaving a residue of prickling memories like cactus barbs beneath the skin: the red-brick high school where I had spent some of the worst and best moments of my life; the small city park with its oversized swimming pool and its undersized bandstand, beneath which, during my sophomore year, I had finally understood the delightful difference between boys and girls about which my friends and I had been lying for years.

Melissa Arenson. Bright, intense Melissa. Beautiful Melissa, desire finally overwhelming fear in her wide dark eyes, deft fingers and murmuring lips urging me on, guiding me into the realm of an early manhood I wasn't capable of handling. It had been she who had held me afterwards, soothing my very unmanly terror at the enormity of what we had done, the possible appalling consequences.

It had not been the first time for me. Some of the younger hands on my father's ranch had attended to that on an overnight trip to a Fort Worth rodeo a few months before. But that had been a casual cash transaction, and I had been beer-drunk enough not to remember exactly what had happened, sometimes found myself wondering if in fact anything had happened at all. In some respects that encounter had the vague inconsistency of a pleasant dream, something that occurred a long time ago with someone not quite real.

But Melissa was real. She was there the next day, and the next, and pride of conquest faltered beneath the twin specters of guilt and shame, and the grim possibility of pregnancy.

But nothing happened, and by the time I got over my scare school was out for the year and she had gone to visit her grandparents in Houston. When school resumed in the fall she started dating Webb Chandler, our varsity quarterback and my best friend, and, as far as I could remember, I had never been alone with her again. Not that I didn't try.

I clattered across the railroad tracks where I'd first encountered violent death. Three classmates the night of the senior prom, racing a high-balling freight to the crossing, seeking a fleeting moment of glory, ended up dying in a fiery blaze of it.

Since that night I've seen a lot of dead bodies, but never any that affected me in exactly the same way. In the winking of an eye I discovered that death was not reserved solely for the old, the feeble, the sick. I felt the sour, hoary breath of vulnerability, and life was never again the same. I began to sense limits to time and space and freedom, an invisible barrier just beyond the perimeter of my perceptions. And along with an ineffable sadness came a growing conviction that I was not quite what I, and others, presumed me to be. I had stature and strength and the respect of my peers, and, if the Saturday morning quarterbacks were to be believed, I was the best broken field runner the Butler Wells Catamounts had ever had. But it wasn't enough; maybe at that age nothing ever is.

I followed a chugging eighteen-wheeler to the top of the Interstate overpass, sat smoking while he waited for a left-turn break in the oncoming traffic. Off to my right the dark waters of Cannonball Lake wound sinuously through a ragged patchwork of lake development prop-erties. From mobile homes to condominiums worth well over a hundred thousand dollars each, the twelve-mile strip of the southern shore that belonged to the town was rapidly disappearing beneath the onslaught of bulldozer, hammer, and saw.

It was said that these new residents accounted for more than half the town's taxes and at least two-thirds of the population growth over the last ten years. Retirees mostly, nice old folks who had fought long and bitterly and unsuc-cessfully the city's crafty maneuvers to annex them into the fold. Understandably irritated at such unseemly ingrat-itude, the city fathers had wielded the long whip of prop-erty assessment against them. As a result Butler Wells now had a spanking new fifty-bed hospital and a junior high school under construction in a picturesque pecan grove near the north edge of town.

Maybe it's still possible to fight city hall and win. But not in a small Texas town. And especially not if you're a bunch of damyankees from up around north Texas.

I made a stop at Elmer Duchin's combination conven-ience store and gas station near the western city limits. I bought enough food for my evening meal and breakfast, planning to be on my way home before lunch.

I wasted a few minutes listening to Elmer bitch about the government's encroachment into the lives of the small businessman, that damn Republican Governor wanting to double the cigarette tax, and the damn fool weekenders buzzing around the lake spoiling the crappie fishing.

As I was leaving, a middle-aged man and a teenage boy came in. The boy was a slender yet muscular youth in his mid-teens, with blue eyes and dark brown hair worn mod-erately long. I held the door for them and the boy nodded his thanks and gave me a quick, friendly smile, his face aglow with the simple pleasure of living.

I drove the rest of the way to the cabin trying to remember how it had felt to be that young, that carefree, that good-looking. I finally decided I never had.

4

THE BUTLER WELLS POLICE DEPARTMENT WAS STILL where it had always been on the first floor of the courthouse. It wasn't a large room, but then it wasn't a large police force either. In my heyday there had been a working Police Chief named Horace Dumwiddie and three additional officers.

A big splay-footed man with an immense belly and acne scars, Chief Dumwiddie had possessed a seemingly endless capacity for forbearance when it came to the youth of the town. We had striven to make his life miserable in our innocent adolescent way, but beyond a gruff fatherly lecture and an occasional kick in the ass, he had rarely retaliated in any meaningful way.

Long dead from a heart attack, he had pleasantly colored my image of what a police officer should be and may have contributed, subliminally at least, to my choice of that profession as a career.

The room appeared to have been freshly painted. Sunflower yellow. Venetian blinds draped the tall windows and a half-dozen sand-colored metal desks were grouped neatly in the center portion of the room. Along one wall a cork bulletin board the size of a schoolroom blackboard was festooned with evil-looking mug shots, telex flimsies, and various memoranda, some of them yellowed and curling with age. One corner of the room had been partitioned with waist-high plywood panels topped with translucent Plexiglas. A somewhat superfluous sign reading COMMUNICATIONS dangled over the open doorway.

A young woman with short, blonde hair sat slouched before a modern-looking communication console inside the enclosure. She wore the silver and gray uniform of the Butler Wells Police and looked unutterably bored. An open magazine lay on the narrow ledge in front of her and she raised cool green eyes to watch my approach, her face as blank and unreadable as a Nixon Halloween mask.

I stuck my head around the door. "Looking for Chief Chandler," I said.

She stared at me silently for a moment, then raised a slender rounded arm and pointed at the tip of my left shoulder.

"See that door over there with the sign painted on the glass? It's C-h-i-e-f. That spells Chief. I'll bet if you opened that door chances are you'd find him. What do you think?"

I glanced over my left shoulder, then turned back to her and nodded. "So it does. The only thing is the last time I was in here that door opened on a couple of small jail cells where they took people and beat them bloody with rubber truncheons—that's a club—made out of old truck tires." I leaned against the doorjamb and took out my cigarettes and lighter.

She returned my nod without appreciable change in expression. "That was before my time. We use oak batons now and we've moved the cells to the basement. It's

31

soundproofed. You'd be surprised how much it cuts down on the noise." Eyes glinting, she watched me light up, then pointed to a NO SMOKING sign on the wall behind her.

"I've always wondered," she said. "Is it difficult going through life not being able to read?"

I barked a reluctant laugh and retreated, weaving my way through the clutch of empty desks, leaving a defiant trail of smoke and wondering about this new generation of world-weary cynics, our future world leaders, coldly logical and blase, desensitized by TV violence, X-rated movies, and the bomb. A disproportionate number of them seemed to be wiseasses, a wretched condition I attributed directly to a loss of wonder, a lack of imagination, and an active contempt for anyone over thirty.

But the testy young lady officer had been right about one thing: Chief Webb Chandler was on the other side of the door marked Chief.

He too appeared to be reading, booted feet holding down one corner of a battered wooden desk, matching swivel chair shoved back against the wall, the big blunt-fingered hands holding a strange-looking magazine loosely propped on a waistline that seemed no thicker than it had at eighteen. A thatch of brown hair liberally streaked with gray curved across his wide forehead. His eyes were closed, the well-formed mouth pursed in a soundless whistle of surprise or shock. Or maybe he was snoring; but if he was I couldn't hear it.

I rattled the doorknob and closed the door loudly. He snapped awake without moving, the dark blue eyes momentarily dazed, unfocused, staring at me without comprehension, no sign of recognition.

I grinned and faked a move to the left, went to my right and leaped more-or-less gracefully off the floor and snagged an imaginary ball and tucked it into my side, bobbing and weaving—

He yelled, the magazine flying, boot heels cracking on asphalt tile as he hurled himself around the desk, long arms widespread, face red and beaming.

"You sonuvabitch!" he bellowed, catching my shoulders, propelling me into a bearish embrace, pinning my arms against creaking and groaning ribs.

"I love you, too," I said shakily, "but what'll people say?"

He pushed me back to arms' length, hands biting into my shoulder caps. "Goddamn! You old no-good bastard. Christ, you don't know how many times I've thought of you since high school!" His eyes were moist and for one terrifying instant I believed he might kiss me.

He shook me instead, then dropped his hands and grinned unabashedly. "You can see I still get carried away sometimes." He took a step away. "And I can see you're still old Demonstrative Dan, the stoic of Butler Wells High."

"It's a failing," I admitted, "but I don't have all that many that I want to give up one."

He laughed. A little too loudly, as if he hadn't laughed much lately. He bustled around behind his desk. He picked up the magazine and dropped it on the desk, then shoved his padded chair around to me.

"Here, use this. I'll get one out of the squad room. I don't keep a visitor's chair. Discourages loitering." He laughed again and went out the door.

I reached across and picked up the magazine.

Pulp. Dated January, 1936. A cover layout of a hunched figure in a swirling black cape, black hat, and a mask. Two huge black automatics spouted flame from the folds of the cape, and a bloated, baldheaded oriental wielding a scimitar three feet long reeled away from a trussed-up, flaxon-haired woman with impossible thighs and breasts. A large black spider dangled companionably near the masked man's head.

Webb came through the door pushing a swivel chair, a large glass ashtray in one hand.

"I see your taste in literature has improved some," I said. "The last thing I remember seeing you read had lots of pictures and came through the mail in a plain brown wrapper."

He grinned and nodded. He gave me the ashtray and moved his chair a few feet away. "Pulps. Thirties and forties. I found three big boxes full of the things in our attic after Dad died. The Spider and The Shadow, Black Mask, Doc Savage, Spicy Adventure, Spicy Detective—Christ, there must be fifteen, sixteen hundred of them."

"Sexy?"

"Naw. Lots of half-moon globes, alabaster thighs, pearly bosoms, stuff like that. Sunday school stuff by today's standards. But the thing is, it's action without all the other crap. Richard Wentworth—that's the Spider, is probably my favorite. He finds out some asshole needs killing, he goes out and blows the scud away. Simple stuff; earthy."

I tossed the magazine on the desk. "Not the kind of thing you'd fall asleep over."

He grinned again and shook his head. "The last few days have been real pissers." The grin faded. "I don't know if you've heard or not, but an old friend of ours has committed suicide. Do you remember—oh, hell, of course you do. Clay Garland."

I nodded. "Yes, I heard about it."

He sighed. "And then there was Mr. Ardell Boggs. You might not remember him, but you'll remember his wife—"

"She came to see me," I said.

He stared at me, his eyebrows bunched. "Came to see you," he echoed inanely. "In Dallas?"

"No. I was at the cabin."

"You mean she came visiting, or . . ." He let it trail off, a hint of annoyance in his dark blue eyes.

"Or," I said. "She doesn't believe her husband fell off Scales Bluff. She makes a pretty good case."

"You mean the acrophobia thing? I couldn't substantiate that, Dan. None of his neighbors or friends knew anything about it. Dr. Lew Ragen. He's been Boggs's doctor for years. He didn't know anything about it, either."

"He was ashamed of it."

"I know. She told me that, too. But I find it hard to believe he could live in a town this small and have nobody know anything about it except his wife. It's not a shameful disease. A lot of people have phobias."

"He thought it was."

He rolled wide shoulders in a shrug. "I guess."

"How about the snakes? Are there snakes along the top of the bluff?"

"I'm sure there probably are. Some. I didn't find any when I went out and kicked around, but that doesn't mean anything. They hole up and you never see them. But they're not crawling all over the place like she seems to think. And she's right, I wouldn't want to go strolling through there without boots on, particularly at night. There are paths where fishermen go back in there sometimes. And teenagers. They congregate there all the time. Once you get through the thicket there's a pretty wide open area. The kids go there to drink beer and make out. Nobody's ever been bitten that I've heard about." He chuckled suddenly,

35

a broad smile brightening his solemn face. "At least by snakes."

"How about the autopsy?"

He nodded slowly. "Lew Ragen's the county coroner. He did the autopsy himself. He said Boggs evidently went over headfirst into the rocks. Broke his neck and smashed in his skull pretty good. You've probably noticed the lake's down about seven or eight feet. Otherwise, he probably would have survived the fall. He may have drowned, but at least he wouldn't have opened his head on the rocks."

"Any water in his lungs?"

"No. There was some in his throat and mouth, but Doc Ragen figured that came from wave action. He was lying on his back in about ten inches of water."

"No water? That doesn't surprise you?"

"No, not really. Death had to be instantaneous. If you'd seen his head, you'd know what I mean."

"You'd think he would have taken at least one more breath, reflex action if nothing else."

He grinned crookedly. "You're thinking he could have been dead when he went over."

"It seems like a possibility."

He sighed and shook his head, his square face sobering. "I know where you're coming from. She almost had me convinced, too. I found myself thinking about a mad killer roaming around Butler Wells, killing seventy-five-year-old men." He paused, the lopsided smile returning. "And thinking in terms of murder finally brought me around to the most logical suspect." His eyes glinted with a sardonic humor, the smile broadening into a grin.

"Mrs. Boggs herself," I said.

He chortled and slapped his thigh. "Exactly. You're still quick on your feet, Dan'l."

"You don't really think—"

"Of course not. Boggs talked to Emil Prescott, his next door neighbor, around six o'clock. He was just starting his nightly stroll down toward the marina. He mentioned to Emil that Mrs. Boggs was abed with the vapors, which meant to everyone who knew them that she was probably passed out in her bed. Everyone in the neighborhood knows she drinks, but like decent upright folks, they ignore it. Anyhow, you can't keep something like that secret in a town this size. She began when she retired and kept working at it until she's become a lush."

"Boggs leave any insurance to speak of?"

"Burial policy and a five-thousand-dollar paid-up life policy he evidently had for years."

"What's your best guess, Webb? Did he walk over that cliff?"

He spread his big hands and shrugged eloquently. "A guess is what it would have to be. I know it's hard to swallow if she isn't exaggerating about the acrophobia. But people that old have lapses. Maybe he forgot he was afraid, maybe became disoriented, turned around and went the wrong way and ended up on the bluff. It's anybody's guess, Dan. But there's one thing we haven't talked about."

"Suicide," I said.

He nodded soberly. "I guess I really believe that's the most likely possibility of all. Life wasn't easy for the old boy. He had health problems, his wife's drinking which he hated, the fact that he was probably a homosexual—"

"How do you know that?"

He looked past me toward the window, his broad face screwed up into a grimace. "I probably shouldn't tell you this, Dan, and I wouldn't if I didn't know it wouldn't go any farther." He stopped, heavy eyebrows bunched inquisitively.

I nodded. "You've got my word."

He leaned back in the swivel chair and crossed his legs. "Almost three years ago. Right after I became Chief, we had a clerk in the County Treasurer's office run off with a bundle of money. Not a hell of a lot—five thousand or so. But come to find out she had a record in Dallas, had even done a little time for fraud. Naturally, the city fathers were highly incensed and decided in all their wisdom that we had to run a check on all city employees. A real check, background, FBI, the whole bit. Boggs was still working at the library, and it turned out he had been arrested a couple of times. Three times, to be exact. Twice in Houston, suspicion of sodomy. Once in Dallas for the same offense. He had been fined in all three cases. I thought about it for a while, then lost the sheet. I had a chat with him, suggested it was high time he was retiring. He was about five years overdue. He agreed, but I had the feeling that knowing I knew did something to him. Maybe I should have handled it some other way. Hell, I don't know. It seemed the right thing at the time."

"You think Mrs. Boggs knew?"

"I don't know. I don't have any way of knowing without asking her. I'm not about to do that." He locked his fingers together and rocked gently in the chair, his expression pained. "She's hungup on the idea that somebody did him in. Maybe that's easier to accept than the thought of suicide."

"I imagine it would be."

He sighed again, a heavy sound of unfeigned exasperation. "I worked at it, Dan. Put aside all my preconceived notions of accidental death and suicide and tried to find just one thing that would hint murder. There's nothing.

Granted, I'm a small-time cop in a small town, but I worked homicides in Frisco the last two years I was there and I know a little something about it."

I lit a cigarette and puffed a ball of smoke at him. "I don't want to come right out and ask you why you came back here, so why don't you volunteer to tell me."

He laughed. "Subtlety never was your long suit." He rubbed his chin and squinted reflectively. "Three things, I guess. Frisco is a weird town full of weird people and weird politics. A lot of gamesmanship going on in the cops. I never could find the right asses to kiss, I guess. It took me eight years to make sergeant and get into the detectives. Luckily, I landed in homicide. I never had to work vice, by God. That was a nightmare."

"Pretty much the same everywhere."

He nodded. "Secondly, I got a divorce about four years ago."

"Kids?"

"No. I had a stepson. He was eight when I married her. Too old to ever see me as a father. We were two natural enemies living under the same roof, vying for the attention and love of the female of the house. It lasted seven years, the last three of which were miserable." He followed the intricate design on his boot top with one long blunt finger, his eyes clouded with recollections of painful times.

"You said three things," I prodded gently after a while.

He stared at me vacantly for a moment, then the broad boyish smile returned. "Nostalgia, I reckon. That's as close as I can come to the way I felt. I wanted to see real people again, talk about something besides crime and corruption and the homosexual problem. I wanted to see a prairie, shoot me an eight pointer in the fall. I wanted to catch crappie in the spring, string a trotline for catfish, eat some real honest-to-gosh chili.'' He paused, stroking his long straight nose thoughtfully. "I wanted to see a working oil well again, banging away out in somebody's field, surrounded by white face or Black Angus. . . . I wanted to hold hands after a movie with some down-home kind of girl, sweet and innocent.''

"By golly," I said. "I never would have thought it. You couldn't wait to get away from this hick town. What happened to law school, the White Knight riding to the rescue of the disadvantaged, the downtrodden, the falsely accused?''

"The same thing that happened to your aspirations to be a jet pilot hero.''

"I got a part of that, at least," I said. "I flew helicopters in 'Nam.''

"I got a part of the law, too," he said. "The asshole.''

We laughed together. I stubbed out my last cigarette and pushed to my feet. "Would you get pissed at me if I poked around a little, talked to a few people?''

He frowned, a perplexed look crossing his face. "You mean about Boggs?''

I nodded.

He came to his feet. "Hell no! Nose around all you want. Maybe you can convince the old . . . girl that we don't have a homicidal maniac roaming around. I can't seem to get through to her. But then I never impressed her much as a student, either. You probably don't know this because I didn't notice it at the time, but you were one of her favorites. You read everything in sight and that impressed her. And she thought you were witty.''

"If that's so, I sure as hell would have hated to be on her shit list. She sent me to the principal on an average of once a week.''

"She came down on you because she knew you could have done so much better, and it exasperated her. You loafed along with the rest of us dum-dums and that broke her heart."

"How the hell do you know so much about it?"

"She told me. A year or so ago. She came in Watkin's Cafeteria and sat down and ate lunch with me. We talked for a couple of hours about the old days. She teared up a time or two. Funny thing was, I enjoyed the hell out of it. She knew a lot about what had happened to you and some of the other kids we went to school with. I found out she isn't such an old harridan after all. She was the one who told me six months or so ago that you had quit the cops and gone private."

I stared at him, dumbfounded. "Christ, she must have a direct pipeline to God. I hadn't been in this area since that happened until a couple of months ago."

He smiled and nodded. "It seems one of her old students is a captain with the Midway City force—"

"Homer Sellers," I said grimly. "Old big mouth himself. He graduated the year before you and I started high school. He and his dad moved to Dallas so he could go to SMU. Only thing he likes better than eating is gossiping."

Webb rubbed a hand along his jaw, his eyes thoughtful. "Sellers. He played ball. I remember seeing his picture in the trophy case in the gym. Big mother."

"Yeah, they were something like 1–9 at the end of the season. That was his team we inherited."

He slapped me on the biceps, then slipped his arm across my shoulders as I moved toward the door. "The Infallible Four," he said. "By God, we showed their asses."

"Yeah," I said. "Two years and acres of pain, but we

41

showed their asses.'' I turned to look at him, grinning. ''Was it really worth it?''

He nodded solemnly, his eyes moist again. ''Yeah,'' he said gruffly. ''It damn sure was.'' He cleared his throat. ''It's the only thing I ever did in my life that somebody cheered.''

5

I THOUGHT ABOUT WHAT WEBB HAD SAID WHILE I DROVE across town to the library. They had indeed cheered us, screamed their throats raw under the crisp autumn skies, screamed with savage joy and exultation: fierce ritualistic incantations as young warriors ripped and tore at each other in the name of honor and victory. It was heady stuff to hear hundreds of voices chanting your name, to have strangers want to shake your hand, little kids want to touch you.

It had not always been thus. At the end of our freshman season the Butler Wells Catamounts had finished second from the bottom in the rankings. On a good Friday night we might have a hundred fans in the bleachers. Our sophomore year wasn't much better. We finished fifth from the bottom. That was the year a *Gentryville Courier* sports writer named Daniel Roman, Webb Chandler, Clay Garland, and Zeke Fairlee the Fallible Four. We were all sophomores, all backs, and were catching from a senior quarterback named Clive Wells. Almost catching, that is.

Clive Wells was undoubtedly the worst quarterback in

the history of Texas high school football, and we weren't doing a lot to make him look any better. But his father was the local banker, a member of the city council, and the president of the chamber of commerce. Coach Reuben Stallis was a practical man. He farmed a marginal three hundred and twenty acres during the off season and frequently found it necessary to tap the till at the bank for operating expenses. It was said that as long as Clive was in high school and played at being quarterback, Reuben Stallis received his yearly loan at a remarkably low rate of interest.

But time has a way of moving on and bringing changes. Clive Wells graduated. Webb Chandler moved into the quarterback position and I became a nervous fullback. With Clay and Zeke as wide receivers, the offensive line beefed up with a matched set of two-hundred-and-ten-pound brothers transferred in from Waco, we figured we had a fighting chance at winning a game or two.

We won the first five going away.

With the Hudson brothers breaking trail and Webb's machinelike, precision delivery, I discovered I had capabilities that hadn't been apparent as a wide receiver. I had body strength and good moves and I could hit and run. Not the fastest back around, I had to rely on agility and timing and muscle.

By the sixth game, a home game, Webb was calling his own plays and the bleachers were filled to overflowing. Everybody loves a winner and the town caught fire.

Snooky Windell, owner, editor, and chief reporter for the *Butler Wells Bulletin* dug out the old article from the *Gentryville Courier*, ran it on the front page, added a few derisive comments relative to the gender of the Gentryville Warriors, and renamed Clay and Webb and Zeke and me the Infallible Four in bold blackface type.

The other members of the team weren't exactly ecstatic, but we were winners, we were kicking ass for the first time in our ball-playing careers, for the first time in Butler Wells history. There was more than enough glory to go around. Friday night heroes, we modestly accepted the adulation of the masses while we boxed groceries, made deliveries, and mowed lawns on Saturday.

Webb led us into the regional playoffs that year. Sure-footed as a cat, the eye of an eagle, the arm of a young Atlas was the way Snooky Windell put it in one of his more subtle articles. We were nosed out in the second game of the playoffs 21–20 by Gentryville, our legendary nemesis.

The last year, our senior year, we were undefeated in the regular season. Our offensive line was bigger, stronger, and had experience. Webb couldn't seem to miss and my running game had never been better. Zeke and Clay made catches that became legends and the Hudson brothers allowed only a dozen or so quarterback sacks the entire season.

We went into the playoffs riding a gigantic wave of confidence, the entire town howling at our backs. We lost the state championship in our division by two points, a field goal in the last ten seconds that we had to stand and watch drift lazily end-over-end through the uprights.

I remembered Miss Imogene Jalesco well. A short, stocky, middle-aged lady even then, she had found delight in my voracious appetite for the written word, and since I lived a few miles out of town she had fractured the rules a little and allowed me to take home as many books as I could comfortably carry. A spinster with a heart-shaped baby face and a sweet disposition, she seemed awed by my seemingly endless capacity and what must have appeared to her a grim determination to consume the contents of the well-stocked little library from cover to cover.

She had weathered time well. Even though she was well into her late sixties, her face was still round and full, the passed years chronicled only by the web of fine lines at her mouth and the edges of her sparkling cerulean eyes. Spectacles still swung atop her ample bosom from a chain around her neck, and once-black hair that had faded to a dull gray swept back severely from her face, ending in a tightly wound ball at the nape of her neck. She wore a simple peasant blouse and skirt and sensible black shoes.

She recognized me almost at once, with a quick glance and then a startled double take as she came out of the stacks near the end of the checkout counter.

"My goodness," she said, snatching the glasses from her bosom, peering at me as I crossed the tiled floor toward her.

"Danny Roman! My goodness, I'd almost given up on ever seeing you again." She beamed at me across the polished wood, blue eyes shining fuzzily through the thick spectacles.

"Hello, Mrs. Jalesco," I said. She was a spinster, but when I was growing up everyone over thirty automatically became Mr. or Mrs., and old habits die hard. I leaned an elbow on the counter.

"You still keeping the naughty books under lock and key?"

She had a delightfully hearty laugh she used often. She used it now, her eyes darting around the room as if in search of someone to share her good fortune.

"Heavens no! I'd have to lock up half the library nowadays to do that. With Robbins and Kastle and Susann—" She broke off and made a self-deprecating gesture. "I guess

46

I'm just an old fogey. I just skip over the dirty words and . . . other things." A spot of color had appeared high on each cheek.

"So do I," I said. "You never would have found any of that dirty stuff in *The Deerslayer*, or Sherlock Holmes. Even old Zane Grey used dashes and exclamation marks."

She gave me a searching look, then evidently decided to take me at face value. She smiled and touched the small black bow at her neck. "Do you still read as much as ever, Daniel?"

"No ma'am, I don't," I admitted, suddenly realizing that the note of regret in my voice was real. "You know how it is. Too many things seem to eat up the time."

She nodded. "You're a detective now." It was a statement and not a question. "I saw you on television once. It was the time that man shot his wife and two children and tried to put it off onto the retarded boy next door. You didn't let him get away with it." Her words ended on a note of grim satisfaction. Justice and society's revenge. It was something everyone could identify with. She either didn't know or didn't want to say that the man had later gotten off on a plea of temporary insanity.

"I'm in private practice now," I said, welcoming the opportunity to get to the reason for my visit.

She nodded, unsurprised. "I know. Ethel Boggs told me when you quit the police force." She looked down, her face tightening, her fingers fussing with the electric date-stamping machine. "I suppose you've heard about poor Mr. Boggs."

"Yes," I said. "It was a terrible thing. I don't remember him very well despite all the times I came here to the library. I don't remember seeing him much."

She sighed. "No. He stayed pretty well in the background. In his office. He was in charge of purchasing new books and he spent a great deal of time reviewing in preparation for the library board meetings. That and negotiating package deals for the library. He was very good at that. He saved us a lot of money which, of course, meant more books for our money. And too, he didn't feel that he was good with people. He thought most people didn't take to him." She stopped and sighed again. "Actually he was a very warm person, a brilliant man." Her voice throbbed with sincerity, a hint of passion, and my cynical mind began pondering the possibilities of hanky-panky among the musty stacks. They had worked closely together a long, long time.

"He was so much more than anyone ever suspected," she said, the throbbing muted, her voice subdued. "Not even Ethel, I think. He came here from Europe, you know. He was an Englishman, but he spent most of his early life in France and Germany." She picked at a ragged cuticle, her eyes downcast. "He fought with Charles de Gaulle in the French underground, but he never talked about it. He was a shy, retiring man."

"He certainly seems to have lived a secluded life," I said. "I didn't know till just yesterday that the poor man suffered from acrophobia."

She nodded soberly. "That's true. He was very sensitive about it. I had an extra set of keys made for the rear entrance so he wouldn't have to climb those high steps out front. It must be terrible to have that affliction. I found him clinging to a row of shelving once, pale and trembling, sobbing. He was standing on a three-foot ladder racking some books. Three feet! Imagine that."

I shook my head in wonder. "And yet he walked off a thirty-foot cliff."

She wagged her head slowly, her small lips pursed in a

curiously defiant pucker. "Perhaps," she said, her voice oddly muted. "And perhaps it wasn't so accidental." Her head swiveled as a woman came out from the back with an armload of books. She smiled and the two women chatted while Mrs. Jalesco stamped her books.

I waited, wishing for a cigarette, wishing I was already on my way home.

"Thank you," Mrs. Jalesco said, short deft fingers filing the inventory cards as the woman clattered toward the door in blue jeans and wedgies.

I moved back up the counter. "What did you mean before? Not so accidental?"

She smiled without looking up. "You're here because of Ethel Boggs, aren't you?"

"Yes. She doesn't believe her husband fell off that cliff either."

"I think I agree with her on that, but that's as far as it goes."

"Meaning what?"

She finished filing and folded her hands on the counter. "I don't believe anyone killed Mr. Boggs the way she does . . . or pretends she does."

"You believe it was suicide then?"

"Yes. Ethel won't accept that, because to do so would mean that she would have to accept at least a part of the responsibility." She was silent for a moment, then added quietly: "Her drinking is what I mean."

"Do you have any reason to believe he might have taken his life?"

"He was distraught a lot of the time. He spent a great deal of time here even after he retired because he couldn't stand to see her drunk."

"He told you that?"

"He didn't have to. I—I knew him pretty well."

"Any enemies that you knew about, heard about, maybe?"

"No. Only himself, perhaps. With the exception of Professor Thisinger I don't think he had any friends, either. Not what you would call close friends."

"Professor Thisinger?"

She frowned thoughtfully. "Long after your time, I suppose. He came here about fifteen years ago from Los Angeles. He taught mathematics and physics. He and Mr. Boggs played chess one night a week. He is considerably younger than Mr. Boggs, but they seemed to hit it off right away."

"Happen to know where he lives?"

Her brow furrowed again. "Either directly across the street from Mr. Boggs or possibly one house over either way. I know they lived very close to each other."

"Well," I said, then turned and looked toward the front of the building. Two bedraggled-looking women herded a group of small children through the double doors.

"A visiting kindergarten class," Mrs. Jalesco said, smiling mechanically, waving at the group. "I'll be right with you," she called out.

"I'll be going," I said. "It was good seeing you again."

She smiled and nodded, seemed to hesitate, then said, "I'm not at all sure what you're doing is a good thing, Daniel. The dead are dead. You can only hurt the living."

"It works that way sometimes. Sometimes it helps."

She pressed her pudgy hands flat on the countertop, her blue eyes fuzzy again behind the glasses. "Is it so important then, this search for truth?"

"Yes," I said. "It's all we've got."

She reached across and patted my arm. "Come and see

50

me again when you can." She moved away down the counter.

"I will," I promised. But I wasn't at all sure she heard me above the chatter of the children.

6

PROFESSOR THISINGER'S HOUSE WAS MEDIUM SIZED. ONE story. Originally a frame, all exposed wood had been covered with shiny, brown metal siding artificially grained to simulate wood. Built in a time when land was dirt cheap in comparison to building costs, the builder had compensated for no-frills architecture by surrounding the structure with at least an acre of tree-studded ground.

A low concrete-slab front porch was bounded with wrought-iron rail and an obviously new concrete ramp extended a dozen feet out onto the front walk. The yard was untidy, threadbare in spots, and stippled with bits of trash.The grass was long and yellowed and curling.

I punched a button immediately below an orange and black sign reading NO SOLICITORS and wondered about the concrete ramp. Ramps usually indicated a wheelchair. Since it was a relatively new ramp and Mrs. Jalesco had intimated that Thisinger lived alone, the logical assumption was that he occupied a wheelchair.

Having made that shrewd deduction, I wasn't at all surprised when the door opened and I stood looking down at a baldheaded, bearded man in a wheelchair. A big man, judging from the depth and breadth of his torso, the long jeans-clad legs that looked full and strong and perfectably usable.

He watched me without speaking, dark eyes glinting beneath the wildest set of eyebrows I had seen since I had shaken hands with Congressman Jim Wright.

"Professor Thisinger?"

He stared at me for a moment longer, then slowly shook his head. "No. Mr. Thisinger, maybe, even David Thisinger, or hey you. But not professor. I am not now, nor have I ever been, a professor."

"Okay," I said agreeably. "Mr. Thisinger. My name is Dan Roman. I'm—"

"Wait." He held up a wide palm, a flash of white coming through the thick mat of hair that extended from his upper lip to six inches below his chin. Unlike his lawn, it was neatly clipped. "Since I assume you can read, I must assume that you're not a salesman. At any rate, salesmen don't dress like you. Offhand I'd say cop, except that I know all the Butler Wells cops. That leaves state and federal, but they don't usually dress like you either. So, my best guess would be the health department. Some asshole in the neighborhood is complaining about my property again. Right?"

"Actually, you're pretty close. I'm a brain surgeon with the health department. After the third warning comes a lobotomy. I came around to check you over, take measurements, and like that."

For a long second I thought I had made a mistake, misread as humor the soft burr in his voice that might have been something else altogether. The gleaming eyes almost hidden in their deep sockets seemed to glare balefully, the broad face beneath its mask of hair unreadable.

Then he blinked and slammed the arm of his wheelchair

and bellowed a laugh. "Brain surgeon! By damn, I like that!" He leaned forward and flipped the latch on the rusty screendoor. "Come on in, Dan Roman, whatever you are." He pressed a button on the side of the chair arm and hummed busily backward.

I closed the door and took his extended hand. It was dry and cool, one quick hard squeeze and gone, the smile flashing again, amusement still bunching the flesh beneath his eyes.

"I'm a private investigator," I said.

He gave me a pleased look. "I wasn't far wrong then. That mean you used to be a cop?"

I told him I had and he buzzed through a wide archway into a sparsely furnished room with worn hardwood floors and yellowed cracking paper on the walls. He motioned toward an old-fashioned, brass-studded, thin-armed sofa covered with a wiry brown material that looked scratchy. A matching chair sat at right angles to the sofa and a high-backed wooden rocker with a pad occupied one corner of the small room.

"Used to be the parlor," Thisinger said. "Useless as tits on a boar hog. One good thing, it's handy to the kitchen." He made a small half-circle with the wheelchair, nudged it backward into the wall by the rocker. Then, smiling a little at my look of surprise, he rose from the wheelchair and stepped to the doorway that led to the kitchen.

"Cup of coffee? Just made it fresh this morning."

"No thanks."

"A beer then? Or maybe a Coke?"

"I'm fine, thanks."

"Have a seat, Mr. Roman. I'll just have my midmorning hit of caffeine."

I picked the chair because of the large glass ashtray on the end table beside it. I took out my cigarettes and got one going, listening to the rattle of cup and saucer and the clink of a stirring spoon. He appeared moments later, moving with the slow measured cadence of a man walking on ice. He sat back down in the wheelchair and balanced his mug of coffee on the wide wooden arm.

"You're wondering about the wheelchair," he said matter-of-factly. He produced a pack of cigarettes and a disposable lighter. "Practice, Mr. Roman. Preparation for what is coming in the not-so-distant future. Not distant at all, as a matter of fact. I find myself using it more and more all the time. Walking brings pain and riding does not. It's as simple as that." He lit the cigarette and sucked smoke greedily. "First one today."

"I'm sorry to hear that . . . about the wheelchair, I mean."

His teeth gleamed briefly through the mat of hair. He shrugged. "Why should you be?" he asked mildly. "We've never met before. You have no interest in my future and I have none in yours. We humans are a curious lot, Mr. Roman. We're programmed from day one to react to specified data in a certain way. We respond automatically by mouthing platitudes at the first sign—"

"Okay," I said. "I don't give a damn about you and your wheelchair."

He chuckled genially and lifted his coffee cup in a salute of sorts before bringing it to his mouth. He watched me over its edge, his eyes as shiny as brown marbles.

"You're here about Ardell Boggs," he said after a moment, the ends of his moustache glistening wetly.

"Why do you think that?"

He shrugged again. "It figures. I'm his friend, his only friend in this town as far as that goes. I'm aware that his wife believes he was killed and that she came to see you. I know you talked to Mrs. Jalesco."

"You know a lot for a man in a wheelchair."

He gave me a wry look. "There's nothing mysterious about it. Mrs. Jalesco called. She said you might come by."

I nodded. "The official version is death by accident. Mrs. Boggs believes, or professes to believe, that he was murdered. Mrs. Jalesco favors suicide, as does Webb Chandler unofficially. They all seem to have their reasons. You were his friend, what do you think?"

"What I do not think," Thisinger said promptly, "is that he took his own life. It's an absurdity, particularly in view of the way he died."

"You mean the acrophobia and the snakes?"

He frowned. "I don't know what you're talking about. Acrophobia? Snakes?"

"He suffered from acrophobia, fear of heights. And he was deathly afraid of snakes. Mrs. Boggs said he wouldn't go near the cliff because of snakes along the top and his fear of heights."

Thisinger shook his head impatiently. "I don't know anything about fear of heights or snakes. He never mentioned either. I'm talking about common sense. A thirty-foot jump, even onto rocks, is no guarantee of death. What it might guarantee is a broken body and a cast for the rest of your life. Ardie Boggs was far too smart to do something as stupid as that. Too smart and too thorough. If he had wanted to die, he would have found a dozen better ways to do it than jumping off a ledge. He was a very cautious, meticulous man. He would not have left anything to chance. A careful bullet in the brain would have been his style." He stopped, his face closed as if the boundaries of his universe had suddenly shriveled. "But he would not do even that. He enjoyed life too much."

"How was his health? And wasn't he upset much of the time about his wife's drinking?"

"He was as healthy as a man can be at seventy-five, and his wife's drinking bothered him very little. Most of the time he simply ignored it. At other times it seemed to amuse him."

"That leaves murder or accident."

He took a drink of coffee, grimaced, then dropped his half-smoked cigarette into the cup. He leaned over and placed the cup on the floor beside the chair. He stroked his impressive beard, staring at me thoughtfully.

"I would have to rule out accident for some of the same reasons as suicide. He was much too prudent to expose himself to danger needlessly. Walking along an unlighted bluff after dark would certainly indicate a degree of carelessness. Not to mention the probable presence of snakes as you pointed out. No. I can't accept that premise any more than the one that has him doing a swan dive over the edge."

"You're a mathematician," I said. "I don't have to tell you that two from three leaves one."

"Murder," he said, his voice as hollow as an echo.

"Can you accept that premise?"

"More than the others," he barked, his brow furrowed with the sudden irritation of a long-suffering teacher with a particularly obtuse student.

"An old man," I said. "An inoffensive little old man of seventy-five. Who could possibly want to harm him?" I hadn't meant it to sound disparaging, but Thisinger was bristling, and I realized belatedly that he must be in his late sixties and probably thought of himself as an old man, though certainly not little.

"What does age have to do with it?" he snapped.

"Nothing . . . probably," I said. "Mrs. Boggs thinks

57

he may have been the victim of some wandering killer; a stranger murder. Someone who gets his or her kicks killing people."

He snorted. "Nonsense. Ethel Boggs's brains are only a fifth of bourbon away from being permanently pickled. Real life to her is what she sees on TV and through the bottom of a bottle. She has no conception of what her husband was really like, the life he led before they married, the life he was leading right under her nose." His own nose, thin and hawkish, seemed to compress at the tip, pull in toward his mouth.

"And you did," I said gently.

His mouth closed, tightened, disappeared behind the salt and pepper bush. "Some of it," he said tightly. "Enough to know that the Friday nights he spent in Dallas weren't for the reason she thought, the reason he gave her. I happen to know—" He bit it off, his face closing down again. I had a distinct feeling I was about to lose him.

I nodded and busied myself lighting another cigarette. I huffed a stream of smoke in his direction and smiled. "She seemed to accept the Friday nights," I lied, forcing a chuckle. "After all, boys will be boys."

The tangles of hair above his eyes shot upward. "Is that what she thought?" He made a sound somewhere between derision and contempt. "Typical woman. Jesus H. Christ. Ardie was way past that kind of thing."

"I don't know," I said doubtfully. "She seemed to think he had a kind of . . . well, obsession about the Friday nights."

"Hell yes, he had an obsession! The same one he had when they got married. She just never took the time or trouble to discover what it was, to help him with it. She thought his interest in the holocaust was nothing but a hobby, something to while away the time in the musty stacks at the library. She treated the whole thing with a sort of amused tolerance. He was haunted by his past and she dismissed it with platitudes about putting it all behind him, beginning a new life. Bullshit! He was obsessed with guilt because he survived and his family didn't—along with six million others.''

"Boggs," I said, feeling an old familiar cold place between my shoulder blades. "That's not—"

"Jewish," Thisinger finished for me. "No. He was half Jew. His father was an Englishman, his mother a German Jew. He was born in England but he spent almost all of his childhood years and early manhood in Germany and the other countries of Europe. His father was a civil engineer, a bridge builder, and they moved about quite a lot. When Hitler came to power they were back in Germany, in Berlin. Ardie worked for the government and his father was still building bridges. Like most of the Jews and near-Jews of that time and place, they closed their eyes to what was going on around them.'' He sighed, the dark, recessed eyes sadly contemplative as though he were suddenly confronted with his own mortality.

"They were English citizens," I suggested after a while just to get him talking again.

"Yes," he said morosely. "And that in part led to their undoing. It gave them a false sense of security, kept them there far beyond the bounds of common sense. Ardie had lost his job with the government, but he was working for one of his uncles, his mother's eldest brother, in the garment industry. His father was away, working on a project in Poland. Jewish registration was well under way and the star of David began to appear on Jewish chests. There were rumors of 'resettlement cities,' quotas, nationalization of certain industries. Jews quietly began to disappear. Jewish businessmen were terrorized, their business ravaged, burned, bombed. And still Ardie and his family hung on, trying to locate his father, hoping the madness would somehow go away.'' His voice dwindled away, and it occurred to me for the first time that he too was Jewish, and I began to wonder what part the holocaust might have played in his own life.

He expelled his breath in a gusty sigh. "As you may have surmised, they waited too long. Ardie's father never returned from Poland. He never found out why. The government seized his uncle's business, posted his entire family of fourteen people for resettlement. Ardie protested, of course, citing his immediate family's English citizenship. It made no difference to the S.S. They were Jews. Their origins had no significance in the grand scheme of things. Ardie managed to contact the man he had worked for in government, a fairly high official who had tried to keep him from getting fired in the first place. The official promised to see what he could do. Two days later Ardie and his family were herded into cattle cars and shipped off to the camps. He was separated from his mother and two sisters and never saw them again. When they reached the camp, Belsen, I believe it was, a German officer with a clipboard went down the line of people, calling out his name. The official in Berlin had managed to help him after all. He had sold them on Ardie's organizational genius. The Germans were a thrifty people. They didn't throw away what they could use. To cut the story short, Ardie was assigned to the Camp Commandant's office, given the chore of organizing the camp's accounting procedures. A method to account for everything from inmate's gold inlays to shoelaces to dead bodies. Somehow, he managed to close his mind to what the figures he worked with represented. He set up the system to the best of his ability, which was considerable. The Germans were so pleased they shipped him off to another camp, and eventually another. During the years of the late thirties and early forties he worked at almost every major concentration camp the Germans had in operation. He told me he made himself into a zombie, convinced his conscious mind that what he was doing was no more sinister than the inventories he had controlled for the government and his uncle's business.'' He stopped and looked at me with a slightly deranged grin, eyebrows high over glittering brown eyes.

"He was doing something else," he said gutterally, his voice high with passion. "Doing it almost subliminally." He paused, then went on, his voice at normal volume. "Boggs had total recall—eidetic imagery—and was almost subconsciously committing to memory each of the German faces he came in contact with at the camps, guards as well as administrative personnel. The names also, but that didn't mean much as things turned out. They changed their names after the war. They couldn't do a lot about their faces. Not enough to fool Boggs's eye, at least." He paused to light a cigarette, his gaze burning at me over the dancing flame.

"And so," I prompted.

"And so." He exhaled a gusty balloon of smoke. "And so after the war he became a Nazi hunter."

7

"THE ORGANIZATION HE BELONGED TO IS CALLED WWNF, World Wide Nazi Find. It's comprised primarily of survivors of the death camps with a smattering of sons and daughters and even grandchildren they can call on for muscle and certain strenuous activities they are no longer capable of doing." Thisinger combed slender fingers through an imaginary thatch of hair on his shining pate, hesitated, then patted his round head fitfully as though irritated to find the hair missing.

"They are a small cell in an organization that exists in every free nation around the world, and in some that are not so free. That is where Ardell Boggs spent most of his Friday nights. He also belonged to a Dallas—Fort Worth writers' club, which happened to meet on Friday evenings. That's where Ethel thought he spent his time. It was a natural cover. He was writing a historical novel set in Germany during the thirties and early forties, the time of Hitler." He stopped and smiled. "He had actually written around three hundred pages, and it wasn't half bad. It's conceivable that he may have made a pretty fair novelist if he had given it a third the time and energy he gave to

WWNF. But he was a driven man. I think that he and the other survivors of the camps expected some cataclysmic upheaval after the war, a gigantic uproar of world condemnation of the Nazis. What they got, about all they got, were the Nuremberg trials in 1945 and 1946, the conviction and execution of fewer Nazis than the victims of one gassing in one shower room in one camp. Time passed and the world wanted to forget, but Boggs could not forget, would not let himself forget.''

"Butler Wells, Texas," I said. "It seems an unlikely place for a Nazi hunter."

He shook his head impatiently. "Where he lived didn't matter. Boggs's function in the organization was an integral one, but one he could perform anywhere he happened to be. He made identifications. Usually from a photo in the beginning, sometimes in person. He would fit a name and a place to a face. If there was doubt, a closer look would be arranged. Almost without exception the suspects would break and admit their former identity when confronted with names and dates and places."

"And then what happened?"

Thisinger smiled faintly. "I asked him that question. He said he didn't know for certain. He pointed out the case of Stefan Welte who was returned a few years ago to West Germany to stand trial as a war criminal. Boggs made that identification. But Welte was one of the bigger fish. Most of the big fish have already been fried or are floating around South America. WWNF has been concentrating mainly on the lower echelon bastards, the SS super jocks and the guards, the sadists who got their kicks on a one-to-one basis with the prisoners, the rapists and sodomites who killed with boots and clubs and bayonets instead of gas."

"Then you think his death could be connected to his Nazi hunting?"

His eyebrows came together in one solid bushy line, a row of sardonic V's crawling up his forehead. "It would have a certain irony."

"I know, but do you believe it?"

"As much as a swan dive or a careless step over a cliff." His voice was sharp with defiant aggressiveness.

"Why? Admittedly what you've told me is interesting, even surprising, but I don't see the seeds of murder in it anywhere." I took out a cigarette, deliberately holding his eyes with mine. "Unless, of course, you haven't told me everything."

"That's right," he said flatly. "I haven't told you everything." He stopped to watch me light the cigarette, looking as smug as a TV evangelist at a porno book burning.

I nodded absently and waited, letting the silence work on him, crossing my legs and studying the pattern of holes in my cigarette.

"Nothing definite," he said reluctantly, disgruntled that I hadn't made a run at his hook. "Just an overall impression I got when he came back from Dallas last Saturday. He was on a high, as high as I've ever seen him. The kind of high one associates with drugs. But Boggs didn't take drugs. He came by late in the day—something he did quite often—and we began a game of chess. But he was too hyper to play. We settled in the den with vodka gimlets and a couple of good cigars he had brought back from Dallas. I set about trying to find out what was giving him such a rush. He was evasive, uncharacteristically so. Vodka usually loosened his tongue, and after several drinks I maneuvered the conversation back around to his trip to Dallas. He simply smiled and said something to the effect that I and the whole of Butler Wells would be knocked on its ear in a few days. Later, as he was leaving, he muttered a few more words. I didn't get it all, but it sounded like: ". . . bastard . . . something . . . right under our . . . something . . . noses."

"A Nazi," I suggested. "Right here under our noses?"

He shrugged. "That's the conclusion I came to."

"If that were so, why wouldn't he have recognized him sooner?"

He shrugged again. "Maybe one he had never seen. He certainly couldn't have seen them all. There were something like twenty-four major camps with dozens of smaller ancillary work camps throughout the entire system."

"Makes a kind of crazy sense," I said. "And has the appeal of a classic—hunted becomes the hunter, and all that."

He gave me a look compounded of one part petulance and three parts irascibility, one big thumb stroking the skin under an eye that looked as smooth as the hollow of an old salt block.

"Just might be true," he growled.

"Might be I ought to take a look at Ardie's things," I said.

"Not today you won't. Not unless you want to break in. Ethel's gone to see her sister in Waxahachie."

"What did Webb Chandler say to all this Nazi hunting stuff?"

"Haven't talked to him," Thisinger said brusquely. "I was at the VA hospital in Houston Wednesday and Thursday. I just barely got back before Boggs's funeral. Chief Chandler hasn't been around." He hesitated. "From what I hear, his mind is already made up."

"Pretty much," I agreed. "But that doesn't mean we can't unmake it."

"You and he played ball together, I hear." His voice was back to affable again.

"Along with nine other guys," I said.

"Ardie wasn't sports minded, but he liked to brag about the Infallible Four and the time you almost won the state championship."

"We were almost infallible," I said.

"Clay Garland and Zeke Fairlee. The other two. Both leading citizens. I was sorry to hear about your friend Clay."

I nodded and stood up. I mashed out my cigarette. "I was sorry to hear it myself. We were teammates, but we were never close friends. How can you be friends with a guy who drives up in a brand new convertible Buick the first day of school?"

He chuckled and wheeled in behind me as I headed for the door.

"How do I get to the road that goes up over the bluff? I was up there when I was a kid, but we always cut across somebody's yard."

"Just stay on Scales Drive here going west. It'll curve sharply down at the foot of the slope and then fork just above Garland's Marina. The left fork goes to the marina and the right turns into the dirt road up over the bluff. You can't miss it. It's rough and rutted but you can drive it all right. Just be careful of glass. These high school kids don't much care where they throw their bottles."

I opened the front door and turned to shake hands. "Thanks. And thanks for the information."

"I trust you'll put it to good use."

I nodded and lifted my hand and went down the ramp. Nazis in Butler Wells? Not damn likely. I'd be less surprised seeing John Wayne doing the funky chicken in drag.

But what the hell did I know? I'd voted for Nixon.

* * *

The fork in the road was just where Thisinger had said it would be, around a sharp bend at the bottom of the hill. To call it a fork though was something of an exaggeration. The blacktop wound on down to the marina; the dirt road veered off to the right along the edge of the small bay. Barely more than a well-defined set of car tracks, it disappeared into sparse thickets of hardwoods that grew in intermittent clumps along the water and up the gentle slope to the back fence of the first house on Scales Drive.

Acting on impulse, I held left, let the pickup drift down the winding road to the marina parking lot. I parked beside an aging rusty Maverick and lit a cigarette. I got out and crunched through shifting creek gravel to the gangplank, trying to figure out what was different about the marina other than its name change from Scales's Marina to Garland's. I decided it looked smaller; but almost everything in Butler Wells had shrunk in size since I was eighteen. That was a matter of age and perspective, but even allowing for that, this decrepit mélange of rusty pipe and styrofoam, seamed plywood, and weeping corrugated metal seemed only half as large as it once had been.

At first glance it appeared deserted, the plate glass window of the small shop where Martin Scales had sold fishing equipment and bait dark and dirty, reflecting my indistinct image and defying attempts to peek inside.

Somewhere nearby an electric motor whined angrily, loading up, then ebbing, accompanied by slurping gurgling sounds like those of an ill-mannered giant eating soup. Water splashed on water.

I flipped my cigarette into the open lake and moved down the dock toward the sounds, the gentle roll and bob of the boats tethered in the slips creating an illusion of oscillatory movement beneath my feet.

The noise of the motor grew louder and I recognized it for what it was: a water pump transferring liquid from one point to another, the first point being the well of a boat, the second point undoubtedly the lake.

I found him in the fourth slip from the end, bailing a twenty-four-foot cruiser that had a cuddy cabin and an imitation teak deck. He looked young, a slender body in faded chinos, a black T-shirt and thin nylon windbreaker. His beard, moustache, and hairstyle were early Willie Nelson; clear blue eyes and a rust-colored headband rounded out the image. He nodded at me and smiled, then held up one finger and went back to poking into the enclosed well with a length of black hose.

The small pump, mounted on a rectangle of heavy angle iron, whined and coughed in turn, spouting intermittent bursts over the edge of the dock as his sucking probe found hidden pockets of water.

While I waited I leaned a shoulder against a round steel post, gazed at the lake, and smoked another cigarette, thinking of things both quixotic and quotidian: happier times and a somehow younger more carefree Dan Roman. The water of the lake roiled and murky from the last rain. Melissa Arenson's eyes. What I was going to have for lunch. Ardell Boggs's lonely thirty-year vendetta. The acrid stench of oil mixed with stagnant water. The heat of Melissa's lithe body in the dappled darkness beneath the bandstand. Root beer. Pearly breasts and alabaster thighs. Silence.

With a start I realized the motor had stopped, and the young man stood wiping his hands on a large checkered handkerchief. His startling blue eyes glinted with a spark of amusement; he bared his even, white teeth in a pleasantly mocking smile. The silence pressed down like mid-day August heat.

"Woolgathering," he said, stepping nimbly to the dock. "I do a lot of that myself. There's something about the water." He put away the handkerchief and held out a hand. "Jake Trumble. What can I do for you, Mr. Roman?"

I shook his hand and my head along with it. "I guess you've got me, Mr. Trumble. I don't remember meeting—"

He wagged his head and smiled wryly. "We haven't. I was in the courthouse this morning paying a ticket. The clerk saw you going down the hall and gave me a five-minute bio. Were you really as good a ballplayer as she said?"

"Probably better," I said. "Local heroes are never truly appreciated until they die."

He laughed and unzipped the windbreaker, lifted a pack of Winston's out of his T-shirt pocket. "I know what you mean. I'm from a small town myself. Tuskohee, Kentucky. Our game was basketball. We made it to the Regionals once." He held out the pack, a wistful look on his young unlined face. "I didn't think so at the time, but I guess that was the best time of my life. Everything since has been sort of anticlimactic and . . . well, kind of sorry.

I declined his Winston and took out another True. "The loss of innocence," I said gravely. "And wonder. Back then the world was well defined and secure. You were a center stage player with an adoring audience of sweet young things. You were envied by your peers, respected by your elders. You were truly alive and life reached to forever. It gets harder every year to hold onto that feeling, impossible after thirty."

"Shit, man," he said admiringly, kicking the iron post

I had leaned against. "You tell it funny, but you got it right. You too, huh?"

I shook my head dolefully. "Not at all. But I read a lot."

He laughed and jingled change in his pants pocket. "Hey, how about a Coors? I've got some in a cooler inside the office."

"Sounds good." I followed him back the way I had come, between rows of boats of all colors, shapes, and sizes, many of them personalized with cutesy names and equipped with the latest designs in sonar stalking capabilities. No longer the exclusive toys of the wealthy, or the near-wealthy, boats were rapidly becoming the status symbol of the masses, misguided souls who fantasized late evening cruises on blue-green water in their very own yacht—never mind the terrors of freeway towing, the heart-stopping expense of tune-ups and overhauls, the sad fact that boats depreciate at an accelerated rate that would make a new car dealer purple with envy. I had owned two boats in my life. Usually it only takes one, but I'm a slow learner.

Trumble disappeared inside the vacant store, reappeared almost instantly, two dripping cans of beer in one hand.

"Here we go," he said, and tossed me one. He yanked the tab and pushed it back through the hole, tilted the can, and drank thirstily.

I pulled my tab and threw it into a nearby trash barrel. I sipped my beer. The first taste was always the worst. After that it didn't seem so bitter.

"Been around here long?" I asked.

"Six months, more or less. I was hiking down to Houston and got dropped out on the Interstate. I went into that tonk called The Tiger's Eye for a beer. That's where I met Clay—Mr. Garland. He needed a good outboard mechanic it turned out, and I damn sure needed a job. I've been here ever since. I kind of manage the place for him, fix the customers' engines, sweep up, like that. At least I did. I don't know what'll happen now that the Madonna owns the place—'' He stopped, the smooth skin above the beard darkening. ''Mrs. Garland, I mean,'' he added carefully. ''I guess they're friends of yours. No disrespect intended.''

''I'm sure not,'' I said, trying to form a mental image of Melissa after eighteen years. It was hard to visualize her in Trumble's framework of a Madonna—the limber body, the piquant, lovely face—but eighteen years could have changed her in a thousand different ways, fleshed the heart-shaped face with dignity, added lushness to the willowy frame.

''He liked to talk about the old days,'' Trumble said, moving to a less contentious subject. ''Especially your high school days. Football, girls, the dumb things you guys did. The usual stuff. But it meant more to him, somehow. Maybe it was the wheelchair. He particularly liked to talk about the Invulnerable Four and your—no, that don't sound right. The Invulnerable Four? Is that right?''

''It's close enough.''

He nodded, the wistful look back on his face. ''They like to give you dumb names. They called me Jake the Rake because I stole so many balls and . . . and for some other reasons.'' He gave me a shamefaced grin. ''Hell, I'm only twenty-three and already I'm waxing nostalgic, as they say.''

''Have any idea why Clay pulled the plug?''

He sobered, squinted in concentration, and combed his grease-stained fingers through the neatly trimmed beard.

''I'm not sure. He wasn't an easy man to get to know.

71

He wasn't a very—" He broke off. "Before I put my foot in it again. Were you close friends?"

"No. To be honest I didn't like him much in high school. I haven't seen him since except a couple of times at a distance."

"Well, I don't aim to sit here and bad mouth him, but he wasn't an easy man to work for. Too picky. Too domineering and too much temper for no reason. No control. I guess being in a wheelchair could do that to you. He wasn't all that old. What? Thirty-nine or forty?"

"Thirty-six. My age."

"He looked older and you look younger than that." He took a slug of beer and gazed pensively at the label. "Misfortune can age a man, I guess."

"Maybe the odds caught up with him," I said. "He always had it wired. All the money he wanted, the new cars, and of course that meant girls. He married the prettiest girl in town not long after graduation and when he was twenty-one his dad gave him a company."

Trumble nodded sagely. "Claybar Tool and Die. Does a lot of work for Bell Helicopter and General Dynamics up at Fort Worth. Did forty-six million last year. Not bad for a town like Butler Wells."

"He tell you that?"

Trumble hooted softly. "Nope. He never talked anything but boats to me. Zeke Fairlee. You remember him?"

"Sure. Zeke and I were good buddies."

"Old Zeke is all right. You'd never know he's a wheel. He owns that cruiser I was swamping out when you came up—oh, and by the way, if you see him before I do, would you tell him he has a cracked fuel line? That transom smelled like a gas station. He needs to get Corcoran's Marina to pick it up, or I could tow it over there. I'm not equipped to handle it here."

I nodded.

He massaged the bridge of his nose, then let his tanned fingers roam through his beard. "I guess now that Clay and his dad are both gone Zeke will move into the president's job. He deserves it. He had to take enough shit off of Clay."

"Walter Garland is dead?"

"Couple of months ago—say, Clay was pretty down over that. Maybe that had something to do with his suicide. I'd never thought of that before."

"Could be," I said. I drank the rest of my beer and dumped the can in the barrel. "You ever notice an old man walking down the dirt road over there along the lake? Probably be some time around dark."

"You mean Mr. Boggs," he said gloomily. "Sure. Most evenings when I hung around past my six o'clock quitting time, and I did that a lot. I've been saving my money so I haven't had much night life and that junky little room I've got isn't something you'd want to rush home to. I'd hang around and fish sometimes. When he saw the light, he'd generally come on around the bay and shoot the breeze with me a while. Nice old codger, interesting to talk to. I was sorry about his bad luck."

"Wasn't his wife usually with him?"

"Sometimes. Not always. She came on board with him a couple of times, but she'd get bored or something and they wouldn't stay but a minute. They always ended their walk on that little rise over there behind the crappie house. If he came on over here, she'd turn around and go back by herself." He hesitated. "I got the feeling that she maybe drank a little. You could smell it."

"A little. It's an occupational hazard."

"For a teacher?"

"For anyone."

73

He laughed. "You've got that about right."

"How about last Tuesday night? Did you see him then?"

He looked startled for a second, his tanned forehead furrowed below the headband. "This last Tuesday?" His brow cleared. "No. I had to take off early Tuesday afternoon. I went to the dentist, Dr. Carlyle. I didn't get back here till dark. That was the same night—" He broke off as a bell tinkled merrily somewhere behind us, a tinny noise that managed to sound musical and strident at the same time.

The sound galvanized Trumble. He upended his beer can, gulped hastily, then tossed it in the direction of the trash barrel. Wiping his mouth on his sleeve, he trotted around me, out to the corner of the dock.

"Got a fish," he said, dropping to his belly beneath the still tinkling bell. He extended both arms into the water, grabbed something, and heaved.

A heavy nylon line split the surface, rose dripping as Trumble climbed to his feet, his shoulders hunched to resist the tug of the trotline with its water-logged droplines spaced every eighteen inches. Using both hands, he heaved upward, looped the line through an open eyebolt screwed into the post.

"Let's see how big he is," he said, grinning. He wiped his fingers on his pants, grasped the taut line lightly between thumb and fingers. He stood motionless, "reading the line," eyes squinted in concentration. After a moment he frowned and shook his head. "Little sucker. Not worth getting out the boat for. I'll pick him up later." He wagged his head and grimaced. "Rang that bell like an old yellow-bellied lunker."

I walked over and placed my hand where his had been. A faint movement throbbed along the line and into my fingers.

"I've never seen a trotline this heavy. That has to be at least a quarter-inch main line."

He nodded and grinned. "There's a reason for that. See that crappie house over there? The other end's tied to the left corner."

"Christ, that must be two hundred yards!"

"That's it almost exactly."

"Two hundred yards. You have droplines every eighteen inches?"

"More like two feet."

"That's still over three hundred hooks. I thought there was a fifty hook limit."

"There is, unless your name's Garland." Grinning at me over his shoulder, he lifted the line out of the eyebolt and let it slice back into the water. "Don't worry, Chief Chandler knows about it."

"It's not Chief Chandler's problem," I said. "What I'd be worried about is the game warden."

"Clay Garland's cousin," he said, the grin broadening.

I shook my head and returned his grin. "I told you Clay always had it wired."

"Locked up and buttoned down," he agreed. "A beautiful wife, the juiciest daughter I've seen in a coon's age, and all that loot. And he pisses it away with a bullet in his brain."

I took out a cigarette and began working my way toward the gangplank. He walked along beside me. "I've never met his daughter," I said. "I've heard she's a beauty."

"Jesus," he breathed, burlesquing a sob. "She's still six months away from being legal. That's the only thing that's kept me from committing rape most foul." He waved his arms and made a pained sound. "Naw, I'm just kidding. She's just too damned sweet and innocent to let loose in this sex-crazed world.''

''Sometimes they fool you,'' I said, thinking of Melissa, the interminable months it had taken to get her under the bandstand, the panting, lusting tigress she had become in that one wild, incredible moment. She had scared the hell out of me, and I was too young and too dumb to be much afraid of anything.

''Maybe so,'' he said, sighing, a painful sigh out of the world-weary experience of his twenty-three years.

We drifted to a stop at the door to the storeroom as if that had been our destination all along.

''This is where he did it,'' Trumble said unnecessarily, his voice muted. He looked at me, his eyes bright. ''You want to see inside?''

I started to decline, then impelled by the same sort of ghoulish curiosity that makes people visit the site of a particularly hideous crime, I changed a shake of the head to a nod.

Trumble opened the door and flicked on an overhead light. I followed him inside.

Long and narrow, approximately twelve feet by sixteen, the outer room contained a squat scruffy refrigerator that had once been white, a sagging tattered leather couch, and a jumble of rods and reels stacked in one corner. Trumble's beer cooler sat beside the door. An ashtray stand at the end of the couch had overflowed onto the dark blue linoleum floor, a profusion of candy wrappers, butts, and something that, at first glance, looked like tongue depressors.

''Back here,'' Trumble said. He pushed open a thin slab door and stepped back to let me go first.

The same length as the first room, Clay Garland's office was even narrower. No more than ten feet wide, it shared the same royal blue floor covering and the same general air of age and neglect.

The smallest wooden desk I had ever seen sat jammed against the far wall, nicked and scarred from careless usage, peeled and cracking from too many coats of paint. An ancient wooden swivel chair, a filing cabinet, two folding lawn chairs, a coffee pot on a frail-looking serving tray, and a cot against the end wall under the window made up the room's meager furnishings.

A gooseneck light and a telephone adorned the desk, and another ashtray, not quite overflowing, was littered with the small flat sticks that I had decided came from ice cream bars.

"Somebody ate a lot of ice cream bars," I said, lighting a cigarette, looking around and wondering if Clay had been rebelling against the ostentatious lifestyle of his parents, expressing contempt for the luxury and impeccable surroundings of his youth. Or maybe it had been only frugality, I thought.

"It was Clay. Eskimo Pies. He was a fiend about Eskimo Pies."

"Fattening," I said, the casual chit-chat sounding forced and hollow in the quiet airless room.

Trumble chuckled, an uneasy sound. "Isn't everything?"

I nodded and turned to go, then noticed a crack in the plastic floor covering running parallel with, and about two feet away from the wall. Two intersecting cracks extended outward from the baseboard to form a rectangle approximately six feet long.

"What's that?"

"Clay's fishing hole," Trumble said. "He liked to sit in here and fish. Somebody said he had it put in after he had the accident. He kept it baited for crappie and catfish.

Did pretty good, too.'' He dropped to one knee and lifted a square of floor covering at the inside edge of the crack. A small brass ring lay flat in a hole countersunk into the thick plywood. He hooked his thumb in the ring, jerked inward, and lifted.

The section of floor rose, opening on murky lake water trapped inside a bottomless box formed by sections of plywood attached to the edges of the opening and extending at least a foot below the surface of the water.

''A little dirty,'' Trumble grunted, and allowed the trapdoor to lean against the wall. He dropped flat on his stomach and stretched a muscular arm toward the debris floating on the water: candy wrappers and cigarette butts, a mangled cigar stub, a stubby pencil with a broken point, and two of the ubiquitous ice cream sticks. His fingers fell short by two inches. He finally managed to snag two of the candy wrappers before he gave it up.

''Too short in the britches,'' he said, climbing to his feet and smiling. ''I'll have to get a minnow dip net.''

''Any way a man could come up through that hole?''

He looked at me quickly, then pursed his mouth and nibbled on the inside of his lip. ''You could swim under the deck to the hole all right. But coming up would be another matter. Unless, of course, someone opened the trapdoor for you. There's no way to open it from underneath without ripping through the plywood. It's a simple spring loaded bolt, but you have to use the brass ring to unlock it.'' He squinted at me, a slow smile widening the gap between moustache and beard. ''You got something in mind?''

I shrugged and turned once more to the door. ''Just curious.''

We shook hands at the top of the gangplank. I walked to my truck with something nuzzling at the edge of my mind, a nagging blip of thought that dodged and weaved and flitted.

I sat thinking until the whine of the pump motor started again. I shrugged and gave up, started the engine and drove back up the rise to the fork in the road.

8

CRAPPIE HOUSE: A TEXAS COLLOQUIALISM FOR A BOXY, shedlike affair mounted on a floating platform which usually, but not always, obtains its buoyancy from tiny beads of polystyrene heated and compressed into blocks or barrels. Constructed from thin sheets of corrugated steel or aluminum, the primary purpose of the structure is to protect its occupants from the vagaries of Texas weather during the peak crappie fishing seasons of early spring, late fall, and winter, to theoretically keep them snug and dry while the dedicated anglers pursue their sport through a large opening in the center of the floor.

As often happens, primary considerations become obfuscated with time, broadened and diffused. People have been known to live in crappie houses the year around, albeit with a certain amount of discomfort.

The crappie house across the bay from Garland's Marina rode low in the water on thick semiwhite blocks of polystyrene. Anchored fifteen feet from the shore by some unseen method, it sat squat and ugly and obviously untended.

Huge spider webs triangulated the corners from eave to rail to cabin, and willow and oak leaves commingled in moldering patterns along the dirt-encrusted deck. Bird droppings pimpled every exposed surface like ripe chancres from some exotic pox.

I topped the small rise behind it, then braked on the downward slope as my eyes caught a warning flash of reflected light. I recalled Thisinger's caution about broken glass and eased the truck forward, searching the twin tire lanes intently in an fervent desire not to puncture one of my new belted radials.

I found the source of reflection at the bottom of the slope, two throwaway pop bottles that appeared to have been deliberately smashed together. I had read somewhere that throwaway bottles were made from a "soft" glass too frangible to injure tires, but empirical hokum or proven fact, I wasn't about to risk it.

The wash was a low, flat spot in the road, an overflow from the shallow ditch that ran along the bottom of the slope. Bits of refuse clung to the brush and matted grass, and in addition to the glass I found tangible evidence that the spot also served as a clandestine lovers' lane: used condoms and wads of blood-stained tissue, several soiled tampax, a balled-up handkerchief with dark rusty stains, a smoky-gray lens from some eager young stud's sunglasses, and a pair of ruined pantyhose.

I picked up the larger shards of glass and the gray-tinted lens and kicked the smaller bits and slivers into the brush at the side of the road. I dumped my handful of tire-killers into a small washed out depression and covered them with dirt. Maybe they wouldn't do much damage to hard resilient rubber, but they could sure as hell slice into a bare foot.

The rest of it, the effluvium of adolescent passion, I left where it was.

From the wash the road sloped upward gently, the dingy

waters of the lake gradually falling away to my left, the row of houses along Scales Drive drawing ever closer, lower, on my right. By the time I passed the last house on Scales Drive—the Boggs's residence—the road had almost leveled out. Directly ahead I could see the sharp incline that led to Scales Bluff, and I was beginning to accelerate when I heard the blat of a car horn behind me.

I eased up on the gas and glanced in the rearview mirror. All I could see through the roiling dust was the low-slung silhouette of a sports car, an indistinguishable face through the windshield, and an arm waving a friendly salute out the window. The arm was obviously male, and since he couldn't possibly want to pass, he just as obviously wanted to talk to me. I thought about it for a moment, stuck my arm out the window and waved, then rolled up the glass and gunned the pickup.

Fifteen seconds later I pulled up at a chain stretched across the road between two round metal posts. The road swung out and around the barricade, and continued on out of sight down the far side of the ridge. But I was where I intended to be, the top of Scales Bluff, and I lit a cigarette and waited for the sports car I could see dimly through the blowing dust.

He was still freckle-faced and redheaded. A lopsided smile. But years of good living had erased the rawboned angularity, given him a comfortable-looking roundness. Even the big-knuckled farmer's hands that, along with his listing, shuffling gait had made him appear so deceptively clumsy, were padded with a layer of smooth resilience. Neatly clipped, shiny nails where there had always been a rind of black. Big ears hidden behind carefully coiffed hair. Gunsmoke gray eyes shot with blood. Lines at his eyes and mouth; he had somehow aged to a different clock.

Ezekiel Knute Fairlee. Amiable, adroit: a lazy good nature that had masked a driving ambition only a few had known about. From humble stock, he had grown up hungry.

We pummeled each other, grinning and mouthing obscene nonsense, bearing down on our handshake like two strange kids testing macho on the playground. The handshake was a draw. It almost always is if you know how to go about it.

He had been the fourth member of the Infallible Four. Big and rangy, capable of blinding speed, he had roamed the backfield at will, faking the secondary like a prowling wolf among dogs.

"Damn, cowboy, I've been chasing you all over this town." He had a hoarse basso voice, a heavy smoker's wheezing laugh he used often. It had been one of the reasons I liked him so well in school; he had laughed at all my jokes, snickered at all my smart-ass remarks, and had been the only other ballplayer who smoked.

"Really? I haven't been hiding."

"No, but you've been moving. I ran into Webb Chandler at Washer's Cafe more'n two hours ago. He told me you were in town, that I might find you out at the library. I went out there and Mrs. Jalesco sent me to some old geezer named Thisinger. Thisinger sent me down to the marina. Jake Trumble said he thought you'd gone back downtown. Then I happened to see the top of your pickup down in that wash behind Pete Dixon's crappie house. What was you doing down there, anyhow? I saw you get back in your truck and drive off."

"Investigating the area for evidence of illegal copulation."

He laughed. I still had it.

"Actually, I was picking up broken glass, not that there weren't plenty of signs of illicit hanky-panky."

He grinned, baring large white teeth and a glint of gold far back on his molars.

"It's a good place for that, all right. Only one of these houses that can see down in there is old lady Dawson's, and she goes to bed with the chickens. It's a pretty safe place."

"Experience or hearsay?"

"Hearsay, of course. I've been a happily married man lo these fifteen long years."

I gave him an appraising look. "You have that well-fed married look, all right. I hear you're a big mucky-muck out at Claybar Tool and Die. I'm right proud of you, Zeke."

He looked embarrassed. "I've worked for it," he said, a trace defiantly, I thought. "I started out on the dock, worked my way into the machine shop." He stopped and shrugged. "Clay didn't give me anything."

"No, I don't imagine he did. The Garlands were never famous for their philanthropy."

"Except a chance," he added quickly. "He gave me a chance. I worked my ass off for him—" He broke off and smiled wryly. "Classic story. Poor boy makes good. I went to night school, took college extension courses, and he moved me into management." He looked out across the lake. "Clay wasn't the easiest man in the world to work for."

"I can accept that," I said.

"What're you doing up here? Come up to check out an old make-out spot, or what?"

"Ardell Boggs," I said.

He gave me a hesitant, frowning glance. "You mean the

old codger who took a header off the bluff a few days ago?''

''Is that what you think?''

He shrugged. ''That's what I hear. But I don't understand. What connection do you have with Boggs?''

''Mrs. Boggs. She thinks he may have had some help.''

''No shit? You mean murder?'' A lugubrious expression flashed across his broad features, a mixture of incredulity and humor. ''But what does that have to do with you?''

''It's my job,'' I said, doing a fairly credible impression of Joe Friday. ''I'm a cop.''

He laughed. ''I know you're a cop. Or used to be. I heard somewhere you quit.''

''I'm on my own now. I'm a private detective.''

His eyes widened with awe. ''Gee whiz, with a big gun and everything?'' He threw up his hands in a surprisingly artful expression of disbelief.

''You got it. It don't count for much in this high-tech world, but it's a living.''

He laughed. ''Most anything beats nine to five.''

I dropped my cigarette and carefully ground it into the dirt. ''Want to take a little walk?'' I pointed toward the bluff.

He cast a quick glance at the vines and sawbriars and brush, then down at his whipcord, cuffless pants and tassled loafers. ''Huh-uh. Thanks all the same. That looks too snaky, not to mention the cockleburs.''

''No sweat,'' I said. ''This time of year the snakes are crawling out of their old skin and are lethargic.''

''They're also blind and mean as hell. You go ahead. Maybe your boots will help some. Anyhow, it ain't far to the hospital.''

I snorted derisively and ambled to the thicket, pushed back an overhanging tangle of limbs, and stepped into the narrow path I had noticed earlier. "Hang on, I'll be back in a moment."

I walked without undue haste, but I didn't dawdle either, and a few seconds later I broke through onto a fifteen-foot-wide strip of open ground, hard-packed and rocky, strewn with evidence that others had been here before me, the reasons why glaringly apparent to even the most inexperienced eye: they'd fornicated, guzzled beer, chewed copious quantities of gum, smoked pot, innumerable cigarettes and plastic-tipped cigars, and even defecated in one or two unlikely places.

The bark of a huge elm leaning precariously toward the water bore the crude artwork of a hundred different lovers. The lake swept away in a huge arc to my right, its coffee-colored waters lapping hungrily at the base of the bluff. A flock of gulls swooped and dipped above a patch of agitated water, and a brace of lowslung bass boats trailed peacock-plumes along the northern shore.

I leaned an arm against the tilted tree and peered over the bluff, not sure what I was looking for.

The rocks seemed farther than thirty feet away, jagged and bleached and waiting.

For one heart-freezing second I felt a swirling in my head, a faint insidious desire to leap. My insides tilted, swooped; my torso sagged beneath an incredible gravitational force.

I shoved away from the tree, stumbled backward. I closed my eyes and shook my head and the feeling dissolved, leaving a slick slimy residue of fear, a taste of copper on my tongue.

I breathed deeply and reached for a cigarette, my fingers trembling. Was that what it meant to have acrophobia? Or was it simple vertigo? And were they the same thing? Could that be what had happened to Boggs? Maybe he had been testing himself and felt that terrible drawing feeling inside, that insane compulsion to fly, to surrender to the mesmerizing lure of the bonebleached rocks?

I had never had that feeling before. Not even in the open door of a Bell Huey hovering hundreds of feet above a verdant jungle. Not even in parachute training when we leaped headlong from training towers and from the bowels of planes. I'd had plenty of fear, but fear of dying, not of falling.

"Hey, you all right out there?" Fairlee's voice boomed over the thicket, a lot louder than it needed to be.

"I'm fine," I said. "Coming out." I dragged deeply on the cigarette, then flipped it out over the bluff. A white gull sideslipped out of a raucous formation and dive-bombed the butt, skimming the water then rising, screaming in indignation.

My thoughts occupied with other matters, I made it through the tangle without once thinking about the snakes; the vague stirring that had plagued me before nagged at my mind like an ancestral memory.

"What were you looking for?" Fairlee leaned against the door of his Ferrari, plucking the leaves from a willow bough.

"I don't know. Scene of the crime. That sort of thing."

His expression sharpened with interest. "You think it was a crime, then?"

"Figure of speech. I don't think anything yet, but it does tilt slightly in that direction. Makes more sense than the other two options."

He flipped the denuded branch into the brush and fished out his Camels. "You're the detective, but the consensus of opinion is that he took a dive. Bad health, old lady Boggs a lush, and like that. Christ, who'd want to kill a little old man who never hurt anybody? When the news got out, most folks had to stop and think who he was.''

"You're right, it's probably ridiculous. But you know how it is with us detectives. Our success depends on bits and pieces and being thorough. Don't you ever watch TV?''

He chuckled absently, then frowned and squinted one eye. "But how could you ever hope to prove it? From what I hear, there were no witnesses. Nobody saw him come up here, or saw him at all for that matter. Webb said he thought the old man jumped, although they didn't find a note. For the sake of argument, if you thought somebody did the old geezer in, where would you begin?''

"Okay,'' I said. I leaned against the car beside him and lit a cigarette. "It's not strictly true that nobody saw him. Emil . . . what's-his-name . . . his next door neighbor saw him around six. He was getting ready to take his walk. But let's let that lay for a moment, take a hypothetical case that could fit Boggs's circumstances. I don't believe for a moment that someone dragged him through that thicket and over to the cliff while he was conscious and able to resist. That leaves two possibilities. He was unconscious and still alive, or he was already dead. I'd favor the latter assumption for the simple reason that the killer couldn't be absolutely positively certain that the fall would kill him. If he was already dead then it follows that he was probably killed somewhere else, brought here in some sort of vehicle, carried over to the bluff and tossed over headfirst. I say headfirst because the fatal wound was a crushed skull. But one crushed skull looks pretty much like another unless the autopsy is thorough enough and sophisticated enough to detect the presence of different particles which could indicate two wounds, one on top of the other. Maybe metallic traces if the killer used a crowbar or a piece of pipe.''

"They can do that?''

"And more. A good forensic man with the right equipment can track a fly across a wall."

"Okay, so where does that get you? I doubt if Doc Ragen could do anything like that. Anyhow, Boggs is already buried."

"That's not a big problem. He could be exhumed if necessary. But I sort of digressed, as they say. I started out to make the point that if Boggs had been dead for any length of time, and had been lying in a different position other than the one they found him in—on his back—then there would be evidence of that. It's called post mortem lividity, and simply means that blood begins settling to the body's lowest point soon after death."

"What kind of evidence?"

"Dark reddish streaks in the skin. Striations, they're called. The surface area involved and coloration would depend on how long he laid in that position." I was showing off a little and we both knew it, but he seemed interested and I wasn't above a little grandstanding now and then.

Would Ragen have noticed that, do you think?"

I shrugged. "That would depend on a lot of things. The extent and intent of the autopsy. What he was looking for. How perceptive he is. Maybe even how well he can see. If it was a cursory examination to confirm preconceived notions of cause of death, it may not have been much. I know he checked the lungs for water. I don't know what else he did. I haven't seen the report. I will, though, and I intend to talk to him."

"This is all great stuff," he said soberly. "But it doesn't tell you why."

"When I know the if, I can find out the why. I have two possible motives already."

"What?" His head swiveled, gunpowder-gray eyes widening in astonishment.

I shook my head, grinning. "Sorry, Zeke, I can't tell you. At this point it'd be an invasion of privacy. Besides, all this is theoretical, remember? A hypothetical case. The odds against it happening the way I said are astronomical."

"Wouldn't it be a kick, though," he said, returning my grin, "if it happened the way you said and you could prove it. Some asshole sitting back feeling smug and superior, figuring he's pulled off a perfect murder, and old Dan the Man ambles along and sacks his ass."

"The heady stuff of dreams," I said.

He grinned and bobbed his head, then pushed abruptly away from the car. "Hey, how about a beer? All that detecting stuff, you must be thirsty."

"Sure, where do we go?"

He reached inside the car and took out the keys. "Nowhere, unless you just want to. I always go prepared." He grinned and opened the deck of the car, a small cramped space packed with a jumble of sporting equipment. He rummaged, displacing framed tennis rackets, jogging shoes, two aqualungs, and a neatly folded pair of black pants and a striped shirt, coming up with a small foam cooler not much larger than a lunch pail.

He opened the cooler and triumphantly flourished two dripping cans of beer. "Not ice cold, maybe, but they're still cool." He snapped two tissues out of a box wedged in a fender well and blew his nose lustily. "Damned hay fever," he said and blew again.

I accepted one of the cans and stripped the moisture with my forefinger and thumb. "You do much scuba diving?" The beer was barely cool, but it beat nothing.

He grunted and looked out at the lake. "Not much here. This isn't a good diving lake. I generally go to Possum Kingdom, or down to the coast. I've been giving Josh—that's my thirteen-year-old—some lessons, but this damn lake's still too muddy to do much. I need to get this stuff put away for the winter, anyhow.''

"What you need is a panel truck or a station wagon to carry all this junk. What's the referee's outfit for? You officiating now?''

"Some Little League stuff and I've been helping out over at the junior high. Coach Spellman cracked an ankle bone and I've been coaching the track team. Josh is by far the fastest thing we've got going for us this year. He can fly, that boy.'' He said it with quiet pride, then looked a little embarrassed. "Not enough meat on his bones to play ball, though," he added sadly and chug-alugged half his beer.

We fell silent again, smoking another cigarette and watching the seemingly aimless circling of the gulls. A blue jay dive-bombed a squirrel high in the leaning elm, and far into the azure sky a tardy V of long-necked geese honked their way south. A wide, flat boat droned out of the marina and sped to the edge of the roiled patch of water. The gulls moved up a few feet, but refused to be intimidated.

Two men and two women in the boat began casting almost immediately, dropping plugs into the agitated water. Streaks of bright silver glimmered as hapless shad sought to escape the sand bass's feeding frenzy, skipping across the surface in a futile attempt to deny gravity and their destiny. As mindless as feeding sharks, the sand bass were sloppy hunters, leaving bits and pieces and crippled shad squirming on the surface. The gulls dipped and scavenged, and far below lazy black bass fed leisurely on what was left.

The four people in the boat had fallen into a metronomic pattern of cast, hook, and retrieve, not bothering to deep well their catch, the bottom of the boat rapidly becoming layered with a seething mass of choking, dying fish.

"Is it a good job, being a private detective?"

"I don't really know yet. I haven't been doing it long enough."

"I don't know. Messing around in murders, poking into other people's lives, dealing with crooks and hoods all the time. It may be exciting, but it sounds so . . . so . . ." He hesitated, unable to find a word.

"Seamy," I said. "Maybe so, but you've got one thing wrong no matter what you hear or read or see on TV. P.I.'s don't solve murders. We find people mostly, and a half-dozen other odd jobs that people can't, or won't, do for themselves."

He unveiled the quizzical grin again. "Then what're you doing messing around in this Boggs thing? Auld lang syne?"

"Wasting time probably." I watched one of the women in the boat reel in a flopping silvery fish, drop it onto the teeming deck and cast out again. Automated fun.

"But you're going to stick with it, huh?"

"A while longer. I have a few more people to talk to. Why not? I didn't have anything planned for this afternoon, anyway."

He glanced at his watch. "Speaking of the afternoon, it's winding on down. I'd better sneak out to the plant, see if I can catch the peasants shooting craps between the machines."

"How quickly we forget. I can remember a boxboy at Clyde's Grocery who once wanted to round up all the slave-driving capitalist bastards in town and hang them on the courthouse square."

He laughed and opened the Ferrari's long curving door. "It's all a matter of perspective."

"It's all a matter of capital," I said, shaking his hand and agreeing with his suggestion that we get together some evening and shoot the bull, drink a few, and catch up on who had done what with whom since way back when.

I waited until his dust storm died down, then followed his tracks down the road as far as the Boggs's residence. I parked behind her six-foot board fence. I got out of the pickup, stomped out my latest cigarette, and walked through the sagging gate into Emil What's-his-name's yard, a sense of defeat and futility pressing down on me like a fundamentalist's vision of Judgment Day.

9

His name turned out to be Emil Prescott. Sixty-eight years old. Retired. A widower. A short, stocky man with bad feet and varicose veins that came from thirty years of pounding the pavements of Butler Wells carrying sacks of junk mail. Two children. A beach-bum son somewhere in California, a sweet dutiful daughter who lived nearby and came to see him weekly. He dipped snuff and hated dogs and thought Nixon should have been stood against a wall at the very least. He thought Ford was a klutz and who was this peanut farmer from Georgia they had running the government now?

His house wasn't much, maybe, but he owned it free and clear and if them money-grubbers down at city hall didn't start futzing with the tax rate or the property assessments, he might just be able to make it another year on his pension. He had hemorrhoids, prostate trouble, and a dropped bladder and would give a pretty if he could take a good shit or a piss without having to think it over first.

All this and more I learned about the voluble little man during the first five minutes of our conversation. Seated face to face on his small concrete slab patio in deep wicker furniture, he prodded my boot with his rubber-tipped cane to emphasize a point or to bring me back when my attention wandered. He had an extraordinary thatch of wavy silver hair and the dry leathery skin of a man who has lived at the mercy of wind and sun. Finally, catching him in the act of replenishing his supply of snuff, I seized the conversation.

"Too bad about what happened to Mr. Boggs," I said.

He made a snorting sound and spat, not adroitly, dribbling amber fluid on his denim jacket, the main glob of spittle splashing against the side of a three-pound Crisco can near the edge of the patio.

"Wasn't any more than I expected," he said, his speech momentarily slurred. "Wandering off up there on that bluff at night, old man like that."

"You mean you saw him go up toward the bluff?"

"Naw. Can't say as how I did. I never saw which way he went, to tell you the truth, I was out behind the fence sickling some weeds. He stopped and we talked a spell. Then I come on in the yard and never did see which way he went. He usually went down toward the marina and he mighta that night too. My guess is he had one of them strokes and went out of his head or something, forget where he was, maybe. Went wandering off up on the bluff and fell over."

"How high is the bluff out there beyond your house?"

"Right now it's about ten feet. Lake's down some, though. Usually only about three or four feet down to the water."

"You said he stopped. That means he must have been walking down the hill to the marina, at least in the beginning."

He turned watery blue eyes toward the gate in the back

fence. "By gum, you're right. He was carrying that little flashlight. He musta been starting his walk when he stopped to gab. Didn't do that often. He was a nice enough old man, but kinda standoffish, if you get my meaning. Been living here next door to him for twenty years, and I didn't know much more about him than that blue jay settin' over there on the fence."

"You ever see him out near the edge of the bluff?"

He gave me a squinty-eyed, quizzical look. "You mean up there on Scales Bluff?"

"No, I mean out there behind his house."

"That ain't hardly no bluff most of the time. Ain't much of one even now with the water down like it is. Naw, don't reckon I ever saw him over there. Ain't much call for it. He didn't like to fish and there ain't nothin' to see but some rocks and sawbriars and weeds."

"His place looks pretty well tended. He do his own painting, tree trimming, things like that?"

"Now that was another funny thing about him. Never saw him with a paintbrush in his hand. That old lady, she slapped it on like a pro. Climb up and down them ladders like a monkey. He mowed the grass. Had him one of them Sears riding mowers, and I'll have to say he took good care of the yard. See them fruit trees? She done all the trimming needed on them too. Oddest damn thing."

"Maybe he had acrophobia," I said.

He looked at me as if I had just denounced Christ, then licked his lips and poked my boot with his cane. "Naw, you're funnin'. He wasn't having any fits or anything."

"Just my little joke." I stood up and stretched.

"You working for the insurance company, I'll bet," he said, a sly, knowing look crinkling the leathery skin.

"They trying to figger out a way not to pay that big policy?"

"Which big policy is that?"

"That policy old Boggs took out about fifteen years or so ago. Told me his wife would never want for anything when he passed on. Told me she'd be set up like a queen for life." A note of either envy or avarice had crept into his voice.

"Did he mention an amount?"

"Naw, but he said if you wrote it down on paper, it'd run into six figgers."

"Didn't happen to mention the company's name?"

"Naw, he just said it that one time. Old Boggs wasn't a talkative feller."

"Did he seem different that evening? Depressed or withdrawn? Upset about something?"

He cackled and slapped his knee. He tried to poke my boot but I had moved out of range. "Lord, I knowed it. They want to make out like he killed hisself, get out of paying that way." A globule of ill-aimed spittle expressed his fine contempt for welching insurance companies.

"It's just routine when there's a lot of money involved."

"Routine my foot! Dang insurance companies is all alike. Right handy when it comes to writing policies, dang scarce when it comes to paying off." He made a hawking sound of deep disgust.

"You may be right," I said. "Did Boggs have any enemies that you knew about?"

"None that I know about." He stopped, both hands folded on the head of the cane, his lower jaw moving sidewise, back and forth in the manner of a ruminate. "Unless, maybe one of them women of his."

"Women?"

"Up in Dallas. Most every Friday night long as I can remember he went to Dallas. A lot of the time stayed over, too. The old woman said it had to do with writing, some club or other. Guess he was just fooling her. He told me he had him some women friends in Dallas. One at a time, I guess, not all at once." He ended on a wry, cynical note.

"He tell you that, or did you sorta pry it out of him?"

He stiffened, his watery eyes glistening with indignation. "I don't pry in anybody's business. He just up and told me. Same way he did about the insurance."

"And you believed him?"

He gave me a startled glance. "Well, why in the world not? Man wouldn't up and lie about something like that. I didn't hold with it none, him being married and all, and I guess he could see that. He never mentioned it again."

"How long ago was that?"

"Oh, I don't know . . . maybe ten, twelve years or so. I reckon he was still doing it. He still went to Dallas every Friday night about."

"At seventy-five," I said doubtfully. "I wouldn't think he'd have much interest in the opposite sex."

He bristled a little, then gave me a positively obscene grin. "Hell, boy, I'm sixty-eight myself. My mind's as active as ever, and some other things is, too. There's a couple of widder women here in town could tell you something about that."

"That's good to know," I said. "Eases my mind."

"Thing is not to burn yourself out when you're young. Man only has just so many times, you know. It ain't the age that matters.

"I didn't know that. I'll have to watch it." If that were true, I thought, at my current rate I'd still be going strong at a hundred and ten.

He seemed highly excited by the idea of sex after sixty-five, and he followed me all the way to my truck, quoting geriatric sex statistics and testimonials about the simple pleasures of fondling.

I shook his hand and left him earnestly extolling the virtues of something that sounded like "sex without penalty or pain."

Time had dealt harshly with Dr. Augustus L. Ragen. Somewhere in his mid-sixties, he looked eighty, a sagging, veined, grooved face fully as ravaged as Ethel Boggs's. I remembered him only vaguely. One of Butler Wells' three medical doctors practicing during my adolescence, he had had the smallest practice, and was the least liked, last consulted of the local medical fraternity despite the fact that he was probably the smartest and best educated of the three.

There were reasons for this, of course: a gruff, intense, nononsense bedside manner, a bearded chin, and a heavy Viennese accent that labeled him instantly as a foreigner and therefore suspect.

My parents had preferred Dr. Teddy Weissbaum, subscribing to the widely held belief that Jews make the best doctors and lawyers.

Sitting now behind an antique wooden desk sagging beneath stacks of patients' medical folders and texts, well-thumbed periodicals, the burned-out stub of a cigar forgotten between permanently stained fingers, he scowled at me with ill-disguised bad humor when he learned the reason for my intrusion into his busy day.

"It's all in the autopsy report," he rasped hoarsely, a voice that went well with his short bearish body. "I'd suggest you see Chief Chandler." Only the faintest trace of his former accent remained.

I nodded. "I saw him this morning. He told me some of it, but at that time I didn't know enough to ask an intelligent question. And now it seems he's gone to Austin for the day and no one else will take the responsibility."

"What's your interest in this?" He sucked on the dead cigar, then threw it at an overflowing wastebasket and took out another. "Or rather, what's your authority?"

"I'm a private investigator. I'm making an inquiry on behalf of his wife." It was a stilted little speech, very close to pompous, and I wouldn't have been at all surprised if he had laughed.

He frowned instead. "What's her problem? The official verdict's accidental death. No problem if it's an insurance policy she's worried about." He had pale blue eyes, with thick, furry brows the frown brought crashing together. "The alternative—now that would be a different story. Most policies don't pay off on suicides." He reamed out the hole in the cigar and lit it with a torch-like flame from a disposable lighter.

"There's a third choice," I said.

He stared at me through the flame and smoke, his ruined cheeks working in and out like a bellows, berry-blue eyes suddenly bright with interest. Satisfied with the coal, he snapped off the lighter and reared back in his chair, blue-gray smoke dense above his head.

"Now that's right interesting," he drawled, all trace of the accent gone.

"Is there anything in your findings that would positively rule it out?"

He shook his head silently, watching his cigar trail smoke, lips pursed, considering the possibilities.

"There rarely are," he said finally, "humans being the devious creatures that they are. Murder is, and should always be, a consideration in an isolated case of accidental death, but I must confess I never considered it in this case.''

"Why is that? Because Boggs was such an inoffensive little man?''

After a moment he nodded, a slow smile parting the sandy-gray beard, a baring of yellowed teeth that did nothing to help his failed face. "That's it exactly, I suppose. The idea is ludicrous on the face of it. It simply never occurred to me that it could be anything but what it appeared to be—an accident. I did consider suicide, but only for a moment. It would take a very stupid man to try to kill himself in such a manner, and Boggs was not a stupid man.'' He crashed forward in the chair suddenly, the smile gone, his pale eyes cold.

"I still believe it was an accident. The thought of murder may be a titillating concept perhaps, but all the facts support our verdict of accidental death.'' He rolled the cigar to the other corner of his mouth. "Unless, of course, you have evidence to the contrary.''

"No hard evidence, but did you know he suffered from acrophobia?''

He shrugged and spread his hands. "Chief Chandler asked me that. I was his doctor, and I knew nothing about it. Don't you agree that is odd?''

"Maybe,'' I said. "Maybe not. Not many people knew. He was ashamed of it. It makes sense that he probably sought medical advice at some time or other and discovered that it was a psychological problem. You're a medical doctor. He probably figured it would be pointless to tell you about it. I don't know what his thoughts were on the subject, but there is evidence to support a conclusion that he did in fact suffer from acrophobia.''

"It changes nothing. Conjecture not supported by medical facts. At least none that I am aware of. Even so,

101

it would still prove nothing. A temporary mental aberration, a sudden severe depression, a light stroke—there are numerous afflictions that could temporarily override such fear, bring about loss of orientation, dissociation from reality . . ." His voice trailed away behind his cigar, and his eyes glinted with a combative light.

"Okay," I said genially. "Let's try this one. Did he have a number tattooed on either of his forearms?"

His eyes seemed to widen slightly, then narrow, something glimmering. He pursed his lips and shook his head.

"No." He gave me a moment to digest that, then, "But he did have a scar on his left forearm, roughly two centimeters wide and five centimeters long."

I did some mental conversions. "Roughly three-quarters of an inch by two inches?"

He nodded. "An old scar. If I were guessing, I'd guess twenty to twenty-five years old." We stared at each other for a moment. "A fairly neat surgical scar. Something removed, I would venture." It was a statement, but his tone invited enlightenment.

Instead, I asked another question. "He was found on his back, I understand. Were there signs of lividity anywhere else on his body?"

He shook his head slowly, brows knitted again. "No. I wasn't especially looking but I would have noticed." The frown smoothed into a mocking smile. "This was not my first autopsy, Mr. Roman."

I nodded, hiding my disappointment. Despite the long odds, I realized that I had been halfway expecting him to say yes. So much for the power of positive thinking. Fairlee's expectation for Dan the Man to sack somebody's ass had just taken a belly flop and suddenly I was weary of the whole damned thing, this amorphous fractured image of Ardell P. Boggs that had no more substance than a puff of wind-driven dust. Contradiction and guile. Husband, lover, Commando, freedom fighter, Nazi hunter, sodomite, and adulterer. And what about the years he had spent inside the German concentration camps making the Jew-killing machine work more efficiently?

How could he have been a Commando with the British and a freedom fighter with the French at the same time? The more I learned about him the more impossible it all became. Each person I talked to seemed to be talking about a different man. Shy hero or depraved charlatan? Zealot or self-righteous hypocrite? Pathological liar?

Would the goddamned real Ardell P. Boggs please stand up?

Dr. Augustus Ragen cleared his throat and shuffled his feet, placing his hands flat on the desk and leaning forward in a rising posture.

"If there's nothing else, Mr. Roman, I'll have to ask you to excuse me. I have patients waiting."

"One other thing, Doctor. Were you able to establish time of death?"

"That one's easy," he said, pushing to his feet. "We happen to know that he had a ham and cheese on rye and a pickle at approximately five-thirty that afternoon. Food digestion follows a fairly predictable pattern, and based on that I placed the time of death at somewhere around seven o'clock, give or take an hour."

"That's a two-hour leeway."

"I said fairly predictable, not precisely predictable. Digestion varies somewhat with the individual, the type of food consumed, the condition of the salivary glands, the pancreas, and the stomach itself. Certain foods stimulate the production of gastric secretions, certain others inhibit the process by stimulating production of hormones which actually delay the secretion of gastric juices and therefore retard digestion.''

"Thanks," I said. "I'm sure you took all that into account."

He grinned his yellow wolfish grin, advancing around the edge of his littered desk, short and broad and formidable, exuding, for one chilling moment, a kind of benign malevolence.

"Routine," he said. "It's actually easier than it sounds." He was back to genial again.

"Isn't everything?" I felt a fleeting spasm of self-loathing for hiding behind flippancy.

He laughed and slapped me on the back, bringing his hand to rest on my shoulder, guiding me gently but firmly toward the door.

"Dan Roman? Raised around here, right? Used to play football?"

Caught in the act of lighting a cigarette, I nodded and grunted affirmatively.

"Thought so. Silly damned game, football. I prefer soccer myself. Now there's a game that requires speed and dexterity. Skill and brains. It takes both to be a good soccer player. Players here just can't seem to get the hang of it."

"Big feet help," I said. "And hard heads."

His eyes glinted. "Soccer is a gentleman's game. Perhaps that's why it never really caught on here in the States."

"Yeah, I read somewhere that Hitler and Himmler and Goering never missed a game if they could help it. That in itself gives it a certain panache."

He slapped my back again, his hoarse chuckle following me across the empty outer office, somehow more provocative than jeering laughter. I no longer wondered why the good doctor had so few patients: he probably had been forced to accept the thankless position of county coroner in order to keep body and soul on the same plane of existence.

10

I MADE ONE STOP ON MY WAY TO THE CABIN. I PICKED UP bread and a quart of milk, a six pack of Bud, a thick steak, and a package of frozen french fries. I had somehow missed lunch, and the sight of the marbled red meat started a flow of juices. Nothing wrong with my salivary glands.

I put the steak on to broil, heated a pan of polyunsaturated oil for the french fries, and while I waited, flushed out my mouth with the last cold beer from the refrigerator.

Famished, dejected, seething with futility, I tried to ponder pleasant thoughts, to contemplate things earthy and restorative: the ten-acre oasis of forest around me that had been grudgingly spared the monster coal-eating machines; the twinkling spring branch behind the cabin that chirruped and gurgled its way to feed the three-acre lake below the hill; trout; money in the bank; the cooking steak; the sharp refreshing taste of beer; the aromatic spice of sun-heated cedar and moldy pine cones; long-ago sex with Melissa Arenson-Garland.

But nothing worked for long. The gloomy ghost of Ardell P. Boggs lurked in accusatory silence around the shadowy corners of my mind, his presence as intangible as imagination, yet as real as dust motes in a shaft of blazing sun.

I lit a cigarette and went back over the day's events, rethinking my position, trying to assimilate the things I had learned into some sort of pattern. By the time I finished the cigarette, I realized I hadn't the faintest idea of what I thought beyond the fact that Boggs had either been a genius or crazy or both.

At any rate I was done with it. Finished. *Kaput. Fini.* I had more than discharged my tenuous obligation to Ethel Boggs, if indeed there had ever been one.

On the other hand it hadn't been an entirely wasted day. I had seen a couple of my oldest friends, learned that there was sex after sixty-five, and discovered my salivary glands were good for something besides spitting.

I sat by an open window in the kitchen area, eating steak and french fries washed down with milk, listening to the lulling drone of cicadas, and feeling a sense of liberation now that the decision had been made.

I would spend one more night at the cabin, see Mrs. Boggs in the morning, then head north for Dallas and Midway City.

I thought of my house, 1800 square feet of modern living enclosed in Old English brick and topped with cedar shakes. For a long time it had been a home. Then my wife Barbara had died and a year later my fourteen-year-old son Tommy had wasted his life against a bridge abutment chasing hallucinogenic visions in a stolen car. It became a house again.

With the need for revenge burning in my gut, I had spent all my free time stalking the pusher who had sold Tommy drugs. Thomas Cody Roman, my dead son. Almost exactly a year after we had lost his mother to cancer, he had wasted his life hustling down a country road in a stolen car. PCP. Angel dust. It could have been any one of the others. Nine months later I caught my pusher in the act of selling to school kids, and I arrested him, prodded him into resisting, then beat him unconscious with a cold calculated fury.

It wasn't so much the excessive force used in the arrest that brought disciplinary action, although that was the reason cited. It was the fact that I was lieutenant in Homicide and had been warned to stay away from the pusher, leave him to the narcs. But the call for retribution had been too compelling, the narcs too slow. Police Chief Cliff Hollister had taken my insubordination personally, and I had been suspended for thirty days without pay.

And so I had quit. Much to the dismay and disgust of my boss and best friend, Captain Homer Sellers. He had considered my resignation a minor catastrophe, equating it with withdrawing under fire. For a time our friendship had been sorely tested, but he had eventually come around as I had known he would.

Somewhere nearby a turkey hen shrilled a warning. A thrashing of wings, crashing of brush, and a flock of wild turkeys boomed up the slope from the lake, slow and awkward, as ungainly as Howard Hughes's Spruce Goose. The young toms gobbling with excitement or fear, they circled the cabin and headed toward the Circle Bar C ranch and its hundreds of wooded acres that bordered my land on the west.

Seeing the turkeys turned my thoughts to hunting, the fall season less than a month away. Thinking of hunting brought me back to Homer Sellers, to Tom Jeffers and Lee Swain, my hunting partners since our dreary days together in Vietnam. Because of the coal harvesting, this would be our first hunt on my property since the earth-raping machines had smashed the land bare, opened her bowels and stripped her veins of the soft black gold that was supposed to be our answer to OPEC. Lignite coal.

It had eventually brought me a lot of money, more than one hundred and fifty thousand dollars. Monopoly money that had no real meaning to me beyond the modest yearly income it earned from judicious investments, which in turn provided a certain freedom of choice in the number and type of cases I accepted.

I had decided almost at once that finding people was the only thing I wanted to do out of the many things a private detective does. It is tedious and dull at times and involves a lot of traveling, but it can be interesting, and I meet a lot of unusual people. But finding them is all I do. I never take them anywhere they aren't willing to go. And sometimes, when in my omniscient wisdom I judge that they have found something far better than they had before, I don't find them at all. I simply walk away and leave them to make their own destiny, which is usually why they ran away in the first place. Arbitrary behavior and probably morally reprehensible, but I sleep better nights.

I cleaned up the table and watched the five o'clock news on a snowy Dallas station. Listening vaguely to the day's accumulation of rapes, robberies, murders, and skulduggery in high office, I decided there was one more thing I could do before I definitely, absolutely, irrevocably closed out the Ardell P. Boggs affair.

I sighed, lit a cigarette, and picked up my shiny new phone.

"Sellers." Fully as hoarse and rasping as Augustus Ragen's had been, Homer's voice had a nasal quality all its own, the result of chronic sinus problems and allergic reactions to almost everything that pollinated or discharged spores.

"Hi, Homer, it's me."

"Well whoopteedo! The hunter home from the hill.

Dang, boy, I wish you'd let me know sooner. I'da rousted out the Trinity High marching band, got the mayor over here, and gave you a real rousing welcome.'' I waited until his wheezing laugh subsided.

"You can cut out the crap, Homer. I'm not at home. I'm still down at the cabin.''

"Don't lie to me, little buddy. You may not be home, but you ain't got no phone in that cabin.''

"I have now. I just had it installed. At great expense, I might add.''

"About time, too. Maybe I'll go down there more often now that I don't have to drive twenty miles just to check with my stockbroker.'' Another wheezing chuckle. He appeared to be in an abnormally good mood. I had a feeling I was going to change that.

"Homer, do you remember our old English teacher? Ethel Boggs?''

"Of course I do. She's a second, third cousin of mine on my mother's side. Matter-of-fact I talked to her not more'n six, seven months ago. Why? She die?''

"No, but her husband Ardell did.''

"Ardell. I remember him, but not too plain. Hung around the library a lot.''

"He worked there, Homer. Assistant Librarian.''

"Well, that's a shame. Tell Ethel I'm sorry. I'll send some flowers. When's the funeral?''

"He's already buried. He died, or was killed, last Tuesday night.''

"Or was killed? What do you mean or was—?''

"Just what I said. Mrs. Boggs thinks he may have been murdered.''

"Well, I'll be damned! Ardell Boggs? Murdered? Son, I'm having a little trouble with that one.''

110

"Yeah, so am I. Which brings me to the reason—one reason, at least—for this call. We need your help."

"We? What do you mean, we? What do you have to do with it?"

"She asked me to nose around a little."

He grunted. I heard the rasp of his lighter. "You got the nose for it all right. But what's the matter with the police down there? What do they say?"

"Accidental death. They think he walked over a thirty-foot bluff. Scales Bluff. You remember Scales Bluff?"

"Course I do. I remember it when there wasn't any lake, when that piss-ant little Cannonball Creek ran along through there. We used to go down there and catch—"

"I've picked up a lot of conflicting information, Homer, and there's something I need your help with."

"When? I got off duty an hour ago. I was just cleaning up some—"

"Right now. Don't give me that off-duty crap, Homer. The law never sleeps, remember? It's the only thing between us and the jungle? Without the law the whole world would be in chaos? Remember that little speech you gave me?"

"Pity you didn't remember it before you heisted your leg and pissed all over your career." He went silent for a moment. "Hey, I like that."

"You got me there, Homer. I can't stand up to that pithy tongue of yours."

"Pissy tongue? That don't make no sense at all. If you're going to trade—"

"Are you gonna help us out or not?"

"You'll have to tell me what it is first. It depends on that. If it don't take too much time. I got a date."

"Congratulations. With your connections it shouldn't

take much time at all. Actually, there are two things. Do you have your Dallas phone directory handy?''

I heard a grunt, a squeaking drawer, the slam of something on metal.

"Yeah, got it right here. Shoot."

"WWNF. Acronym for World Wide Nazi Find. I doubt if you'll find it in the yellow pages."

I heard paper rattling, a pause while he blew his nose, a nasty wet gurgling sound.

"Warn me next time, will you, Homer?"

"What?"

"Never mind."

"Yeah, here it is, WWNF. That's all. No name. Located way out on Harry Hines Boulevard."

"Give me the phone number."

"It's 555-9802. 214 area code, but I guess you know that."

"Thanks. Now the other thing is Boggs himself. That's Ardell P. Boggs. I don't know what the P. stands for. He was born in England, English father, Jewish mother. The way I understand it, he spent most of his life in Germany, even worked for the German government for a while. I hear conflicting stories about what happened to him during the war years, but he came to the States right after the war was over. He married Ethel shortly after that."

"I remember that," Homer said. "Ethel's first husband was killed at Pearl Harbor. They had one kid, I think. She married Boggs in 1946, the year I had the measles. I think she met him in a museum in San Francisco. She was on one of them Sabbaticals they're always talking about. As I remember, everybody was scandalized when she came home married. But hell, her husband had been dead five years by then."

"You've got that cousin in the Justice Department. It shouldn't—"

"State Department."

"Same difference. That's even better. I need to know what actually happened to him during the war. There must be a record some place. He'd have to make application for citizenship—"

"Yeah, I know. I damn sure can't get it for you tonight. Maybe tomorrow, if I can get hold of Ken. They've probably got Boggs on a computer somewheres."

One thing about Homer, I thought fondly, once he gave in he didn't ask a lot of damn fool questions. I told him so.

He snorted. "What's the use? I always end up doing your work for you anyhow. Why waste a lot of time?"

"You're right, and you know I appreciate it."

"You could have worked through the police in Butler Wells, you know. It might take them a little longer, but they could get the same information."

"I know, but for the time being I'd just as soon go at it from another direction."

"What's the matter? You don't trust the police down there?" There was a note of undisguised belligerency in his voice. To him a cop was a cop and therefore trustworthy. Impeccably honest himself, he possessed an esprit de corps second to none and grudgingly acknowledged only the rankest kinds of chicanery and malfeasance among his brother officers. Fifteen years of police work had done nothing to rob him of his curious naiveté, his belief in country, in government, in friendship, in the basic goodness of the homo sapien. He still could not believe a friend could look you in the eye and lie; over the years I had taken shameful advantage of that weakness.

I decided to change the subject. "Hey, man, you know it's less than a month until deer season?"

"I can read a calendar," he growled, unmollified. Then he took a long deep breath, changing gears. "Yeah, Swain called me last week. Wanted to know what we were going to do this year. Jeffers has five hundred acres lined up down around Comanche, but it'll cost us an arm and a leg. Bastards want a hundred a gun for the first week, or six hundred a gun for the season."

"Forget it, Homer. We'll hunt on my place. And I won't charge you half that much."

"That piddly little old ten acres? You drinking again, Daniel?"

"The price just doubled," I said. "No, Homer, that strip along the west side that borders the Circle Bar C is coming back strong. Willows and mesquite already ten feet tall, a lot of sumac, and new growth hardwoods anywhere from a foot to waist high. Rubs all over the place. You know how they like browsing that new growth."

"Lots of rubs, huh?"

"All over the place. That section is about a mile long. You think the three of you can keep from blowing each other's asses off?"

"Where you gonna hunt?"

"I'll hunt the hill, the ten acres. That's where the turkeys usually are. I'd rather take a gobbler any day. Easy to gut and they don't weigh much."

"Sounds pretty good. There's some good bucks on that Circle Bar C ranch. I know some cops who've hunted down there." Enthusiasm had crept into his voice, and I could picture him on the other end of the wire, reared back in his chair, phone cramped between one florid jaw and a beefy shoulder, his right hand pawing through a tangled thatch of mud-colored hair, guileless blue eyes sparkling behind smoky-gray bifocals. "Damn, boy, I've had the fever ever since that first cold snap." He uttered a gruff, barking laugh. "I've been hearing buck snorts in my sleep."

"We'll have to get humping. You guys better get down here this Saturday and get up your stands. I set mine up on the north slope above the lake."

"You gonna stay down?"

"I'm planning on coming home tomorrow sometime, but I'll come back with you if you want."

"I'll get in touch with Jeffers and Swain, see if they can get kitchen passes for Saturday. Jeffers' new wife don't take much to him running off without her."

"Hell, tell him to bring her along. The cabin needs a good cleaning, anyhow."

He guffawed. "By God, I will. Might do her some good. She's kinda feisty. One of them female libbers, it seems like to me."

"Chauvinist pig."

"You damn betcha."

We talked a while longer about the appalling inroads the fairer sex were making into masculine territory. Mostly I listened. An avowed chauvinist of the old school, he could expound for hours on God's original plan for man and woman, the woman's ordained niche in the home, in society, and the world. I didn't listen long before I cut him off. I had heard it all before; comfortable man talk around a campfire or over a beer. Defensive prattle to compensate for insecurities that went all the way back to the first time Mama slapped a tiny male hand for fiddling around with his peepee.

11

I OPENED A NEW BEER AND, ON THE OFF-CHANCE THAT NA-
zi hunters didn't keep regular hours, dialed the number
Homer had given me. It rang five times, clicked,
hummed, and then clicked again, and just when I thought
I had been disconnected, a female voice came on the
line.

"Yes."

"Is this WWNF—World Wide Nazi Find?"

"Where did you get this number?"

"Out of the phone directory."

I heard a delicate hissing that sounded like an annoyed
sigh. "Would you state your name, please?"

"Dan Roman. I'm a private investigator. I'm calling
in regard to one of your members, a Mr. Ardell P.
Boggs."

"What makes you think he's a member of WWNF?"

"I have reason to believe that he is—was."

"Was?"

"Yes, ma'am. He's dead."

A soft intake of breath. "I'm sorry, but I'm afraid you
were misinformed."

"He was not a member then?"

She didn't answer; I could hear the faint rustle of her breath.

"My source is impeccable," I said.

"You have no legal right to do this, you know?"

"To do what? All I want to know is if Boggs was a member."

"I can't tell you that. Anyway, I don't know if you are what you say you are."

"Look, I don't understand. Why all the secrecy? Your number is in the book along with your address." I paused. "Maybe it would be better if I came by, talked to you in person."

"That address is an office building. You won't find anything there connected with WWNF. Neither will you locate us through the phone number. We have a call forwarding service."

"Cagey," I said. "But why bother at all?"

"I agree with you. But I'm only one member. Our chapter leader feels we need a viable contact with the population. I was voted down. Personally, I feel that even this much is dangerous."

"Dangerous? Dangerous to you?"

"There are people out there, Mr. Roman, who do not wish us well. A lot of people. You can accept my word for that."

"Well, if you can't tell me about Boggs, will you answer one single, little question? It won't compromise you in any way. I promise."

The silence again; quiet waiting.

"Do you by any chance have a suspect . . . or a prospect, or whatever you call them, in the Butler Wells area? That location is about ninety miles or so southeast of Dallas."

117

"I can't tell you that."

"Why not?"

"For obvious reasons, Mr. Roman. I don't know who you are."

"Then you do have a suspect in that area."

"You are free to believe whatever you wish."

"I can go to the police and eventually find you through this number."

She sighed. "Yes, I know. That is why I fought against having a number in the book."

"You *are* looking for Nazis? The ones who ran the concentration camps?"

"I believe our organization's title is self explanatory."

I couldn't stop a chuckle. "You don't give away much, do you?"

"I m sorry, Mr. Roman. Other than your persistence, I still don't know anything about you."

"I could give you my P.I. license number. I'm licensed by the state."

"I'm sure you are."

I laughed. "Okay, I give up. But there's something I don't understand. How do you get information if you won't talk to anyone?"

"I'm talking to you. If you have any information I'll be happy to accept it, and I can assure you we'll check it out."

"I don't give away anything, either. But I'll be happy to trade."

"I'm sorry."

"All right. I know when I'm licked." I paused long enough to light a cigarette and give it a little thought. "Okay. One thing. It's just possible that your man in the Butler Wells area knows that he's been made—if you have a man, that is."

118

"Thank you," she said, as cool and unemotional as a turtle on a rock.

"You're welcome."

I broke the connection.

I finished my beer and stared gloomily into the gathering twilight, only vaguely aware of the subtle sights and sounds that heralded the fall of night: a pair of doves rocketing in to roost in an oak; the erratic movements of an armadillo crossing the clearing behind the cabin in fits and starts, nose to the ground, oblivious to anything that didn't wriggle, crawl, or burrow in the earth; the bell-like call of a bobwhite gathering the clan for safety in darkness; the flutter and chirp of nightbirds finding their favorite limb; the faraway call of a loon.

Defeat and futility. It was on me again, the last call adding focus and dimension. I had shot my proverbial wad. I was truly finished with the Ardell P. Boggs enigma. No matter what Homer came up with from his cousin. If he proved to be Genghis Khan reincarnated, it didn't matter; Hitler himself in disguise, it still didn't matter. I had been flitting around like a brainless twit, wasting everyone's time trying to find out if the old fart jumped, fell, or was pushed, and my chances of doing that were about on par with a crippled sparrow's in a snake pit. And who really gave a damn? . . . except Ethel Boggs, of course . . . and maybe Mrs. Jalesco . . . and well, to be honest, David Thisinger.

But they didn't matter, either. I had sensed no passion in their fealty, heard no stentorian demands for justice, no rallying to the cause. Boggs had apparently not been a man to evoke deep emotional reactions in others. I suspected he had discovered that fact at some point in his life, had found it intolerable, and began rewriting his personal history to include feats of derring-do that would most likely strike a responsive chord in the people around him.

To Ethel Boggs, an Englishwoman once removed, he had been the brave British Commando, writer, and intellectual. To Mrs. Jalesco, Frenchwoman, he had become the heroic freedom fighter with the Maquis. To Thisinger, the Jew, he had been a survivor of the death camps, intrepid Nazi hunter through all the years since. To Emil Prescott, the lecher, he had pictured himself a womanizer, and I found myself wondering if the acrophobia could have been some obscure gambit in the same incomprehensible game?

Who knew what else to how many more? And most incredible of all, he had gotten away with it.

Night came with a silent rush, blending shadows, blurring distinctions. I caught the last few minutes of the six o'clock newscast. I learned the Cowboys had lost another one, that we had a twenty percent chance for thunderstorms during the night. I was restless, jittery, a gnawing in my stomach that couldn't possibly be hunger. I threw another beer at it, then discovered what the feeling was during an asinine commercial for a popular antacid.

I was lonely. The way you sometimes are in the clutch of a crowd, or the centerlane on a freeway choked with cars. I had been with people all day, one after the other, and yet I was lonelier than I had been for months. Undifferentiated needs and nondescript emotions. I was in the land of my youth and yet I was among strangers. Strangers who pumped my hand and slapped my back and didn't give a damn if I failed or prospered or ever again experienced the love of a good woman. Poignant memories prowled my mind like ancient ghosts stalking a forgotten cemetery. I was decaying with the sickness of an empty life and my only surcease lay in the arms of an auburn-haired woman who was forever lost.

The thought shook me, flooded me with uneasiness, chilled my blood like an icy hand around my heart. Had I been alone too long? Mourned too much? Barbara had been dead three years, Tommy almost two. How long was enough? Too much? And where was it written down?

Maybe it was time to rationalize, to make a clear-cut distinction between life and death and, like Moses coming down off the mountain, establish a new set of imperatives, rules to guide me through the rest of my life.

The idea cheered me, but it was still a melancholy notion.

12

An hour later Webb Chandler and Zeke Fairlee yanked me out of a sound sleep in front of the TV, banging on my door and shouting suggestive obscenities that must have carried all the way to Butler Wells.

Webb's hands were filled with six packs, and Zeke carried a paper sack bulging with something that clinked glassily. Zeke's red face and squinted eyes told me he was already one sheet into the wind, and Webb's loose features suggested he wasn't far behind.

"We was having a drink down at Missy's Box," Zeke said, grinning hugely, "and your name come up. We put it to a vote and here we are, by God."

Webb grinned over Zeke's shoulder. "It wasn't my idea," he said.

"Shit. Don't let him kid you. He was all for it."

"Hey," I said. "Great idea. I'm glad you guys thought of me." I took the six packs from Webb and put them on the kitchen table.

"Why don't you stick them things in the freezer for a minute?" Webb said. "I like my beer frosty."

"Good idea." I slid the beer into the almost-empty

freezer compartment, then scooped three cans off one of the lower shelves. "These are not ice cold, but they'll do for starters."

"Hot damn!" Zeke hooked a chair away from the small chrome dinette and fell into it. "The Infallible Ones, back together again." He slapped the table with a thick, freckled hand. "Damn I wish ol' Clay could be here."

"Everybody's dying," Webb lamented. "You remember Pete Shoals, played center for a while? Deputy Sheriff over in Ralston County for about ten years? His old lady left him, took the two boys. Month later he ate his .357. Never would have figured old Pete for something like that."

"I never would have figured Clay for a plug-puller, either," I said. "Wheelchair or not, he still had all the things that ever mattered to him, name, money, power . . . and Melissa."

Webb chug-a-lugged the rest of his beer and leaned back in his chair to reach inside the refrigerator.

"His pa dying had a lot to do with it," Zeke said. "He took it hard. And that was kinda funny, I always thought he hated the old man's guts. He'd turned the whole she-bang over to Clay, but he was always looking over his shoulder, second guessing him. I thought Clay would be relieved to see him go, but you never can tell, I guess." He shrugged thick, round shoulders. "I couldn't tell any difference in him that night. He was his usual ornery self."

"The night he did it, you mean?"

Zeke grinned suddenly and looked at Webb.

"Old Man Law and Order here was writing him a ticket when I left, busting his ass for shooting that .32 of his inside the city limits."

Webb grunted and took a drink. "He'd had three warnings. That's about two more'n I'd give anyone else. Besides, it was dangerous. Small bullet like that hits the water wrong and it caroms. Mrs. Dawson already had one of her prize pots from Mexico busted by a ricochet.'' He scowled at Zeke. ''You're damn lucky I didn't give you one.''

Zeke threw up his hands in mock-surprise. ''Hey, wait a minute. I didn't fire no gun.''

''No, but you would have if I hadn't got there when I did.''

Zeke grinned at me and winked. ''You can't bust a man for bad intentions.''

''Are you talking about the marina?''

''Yeah,'' Webb growled. ''Them two yo-yo's idea of a good time was to get drunk and shoot at tin cans in the water off the gangplank. I'd warned Clay three times already and numbnuts here twice before to cut it out. That marina's inside the city limits. So Clay decides he'll outsmart me and has one of his machinists make him a silencer for his .32. Old lady Dawson may be old as sin, but she ain't dumb and when she sees these two out on that gangplank, she gets her binoculars. She can't hear the gunshots, but she can see the water spout and the gun in Clay's hand. So she rings me up as usual.''

''So that's who it was,'' Zeke said. ''Clay had a hunch somebody was ratting on us. I didn't think it was her. Her husband worked for him and his daddy for twenty years.'' He shook his head and cupped his chin in one thick hand. ''Clay could be sorta vindictive about little things. One day we were out on the gangplank. We could see her sitting up there watching us. Clay wanted me to get my starter gun out of the car and fire off a few rounds, see if Webb or anybody showed up. That way we'd know if it was her. I told him I was out of blanks.'' He turned his attention back to the window, as if the answer to human foibles lay somewhere out there in the darkness.

"How'd he react to the ticket?" I emptied my can and slowly squeezed the air out of it.

"Bad," Zeke said, "As usual. You gotta understand, though. Clay couldn't stand anyone opposing him. He'd been top dog too long, I guess. Webb laid that ticket on him, he about come unglued. Lousy fifty dollar ticket didn't amount to a shit. But he took it personal. Got loud and nasty. So nasty I tried to get Melissa to leave with me, but she wouldn't. She was trying to quiet him down. Embarrassed, I reckon. Some of their friends were out in one of the slips fishing out of their boat. So, I decided to hell with it and left."

Webb glanced at him and smiled faintly. "He run your ass off. When he got going, he didn't give a damn who he hurt."

Zeke colored. "I don't remember it that way."

Webb shrugged. "Maybe not. You were drunk as a coot, anyway." He leaned back and scrubbed a big hand across his forehead. "Zeke's right, though. He got loud and nasty. So bad, finally, that Melissa left, went out to talk to the Garfields. I got him calmed down some before I left. He wasn't nearly as bad when he didn't have an audience. Clay put me in mind of an old dog I had once. He wouldn't bite much, but he sure as hell loved to bark."

Zeke's head bobbed up and down busily. "That's him, all right. But he bit often enough to keep you guessing." He rolled the beer can between his huge palms and stared at his image in the darkened window. Then he grimaced and gave me a shamefaced grin. "I shouldn't be talking about him. All in all, he treated me right all these years."

Webb looked as if he wanted to say something. He took a drink instead, thumbing the corners of his mouth and fishing in his shirt pocket for cigarettes that weren't there. He reached across and took one of mine, smiling apologetically. "I still like one with a beer now and then." He lit up and inhaled deeply, wincing with either pain or pleasure. He looked at me through the pale exhalations, his face suddenly drawn.

"You don't reckon giving him that ticket woulda had anything to do with it, do you?" His voice was as strained as his features; it was obviously not the first time the thought had occurred to him, and from Zeke's reaction, not the first time he had voiced it.

"Aw, come on, man," Zeke said, half-angrily. "That ticket didn't mean shit to him, except for making him mad, maybe."

Webb continued looking at me. "What do you think? He killed himself about half an hour later."

I shook my head. "I can't make a judgment call like that. I don't think it would have made any difference—for what it's worth." A thought struck me. "Are you sure it was suicide?"

They both stared at me for a moment, their faces vacant. Then Zeke slapped the table and hooted.

Webb smiled crookedly and nodded. "It's a legitimate question. But I'm afraid there's no doubt about this one, Danny. Clay was alone in his little office behind that old tackle shop. The Garfields and Jack Boarman . . . and oh, that handyman, Jake Trumble, heard the shot and rushed in and found him. He'd shot himself in the head with that same .32."

Zeke made his right hand into the shape of a gun and pointed it at his right temple. He looked at Webb. "Right about there, wasn't it?"

Webb nodded. He stubbed out the cigarette, his handsome features pale. "Soft-nosed slug. Did a lot of damage inside. Tore a hole big as a half dollar coming out." He took a deep breath, the crooked smile returning. "I guess

I wasn't cut out to be a cop. I never get used to things like that."

"Few people do," I said, "How about a way in? Back door or a window?"

"No door," Zeke said. "There's a window, but I don't ever remember seeing it open."

"I checked it," Webb said. "It's been painted shut for years. Clay had a small air conditioner mounted in the wall." He reached across and stole another cigarette, this time from Zeke. He took one puff and grimaced. "Jesus Christ, what's in these things?"

"Tobacco," Zeke said. "It's a man's cigarette."

Webb puffed for a moment without inhaling. "I'd just pulled into Melissa's driveway when I got the call," he said. "Melissa needed a ride home and I guess it took an extra ten minutes to run her out to the Wilshire addition. That would have put it close to half an hour from the time we left to the time Clay shot himself. Jack Boarman said he called in immediately on Clay's phone. Melissa heard my call and insisted on going back with me. Unfortunately—or maybe it was lucky in a way—I had a flat on the way back and Stan Monroe, the officer on duty, had things pretty much under control by the time we got there. The coroner was there, and Stan had an ambulance standing by waiting for him to finish. They had Clay covered up, and I guess that helped Melissa some."

"No chance of someone going in after you left?"

Zeke rolled his eyes and chuckled. Webb sighed and smiled faintly. "Not according to Boarman, Trumble, and the Garfields. The front door was closed, in plain sight of all of them. They were all pretty definite about it."

Zeke grinned. "Give up?"

I shrugged. "Just doing the devil's advocate bit. You guys are the ones who knew him as an adult, and you seemed to be having trouble believing he'd kill himself. I haven't seen him since high school. People change a lot in eighteen years, but when I knew him he wasn't the suicidal type." I stopped and stared through Zeke huddled over his beer like a bloated praying mantis, one thought segueing into another like brittle links in an endless chain.

Something was wrong. Something was missing. Somewhere in their tale a T had not been crossed, an I dotted. I puzzled over it, feeling Webb's curious gaze: until enlightenment came like a teacher's kunckle behind the ear.

"Whoa," I said, trying not to sound fatuous. "You said the gun had a silencer. How'd they hear it out on the deck if the door was closed? They make some noise, but not enough to carry very far. Was it defective?"

"I confiscated it," Webb said gravely. "It's illegal. I have it in a locked drawer in my desk along with the gun and some switchblades and Saturday night specials I've picked up over the year. Once a year we take them out in the lake and dump them."

Zeke spoke from behind his hand: "Takes 'em into Dallas and sells 'em, he means."

Webb laughed. "I hadn't thought of that."

"Why didn't you confiscate the gun that night before you left?"

"He had a permit."

"Attached to a silencer it would be illegal."

"That's splitting hairs, Dan." For the first time Webb looked irritated, and I decided I had pushed it far enough. Judging from his suddenly darkened face, he had already thought of that, probably wondering guiltily if his small dereliction of duty had played a significant part in his former teammate's death. Obviously it had, but not one he could possibly have foreseen.

"All right already," Zeke roared. "Enough of this

twenty questions crap. We came up here to bullshit about the old days, get drunk, and wax nostalgic about the days of youth and glory and kicking ass.'' He turned to me. "Come on, Dan, now tell us the truth, boy. You ever get into Tillie Craddock's pants—?''

But the night had gone flat, as sour as Dom Perignon on a palate born to Pepsi and Coke. We tried to flog it back to life with boisterousness and camaraderie, but the heart of it had died, killed by a mean-spirited man none of us had really liked, had only grudgingly respected because he sweated and bled and strove for excellence along with the least and the best of us. His father's money could not buy him that, in truth almost lost it for him. Deep within our grubby little secret hearts we did not want to see him win, did not want to share with him who had so much one iota of the hard-won adulation spilling out of the bleachers on those magical Friday nights. But he had persevered, worked harder and longer than the rest of us, earned his niche among the ''stalwart lads'' as Snooky Windell delighted in calling us.

Once, in a futile effort to bring back enthusiasm, Zeke unsacked his offerings: half-pint bottles of bourbon and vodka, brandy and gin, one squat bottle of cognac. Toiling painstakingly amidst taunts and obscene imprecations, raiding the fridge for Worcestershire sauce and ice cream left over from Labor Day, ransacking the cabinets for tomato puree and chili pepper, cinnamon, and paprika, he constructed what he called the ''Fairlee Bomb.''

The drinks he eventually set before us had the consistency of sludge, the color of pus-streaked blood and a surprisingly pleasant pungent odor.

''It'd take a hundred dollars and a junky with a gun to make me touch that thing,'' Webb declared, pushing the drink away with a long, spatulate index finger.

I feigned a grateful smile and respectfully declined on the grounds that I had a couple of hundred more pages of *Gone With the Wind* I wanted to read before I went blind. I had instead a couple of vodka gimlets, which, on top of all the beer, turned out to be a cruel mistake.

"Chickenshit cowards," Zeke muttered around a straw, slurping mightily, somehow managing to keep a blissful expression on a face slowly turning maroon, glazed eyes growing dim with incomprehension.

Webb finally drank a sip or two of his; Zeke finished the other two, jeering and caustic right up to the second his eyes locked, rolled back into his head, and he began to slide sideways out of his chair.

Webb snorted and caught him with one big hand. "Old Knute the Chute, tough as a boot," he said, quoting one of Snooky Windell's more fanciful superlatives. "He may have been a hell of a running back, but the dumb shit never could hold his booze."

I helped shoehorn him into the passenger side of the Ferrari and watched grinning as Webb fought his way into the midget seat behind the wheel.

He careened wildly down the moonlit slope, either unable to find, or forgetting, the lights until he was on the blacktop heading east to Butler Wells.

13

I WAS AWAKENED THE NEXT MORNING BY THE VILE screaming of blue jays fighting for territorial rights somewhere in the trees above the cabin.

Shocked out of uneasy concupiscent dreams featuring darkhaired nubile maidens and shrieking macaws hurling obscene encouragement into my ears, I thought for a heart-freezing second that I was still in Vietnam, locked for all eternity in a stinking bamboo cage along the brush-infested shores of the glittering Song Bo River.

Then I made the dim, groping connection between my perforated, off-white, sound-deadening ceiling and a nifty, two-room cabin on a hill in Texas, and relief as sharp and vivid as coruscating fireworks flowed soothingly along my twanging nerves.

I dozed, closed my matter-encrusted eyelids and tried without hope to regain my delightful dream, unmindful of the warning pressure somewhere behind my loins. Jolted awake again by the jays's next encounter in the never ending war for aerial supremacy, I got up and staggered into the bathroom and sat down, too enervated to stand.

While I waited for the compressed valves to open, I held

my head in my hands and tried to think what I had planned for the day. Going home was first and foremost on the agenda.

I had had it with peace and solitude for a while, had it with hometowns and self-righteous people so bored with life they were tossing it away like biodegradable pop bottles along a busy highway. I'd had enough of bathos, and of nostalgia, which was nothing more than the dreary years of childhood resurrected with all the feculent matter removed. I'd had more than enough of Ardell P. Boggs, why he died and how. Nobody really gave a damn, including me.

Judging from the angle of sunlight slashing through the sagging bathroom curtain, I decided it was well on the way toward noon. I listened to the roll and seethe of my stomach and made a wise decision to skip breakfast, to make my courtesy call on Ethel Boggs and pick up a bite on my way home.

I needed something, however, to cut the gritty, gummy coating inside my mouth, something tart and refreshing to fuel the old machine, open the pores, uncloud the eyes. When I finished in the bathroom I rummaged in the fridge and found one single solitary lonely-looking can of beer. Life wasn't all bad.

Once, when I was eight or so, my grandfather advised me that one sure way to avoid a lot of fuss and fret in this life was not to delay what needed to be done.

"If you've got it to do, then get it done," was the way he put it, leaving it up to me to figure out if he was talking about the quotidian or the more worrisome things of life.

A long-time widower at age sixty-nine, he had died in the bed of a neighboring widow lady a month later, and I had wondered then if that had anything to do with his list of things he needed to get done.

I had spent a lot of time puzzling over it, questioning his logic in leaving a perfectly comfortable bed in his own room to spend the night with a skinny old lady with buck teeth and hair on her lip.

I eventually understood it, of course, but that understanding came only at a later age when his actions no longer seemed illogical.

That particular bit of advice had lingered, however, eventually becoming entrenched in my psyche, or id, or whatever it is that compels us to do things that are necessary but unpleasant.

And telling Mrs. Boggs that I was abandoning her quest for truth in the death of her husband I found to be both necessary and unpleasant.

But I had to do it, and I resolutely turned the nose of my pickup east toward Scales Drive when I reached Butler Wells, driving leisurely, but not dawdling, my mind curiously blank, refusing to cooperate in my search for specious arguments, soothing rationalizations.

Ethel Boggs's home needed painting. A duplicate of Thisinger's house across the street without the metal siding, its narrow boards were cracked and warped in places, and long curling strips of paint dangled off it like the shredded skin of some gigantic insect in the last stages of ecdysis. Potted flowers crowded the porch railing, and an antique oaken swing hung listlessly from eyebolts in the shiplap ceiling. Worn floorboards squeaked in vague protest as I crossed the narrow porch and knocked on the door.

She looked somehow different in the light of day. Better. Younger. Some of the cracks and crevices deleted by the more or less artful application of pancake makeup. A blush high on each check. Tasteful pale pink lipstick. Blue eye-liner that was evident only when she blinked. I couldn't help wondering why she bothered. But she was a widow now, and maybe hope really does spring eternal.

"Why, Daniel, my goodness, I really didn't expect to see you so soon." She clinked and jangled from bracelets and chains as she ushered me into a room that could well have been my mother's parlor: high-backed, curving furniture, tiger's paw legs, and a lot of dark polished wood. These were scratchy, thinly padded, uncomfortable as hell, and for that reason would last forever, because nobody could stand to sit on it for long.

"I just came by to say—"

"Sit down, sit down. My goodness, I'm forgetting my manners." She gave me a ghastly smile and bustled around like a nervous mother hen. "I was just brewing a nice cup of tea. I prefer it to coffee, don't you? And it's so much better for you, don't you think? All that caffeine. Does it keep you awake nights? I'm sorry I don't have any beer. I'm sure you would prefer beer, wouldn't you? Mr. Boggs always preferred a beer. He said tea and coffee were sissy drinks, okay for women and youngsters and . . . ah, certain other types we won't mention, but that real men preferred beer. What do you think?"

"No, no, no, yes, and yes," I said.

She gave me a startled look, rheumy eyes popping out of their padded cells, bright and shiny with fun. Then she giggled like a thirteen-year-old meeting her first rock star. "Oh, you, you're teasing me again," she trilled, and whisked out of the room before I could confess.

Resigned to my fate, I looked around for an ashtray, found it finally on the plate glass coffee table in front of me. A large handcrafted brass plate with curled edges, it showed signs of recent usage, a half-dozen stubbed-out filter cigarettes with a ring of bright red lipstick. A large manila envelope lay beside the ashtray, its sides bulging. Across the front someone had written in large block letters: POSSESSIONS OF ARDELL P. BOGGS.

"Here we go," Mrs. Boggs said happily. "I found you a beer after all. It was hidden behind some jars of preserves in the icebox." She set a small metal tray containing the can of beer and a napkin on the coffee table. She slid a spindly looking wooden chair away from the wall and sat down across from me. "I'll just wait a few more minutes on my tea. I like it to steep, don't you?"

"It's much better that way," I said. I reached for the pull tab on the can and found it already gone. I took a drink and set it down.

"That envelope," I asked, for want of something better to say. "Did it come from the police station?"

"Yes." She absently smoothed the shiny fabric of the high-necked gray dress she was wearing. "Yes, those are Mr. Boggs's things. You know, the things he had on him when . . ." She let it drift away.

"I nodded. "I thought it looked sort of . . . well, official." I took another drink, trying to decide the best way to tell her.

She picked up the envelope. "It just arrived this morning. That nice Shillings boy brought it in his patrol car. We had a nice little talk. He had a very high regard for Mr. Boggs. He said he hoped someday he would be able to match his achievement."

"Which one was that?"

"Karate. Mr. Boggs had a black belt in karate."

"Oh, I didn't know about that one."

"Few people did," she said wisely. "Mr. Boggs wasn't one to brag about his accomplishments. He was a very humble man."

"So I'm finding out," I said, watching her long, bony fingers work loose the seal on the envelope, tilt it over the table, and let the contents slide out onto the glass.

Most of the bulk came from a neatly folded short-sleeved shirt and a pair of yellow walking shorts. They had obviously been laundered, but the detergent had failed to remove a large rust-colored stain on the left leg of the shorts. A similar stain, not as large, was less noticeable on the left shirt pocket.

"Shorts?" I asked. "In October?"

"Oh, yes. Mr. Boggs was a very hardy man. At any rate, if you'll remember, last Tuesday was a very warm day."

She picked up a thin brown billfold, fingered the contents gingerly, then extracted a small sheaf of bills. She fanned them out on the table—a ten, a five, and three ones.

"Eighteen dollars," she said. "He never carried much money. He said it wouldn't do. That way he wouldn't be tempted to harm someone if they were foolish enough to try to rob him."

"I never would have thought of it that way," I said.

She nodded sagely. "Mr. Boggs had a very unique way of looking at things. I found him continually amazing." For the first time there was sadness in her voice.

And you believed him, I thought. All the shit he told you over the years. I took another sip of beer. Well, why the hell not? If it made her look up to him, respect him more, brought a little something extra into what had to be a lackluster, uneventful marriage. What mattered a few harmless lies, self-aggrandizing or not?

Her thin fingers were working gently on a tortured, twisted pair of spectacles, the ear stems bent and curled, the right lens starred, the left one missing.

"His glasssses," she said unnecessarily. "He really didn't need them. He felt they gave him dignity, the look of a scholar. If Mr. Boggs was anything at all, he was a scholar. I think I told you he was writing an in-depth psychological profile of Adolph Hitler, didn't I?"

"I think so." I picked up the envelope and shook it to make sure everything was out.

"And after that he was going to do Joseph Stalin and perhaps Mussolini." She sighed. "And now this."

The only remaining items were a neatly folded handkerchief, a felt-tipped fountain pen, and a comb. She stacked them all in a tidy pile on one corner of the table.

I lit another cigarette, wondering once again how I was going to tell her that I had no more idea how her husband had died than I had in the beginning. Less even. At least at the start I had had her suspicions to work with and a fresh unprejudiced approach.

She folded her hands in her lap and sat quietly, guileless, old eyes boring expectantly into mine, penetrating and intimidating.

I finished my beer and put out my cigarette. I crushed the can, reducing it carefully and methodically to a small, thick circle of reclaimable waste. I cleared my throat.

"Well, Daniel, do you have anything to tell me? I assume you didn't come here just to socialize with an old lady."

"What's wrong with that," I said and chuckled hollowly. I picked up the felt-tipped pen, read the advertisement on the side, put it down. "I've been talking to a lot of people who knew your—husband. He, ah, seems to have been a remarkable man."

She nodded placidly, eyes glinting, the "I told you so" plain to see in her face.

"I . . . uh, talked to his friend David Thisinger. He

137

thought a lot of your husband.'' I picked up the comb and ran it through the hairs on my arm, put it down.

"Didn't I tell you," she said.

"I talked to Mrs. Jalesco and that mechanic down at the marina—what's his name—" I picked up the spectacles and began straightening the ear stems, my hands beginning to sweat. What the hell was I afraid of? The only way to do it was to tell her, come right out and say it, "Look old girl, I've done all I can do, a lot more than you have a right to expect under the circumstances."

"Jake Trumble," she said. "He's a nice young man. His ambition is to drive racing cars. He was always pestering Mr. Boggs to give him pointers."

"Mr. Boggs drove race cars, did he?" I sighted down the stem to see if I had it right.

"Formula One. And he won the Italian Grand Prix back before the war."

She pronounced it "pricks," and it was just one thing too many, and I felt a bubble of mirth burst in my stomach, stream upward toward my throat, wrenching gasping laughter that I knew from past experience would leave me a shuddering helpless mass of protoplasm.

I closed my mouth and stopped it, covered it with a paroxysm of coughing that scourged my throat.

I got my handkerchief out and over my mouth, then watched in horror as the eyeglasses slipped through my nerveless fingers and bounced off the coffee table, the broken lens coming apart, the pieces skittering across the polished hardwood floor like tiny silver bugs.

"'Oh God," I gasped between spasms, "I'm sorry."

"You'd better see about that cough, young man," she said grimly, already flitting around the room picking up pieces of glass, casting suspicious glances at me from time to time.

I dried my eyes and got down on my hands and knees to help her, too unsure of my control to trust myself standing.

"Never mind," she said sharply. "Get up from there. You'll cut yourself. I'll get it with the sweeper. I just want to pick up the larger pieces."

"I see one," I said, crawling toward a triangle of glass glittering in a shaft of sunlight slanting through the side door window. I picked it up carefully, looked at it, wiped my eyes, and looked again.

"No, I guess not," I said. "You must have broken something else. This piece is dark, smoky."

"No," she said, a hint of the irritation I remembered so well in her voice. "These were Mr. Boggs's new glasses. They turn dark in the sunlight, turn into sunglasses, then clear up again when you come inside."

"What'll they think of next," I said, climbing slowly to my feet, avoiding her eyes, feeling the laughter lying in ambush deep in my diaphragm, coiled tightly, as unpredictable as Texas weather in May. I felt riven, irreverent, vulnerable. A wrong look from her or another relevation about Ardell P., and I would be reduced instantly to shambles, a gibbering idiot completely out of control.

"Well, back to work," I said crisply, making for the entry hall and the front door. "The day is getting away from me."

"Wait," she said, padding along behind me, surprise and alarm in her voice. "You haven't told me why you came."

"Just a visit," I hurled over my shoulder. "Progress report." I trotted down the drive past her small Toyota, leaped into my truck, and hurtled away from the curb.

Halfway down the hill I bounced against the curb, braked. Palsied, odd sounds oozing past tightly clenched teeth, I dropped my head forward onto the steering wheel and began to howl.

14

"Danny! Hello!"

The voice was low and soft and sweet and almost failed to penetrate the cacophonous barrier of lunch time clamor in Cash Dugan's Cafeteria. Immersed in moribund self-disgust, thoughts of cringing cowardice, and failed chances, I looked up from my Businessman's Special into violet eyes that peeled away the years the way a summer sun strips snowcapped mountains.

"Melissa," I said, the word stiff and awkward in my throat, an echo in my heart.

"Danny," she said again, a smile tugging at tremulous lips. She held a tray balanced on the back of the chair opposite me, the face that had haunted countless empty seamless nights as untrammeled as freshly fallen snow, as serene as Christian piety.

I almost said her name again before I realized how ri-diculous that would be. Instead I clambered to my feet, feeling overgrown and boyish.

"Are you alone?" I peered anxiously behind her, old fears of rejection bringing a rush of heat to my face, per-spiration to my palms.

"I'd be delighted," she said, as if I'd just issued a formal invitation, and set about transferring her meal from the tray to the table.

I held her chair and ditched the tray, using the precious seconds to recoup my equilibrium, collecting cool with each tick of the clock. By the time I reclaimed my seat I was smiling easily, unfolding the napkin I hadn't been using, sipping water for dryness of mouth, my mind searching frantically for something witty and appropriate.

"Well," I said. "How's tricks?"

Her laughter burst forth, a short-lived gust of genuine mirth, sparkling eyes, and the lovely, beguiling smile with book-end dimples that had always made me weak in the stomach, simple in the head. She had always known its power, had known all those years ago that she owned me, lock, stock, and zits.

"I'd have bet on it," she said, still laughing, stretching the moment. "The perfect opening line after twenty years."

"I thought it was eighteen."

She shook her head slowly, the curling bank of her chestnut hair stroking her neck and throat, waving slightly above wide and gently mocking eyes. "For us it's twenty, Danny."

"I guess so," I said. "We were sophomores."

She ate a piece of fish, a bite of salad, a sliver of bread. I went back to my roast beef special.

"I guess Webb Chandler beat my time," I said, after a while.

"Not really," she said promptly, as if she had been expecting the question and had the answer at hand. "You said you would write to me in Houston. You never did. My grandparents took me to Padre Island for a week in August that year. Webb and his parents happened to be there. We sort of hung around together. I came home right after that, two weeks before school. You must have known, but you made no attempt to see me, call me or anything. I assumed from that, that what happened under the bandstand that night had turned you against me." Her skin was pale olive, the kind that turns to honey under the tanning rays of the sun. She had always blushed beautifully. Right then her cheeks had highlights like the first rosy glow of ripening apples, her depthless eyes more defiant than apologetic.

"It was a busy summer for me, too. I went to Tennessee to visit a cousin of mine. I didn't get back until a week before school opened. Webb knew that."

She smiled across a glass of tea. "He never mentioned it. I waited for your call. It never came, but Webb's did."

"It was a long time ago," I said, wanting to tell her not to make more of it than there had been. Maybe I had been the first as she had said, but I had never been convinced. Once past the point of token maidenly resistance she had been eager and unrestrained that night, dark eyes wide and luminous and demanding, burning up at me with a wild and ancient knowledge.

Seven months of groping in cars—sweating and freezing in season—wrestling on sofas in parlors, topped by one night of sizzling love under a bandstand was hardly the stuff of nostalgic dreams. But I had never forgotten and, seeing her again now, I understood why.

"I went to your father's funeral, Danny. It was so sad. I'm sorry; I liked him."

"And he you," I said, thinking of all the ridiculous, intricate maneuvering I had done to keep her from seeing him drunk. As if the whole town hadn't known by then.

"I saw you once," she went on, her voice soft again. "Right after you came home from the war. But you were at your father's grave and I didn't want to intrude." She picked at her filet of sole with her fork. "Clay was with me. We were putting fresh flowers on his mother's grave. Clay said it would be better not to intrude, that it might embarrass you."

"I didn't realize Clay was so . . . so sensitive."

She smiled wryly. "He wasn't. He was jealous of you. He always was. And Webb."

"I was sorry to hear about his death."

"Yes," she said simply, the violet eyes downcast. She made another sortie around her plate, tiny ladylike bites, masticating with a barely perceptible movement of her jaws. Then a sip of tea, a fleeting moistness on her lush lower lip. I remembered suddenly how they felt, tasted, a million synaptic switches tripping in my brain, bringing in the memory sharp and vivid.

We were silent for a minute, eating. The silence didn't seem to bother her, but I found myself shoveling food in a way I hadn't since basic training. I slowed down, began chewing again.

"I heard about you from time to time, Danny. Your life. The things that were happening to you. Some of it was sad, but a lot of it sounded exciting. You got away from Butler Wells. That's one of your greater accomplishments."

"Doesn't say much for my life, does it?"

"I'm sorry, I didn't mean it that way. I meant to me leaving Butler Wells would be a tremendous achievement. I may just accomplish that now."

"Clay never wanted to leave?"

She gave me an incredulous look, humor and irony warring for supremacy in her face. "My God, would you, if you had your own kingdom? The crown prince all those years waiting for the throne. Two-thirds of the people in this town depend directly or indirectly on Garland Enterprises. And don't think Clay didn't know that all his life. The only thing he ever wanted and couldn't have was . . . me.'' She looked down at her plate. ''And then he got me,'' she added flatly. The wry smile was back again, the dark eyes big and intensely glowing, a look I had found entrancing as a hedonistic youth. Maybe I had grown into a hedonistic adult, but I still found it enthralling. But not so diverting that I didn't wonder at her choice of words.

''Got you . . . you make it sound like a warlord raiding the local village for a comely maiden to bed.''

She smiled without mirth, the edges of clean, white teeth faintly visible through barely parted lips. The smile lasted only a second, then she switched subjects on me.

''You're not a policeman anymore, I hear?''

''Yes, that's right.''

''Why not? I also heard that you were a good one and that you loved it.''

''Loved it is a little strong. Liked it, I guess. Most of it. At least some of it.''

''But you quit?''

''Yes.''

''And now you're a private eye.'' Her smile was back, impish and provocative. ''I suppose I consciously knew that private eyes existed outside books, TV, and movies, but I somehow lumped them in with the other fable heroes, white knights, old-time western gunslingers, the Texas Rangers.''

''That's good company. They were all real, but there were few heroes.''

''You were a hero once.''

''Say what?''

''That last year, that magical year. You almost won the state championship for us.'' She had gone beyond

145

teasing, the same light in her eyes I had seen in Webb's, in Zeke's.

"I had a little help," I said dryly. "I made the last touchdown if that's what you mean. Come to think of it, the last touchdown of my life. Not a bad way to end it."

"God, I loved you that day," she said, punching holes in her fish with short jabbing motions of her fork. "You and Webb and Zeke . . . and Clay, of course. The Infallible Four. What a silly name, but we all believed it that day."

"Young Gods," I suggested. "Righteous warriors on the field of honor."

She glanced up, face rapt, vacant eyes climbing slowly out of reverie. "You can make fun, Danny, but it was a magic day, a glorious year for all of us."

"No," I said sharply, suddenly weary of other people's wondrous memories. "My mother died that year, my father was well on his way to being the town drunk. We lost half the ranch because of the drought and my father's mismanagement. I watched my chances for college pour out of the mouth of a whiskey bottle. No, Mel, it wasn't a magical year for me."

"I'm sorry," she said simply. "I—I guess I'd forgotten."

"No. I'm the one who should be sorry. You didn't know most of it beyond my mother's death. It's just that all I've heard the last couple of days is rhapsodizing about the jolly old days of youthful glory. Bull. We played good football that year, that's all. We had some good luck, and we almost won it all. Somebody always wins. There's nothing miraculous about it. I guess I just don't understand this preoccupation with a time that was more miserable for me than not."

"Miserable?" Her eyes touched me like a physical caress. "Why? Because you and I—because we broke up?" There was something beyond curiosity in her voice. Hope? The simple human need to be missed, to be wanted, to be the object of unrequited love.

I shrugged, then chuckled, refusing to give her the satisfaction of knowing she was more right than wrong. I pushed back my plate and lit a cigarette, not bothering to ask her permission. I'd been here first.

"It just seems," I said dryly, "that that glorious year was the highlight of a lot of lives in Butler Wells."

"Our horizons are more limited, Danny. Our focus sharper. Small achievements tend to become great victories. We have no yardstick beyond our imaginations."

"Even Webb," I said. "He was gone for years, but he seems to look at things the same way Zeke does, the way, I suspect, that you do."

Eyes downcast, she concentrated on puddling the gravy in her mashed potatoes, fork gripped loosely in one shapely hand. For the first time I noticed that she had already removed her wedding band, leaving a wide white ring around her tanned finger.

"Webb never left, Danny. Not really. Not in his heart. A part of him was here. He just didn't know it."

It was a curious thing for her to say, and I waited for elaboration. But she looked up suddenly and turned on her smile, full wattage, and a small warm hand gripped me gently in my chest.

"What did you have planned for this afternoon, Danny? I feel closed in. I need action, movement, laughter. I want to feel young again, gay—I'd like to drive out along the lake, feel giddy, and talk about inconsequential things. I promise I won't bring up the past, not even once."

"I take it that's an invitation?"

"You take it right, Mr. Roman. Are you game?"

147

"I'm about as gamey as you can get without stinking."

Her laughter burst forth again, heartwarming, stirring old memories despite her promise. The warm hand began to move downward.

15

I HAD GONE THROUGH THE ENTIRE RANGE OF HUMAN EMO-
tions that junior year when Melissa began going with Webb.
I had labeled her with a lot of names I had heard but had
only the vaguest notion of their meaning. Out of spite; out
of envy; out of heartbreak, the cruelest emotion of all. But
time assuages the human spirit, and I had later sorted it out
through endless bouts of rationalization and convoluted
reasoning which ultimately had me dropping her because
she was easy, a wanton woman.

I arrived at this conclusion by blithely ignoring the seven
months I had spent in an almost constant state of agitation,
trying every scheme I had ever heard about, or read about,
or even dreamed about. I used subterfuge, made up lies,
created diversions, pled imminent insanity. Nothing had
worked until that fateful night under the bandstand. And I
never knew why. I had excoriated myself a thousand times
for my knavish cowardice, come to believe that I had failed
her also in some subtle physical way.

But finally I had hammered the memories into some
kind of acceptable shape, filed them away in a form least
likely to cause damage. Over the years when I thought

of her, I did it fleetingly, always with humor and vague musings about the vagaries of youth. I had never called up the memories and browsed through them the way you might an old yearbook; the veneer was too fragile, the core too soft.

And now we were flying along the rim of Cannonball Lake in my pickup, Melissa posed against the other door, one arm cocked in the open window, the other across the back of the seat, chestnut hair flying, flailing rosy cheeks and smiling lips until she rummaged in her purse and found a bit of ribbon, pulled it back into a ponytail.

She wore black designer jeans, a yellow silk blouse, and a white cardigan sweater almost identical to the one she had worn in high school so often. Small-breasted and slender, time had lavished her with loving care, subtly rounding the planes of the once pretty face, smoothing the angles, creating beauty, adding mystery.

We had driven that road a hundred times before, usually ensconced cheek to cheek, hip to hip, in my Dad's old '51 Mercury, less often in one of the ranch's two rattling pickups. Our destination had always been the same; the ubiquitous Lookout Point. Every lake has one, or its facsimile.

Ours had trees, one stone picnic table, and a metal plaque commemorating Cyrus T. Cannon whose zeal and farsightedness had done much to bring about the miracle of the shimmering blue waters. The oldtimers in the area felt there should have been a postscript: "To Cyrus T. Cannon who forever solved the problem of water on his Circle Bar C ranch."

But nobody had really minded. The government and the state had paid the bill, the lake had brought a measure of prosperity to Butler Wells, untold thousands in new taxes, a first-rate scenic viewpoint high above the blue waters, and the squat hulking concrete dam. Some Saturday nights there would be as many as twenty cars parked among the trees and not a single solitary figure strolling the walkway by the bluff.

I nosed the pickup in close to the safety railing, locked the handbrake, and let the motor die. I lit a cigarette and rolled my window all the way down, watching her untie the ribbon, raise both hands to fluff out her hair the way she had always done in those anticipation-riddled moments before our first clench. She lifted her face, the sun firing her skin with color. She breathed deeply the crisp, autumn air, then turned to me with a smile, a faintly sheepish expression, violet eyes wide and strangely limpid, luminous.

"It takes you back, doesn't it, Danny? I haven't been up here in—God, I don't know how many years."

"You wanted to feel young. This is about as young as it gets around here, unless you want to go play on the teeter-totter."

She laughed and brought her left leg up onto the seat, hooking her right knee over her ankle, backing against the door to face me. "You remember the very first time we came up here? The very first time you kissed me?"

"It's engraved in stone. I not only missed your mouth, I was puckered up like a kid kissing his old maiden aunt. Jesus, I was dumb."

"Not dumb, Danny, just inexperienced." She wrinkled her nose. "I taught you, though, didn't I?"

I nodded and grinned, remembering the shock of hot wet lips opening over mine.

Then came instruction, experimentation, frenzy. I had reached the first great plateau in a climb up a mountain I had only heard about. A high difficult mountain, I was to find out, but one well worth the effort.

151

"You turned out to be a terrific kisser," she said, a teasing light in her eyes. "I claim a great deal of credit for that."

"You changed my whole life. I thought kissing was something you did when you couldn't get by on a handshake." I had an uneasy feeling she was going to take it all the way to the bandstand, the way an old dog digs up and worries a buried bone.

"You were a fast learner. How many hours do you suppose we spent kissing in your dad's old car and my parlor?"

"And squirming and groping," I said, to put it in proper perspective. "Enough to wipe out the federal debt at minimum wage."

She sighed. "I guess I was pretty awful. I know you went away hurting and angry a lot of times. And I'd go in my room and cry and cry." She smiled tremulously. "It all seemed so tragic at the time." The smile widened. "And wonderful."

"I'd hate you for about five minutes, swear I wouldn't ever talk to you again. By the time I got home I'd be planning my next strategy in the assault on the Iron Maiden." I flipped the cigarette through the open window, clearing the railing, watching it drift toward the water.

"It was hard on me, too," she said, a pout in her voice. "I had so much more to worry about than you. My reputation, getting pregnant, Mama and Papa—my God, Mama and Papa worshipped me. I was their saintly little princess. They would have hung you from the ridge pole in the barn the way it was."

Oh, I don t know. They were young once. I don't imagine they thought we were exchanging school gossip or telling ghost stories out there in their parlor."

"That night," she said, her face as soft as her voice. "I've never been sorry it happened, have you?"

"Yes," I said, some inexplicable swell of conscience forcing me to be scrupulously honest with her. "I was incredibly happy and I was sorry, too. I'd never thought of myself as a coward, but I found out that night that I was. After all the pain and frustration and the glory of success, I came apart. Afterwards, I wanted to find a hole and hide. I guess I was ashamed. Even today I still don't understand exactly what happened." I stopped and shrugged. "But you knew. You were there."

"No, I didn't," she breathed, leaning forward, her face anxious. "I thought—oh, I don't know what I thought. I was too caught up in my own fears, I guess. You didn't *show* anything, Danny. You never showed anything. You were sweet and gentle, and I was happy to finally make you happy. I knew you were worried because we went sort of crazy and didn't take precautions, but I didn't dream you were that . . . upset." Her hand came out and grasped my arm tightly. "Is that why you didn't write me, call me that summer?"

"It was twenty years ago, Melissa. I'm not sure anymore." We weren't remembering it the same way, but time has a way of filling holes, smoothing edges, shading meanings. That would work for me as well as her, and who knew who was right?

"You know what I thought?" Her soft voice was edging toward roughness, the heat from her fingers beginning to penetrate the thin material of my windbreaker. "I thought I had failed you in some unknown way. And then I came to believe I had made a terrible mistake. You weren't like the other boys, Danny. You were a square in a lot of ways, more intense, more honest, a weird sense of honor. I never

153

had to worry about stopping you, you always stopped yourself—"

"Strategy," I said. "Disarming guile. I plotted constantly."

"But you always stopped yourself. I've tried to believe otherwise, but I know that I took the initiative that night. I guess I was afraid you'd lose interest in me over the summer—no, I'll tell it like it was. I wanted to do it that night, maybe more than you, much more than I had ever wanted to before. I consciously made a choice, and I guess I made the wrong one."

"Hindsight. The trouble with hindsight is that we always see it from the rear. It's usually uglier back there."

"Don't kid about this, Danny. It's important."

"Not any more, Melissa. It's been twenty years. We were kids. Nobody expected us to make adult rationalizations."

"We were adult enough to make love." Her fingers relaxed and drifted away.

"That doesn't prove anything. Children and dogs can make love—and do."

"Are you really so cynical? Are you really? I don't believe it."

"Maybe. But maybe more practical. I wasn't then. You're right, I was a square. We made making love such an unattainable goal that when it finally happened I felt this awesome responsibility to you. I was naive enough to believe that the act itself would bind us together forever and ever. It was actually pretty funny." I chuckled and dug into my shirt pocket for a cigarette.

"You're bitter," she said, awe in her voice. "After all this time."

I laughed; it sounded shaky, but I covered by lighting

the cigarette. She was digging into my neatly compart-mented memories, scratching deep, scrambling them be-yond recognition, striking chords meant never to be strummed again. I didn't like it.

"Bitter? No, I don't think so, Melissa. It was kid stuff, breathless undying love and all that. And I was out of step with the times. I guess I read too many books. The old ones, before the four-letter words and steamy sex. I believed all that stuff about honor and integrity; the only problem was, I couldn't live up to it and sometimes that made me a little crazy. I was as base and conniving as the next punk with his brains between his legs. It just took me a little longer than most to sort it all out, to accept that I was pretty much normal and not depraved and dirty." I looked out across the lake. The gulls had found another school of feeding sand bass, and were dip-ping and swerving and diving in the throes of their own feeding frenzy.

"I felt betrayed, I suppose," I said into the silence be-hind me. "When you began going around with Webb I thought my world had ended. It was all very dramatic—breast-beating and anxiety time." I chuckled again, smoke jetting out of my nose in irregular puffs. "At that age emotions flame high and burn deep; they just don't last very long." I took one last pull and flipped the cig-arette over the railing. "It all seems pretty damn silly now."

"Danny." The word was all the warning I got, dry and cracked and oddly muted. I turned to find her coming across the seat, and once again I felt hot wet lips cover-ing mine.

Nothing much had changed: I shuddered. But for com-pletely different reasons.

* * *

We made the fifteen-mile run to my cabin in wordless silence. Shoulder to shoulder and flank to flank. She hummed something about "love being better the second time around" in a husky offkey voice, and I chain smoked. I wasn't exactly sure what was happening, and didn't even pretend to understand why. She had broken away in the middle of a stormy kiss, shyly confessed an urgent need to use a bathroom, and when I suggested the stone building near the edge of the park, she had politely demurred and made a suggestion of her own: the bathroom in my cabin.

Inside, she headed unerringly in the right direction. Not a difficult task since it took up a third of my bedroom. She was gone a long time. I heard the sound of water, the whine of my electric pump motor and cleverly deduced she was taking a shower.

I moved around the cabin aimlessly, picking up things, putting them down, taking them up again on my next pass. I washed my hands twice, checked my shorts for holes, my underarms for odor. I raked a hand across my day-old beard and almost panicked.

On my next turn around the cabin I found cigarettes burning in two different ashtrays and discovered one in my mouth. I made a vodka gimlet with Zeke's leftovers and almost took a swig before I remembered she had hated the smell and taste of alcohol. I poured it down the sink and rinsed out the glass, hid the bottles under the cabinet.

I sat down then and congratulated myself on keeping my cool. I lit another cigarette and wondered if maybe I wasn't jumping to wrong conclusions. Maybe she really had to use the bathroom, and maybe decided on the spur of the moment that after all the heavy breathing and smooching that a shower would be just the ticket to restore equanimity? She might at this very moment be getting dressed in her designer jeans, silk blouse, and cheerleader sweater . . .

The door opened; she came out wrapped in a towel. Rosy cheeks and a demure smile.

"Next," she said.

She made it a question, but I took it as a command. Five minutes, and I was donning my own towel, unshaven, but squeaky clean, my teeth brushed and my hair pushed into some semblance of order.

I caught a fleeting glimpse of my face, the set strained look of a man awaiting execution. I relaxed and smiled, trying to find the boy in the not-so-handsome features of the man. But he was long gone, the same way Melissa was no longer the girl.

So we were just two strangers after all, coming together on the crumbling sands of almost forgotten memories, as uncertain and afraid as we had been that other time, but not, heaven forbid, as immature.

The small warm hand was back in my vitals, radiating heat.

She was standing where I had left her, hands lightly curled at her sides, a crooked smile that reflected my own anxieties. The color had receded from her cheeks, the violet eyes big and dark, startling against the wanness.

Like lovers in a dream sequence, or a hokey grade-B movie, we moved to within a foot of each other, stood there without touching, without moving, without sound.

Then, not appearing to move, she dropped her towel. I dropped mine. And still we stood.

Her cheeks flamed suddenly, the thin nostrils flaring above dry parted lips. Her eyes grew wide and shadowed, lustrous with raw emotion. The tip of her tongue came out and wet her lips.

The small warm hand inside me moved, contracted into a hot heavy fist.

"Now," she whispered, swaying forward, her voice dry and tense with feeling. "Touch me, Danny! Touch me now!"

"Where?"

16

My contentious blue jays roused us an hour later, shrieking ill will, sounding their clarion call to battle, to grim encounters of the violent kind.

I felt her head stir on my arm, a long soft intake of breath, a gusty sigh. She peeked at me through tousled hair, her face relaxed, her features almost formless. She smiled a dreamy knowing smile.

"You're really a bang-up lover, Danny. Did you know that?"

"Yeah, I know," I said. "Everybody needs one thing they're really good at."

She chuckled, but not deeply. "I'm not kidding."

"I'm not either. It's all in the hips. They didn't call me ol' swivel-hips for nothing, you know."

She nodded, her face serious. "That's right, they did. Among other things. Dan the Answer Man." She lifted her head and brushed hair out of her eyes. "I always thought that was a little bit . . . much." Her head drifted downward again.

I looked at her downcast face, wondering at the faint trace of waspishness until I remembered that the name had come after we broke up, that I was going with Jenny Lee Phillips that year, that Melissa had always had a tendency to denigrate anything from which she felt excluded.

"I agree with you," I said. "I thought it was silly and childish. But I didn't give it to myself. No more than Zeke started calling himself Knute the Chute, or Webb, Spiderwebb."

"Knute the Chute? I don't remember that one."

"Knute is Zeke's middle name. I guess Snooky Windell couldn't find anything to go with Zeke. And Knute worked out better, anyway. That was Zeke's battle cry at scrimmage: 'put her down the chute, Webb, baby, I'll be there.' He always said it, no matter what play we were running. He thought it unnerved the other team. May have, as a matter of fact. They double-teamed him a lot. Some of the guys had been calling him Chute a long time before Snooky picked up on it."

"I didn't know him very well. He ran around with another crowd. I always thought he was kind of . . . well, tough."

"Zeke? Compared to who? Me and Webb used to whip his butt regularly when we were kids. Zeke had a tough time as a kid. I'm proud as hell of him. He's gone farther than any of us. But you know that already, he's your employee."

"I still don't know him very well. He and Clay were buddies, but he never came to the house much. Business parties sometimes, and once or twice a year Clay would bring him home to dinner."

"Is he going to get the president's job—no, strike that. It isn't any of my business."

She shook her head. "I don't really know. I think so. He's the logical one for the job, but it'll be up to the board of directors." She moved restlessly, running a splayed hand down across my chest, switching subjects in midair the way a cat swaps ends. "Smooth as a baby's bottom," she murmured. "I'd forgotten that you don't have any hair on your chest."

"Sign of virility," I said. "Same as baldness. You ever notice Tarzan don't have any hair there? Flash Gordon? Superman?"

She started a laugh that dwindled into a giggle. "You were touchy about it twenty years ago, too. Don't worry, I don't like hairy men." She snuggled closer, pressing warm breasts against my side. "I like men who are sleek and well fed."

"I'm well fed. Sleek, I don't know about. Seals are sleek."

"I want you to know something," she said, suddenly serious again. "Clay and I hadn't made love since his accident. Four years, almost. I was pretty wild today and I don't want you to think I'm some kind of . . . of nymphomaniac, or something, that I just jump into bed with the first man who comes along."

"I haven't had time to give it any thought at all, Melissa. I was as wild as you, and it's only been a year for me. So what's the big deal. You're entitled."

"All right," she said, "but I wanted you to know." Her head fell back against my arm. "It's just so soon, is all. I know this is the same old story, but Clay and I never had much of a marriage. But the town doesn't know that, and they expect a respectable period of mourning."

"I hear you have a beautiful daughter."

She was silent a moment. "Yes, she is. Candy's very beautiful."

"Like mother, like daughter."

"Thank you, but Candice is too beautiful, I think. It's

161

not always a blessing.'' She laughed softly. ''Let me amend that: it is seldom a blessing.''

''You did all right. The richest boy in town and maybe the best looking. I knew he was crazy about you, but I didn't think you were too impressed with him. I always figured you and Webb had it wired—'' I broke it off again. I was blithely cruising into uncharted waters without so much as a sounding. ''Scratch that, also.''

She stirred, rubbed a shapely foot along my shinbone. ''I don't mind telling you. We simply couldn't agree on our future. I wanted to get married right away after graduation. Webb didn't. He wanted to wait until he had finished at least two years. Two years. That was a lifetime at eighteen. Then he had to move to Dallas to go to college and he couldn't afford to come home very often. Things just seemed to get all stretched out of shape. We fought almost every time we saw each other. I wanted to go to Dallas, get married, and go to work. He said no. You know how stubborn he can be sometimes. Well, I can be stubborn, too, and it all seemed to come apart around Thanksgiving that year The details are too tedious.'' She was silent for a moment. ''Clay was there. Clay was always there somewhere it seemed. I suppose I decided that if I couldn't marry for love I would marry for money. It's too long ago. I can't remember.'' She nuzzled my arm. ''I wonder how much different it would have been if . . .'' She didn't have to finish it. I knew what she meant.

''What if's and should have's and could have been's,'' I said. ''It's dead-end thinking. It's all a game of chance. We have to play the cards we're dealt. Sometimes we can make a lucky draw, fill an inside straight or a flush. But mostly we have to go against the game with what we've got. There are a lot of people who'd disagree with that. They're mostly rich and mostly self-made bastards.''

She made the smile I had been angling for, bringing radiance to her solemn face. I tilted her head and kissed her, tasting for pleasure, testing for passion.

I found both.

I dropped her at the rear bumper of her green Cadillac a few minutes before dark. Subdued, violet eyes languorous, she stretched to kiss me full on the mouth, unmindful of the customers crisscrossing Cash Dugan's Cafeteria parking lot. Sometime during the long afternoon she had evidently given up worrying about what the staid populace of Butler Wells might think.

She lingered a moment, one small hand gently kneading my thigh, relaxed yet hesitant, as if the moment called for something more and she wasn't exactly sure what.

Finally she sighed. "Thank you, Danny."

I shook my head in wonder. "You're thanking me? That's kinda like the honey thanking the bear, the rabbit thanking the hound."

Her eyebrows lifted above a tremulous smile. "I'm not sure what that means, but I'll take it as a compliment of sorts." She patted my leg and slid across to the door. She smiled again and lifted the handle. The door clicked open.

"Is this it?" I said, my voice light but as dry as husks. "Or do we meet again twenty years from now?"

She looked straight ahead, her face suddenly working with emotions I couldn't pretend to understand, a hollow feeling in my gut telling me I didn't want to try.

"I don't know, Danny. I'm sorry. I—I don't know." And then she was gone, the dull snick of the closing door as final as the sound of a cleaver striking bone. I watched her duck into the Cadillac, the chestnut ponytail bobbing like the question mark at the end of life.

And I tromped the accelerator. Exactly the way I had

done when I was sixteen, lifted the light rear end of the pickup in a series of screaming bucking lurches, blasting the tranquil twilight in my adolescent fury, my monumental, ego-bruised frustration.

Damn her! She was doing it again—and just when I was beginning to forgive her.

I saw the car while I was still a mile away. Highlighted against the darkening sky, the light bar across the top identifying it as plainly as neon. I glanced automatically at my speedometer. Forty-five. A respectable speed in any man's county.

After a moment, I decided it couldn't be a speed trap. He was parked on the brow of a small hill, a mile or so outside the city limits. That eliminated city police, and every county mountie I had ever seen preferred the curves and gullies. The state police rarely patrolled the lowly secondary roads, and when they did they were usually running on a call.

Nevertheless, I slowed a little more, drifted by the dark silent car at a sedate forty miles an hour. I caught a fleeting glimpse of a sharply defined profile, heard a yell that sounded like a curse, and seconds later saw the night light up behind me as the car's headlamps blazed, the whirling lights not far behind. A siren whooped once like a dying crane, and the car swung in behind me.

I did some cursing on my own, quietly, and drifted onto the shoulder. I killed the engine and lit a cigarette before stepping out to meet my fate, the twin beams blinding, pinning me to the night like some helpless skewered bug. I walked to the pickup's tailgate and stopped, smiling, arms akimbo to let him see that I wasn't some drug-crazed degenerate roaming the country roads looking for sheep to rape or calves to abuse.

A car door closed, a few grating footsteps, and he stood between me and the headlights, tall and wide-shouldered and slim-hipped. Familiar. But not nearly so familiar as the listing, stiff-backed, John Wayne walk as he came closer.

"Shit! You peckerhead! I thought sure some county mountie was filling out his quota."

No laugh. No sound at all. He just stood there, his face in shadow, limned by fire. Hair mussed, flying in the breeze. Swaying, hands on hips. A faint wafting odor of alcohol. Menace in the air so heavy I could taste it.

Cold fingers gripped the back of my head; my stomach swooped suddenly, bottomed out with a sickening thud. And even before the words came, thick and choking, I knew.

"You were with her . . . with her this afternoon. You—you took her—you went to—goddammit, answer me!"

"Take it easy, Webb," I said quietly. "It was free choice, man."

"You son of a bitch!" he howled and, as if in punctuation of the expletive, turned and vomited into the road, his big body broken at the middle, tottering on widespread shaky legs. It went on for some time, intermittent and foul, interspersed with snarled curses and unintelligible sounds.

Finally, he braced himself with one forearm on his fender, the other still pressed against his stomach, the backspray of light playing ghastly tricks with his pallid face, a rind of vomit speckling his mouth, flecking his square chin.

"You—you can't do—do it, Dan. Not after all—all the years I waited. You can't just—just come back and take her, goddammit!" He ended in a howl of pure fury, straightening to stand wavering on uncertain feet, sucking air rasping like the breath of a gored horse.

165

"Take it easy, Webb," I said again. "I'm not taking anything of yours." I stressed the last word, feeling my own drumbeat of anger, anger at my unreasoning fear a few minutes before, anger at him, at myself, at Melissa.

"Oh, yeah, man, you are," he said, his voice deep and resonant again. "She's mine, right enough. She—she's always been mine."

"Not always," I said, smiling thinly, the drumbeat becoming a drumroll, pulsing in my ears, flooding my body with adrenalin, swelling my veins with righteous power. I knew the feeling. I turned my head and breathed deeply, feeling the cold, searing light of the moon on my face.

"I've waited, man. You know how long—Jesus! Twenty goddamned years."

"Nineteen," I said, knowing it was stupid to goad him, to pour acid into a running wound.

"I want your promise, Dan. Okay? I want your promise you won't see her, call her, go near her."

Anger blossomed in me like a shout. I wanted to laugh, to purge that hidden pocket of enmity that had been lurking inside me for nineteen years, pouched and festering without my knowledge.

But there had been more pleading than command in his voice, and along with anger came a kind of empathic understanding. Not much, but a little.

"No," I said. "I won't seek her out, but if she comes, I won't turn her away."

He stood swaying, digesting my words, sifting them through the alcoholic haze in his brain—and finding them wanting.

He charged with a roar, arms spread wide to gather me to his chest, shoulders bunched with waiting power, handsome face ugly with purpose.

I watched him coming and knew I couldn't take a chance.

Once inside those massive arms and I'd be wrung out like hand washables. I couldn't hope to fight him muscle to muscle, and I didn't intend to try. I could outbox, outmaneuver, or outrun him; I had a choice to make.

I made it; I went to meet him.

One step, two steps, and I could almost feel his breath, the long arms beginning to close, upper torso tilted forward in eagerness, features caught in a rictus of howling rage.

Almost inside, I dropped, rolled, threw my hips into his charging legs.

He tried to leap, to slow down, and did neither, his toes catching my hip, momentum carrying him forward in a headlong, helpless rush, driving him headfirst into the tailgate of my pickup with the sound of a sledgehammer on untempered steel.

A car nosed over the rise, slowed to a crawl, headlights flicking to high beam as I pulled Webb away from his dazed clinging hold on the tailgate.

I took my time and did it right, slammed my fist into his solar plexus, the softest, most damaging place I could think of without doing real harm to him or my fist.

The car accelerated, tires squalling; I heard a faint teen-age rebel yell: the hated fuzz finally getting his.

I turned him loose and let him fall, drifting brokenly to his knees, arms loving his stomach again, mouth gaping in horror and surprise, or maybe only trying to breathe.

I leaned against the pickup's fender and lit a cigarette. I sucked the smoke deep into my lungs and tried to find human meaning in the black void between the pinpricks of long dead stars, in the pale inscrutable face of the moon.

How quickly it changed. Baffled by my own inability to prevent friendship from turning into raging confrontation, how could I hope to understand Webb? He, at least, had the excuse of being drunk.

I watched him slowly uncurl on the pavement, retching again.

I felt a swift curling lick of self-disgust. I had wanted it. Hard fist smashing into soft living flesh. I had felt a hot surging thrill, reason gone for those few seconds, instinct and compulsion demanding righteous retribution, demanding dominance, enforcing fealty. Hundreds of years of civilization's veneer vanishing in the batting of an eye, the thrust of a fist. Violence in the genes. It hadn't changed since primeval man.

The smoke burned my mouth, my throat. I threw away the cigarette and stepped to where he had crawled on his hands and knees, head dangling, ropy strands of spittle binding him to the dark pavement. I took out my handkerchief and wiped his mouth.

"Come on, man. Come on, Webb, get up off the pavement."

He swung his head and glowered at me, eyes shot with blood, his skin the color of sickness.

"You couldn't have taken me if I wasn't drunk."

"If you weren't drunk, I wouldn't have to." I slipped my hand across his shoulder and under his arm. I muscled him up to his knees, heaved again, and he was tottering on baby legs, bowed and limber. We worked our way to his car.

I took off his gunbelt and handcuffs before depositing him in the seat. I shoved his arms through the spokes of the wheel, down under the steering post and cuffed him. He watched me, confused and unresisting, his eyes going in and out of focus like a yellow blinking light.

"What the hell—hell you doing?"

"I don't want you following me, Webb. When I get to the cabin, I'll make a call. If I forget or the phone's out of order you'll still be here in the morning when I head for home. I'll turn you loose then.''

His face brightened, came together in some semblance of order. ''You going home?''

I nodded.

He stared up at me, grinning foolishly. ''Then you . . . you don't want her?''

I looked away, then back again, wanting to return the silly smile, willing cool and nonchalance into a face that felt like it was shrinking, wanting to tell him that I wasn't giving up anything because I had nothing. One afternoon of love so hot it took the breath away. But nothing more, not even a promise.

''No,'' I said, breathing deeply, smiling weakly. ''I don't want her.'' I reached through the window and tapped him on the chin—not lightly. ''See, dumbass, this was all unnecessary.'' I lifted a hand and wheeled toward my truck.

''Danny!'' Framed by the window, his face gleamed starkly white. ''Thanks, man. I'm sorry.''

''Forget it,'' I said, without slowing stride. Maybe, just maybe, we were finally even.

17

WHEN I GOT TO THE CABIN I MADE THE CALL TO THE Butler Wells police then rummaged beneath the kitchen sink and found Zeke's almost-full bottle of Jack Daniel's. I set it in the center of the kitchen table, lit a cigarette, and sat looking at it.

It was a game I had played a lot during the months following Barbara's death.

Sometimes I won and sometimes I lost.

That night I lost.

The light was blinding, the fingers digging into my shoulder poison with pain. I tried to fit them into my dream about whispering streams in cool mountains, moon-silvered maids frolicking nude and unashamed. But the contrast was too startling, the transition too abrupt, and I struggled out of sleep to jeering twangy voices as thick as cold molasses on rice.

"Shit, Mingo, this mother's drunker'n a coot. He smell like a brewery. This gonna be easy, man."

"Watch the name, stupid! He ain't that drunk." Mingo's voice flowed into my face, his hands shook me. "Hey, man, come on, wake up!'' I heard the sound of a slap and it took a second to realize that I was the slapee.

''Hey,'' I said and put up a hand, more to block out the light than to ward off another blow. Moments later I found myself tumbling through space, bouncing loosely on the thinly carpeted floor. ''Hey . . . shit!'' I said, groping for something with more dignity, something sterner. ''Hey, dammit!''

The lights came on as somebody found the switch, and strong arms slipped beneath my shoulders, lifted. A voice as coarse as cornbread crumbs snickered in my ear: ''Hey, cowboy, better hike up them drawers. We lookin' right at your pee-pee.'' A rough hand slid down my side and tugged my shorts downward.

A bulky, redfaced man stood beside my bed, hands on nonexistent hips, stomach bulging like a medicine ball. He shook his head in disgust, small round eyes on the man behind me.

''You a sorry asshole, Seth. You know that? Sometimes I think you fruity, the things you do.''

''Bullshit,'' Seth said, propelling me back toward the bed.

I billowed like a windblown sheet, one thrashing hand catching a bedpost, slowing momentum, twirling me almost gracefully around to sit on the end of the bed. Shaking with cold and injured dignity, I looked around the cabin to see how many there were. Only two. My eyes came back to focus on the one called Seth, a smaller, even more decrepit version of Mingo. They both wore bibbed overalls and dark cotton shirts, heavy boots and baseball caps advertising Ford. Stained yellow teeth peeking through lips that didn't close. I decided they were brothers.

''Get your clothes on, bubba,'' Mingo growled, gesturing with one thick, hirsute hand. "We got us a date to keep."

"What do you guys want?" I asked politely. "I have about a hundred and—"

Seth guffawed. "We'll take it."

"Get your clothes on, bubba," Mingo repeated, more softly this time, but hardly more reassuring. The little eyes were rounder, bigger, the womanish mouth pursed. Somehow it made him look meaner, evil.

"Listen," I said without the faintest notion of what I was going to say. But I needed time. The tight band around my head was slipping, dissolving, spilling energy and painful knowledge. I licked my lips and looked at their empty hands.

"Listen, I don't think I'm gonna go anywhere with you guys. Okay? Now I've got a hundred and fifty bucks you can have. Free and clear. Man takes a chance like this, he deserves a little something for the risk he's taking. I understand that. Another thing. I have to tell you that as of right now I'm not drunk any longer. I think I can take both of you. But . . . ." I climbed slowly to my feet. "But I feel it only fair to warn you that I have a black belt—"

"No shit," Mingo said, and yawned. "Then you better be puttin' it in the loops of them pants you're gonna put on." He brought his hand out from the front of his overalls, held out a Smith and Wesson Airweight five-shot that looked exactly like one of mine.

While I was getting dressed, I wondered if it was.

They took me to a boat landing I had never seen before, sat me in the center seat of a battered old Lone Star aluminum fishing boat, took off my boots and lashed each foot to a cinder block with thin nylon twine.

"Just so you won't get no ideas about jumpin' in and swimmin, off," Mingo explained.

I watched Seth bolt an electric trolling motor to the transom.

"What're the other two blocks for?" I asked Mingo.

He grunted. "Ballast."

Seth snickered and held a kitchen match to the double mantles of a Coleman lantern.

"All right, let's move it." Mingo shoved the boat away from the ramp, metal grinding on concrete. He tried to leap inside without getting his feet wet and almost turned us over, ended up dragging both feet in the water as the boat coasted slowly away from shore. He glared at me when I laughed, the mean look coming over his face. But he took his anger out on Seth.

"Come on, you dumb asshole! Get that motor going."

"What the hell you mean? Sucker is going. All she'll do."

Mingo swore. He produced the gun from somewhere in his clothing, leaned forward and tapped my knee with the barrel, his rabbit features in shadow, black, beady eyes deeply imbedded, shining at me like tiny animals in ambush.

"You gonna oar us, bubba. We'll be all the damn night this way. Just lift them oars easy and drop 'em in them little holes there."

"I should turn around," I suggested politely, suppressing an urge to chuckle at his stupidity. Somewhere on the drive from the cabin the alcoholic fog had closed in on me again, and the entire thing had taken on the atmosphere of a boyish lark.

He looked at me thoughtfully. "Yeah, I guess you're right. Okay. Just squirm around there and face old Seth. That's better, anyhow, cause I got the gun."

I gripped a block in each hand, lifted and swiveled on the seat. Seth grinned at me. I dropped the oars into place, squirmed, and took a tentative pull. We moved perceptibly faster.

"There you go." Seth laughed his crazy, whinnying laugh. "Put yore back into it, boy."

I nodded and fell into an easy rhythm, breasting the almost nonexistent chop, doubling our speed, letting Seth do the guiding, concentrating on my stroke, feeling more euphoric by the minute, a small part of me looking on with incredulity and dismay.

He said he had the gun, I thought languidly, watching the lights on the surrounding hills pull away. That means there's only one. I felt my brow wrinkle. Why was that important?

The answer eluded me. I shrugged it off and put my back into my rowing like Seth had said, proud of my ability to propel our battered craft through the dark silent water. I felt powerful, thrumming with energy, the moon a bright silver disk, luring us onward into the night.

"Snake, Mingo! Right side!" Seth's voice shrilled with excitement, eyes shining, buck teeth bared in a mean, spiteful grin.

"Goddamn!"

I felt the boat lurch to the left, tilting dangerously, then the clatter of metal on metal and two percussive claps of thunder that almost lifted me out of the seat.

"You got'em!" Seth yelled. "Got that mother right behind the head!"

I shipped my oars and watched a writhing coiling body slide by the boat.

"An old brown watersnake," I said. "He'd never hurt nobody."

"Aaaah." Mingo's voice was raw and shuddering. "God, I hate them mothers."

"He got bit," Seth said knowingly. "When he was seven. Got him right above his pecker. Swole up so bad he couldn't piss for a week. They had to slip this little plastic gismo—"

"Shut up, Seth, goddammit! You gotta tell every damn thing you know?"

"He ain't never heard it," Seth said sullenly. "Don't make no damn difference."

"Gunshots carry over water," I said. "Especially at night. Probably a hundred or so people heard those shots—"

"Shut the hell up! Just get back to your rowin'."

"Who're we going to see?" I asked, making no move to resume rowing, looking over my shoulder at Mingo's mean puckered face, cold reality nosing through cloudy delusion, the sibilant sound of the Coleman lantern a prelude to a rising crescendo of alarm.

"You ever hear of Davy Jones?" Seth guffawed again, pounding his knee and rocking, his swarthy face dark with glee.

"This is as far as I go," I said, releasing the oars to swing free in the water, wiping my hands on my pants legs, calculating my chances with two twenty-pound cinder blocks—

"Maybe you're right," Mingo said, his eyes sweeping the distant shore, his voice flat and hard. "Might be you're right about them shots, too."

I let my right hand drift back to the oar, turned slightly in my seat to look at him. If I could drive the butt end of the oar into his face, his throat, his groin—

He took out the gun and grinned. "Ship them oars, bubba. Easy. I'd as soon shoot you as not."

"Why?" I eased the oars into the boat, placed them

175

along the inner curl of the gunnel. "I don't even know you."

"Shut 'er down, Seth." Mingo reached behind his legs and produced an anchor from under the seat. He let it slip into the water, playing out the rope with his left hand.

"Why?" I asked again. "A man has a right to know that."

He nodded, his face thoughtful. "You're right. A man ought to know that, at least. I wish I could tell you." The boat drifted, then caught on the anchor, slowly circled.

"You must know who hired you. You were hired, weren't you? Or are you two degenerates getting your kicks?"

"What's a degenerate, Mingo?"

Mingo scowled. "We ain't none of them. I ain't least-wise. Sometimes I don't know about brother there."

"Up your ass, Mingo!"

"Who? If you're planning to kill me, does it matter?"

"Can't do that, bubba. Like you said, sound carries over water. Besides, I don't tell asshole back there anything. He chatters like a pregnant hen."

"Up yours, Mingo!"

"All right!" Mingo bellowed suddenly. "Face around there, look at my pretty brother for a change. Seth, I'm gonna pass you these two blocks. You tie 'em to his hands. Tight, hear? I don't want him able to wiggle loose." The boat shifted, rocked as he rose carefully to his feet, Something hard poked against the back of my head. "You move a muscle, bubba, I'll blow it off."

The boat drifted. I could see his shadow, distorted in the rippling chop. I saw him drop the gun in his pocket, lean down to pick up one of the blocks with each hand.

"Here they come, Seth."

Seth stood up, shuffled his feet forward.

"Don't stand up, you stupid—"

But I was already moving, hurling my weight to the left, my right hand locked on the right gunnel, lifting it high, jerking, rocking.

Mingo yelled, cursed, felt his balance going and dove headfirst into the water.

Seth teetered, waving his arms for balance, grabbing the motor handle just as I threw myself back the other way—almost too much—water washed over my hand, splashed against the blocks. The hanging lantern lurched dangerously, spitting and hissing from spattering globules of water.

But the angle was too much for Seth. He lost his hold and, arms windmilling, fell flat on his back, choking on an animal scream of pure terror as the water closed over him.

I duckwalked forward, whirled, and sat down on the rear seat. I flipped the switch on the motor and shoved the rheostat to full power just as Seth surfaced a dozen feet off the port bow, thrashing, coughing, spitting water, and trying to scream. Thrust reaction to his fall had shoved the boat away from him just as it had with Mingo's dive, and I found myself floating at the end of the anchor line, the motor pulling the boat around in a lazy, creeping circle.

Mingo surfaced like an angry bull walrus, blowing water and waving the gun. Ten feet from his brother, he treaded water and stared at the flailing figure with a look of animal fascination.

"Mingo! Help me! I can't—you know I can't—" Seth went under, the baseball cap floating free of his head. He was up again in a second, beating the water like a baby in a pan, his face a pale stricken blob in the dark water, mouth gaping, sucking air.

"Jesus! Mingo . . . I can't—help!—" He went under again.

Mingo waved the gun. "Get the boat over there! Pick him up."

"You get him," I said. "You're closest." I shut off the motor; I wasn't going anywhere.

"Goddammit! Get that boat over there!" He sighted the gun at me and I hit the deck. Nothing happened. I heard a dull click, a curse, and peeked over the gunnel in time to see him yank the trigger again. It went off; the bullet sailed somewhere off into the night. That made it three gone, one dud, and one still in the gun.

"Get it over there!" he yelled. "Pick him up! Next shot I'll blast your ass right through the metal."

"Mingo! Mingo! I can't hold—" He disappeared for the third time, bubbles bursting the surface where he had been, ripples expanding in ever widening circles.

But Mingo was busy, closing the distance between us with long overhand sweeps, the gun still in his right fist, clubbing the water with each stroke.

I picked up an oar.

He drew up a yard away, his face twisted, his small mouth a neat, round O. He grabbed the gunnel with his left hand, lined the gun up with my chest; water ran out of the barrel, leaked out the corner of his mouth, his eyes wide and blaring, as black as the shell of a beetle.

I held the oar like a spear, butt end forward, acid fear melting my insides like cotton candy in a flame.

"Okay, you've got one," I said evenly. "Maybe it'll fire, maybe it won't. If it does you've got no problem except a dead brother. If you try to and it misfires, then I'll beat you to death with this oar. Believe it."

Our eyes met, locked, fused. Cold and calculating, he gaped at me like a defective. An eternity passed. His finger curled, tightened, and uncurled. Once, twice, three times, lips peeled in an unwitting grin.

"Make up your goddamned mind!" I yelled, my stomach crawling, a taste like bile boiling in my throat.

His hand opened; the gun rattled in the bottom of the boat.

"He oughta learned to swim," he whined. "I told him and told him."

I picked up the gun and checked the base of the bone grip. No chip. The gun wasn't mine. I ejected the empty casings and dropped it into my jacket pocket.

"Hey," he protested weakly. "That gun cost me a hunnert and twenty-five dollars." He moved along the side of the boat to the middle, pumped up and down a couple of times in preparation for boarding.

I picked up the oar and tapped him between the eyes. He yelled and clapped his hands to his head and immediately sank out of sight. He was back a moment later, sputtering.

"First we talk," I said.

"I'm freezing." He held up a shaking hand to prove it.

"Who hired you, Mingo?"

"I don't know his name. Just a guy I met down at The Last Stand."

I hit him again, a little harder. I lit a cigarette while I waited for him to surface and paddle back to the boat. A red welt had formed between the piggish little eyes.

"I can keep this up all night. Can you?"

"Come on, man. Let me in and we'll talk. Maybe I can remember."

I tapped him again, a short, solid jab with the butt of the oar. Only a dedicated moron would have let go with both hands a third time. But he did, and immediately sank. He stayed under longer this time, came up blowing weakly. He hung his arms over the side of the boat, sucking for

179

breath, his stricken face seized with belated presentiments of mortality.

I ignored him while I found my car keys and opened the blade of a small penknife stamped with the Bell Helicopter logo, a memento of a courtesy tour they had given me just before I traipsed off to Vietnam to fly their ungainly machines.

He watched me saw through the nylon twine, find my boots, and slip them on. Then I picked up the oar and turned back to him.

"Bremmer," he said quickly.

"Bremmer?" I stared at his pasty face, the round head bobbing earnestly.

"Alex Bremmer?"

The head bobbed faster. "Yeah, that's him. Alex Bremmer. Mean mother owns The Last Stand. You know him?" All at once he seemed eager to please.

I knew him. I had gone to school with him, would have graduated in the same class had he not been thrown out of school for selling pot—among other things. A short, stocky boy with heavily muscled legs, he had played center for Webb most of our junior year. Coach Stallis had caught him stealing from another player's locker and booted him. A month or so later he had been suspended again. He never came back.

"Do you know why?"

He threw up his arms and almost lost his hold on the boat. His hands were visibly shaking, buck teeth clicking on his lower molars. "Man, I don't know nothin about that." He clamped one hand to his jaw as if the chattering embarrassed him. "Man, I'm cold."

"All right, cross your wrists."

I found a piece of the nylon twine and lashed his hands together. I had to haul him into the boat, almost turning us over. I took off his boots and tied his feet to two of the blocks. The other two blocks I dropped into the water.

Seth's plastic hat bobbed jauntily near where he had vanished. I fished it out with an oar and cut a hole in the brim. I sawed through the anchor rope and tied it to the hat. I threw it back into the water.

"What're you doin?" Mingo stared at me dully from the front of the boat, hunkered and shivering, sandy hair plastered to his forehead like crusted strands of blood.

"Marker. You want them to find your brother or not?"

He looked at the hat, twirling gently with the breeze. "He wasn't much," he said, his voice cracking. "But he was my only kin." He began to blubber.

"You brought him up real good, Mingo. You should be proud." I switched on the motor, feeling the boat respond sluggishly. I eased the nose around and headed back the way we had come.

"We wasn't goin to kill you," he said. "Just scare you a little."

"I'm not the man to tell that to," I said. "Maybe you can convince a jury. Good luck."

"Honest to God."

"It's gone beyond that. What you're facing now is murder."

"What? You're crazy. Seth drowned accidental. Anyhow, I didn't have anything to do with it. You did."

"A man died during the commission of a felony act of kidnapping. That's murder. The circumstances don't matter." I lit another cigarette and smiled at him. "Maybe you can cop a plea, turn Alex Bremmer over and slide it down to manslaughter."

He hunched forward, teeth clacking again, crossed wrists against his brow.

"Bremmer's a German name," I said, more to myself

than to him. "Seems to me his folks were naturalized citizens. Any idea when they came to America?"

"I don't know nothin.'"

"Where does he live?"

He didn't reply. I flipped the cigarette at him. It burst on the palm of his hand in a shower of sparks. He yelped and slapped the palm against his knee.

"You want to answer me, Mingo, or do you want to swim the rest of the way?"

"You're gonna have me arrested anyhow. I ain't telling you nothin', you son of a bitch!" His eyes glowed feverishly, something raw and malevolent in their ebony depths.

I shut off the motor. I stepped across the middle seat and sat down, my toes touching the blocks tied to his bare feet. I took out my key ring again, opened the fingernail blade on the penknife. I gave him a friendly grin, a pat on the knee.

"I can find out easy enough, but it's a waste of valuable time and I've decided you're going to tell me. You want to do that now?"

He glared at me, the small mouth curling in a sneer. "You ain't gonna do nothin'. We're in shallow water. It ain't deeper'n my armpit anywhere around—"

I drove the tiny blade into his right instep, slid it out and did it again before painful awareness could overtake disbelief.

He screamed; shock and dismay. The pain would come a little later. I let him howl for a moment, yellow buck teeth bared like a maddened hare. Then I leaned forward and slapped him. Backhand first, then forehand. Back and forth until he shut up.

"This hurts you more than it does me. I did that to get your attention. Now that I've got it, you want to tell me where he lives?"

182

He was blubbering again, hunched in a ball, his bound hands pressed against the oozing puncture wounds, the vast hiatus between the night's expectations and its reality finally catching up with him.

"Over—over the bar," he mumbled. "Jesus . . . this hurts."

"I'm sure it does," I said. "I'm sorry, Mingo." I went back to my seat and switched on the motor.

18

I drove Mingo's old Ford sedan back to my cabin. He sat hunched in the corner against the door, the heater going full blast, all the vents centered on him, the staccato beat of his big yellow teeth gradually subsiding. Intermittently he sobbed, the round carp's mouth puckering as some distressing segment of the night's proceedings presented itself to thought processes not given to energetic introspection. Invariably he vocalized his concerns, his dissonant voice as irritating as mating cats at midnight, his dissimulation a wonder to behold.

By the time I picked up a change of clothes, a badly needed pack of cigarettes, and drove back to the Interstate and the deserted parking lot of The Last Stand, Mingo had spread the blame for his failures from the Pope in Rome— he was a good Catholic—all the way to a little old gray-haired lady in Oklahoma City—his mother who had dropped his brother Seth on his head at the tender age of three months, inducing coma and addled brains, then doting on the little bastard from that day forward, thereby creating untold psychological pressures far beyond those of normal sibling rivalries. The Pope in Rome had failed him by changing the rules—like eating meat on Friday—until a feller didn't know whether he was coming or going.

That was my interpretation of his rambling, sometimes incoherent, monologue. I listened in silence, feeling a glimmer of pity for this unlovely—and probably unloved—lump of human detritus.

The luck of the draw, I thought, remembering my throwaway lines to Melissa earlier. Glib, facile, designed to elicit humor and a change of mood, the words had held at least a modicum of truth. Casual mating. Frenetic coupling in dark places. Random combinations of genes that could make a Quasimodo or a queen.

It was still an hour away from dawn when I eased the Ford to a stop at a metal staircase leading to the second floor of the flatroofed rectangular building housing Alex Bremmer's Last Stand. Constructed from cinder blocks painted white, it had a solid functional look once you were past the neon-encrusted portico, the redwood slab and rose-tinted glass facade that promised topless dancers, waiters, and bartenders, all the booze you could pay for, and a licentious atmosphere to drink it in.

I killed the motor and we sat for a moment listening to it tick. I took out Mingo's reloaded. 38, jacked out the cylinder, spun it, snapped it shut, and placed the gun in my waistband. All for effect; Mingo's small hot eyes followed my movements the way a cobra watches a mongoose.

"You know what you've got to do," I said. "Once we're in, find yourself a nice chair and sit down. Don't speak unless you're spoken to. Got it?"

"You gonna untie me?"

I took out the penknife and opened the blade. I pressed it against the tightly stretched fabric on his thigh.

"There you go already. Screwing up. I asked you a question."

"I got it," he said sullenly. "You gonna untie me?"

"Does a sailor piss upwind?"

"He ain't gonna let me in if he sees me tied up like this."

"See that he doesn't. If he has a door chain, crowd in close. If he doesn't, I'll handle it."

His eyes took on a beady speculative look. "He'll probably take your ass. He's a lot tougher than me."

"He could be a wilted dick and be tougher than you. Just don't get cute, Mingo. I haven't killed anybody in a while. I'm getting the fever."

"You killed Seth."

"Your stupidity killed Seth. Come on, let's go."

I stopped his limping, shuffling hobble at the bottom of the steps. "What's behind the door? Does he have the entire second floor?"

"There's two apartments," he said reluctantly. "He has the one in front. This here door opens on a hall. He'll be down to our right. Far as I know, the other'n's empty." His bound hands massaged his pudgy nose, dropped to a pointed, dimpled chin, then slid thoughtfully along the beard-darkened curve of his jaw, his eyes pouched and hidden.

"We'll check out the empty apartment first," I said cheerfully. "No surprises that way." I took out the gun and raked the sight across his ear. "I'd hate to think you'd lie to me, Mingo."

He rubbed his ear and cocked his head, then looked at me with a shamefaced grin. "By gum, I forgot. He moved to that other apartment. Said it was too noisy—"

"Move." I jabbed a stiffened finger into his back. "Somewhere in that lump of suet you call a brain, Mingo,

186

you've decided I won't kill you. You're right, I won't. But this .38 is loaded with soft-nosed bullets and I'll be right proud to blow something off that lardbucket you call a body. I don't much care what. You better keep that in mind."

He shrugged and sneered and started up the steps, his shoes sliding, grating loudly on the metal grid. I caught up with him in one stride, raked the gunsight across his ear again, harder, bringing a splash of blood and a yelp I smothered with my palm.

"Softly, my friend." I rapped him over the eye with the gunbarrel. It rang hollowly. "One more little thing," I said, reaching around and shoving the gun into his groin, "and you'll be talking in a high girlish voice for the rest of your soprano life."

His head bobbed reluctantly. I released him; we went up the stairs quietly. But he wasn't really cowed and I knew it, too damned stupid to be scared now that he was in familiar territory.

On the landing, I reached around him and opened the door, herded him inside. We were near the center of a long dim hallway that ran the length of the building, ended in blank textured walls.

Four outside windows and a weak covered bulb provided illumination; two doors opened off the hall, both closed and silent. No hint of occupancy.

Mingo turned to the left; I grabbed a fistful of collar and shoved him to the right.

He stared over his shoulder. "I told you—"

"I know what you told me, and I know what you want me to believe. Move!"

We moved, Mingo muttering under his breath, our feet making no sound in the deep shag carpeting. I stopped him just short of the door. I stepped around him and pressed my ear against a dark glossy panel that felt like solid oak. Nothing. But then I hadn't expected there would be. Dawn was still almost an hour away and decent folk were still hard abed. Night owl nightclub owners like Bremmer would probably just be settled in to sleep.

I positioned Mingo in front of the door, slightly to right of center. I flattened myself against the wall, extended the gun to point at his right temple. He stared back at me, his waxy face wooden, the tiny black eyes glistening like drops of dirty oil.

I reached around with my left hand and pumped the bell, hit it three times, then held it down until I heard the muted sound of voices, the faint thud of feet.

Mingo was still staring at me, as if trying to make up his mind about something. I put the gun barrel against the side of his nose and pushed his face forward, held it there.

"Who the hell is it?" A deep male voice, husky with phlegm, a feminine murmur in the background.

Mingo flicked a glance in my direction, his rabbitlike face a study in absurd indecision.

I pressed the gun into the juncture of his thighs and eared back the hammer.

"Dammit, who the—?"

"It's me! Mingo! Everything's gone to hell! Seth's dead and that feller got away!"

More cursing, deep and heartfelt; then the snick of a deadbolt, the rattle of a chain, the click of a knob lock, the door began to open.

I stepped behind Mingo, slammed a shoulder into his back, and shoved. He grunted, then yelled as the door met resistance, his head cracking like a rifle shot against the oak.

I plowed ahead, using him as a battering ram, allowing him to drop as the door swung wide, my heart hammering in my ears, my stomach lurching. I stopped short, trembling like a greyhound at the gate.

A roly-poly blond man sprawled cursing on the floor, sky blue pajamas and dazed blue eyes an almost perfect match. A small, nickel-plated automatic lay on the carpet a half-dozen feet away, and a young, naked black girl watched impassively from a doorway across the room.

Mingo groaned at my feet, blood oozing from a cut on his forehead, bound hands twitching spasmodically beneath his cheek.

I put away my gun and picked up the one on the floor. Holding it loosely, I stood over the blond man, searched the porcine face for identification landmarks and found few. Nineteen years had changed Alex Bremmer, obfuscated the once hawkish features with the overcompensations of middle age: self-indulgence and satiety. Born at approximately the same time as the rest of us, he had somehow managed to age to a different rhythm, a different system of accounting. Fine lines criss-crossed his plump features like the webbing in a net; plum-colored pouches sagged beneath eyelashes as fine as silk.

He stared up at me, recognition swimming in the pale blue eyes, ridiculously tiny teeth gleaming through slowly parting lips.

"I'll be damned! Danny Roman!" He rolled over on his stomach and scrambled to his feet, making it look almost easy. He scampered forward and held out his hand, plump and smooth and carefully manicured. "How the hell you doing, Danny boy?"

I looked down at his hand, then back at his face, watching the blood suffuse the gross features, making my tight smile as insolent as I could manage, letting the awkward silence grow, driving a dibble of uncertainty all the way to his quick.

He took a little step to one side, threw wide his arms. "What is all this? Who is this man? Why do you come breaking down my door at this time of morning? I know you used to be a joker, Danny, but this is a bit much."

Mingo stirred and groaned; blood flowed sluggishly across his forehead and dripped into the beige carpeting. I stepped over him, slipped my hands under his arms, and heaved him to his feet. His legs wobbled and threatened to break at the knees. I dragged him to a tan and brown velvet chair, let him fall loosely. His head bounced, fell to the chair arm, and went on oozing blood. I looked at Bremmer and smiled.

"Hard to get good help nowadays."

"I don't know what you mean."

"Let's talk about it," I said. I dropped the automatic into my jacket pocket and nodded at the naked black girl still standing in the bedroom doorway, nonchalantly watching the white folks carry on. "Who's she?"

He made a vague gesture, his brow wrinkled. "Just some . . . just a hooker."

"Get rid of her."

He looked up, anger deepening the furrows in his forehead. "Don't tell me what—" He bit it off and made another vague gesture, whirled toward the girl.

"Verabelle. You go on and leave, babe. Money's on the dresser. You know how much." He turned back to me, then whirled to her again. "About all this. You forget about it, hear? Listen, what I'll do is, I'll give you double. Okay? Double. You got it? You know where it's at." He turned again without waiting for an answer, sleek and fat and self-assured.

"Hey, Danny boy, how about a little eye opener?" He moved off toward a small mahogany bar across the corner next to the bedroom.

"I usually wait until after breakfast," I said, moving with him. "But I'll keep you company." I came up behind him. "Just keep your hands in sight."

He stopped. "Hey, that little gun is the only thing I got. Come on, man, look for yourself." He stepped aside to allow me behind the bar.

I checked the shelves and the two small drawers. The back bar was a mirror and one long shelf. Plenty of booze, but no guns no knives. I walked around to the front.

"Satisfied?" He smirked and eased his bulk through the narrow opening. "This is still my night. I didn't get to bed until after three. Same every night. Can't trust these dip-shits who work for me not to steal me blind."

I watched his stubby fingers mix his drink. I lit a ciga-rette and waited until he finished. Then I reached across and took it from his hand and poured it down the front of his pajamas.

"Why?" I asked.

He smiled and brushed languid fingers along the dark-ening line down the front of his silk pajamas. He wriggled his chubby body and said "brrrr" and laughed.

"Nothing personal, Danny. Just business. You know." He pulled the wet material away from his crotch and made a leering face. "Headed right for the old tallywhacker."

I felt a faint stir of uneasiness. He was taking it all too calmly, smiling, enjoying himself hugely, doing a little jigging dance that made the tube of fat around his waist roll and bounce, red-faced and gaping like a clown, the pale eyes bright and alive with merriment—or triumph.

Goddammit! Something was wrong.

I whirled and looked at Mingo; he was sitting up, head lolling, eyes unfocused, the oozing blood breaking across the bridge of his nose, winding its way through beard stub-ble to his underslung jaws. No danger there.

I looked back at Bremmer: still acting the fool. I caught movement out of the corner of my eye. The girl leaving—

The girl!

I spun on the stool.

She was back in the doorway, still naked, not more than ten feet away, a shotgun cradled in her slender arms, her dark face emotionless, eyes flat and black, as cold as space.

Behind me Bremmer cackled. "She's a skeet shooter, Danny boy. Double ought in that there gun. You want to try her?"

A double. He had done it right under my nose.

"Just take out them guns, Danny boy. Lay them on the counter real careful." His voice rippled with mirth.

"Nothing personal, Danny boy. You understand. Just business.

He scooped up the guns and danced around the end of the bar, face wreathed in a gleeful smile. He waved a short, heavy arm in the direction of the girl. "Watch him, Verabelle, honey." He looked at Mingo and clucked derisively. "I gotta take care of the genius over here." He whirled and pranced toward Mingo—stirring sluggishly and cursing—small mincing steps, curiously graceful despite his bulk.

19

DAY WAS STILL A HAZY PROMISE IN THE EAST WHEN WE
left the parking lot of The Last Stand in Mingo's old Ford.
Alone in the rear seat, hands trussed behind my back with
another length of Mingo's supply of nylon twine, I was far
from lonely. Almost unconscious from the beating Mingo
had given me the instant Bremmer cut him loose, I stared
with unfeigned bewilderment at the two round heads in
front of me, bobbing, whipping back and forth as they
shouted at each other above the percussive crash of rock
and roll coming from the radio.

Bremmer, driving the car, sleeker than ever in a skin-
tight navy jumpsuit with white piping and a voluminous
quilted windbreaker, hurled imprecations and raised serious
questions relative to Mingo's immediate ancestry, the possibility that his mother may have had more than a casual
acquaintance with a certain large hirsute primate.

Mingo, sullen, malevolent, and obviously intimidated,
responded with a whining recitation of previous accomplishments, a litany of protests relegating blame to his idiot
brother, my cunning treachery, and the new November
moon. A large rectangular band-aid adorned the center of

his bulging forehead, and his rosebud lips worked in and out like a bottom-feeding carp. Eyes lidded, features fixed in a petulant pout, he leaned forward and the booming radio went silent.

I closed my eyes wearily and tried to relax, hurling a few silent imprecations of my own, mostly at myself. Stupidity and carelessness; a generous portion of naiveté. During the few minutes before Mingo roused enough to begin his assault, it had become clear that the black girl, while undoubtedly a hooker, was much more than that. She was Bremmer's current live-in girlfriend, hairdresser, valet, and, in light of recent events, a pretty damn good bodyguard.

Bruised, bleeding, aching in a dozen different places, I pondered my predicament, the utterly unbelievable odds against having it happen twice in as many hours, captive and helpless, on my way to an uncertain fate.

But was it uncertain? To believe that, I would have to believe what Mingo had told me, that they had only planned to scare me a little. But to what purpose? An elaborate hoax by Webb in retaliation for his defeat on the highway? Even more unbelievable. This wasn't Webb's style. He would simply have waited until he was sober and come at me head on. And besides, we weren't enemies. We were two aging lotharios caught in the oldest triangle of all. And not even that. I had made it plain I was withdrawing, leaving the field to him. He knew me well enough to know that I wouldn't have lied to him, not about something like that.

Not Webb. Then who? Then why?

My head hurt. A growing sense of dread, of impending catastrophe, kept pace with the steady thrumming of the car's engine. The last vestige of alcoholic buffer had vanished long ago and there was nothing between me and steadily rising panic except the pain.

We left the Interstate. I recognized the increased susurrus of the tires, the heavier vibration on the rough-textured county blacktop. We crossed a bridge and perhaps five minutes later turned onto a gravel road.

The car seemed to pick up speed, tires grating, a drumroll of pebbles pounding the underbelly of the Ford.

I opened my eyes into the oppressive gray of a cloudy dawn, a blur of ragged vegetation whipping by the windows, petalless sunflowers, sumac, and thin stunted thickets of post oak.

I struggled erect, noting for the first time that my hands were numb, my arms burning with fatigue.

Mingo caught my movement and immediately wrestled his bulk around in the seat and hammered a knobby fist into my thigh, his beefy shoulder jostling Bremmer. The car swerved.

"Watch it, you dumb shit!" Bremmer cursed and fought the wheel. I felt the rear end float on loose gravel. "Dammit, Mingo, leave him alone! You had your fun, now cut it out. You want to wreck us?"

"Crummy mother killed my brother!" Rabbit teeth bared in a crippled grimace, the malevolent eyes burned at me like a curse. But he desisted, flopped around in his seat mouthing obscene promises of arcane and probably impossible atrocities to come.

Any doubts I may have had as to the seriousness of my condition abruptly vanished. His intentions were as easy to read as my effigy nailed to a post and criss-crossed with pins.

Whether or not they had planned on killing me in the beginning, they were going to do it now. Maybe Seth drowning had made the difference, taking it beyond the scope of kidnapping and terrorizing and into the realm of felony murder as I had so glibly explained to Mingo in the boat.

But it wouldn't have mattered. Bremmer would have known that, would have recognized instantly the necessity for tidying the snarled backlash his inept henchmen had created. He may have been a thief in high school, and undoubtedly still was, but nobody had ever questioned his intelligence.

"How far we going?" Mingo broke the lengthy silence, twisting to give me a murderous grin.

Bremmer ignored him, concentrating on the winding road that climbed now through thickly forested hills, hardwoods and pine, and underbrush as impenetrable as the Maginot Line. It all seemed vaguely familiar, a primitive landscape indistinguishable from a dozen others within a half-hour's drive of Butler Wells.

Surprisingly, the road dipped, began to level out. A chasm yawned to our left, a rock-infested slope and a trickling stream gleaming darkly in the rising light.

"Almost there," Bremmer said cheerfully, catching my glance in the rearview mirror and laughing. "Ever hear of Clawhammer Mine, Danny boy?"

I had and he knew it. Abandoned since the late eighteen hundreds, some said its main shaft dropped a thousand feet straight into the bowels of the mountain; wiser heads made it less than five hundred. An uncontrollable shudder rippled through me, leaving a cold damp spot between my shoulders.

Mingo cackled. "You got his attention there, Al."

Bremmer shrugged plump shoulders. "Just a job, Danny boy. Want you to know that. I got nothing against you personally. Fact is, I always kinda liked you in the old days."

"Then who, Alex?"

He shrugged again. "A favor for an old friend. An old debt."

"Who?"

The canyon had deepened, the walls more sloping, speckled here and there with huge boulders. The mine was coming up fast. Around the next bend in the road. The road ended there; so did my chances.

"Sorry, I can't tell you that. Not with numbnuts here in the car.

"Hey," Mingo said, turning from me to face Bremmer, his lagomorphic features struggling from hilarity to indignation. "Who the hell you call—?"

That was as far as he got before I slipped down in the seat, whipped my leg upward, and slammed my right boot heel into the hinge of his jaw, feeling the hard leather heel tear at flesh and muscle, glimpsing a splash of cascading blood and hearing his unearthly howl, the crack of his cranium against the window.

Almost drunk on a surging rush of adrenalin, I turned my attention to Bremmer, wide-eyed and cursing, one hand off the wheel and out of sight.

I saw his shoulder lift as he tugged at the gun in his coat pocket and rolled to my left behind him, swinging my foot along the seat back and driving the toe of my boot into the side of his sleek, blond head. I jerked it back and did it again as his hand came into sight with the gun.

He screamed and threw up his arms protectively, the gun forgotten in his agony, his high, thin voice vying with Mingo's howl.

The car lurched, fishtailed, hit a rock or a rut, and bounced, rear tires spewing gravel in a valiant effort to gain traction, to do what Bremmer's heavy foot commanded it to do. It spit and coughed, the rear tires juddering sidewise, catching, moving us forward again.

I saw daylight through the windshield, open space, a chunk of sunrise.

197

I jerked my foot back and kicked upward at the door handle, missed, and kicked again, frantically, as I felt the center of gravity shifting, tilting, the front end dropping with a sickening crunch of metal on stone, the car's residual momentum inexorably carrying us over the edge.

I kicked again and the door snapped open; I saw it whip backward and tear away with a shriek of rending metal as the heaving capsule rolled on its side.

I tumbled helplessly, feeling rocks and grass and prickly vegetation as the open door became the floor, then caromed off cloth and glass and plastic-covered foam rubber seats as the car swapped ends again.

We rolled and skidded and bounced, boulders arresting our headlong flight, abruptly changing our direction, hurling us into the air for endless seconds of thunderous silence broken only by the whimpering curses of human voices, the scream of surrendering metal.

Then crashing to earth again, jarring bone and brain pan alike, darkness swooping and receding, beckoning, threatening oblivion.

Finally, my head found something hard and unforgiving, exploded into a pinwheel of sparks, cold pitiless stars that in turn gave way to warm dimpled darkness that didn't go away.

I awoke to pain and the raw stinging smell of gasoline. I lay inert for a moment, gathering my scattered wits, something hard and smooth and sun-warmed against my left cheek, another something sharp and spiteful digging into my back.

Even before I opened my eyes I took mental inventory of my various parts, sensing that I was, against all odds, still in one piece, feeling no one great pain standing out above the others. The most discomfort came from my back, but that would be a simple matter of changing position.

I opened my eyes to sunlight, slanted and warm. Judging from its position, I had been lying there for some time, maybe as long as an hour.

I raised my head gingerly and looked around. Scrub brush and a cactus. Two large boulders. I had somehow managed to roll or drop between them. I tilted my head and looked behind me. Nothing but outcroppings of rock, sagebrush, and sawbriers looped along the slope.

I shifted my position and felt the pain in my back move elsewhere. I took a deep breath and sat up.

My head rang; darkness closed in, pulsating, leaving a long dim tunnel sprinkled with stars. I leaned against the larger rock and waited it out, focus slowly returning, the stars dimming, the tunnel widening, fading.

I leaned forward a trifle, looked to my right and saw Mingo. He was lying there quietly watching me, obsidian eyes fixed and unmoving, head propped on his chest, the bloody flap of meat I had kicked loose standing out from his cheek like the cowl of a cobra.

It took a dozen cataleptic moments to realize that he was dead.

I expelled my breath and looked away, craned my neck over the other boulder and saw the car fifteen yards away at the bottom of the ravine. It was upside down beside the creek, flattened and mangled, windows gone, the door I had fallen through gaping like a toothless mouth.

I wondered if Bremmer could still be in there, and once again became aware of the stench of gasoline. Tank punctured, I thought, and gas draining down into the car. A thousand wonders the thing hadn't gone up in flames.

Pain closed in like a fist while I thought about what to do. First order of business would be getting my hands free to find out if they still worked. I studied what I could see of my two rocks. No sharp edges, no splintered cracks suitable for fraying nylon twine.

I looked around at creek gravel, innumerable stones of all shapes and sizes, all smooth as a baby's butt. I was beginning to wonder if I might have to creep down to the car to find a jagged piece of metal when I scooted backwards and discovered what had been doing the job on my back. A ragged crescent of stone protruding two inches out of the earth, saw-toothed edges as suited to my task as a Cro-Magnon man's skinning knife.

I squirmed into position and sawed away at Mingo's twine, working by guess since most of the feeling had bled from my hands. A couple of minutes later my bonds parted and I cautiously brought my arms forward, ignoring the stabbing pain in my shoulder joints.

My hands were an unhealthy looking gray below the bindings, flushed and swollen above. I unwound the cord from my wrists and flexed my fingers. Numb, but functional up to a point, new needle pains rushing to join the rising crescendo in my body.

I sat perfectly still for a moment, wallowing in it, enjoying the uniqueness of it, glancing at Mingo's grotesquely distorted body and feeling more alive than I had ever felt in my life, feeling invincible and immortal, a favorite of the Gods.

I managed to light a cigarette, sucked the sweet smoke into the only part of me that didn't hurt. I stared out across the canyon, bemused, lethargic, quietly astonished that I was alive and still in one large wholesome piece.

I sneaked another glance at Mingo's cruelly juxtaposed body, head lying on his chest, eyes fixed on me in eternal accusation, and shuddered.

And heard a sound—a cough or a moan, or a clearing of a throat.

I stared at Mingo, horrified. Ready to bolt if he so much as blinked.

Then movement in the corner of my eye and I swiveled toward the car.

Bremmer crawled slowly from a window, blond hair finally disheveled, plastered to his moon face like bloody exclamation marks, the quilted coat dangling in ragged ribbons, a grey ropy strand almost dragging the ground beneath his stomach. One shoe was missing, the natty blue jumpsuit ripped up the side.

I watched fascinated as he crawled away from the car, head held low, wagging back and forth like a man searching for gold nuggets. The smell of gasoline rose like the threat of perdition. Muttered obscenities drifted to my ears. I saw something flash in his hand and realized he still held the gun. I looked around me and picked up two orange-sized stones, all at once feeling vulnerable again, feeble and defenseless and inconsequential.

I hefted the stones and tried to assess his strength, wondering if I should rush him. But I had yet to try out my legs. For all I knew they might be as useless as my hands had been a few minutes before. He appeared dazed and disoriented, but it took very little concentration to pull a trigger, particularly if the target happened to be flopping around on the ground in front of you at the time.

While I was making up my mind, he stood up. Shoving to his knees, grunting painfully. Another squeal and a curse and he was wavering on unsteady legs, arms akimbo for balance, pale eyes sweeping the slope, lighting on Mingo, pausing, moving on, searching for me.

He took a step forward, left hand clutching his paunch,

the coat fluttering in tatters, the ropy strand of gray material I had noticed earlier looping at his groin.

I focused on the dangling strand and felt a thudding shock as I realized what it was—

Intestine. A piece of his gut oozing through a slash across his abdomen. I felt a surge of relief. He was dying. All I had to do was wait, to keep out of sight until he bled to death. The jumpsuit was already sopping below the waist, plastered to his round thick thighs with blood—

"Ah, there you are, Danny boy!" He stood looking up at me, tiny teeth bared in a ghastly, blood-smeared grimace, a wolfish triumphant grin that conveyed his intention clearer than words. He coughed harshly, spat, shaking his head and pawing his nose like a bee-stung bear. He panted for breath, sucking air in huge gulps, expelling it with obvious distaste.

A current of air swirled along the canyon and I understood why.

"You're saturated with gas, Alex. You pull that trigger and you'll go up like a roman candle." I pushed back as far as I could get between my rocks.

He saw the movement and took another step forward. He looked down at himself, at the bloody hand holding the slash in his sagging paunch together. He looked back at me across twenty-five feet of suddenly charged space and shook his head, teeth bared in that bloody insane grin.

"Blood, man. It's only blood. Blood don't burn." He raised the gun and fired.

I'd heard something like it before: the sound of a flame-thrower in Nam. The bullet chipped flakes from the stone a foot from my head; Bremmer went up in a pillar of fire.

I was up and moving when he started to run, instinctively, forgetting my legs, forgetting everything except the man being consumed before my eyes, the raw, throat-searing screams adding impetus to my feet.

His chubby legs churned up and down, hands frantically clawing at the corona of fire around his head, slapping at the synthetic clothing that billowed smoke and melted like cheese.

Choking on the stink of burning hair and flesh and incinerating chemicals, I pounded after him, closing like Mean Joe Green on Staubach, leaping rocks and brush and cactus in a headlong attempt to intercept.

I caught him before he had gone ten paces. My coat off and in front of my face, I dove headfirst into the hissing flames, hit him in a hip-wrenching tackle that carried us out and over the edge of the creek, into a blue placid pool no more than two feet deep, into blessed coolness that laved me like balm, into an oxygen-free environment.

It was deep enough. I rolled him over and over, held him submerged until the last blue flicker died, smoke curling from a hundred smoldering bits of tissue and cloth.

Then I lifted his head and stared into horror, charred and shriveled skin, a flaming, hairless scalp split and oozing fluid like an overripe tomato. One nostril was gone, his left ear crisped into charcoal.

Nausea coiling in my stomach, I picked him up and carried him to the shore.

He was still alive. But just barely. I could see movement in his chest and feel breath against the back of my hand. I sat back on my haunches and watched him, helpless, wondering if I should have let him drown. If he managed to regain consciousness the pain would be horrendous and I might wish I had.

I reached for a cigarette and realized I had left them beside my rocks. I wearily climbed the slope to get them. In the lower reaches of the gulch the fumes had been overpowering, and I wondered what miracle had kept the car from igniting.

Too diffused, I thought, locating my cigarettes and lighter, hesitating only an instant before firing one up. If Bremmer hadn't set it off with his tower of flame, then a lowly cigarette wasn't going to do it.

On the way back I picked up the gun where he had dropped it. A Colt .45 automatic, it had a few scratches from the rocks and the wild ride down the canyon wall, but showed no evidence of having gone through the holocaust of fire.

I knelt beside Bremmer again. He was still alive, a bubble of bloody froth expanding and bursting at the corner of his mouth. His left hand lay curled on his chest, a sliver of bone showing through burned flesh on one finger. The strand of intestine had shriveled to a black, twisted rope of jerky. Fresh coils bulged through a ten inch slash across his abdomen, through layers of yellowed fat that looked like porous cheese.

How in God's name can he still live, I wondered?

And, as if in answer to my unspoken question, his eyes flew open. He stared up at me fixedly, the tip of a bloody tongue coming out to rake across cracked swollen lips.

"Am I . . . all right?" His voice was thick and rasping, almost unintelligible.

"Doing fine, Alex," I said heartily, wanting to squeeze his shoulder or pat his hand, but afraid of starting the pain.

"I don't feel bad, kind of . . . nothing."

"That's great."

"I missed you . . . huh?"

I nodded and shrugged. "Happens to the best of us."

He tried to smile, but couldn't seem to make his facial muscles work. "That's good," he managed finally. "You warned me." His tongue emerged again, shockingly pink against the black lips.

"Would you like to tell me who your friend is, Alex?"

He licked his lips again and winced. His eyes flicked to my hand holding his gun, widened, the puffy lids tumescent, tiny rolls of blood red sausage.

"You're . . . not going . . . going to shoot me?"

"Not a chance." Where was the pain? How could there not be pain?

"Didn't think so. Not your style. Never was." His eyes rolled; he shivered.

"You've paid your debt," I said. "You don't owe him anymore."

Maybe he had been totally numbed by the flames, the nerve endings destroyed, anesthetized by too much trauma. I scratched my cheek with the barrel of the gun. I'd seen people burned in Vietnam, from tracer rounds to napalm, but I'd never seen anything like this. Not anything alive.

His eyes squinted, the angry blistered skin on his forehead trying to form itself into frown lines. His body arched suddenly, convulsed, began to vibrate. Was the pain finally coming?

"Shoot," he said, his voice thick and phlegmy, a hoarse guttural bark, as if his throat had spasmed around the word.

I stared at him uneasily. "Are you sure?"

He attempted a nod. He was having trouble breathing, bulging lids squeezing his eyes to slivers of desperation. He tried to frown again. "Sure . . . I'm sure . . . fairly . . . shoot . . . fair . . . be . . . fair . . ." He was rambling, his words halting, slurred, rapidly becoming inarticulate, feverish, delirious with pain, but single-minded in purpose. "Shoot," he added, a tired breathless liquid sigh. "Fair . . ." his voice degenerated to a choking wheeze.

I clicked the safety on the gun, clicked it again, unable

to look at him, realizing with a sinking heart that there was a moral imperative here I could not escape. Deserved or not, I had brought him to this wretched state and I could no more ignore his pain than I could walk away and leave a gut-shot deer to die in agony.

I pressed the gun against his head, feeling his eyes on my face.

"Shoot." It was a dry pleading whisper. "Dan, fair . . . be . . . fair . . . please . . ."

It was too much; I pulled the trigger.

20

I FOLLOWED THE SHALLOW ROCKY CREEK BACK TOWARD the Interstate, wading a few knee-high pools, detouring a couple that were too blue and choked with deadfalls that looked snaky.

When the creek took a sharp bend south I left it and crunched through a stubbled field of maize to the highway, crossing the last wire fence a quarter of a mile north of a rustic roadside rest stop consisting of three stone picnic tables and a trash barrel. No restroom, no water, and very little shade.

A middle-aged man and a girl sat at the center table beneath the desiccated limbs of a yellow-green mesquite. She was spreading peanut butter on soda crackers, and they were wolfing them down as if they were Beluga caviar on toast, rinsing their mouths occasionally with something from a gallon thermos. They watched my limping, halting approach with more curiosity than wariness, the man giving me a noncommittal nod as I slumped wearily on the end of his bench.

"Morning," I said. "Had some car trouble over on the

secondary road a ways, I was wondering if you might be going south.'' I trotted out my friendliest grin.

He had big, bony sunbrowned hands and an angular face, squinted gray eyes that appraised me with unabashed thoroughness. Fifty, I guessed, new overalls and a John Deere gimme cap. A failed midwest farmer on his way to the coast and better chances, floods and droughts and auctioneers' gavels a thing of the past, but still fresh and vivid in his memory, dim shadows in faded eyes.

"Yep, I reckon we are.'' He poked a section of cracker heaped with peanut butter into his mouth and crunched methodically, a rotating motion reminiscent of a cow. He swallowed hard, took a drink of water from the thermos.

"Don't reckon we got room for no riders, though. That there little car is loaded to the gills the way it is.'' He slung a hard, square jaw toward a rusty Datsun station wagon parked at the curb, the rear end bulging to the roofline with a jumble of clothing, boxes, and useless mementos they couldn't bear to leave behind.

I nodded and lit a cigarette. I took out my wallet and pinched the edge of a twenty-dollar bill. I leaned down the table and placed it beneath the peanut butter jar.

"We could maybe make room,'' I said. "It's only fifteen or so miles to where I'm going.'' I took a drag on the cigarette. "Butler Wells.''

His lips pursed, his eyes fixed on the twenty. "That's not far,'' he admitted. He glanced at the girl masticating unhurriedly on a bit of cracker and peanut butter. "I reckon we could scrunch up a little.'' He wrenched his eyes away from the money and stared toward the traffic streaming by on the Interstate. "On the other hand you could wait for someone else to come along. Bound to be somebody soon.''

"That thought had occurred to me, also, but my ap-

pearance wouldn't exactly inspire confidence in your typical American tourist.''

"You look purty beat," he said, the wide mouth curling
slightly at the corners. His gaze returned to the money.
"Well, what about it, Petal? We could get us some baloney
and cheese to go with them crackers.''

We both looked at Petal.

She looked at me, ice-blue eyes and a tiny pug nose,
bleached white hair shorter than a boy's. Despite the crispness of the autumn air she wore shorts and a halter, midcalf
men's socks and tennis shoes. Her face was as angular as
the man's, but a hell of a lot more attractive. I judged her
to be somewhere around twenty.

After a while she nodded and immediately got up and
began clearing away the remnants of their simple meal.

We made room. Petal crawled over the seat and into the
jumble of clothing and bedding and curled up like a sleepy
kitten.

Five miles from Butler Wells we topped a hill and I saw
the wink of sunlight on my cabin windows in the distance.
I pointed it out to my unknown Samaritan.

"That's where I live. On that hill. There's another
twenty in it if you'll take me there.''

"How far off the highway?''

"Twelve miles or so.''

He hunkered down behind the wheel, licking his lips,
undoubtedly envisioning Colonel Sander's drumsticks, cole
slaw, and french fries.

"You got it, mister.''

I drank a cold beer while I laved myself with all the hot
water in the thirty-gallon tank. Cuts and scratches stinging,
abrasions and contusions smarting, I fell into bed the way

Edward Mathis

a chainsawed redwood topples in the forest: dead to the world before I reached a horizontal plane.

I awoke at four in the afternoon, dragged out of sleep so deep I felt like Lazarus rising up from the dead.

Cool soft hands and a chiding murmur; compassionate clucking.

I teetered on the edge, waffling between dream illusion and reality, longing to sink back into that soundless, painless void.

"My God, Danny, what in the world happened to you?" The words resonated in an empty brain, bringing cohesion to scattered wits, coherence to chaos.

I opened my eyes to Melissa's lovely worried face, to bright afternoon sunlight and shivering motes of pain.

"You look terrible," Melissa said, and made another throaty clucking sound. "Have you been fighting?"

"You ought to see the other guy," I croaked, then wished I hadn't. The images the words evoked weren't exactly pleasant.

"These terrible bruises." She was murmuring again, gentle fingers tracing my ribs and abdomen, hip and thigh. My mind followed the wandering of her soothing touch, assimilating the information sluggishly, comprehending finally and jerking me wide awake to stare with unfeigned consternation at my naked body sprawled across the counterpane.

I grabbed wildly for a pillow.

She laughed merrily, one finger touching the cleft in her chin, her eyes sparking gleefully.

"You're a little late, Danny. I've seen it all. You have no more secrets, big or small." She went off into another gale of laughter, shoulders shaking, inrushing blood stain-

210

ing the upper reaches of her cheeks, violet eyes narrowed to tiny glowing slits.

It was impossible not to respond. It was the way I remembered her best, completely at my mercy in the throes of helpless laughter, protesting weakly my wandering tickling hands, my searching lips. It was one of the reasons I had loved her. Maybe the best. Whatever my mood, watching her laugh had always made me feel good, witty, important.

"How did you get in?" I said grouchily, unable to keep from smiling. "Did I leave the door unlocked again?"

She nodded, wiping her cheeks, winding down to throaty sobs and muted burps, refusing to meet my eyes, wavy chestnut hair spilling forward across rounded shoulders, sun-fired glimmering gold, finely wrought to complement her lovely face.

"And you just made yourself at home, come waltzing in here and spied on a poor defenseless fool who couldn't so much as suck in his gut."

She nodded again, still without looking at me, her color dangerously high.

"Well," I said, scooting off the bed, tossing the pillow aside. "I'll give you a good look. You haven't seen my backside yet."

With some difficulty and very little grace, I marched across to the wardrobe that served as a closet. While I dressed in clean clothing I whistled softly through my teeth, ignoring her candid gaze, the slim hand that was once again covering her mouth.

I found my cigarettes and lit one, sat down on the edge of the bed next to her to put on my boots, stoically enduring prickles of pain, minor shrieks of agony as my blistered feet encountered leather again. I stamped each one firmly.

"You didn't have to do that," she said, meeting my gaze finally with too bright eyes and a quizzical half-smile.

I didn't have to ask what she meant. "You're wrong, Melissa. It's exactly what I had to do. Another couple of minutes and we'd have been breathing heavy, another five and we'd have been doing something we have no business doing."

"Why?" she asked earnestly, her voice thready with bewilderment. "Are you forgetting yesterday afternoon?" Her hand came to rest on my thigh, the band of white around her ring finger a circle of fire.

I barked a mirthless laugh. "Not likely. Not in this lifetime."

"Then why, Danny? I thought—"

"Are *you* forgetting yesterday afternoon?" I asked harshly. "I can't stand uncertainty, Melissa. I'm a grown-up adult male. I can't handle adolescent games anymore. You've been playing them, with Webb and with me. He's so damned crazy about you, he's . . . he's, well, he's crazy. He's always felt that way about you."

She bit her lip. She slowly withdrew her hand to meet with its mate in her lap. "I know that," she said quietly.

"And you've been seeing him."

Her head lifted sharply, the violet eyes defiant. "Yes, I've been seeing him. Once in a while. I told you Clay wouldn't make love. I'm only human, Danny."

"We all are," I said. "And maybe we deserve better."

"I don't understand."

I shrugged. "Did it occur to you that maybe Clay *couldn't* make love? You lived with him for eighteen years. Did it occur to you that maybe you owed him something? Something simple like loyalty?"

She jerked as if I'd slapped her, face fighting for control, eyes blazing with scorn. "You don't know anything about

212

it! I owed Clay Garland nothing! Except years of misery!''
Tears erupted.

I stared at her, unmoved. ''You married him for his
money. You told me that yourself. There's probably some
earthy old maxim that goes along with that, but I can't
think of it at the moment.'' Even as I attacked her, I had
a sinking, defeated feeling, a welling of deep emotion that
bade me stop, that demanded I take her in my arms and
salve the ugly wounds. But a familiar dark perversity
gripped me, an old feeling compounded of fear of rejection, frustration, and despair. She had rejected me once and
now my pride demanded defense, heaped me with ridicule
for making myself vulnerable again.

I watched her wrestle for control. She blotted tears and
stared at me with wounded eyes, dark and liquid, and
glowing.

''I'd like to tell you something. If you'll listen.''

''That's what I do best,'' I said.

She smiled crookedly. ''Second best, remember?''

''Okay, second best,'' I said, the effort to keep my voice
cool and indifferent almost more than I could handle.
''Shoot.''

She looked away, then back again, let her eyes meet
mine, hold me with a sudden mesmerizing force.

''I told you the truth, the partial truth,'' she said slowly.
''I didn't marry Clay for love. But I didn't marry him for
money, either, or any of the things that go along with it.''

''That leaves precious little. Pity. Or . . .'' I took out a
cigarette, studied it for a moment. ''Or pregnancy.''

I saw her head bob out of the corner of my eye. ''Yes.
I was pregnant all right. But only two weeks and nobody
knew, not even me.''

''Webb?''

She nodded. ''Thanksgiving week. He came home from

213

Dallas. We spent the whole week together almost. We fought and we made love. We were both angry when he went back to school, but neither of us dreamed it would end the way it did.''

"Candice is Webb's daughter," I marveled. "That's what you meant when you said he left a part of him here."

She smiled gently. "I suspected it all along, but I wasn't really sure until she grew older. I could see Webb in her. I always wondered why everyone else didn't."

"How about Clay? Did he suspect, do you think?"

Her face tightened. "He knew all along. Even when I was pregnant. He knew for the simple reason that he was sterile. He had the mumps when he was sixteen. They settled in his groin. Both sides. He almost died. Afterwards the doctor tested him. He never told anyone, not even his parents."

"Not even you?"

"No. Not until . . . not for a long time."

"Does Webb know?"

"Yes. He does now."

I lit the cigarette, studying her downcast face for some clue to her thoughts.

"All right," I said, after a silence broken only by a bitter outburst from my ferocious blue jays. "Why did you marry him?"

She raised her head, her face pale and strained, dark eyes shadowed with painful knowledge, firm lips set in a tight inscrutable line.

"Fear," she said simply. "Fear and cowardice."

21

It was the first of December, just a few days after Thanksgiving. I was maid of honor at Priscilla Maroney's wedding to Steve Clinton. Webb was back at school, and I went to the wedding with one of the other girl's family. It was a big wedding, a nice wedding. That made me feel even worse about Webb and me. Two more years. It seemed like such a long time." Her voice ebbed, stopped while she bit distractedly at a hangnail.

"I didn't drink—you know that—but someone spiked the punch bowl or tea pitcher or something. An hour after the wedding I was smashed. I didn't know it, but that's what it was. All I knew was that I felt funny, light-headed and carefree, reckless, daring." She paused again, her soft lips curving wryly. "We all were, all of us girls. We were acting silly, like a bunch of simps. And when Clay asked to drive me home, I never gave it a second thought. I knew he was crazy about me, and I knew he would try something heavy on the way home. But I could handle him. I always had before, the few times I had gone out with him. Besides, he had received a brand new Buick convertible for his graduation present, and I guess I wasn't immune to that. In fact, I made that a condition. He would have to let me drive. He agreed. A little reluctantly, but he agreed, and I was driving when we left Priscilla's dad's house.'' She stopped again and sighed, her eyes seeking mine, dark and haunted, weeping without tears.

"That was the last thing I remember until I woke up in Clay's car out on Stanton Road. Zeke Fairlee was washing my face and Clay was unconscious on the seat beside me. I could smell smoke and gasoline and . . . something else burning.'' A shiver rippled through her, tanned hands wrestling in her lap.

"There were three people in the other car," she went on, her voice a dry flat monotone. "They were dead, burned to death. The car was on its rear end, leaning against the bank of Cannonball Creek. It was still burning, but the people had been dead a long time. Zeke came along right after the wreck and he said they were dead when he got there. A woman and two children. My god. And I thought I had killed them.''

"Thought?"

She nodded dully. "I was convinced of it. I had no reason to question it. I woke up buckled in the driver's seat, Clay in the passenger side. It never entered my mind that Clay could do such a thing. Or Zeke, for that matter.''

I stared at her, bewildered. "I heard about the wreck,'' I said. "But I thought Clay was driving.''

She nodded again, her face empty of emotion. "He was. He was pretending to be unconscious. It was a sham, a con, or whatever you call it. He was never unconscious. He had taken over the wheel before we had gone a mile from Priscilla's. I guess I just passed out driving. He got us stopped and made the switch, and a few minutes later he drove over the rise on Stanton Road on the wrong side of the road. He sideswiped the other car in the center of their lane. She lost control and skidded into the creek backwards. They said her gas tank hit some rocks and exploded.''

''And Clay was going to blame you?''

She smiled a thin mirthless smile. ''Clay did blame me. He let me believe I was driving. And Zeke backed him up by keeping silent. I don't suppose you have to wonder why considering how well Zeke has done with Claybar Enterprises. They made their deal before I woke up. Zeke took his hot rod and laid rubber all over the road. He confused the skid marks so well they never could prove it was Clay's fault. After Zeke finished and left to go for help, Clay made his pitch to me. He was sweet and humble and told me how much he loved me, that he couldn't bear the thought of me going to prison for . . . I think he called it vehicular something.''

''Vehicular homicide.''

''He said that me being drunk would count heavily against me, that I could get as much as ten years . . .'' Her voice faded. She bit her lower lip.

''But if you married him he would take the blame.'' I took out a cigarette. ''He would gallantly take the blame but you would have to marry him because a wife can't be made to testify against her husband. Something like that?''

She nodded, the bitter smile back in place. ''Almost exactly like that. And I bought it all. I was so frightened, Danny, I would have promised anything, done anything. All I could see were my parents' faces, my daddy trying to preach to a congregation who knew he had a daughter in prison for . . . for murder.'' The chestnut hair rustled as she shook her head. ''I was so dumb, so out of it that I didn't even wonder what Zeke was doing up on the road with his hot rod. I thought he was trying to reenact the accident. It didn't occur to me for months that he was simply destroying evidence, that Clay wasn't going to take the blame for anything really since nothing could be proven. They only had Clay's word for what happened and Zeke would help back him up.

"All this time there was no other traffic?"

"Oh, the road was closed. They were working on the bridge over Cannonball Creek. They had barricades up but Clay knew they had a temporary truck crossing. His daddy's construction firm was handling the job. The lady I— he hit lived back in there."

"And you've believed all these years that you were driving?"

She sighed. "Yes. I've lived with that. But I've already told you I'm a coward."

"How long have you known the truth?"

"Not long. Since Clay's accident."

"Why didn't you leave him?"

Her eyes drifted back to her lap, the white-knuckled hands. Her lips curled as if she might grimace, but she smiled faintly instead. "It was a little late for that. And too, I couldn't face what people would have said. That I left him when he became a cripple. And then there was Candy. She doesn't know that Clay isn't her father."

"I don't know about you being a coward," I said angrily, "but I do know you're a fool."

Her head jerked sharply again, color rushing back into her face. Her lips formed a tight intransigent line, then quivered and relaxed into a gentle half-smile.

"I've called myself that many times over, Danny. Why should I get angry with you?"

I got up and went into the kitchen for a beer. She hadn't moved when I came back. I sat down on the imitation leather chair by the window, lit the cigarette I'd been toying with for five minutes. I took a drink of beer.

"I'm sorry," I said, my voice still tight, not fully understanding my anger. "I had no right to say that. I would probably have done the same thing in your place, but I think I would have killed him when I found out."

She shook her head. "Clay wasn't an evil man, Danny. He was kind in a lot of ways—and generous. But he had to have what he wanted. He wanted me. He knew he couldn't have me, so when the opportunity came, he took it. It was wrong and in some ways it hurt him more than it did me. I had Candy and he didn't. He knew she wasn't his. He knew I never loved him. Even when I responded to him physically, sexually, he thought I was faking. He couldn't understand that I could find him physically attractive and not love him. I think a lot of men make that mistake. He was disappointed and bitter and frustrated. He had what he wanted, but he found that it was as elusive as foxfire. When he touched it, it crumbled, there was nothing there."

She fell silent, examining the tips of her fingers, short nails, neatly clipped and highly glossed with transparent polish. She sighed and looked at me with a hesitant smile.

"Ordinarily," she said, as if picking up the thread of a dropped conversation. "I wouldn't have been there on a Tuesday night. I bowl on Tuesdays. But they cancelled. Too many people had the flu."

"Tuesday night?"

She looked at me, blinking slowly. "Tuesday night. The night Clay shot himself."

"Oh." I felt a tiny muffled click as memory plugged in. "Tuesday night. The same night Boggs died."

Her lips pursed for a moment. "Yes, I suppose it was. Poor Mr. Boggs. But he was old. From what I hear, he had a full life. Maybe it's best to go suddenly when you're that old."

"Maybe," I said and finished the rest of my beer.

The blue jays were at it again, shrill and abrasive. I could see them through the window, a small, fluttering clutch harassing a squirrel. I brought my gaze back inside, to a strained face and downcast eyes, cheeks that still managed the delicate bloom of youth, a curving mouth that I could feel, the taste as vivid as a dollop of honey on the tongue.

I stirred restlessly and jammed out the cigarette. The small room seemed suddenly charged, the atmosphere palpable and electric. A cauldron of undifferentiated longings, desires, and memories, unwanted and unbidden, roamed at will.

"I'm curious," I said, my voice as rusty as a gate hinge. "Why are you telling me this?"

"I don't know," she said, and laughed a low, incredulous laugh. "I'm not sure at all. Maybe for sympathy. Maybe so you'd know that I'm only a coward and not a gold-digging whore. Maybe because it's important to me what you think—more than anyone. I suppose I thought I'd come off as a tragic romantic much abused by fate." Her lips curled in self-debasement. "Instead I came off as a fool."

"I told you I was sorry. I was angry."

She gazed at me curiously. "Why?"

"I don't know why."

She nodded, her expression strained, intense, then began talking rapidly without looking at me, the words tumbling like live coals across taut quivering lips:

"I never stopped, Danny. Even though I loved Webb, I never stopped loving you. Not with Webb and certainly not with Clay. It's been there inside me like a pocket of warmth all these years. I know it's a sign of immaturity, adolescent passion, empty juvenile desires. We're supposed to leave all that behind. But I guess somebody forgot to tell me.'' She looked up then, eyes wide and guileless, candescent. Her lips curved wryly. ''There I've finally told you. I never thought I'd have the nerve again.''

I lit another cigarette and watched the blue jays chase the squirrel along a limb, curiously silent now, a deadly battle no more real and violent than the one raging inside me.

''There's Webb,'' I said finally. ''He loves you, Melissa. You're his whole damned life. You always have been.''

She inclined her head, watching me quietly, her face shadowed.

''He met me out on the highway last night. He knew we had been together. He was willing to fight for you—no, he did fight for you. We . . . talked.''

''What did you two decide?'' she asked, as if we were discussing a fishing trip.

I tried to look at her. I owed her that much, at least. But the dark eyes were too bright and penetrating, too punishing to meet head-on.

''I told him,'' I said, my voice clogged with smoke, ''that he could have you.''

She stood up abruptly, smoothing the brown pleated skirt, her eyes wild and distraught, raking the room as if she had suddenly awakened to find herself in an alien environment, among strangers who might do her harm.

''Melissa,'' I said, but she was already gathering jacket and purse, adjusting her skirt and blouse, absorbed and intent, as if the richness of her life depended on such trivial matters.

Without a glance she turned and walked out of the room, out of the cabin, out of my life.

And I sat there and watched her go, feeling the room

closing in on me, listening to the smooth rumble of the Cadillac's engine until it was swallowed up in the humming of the refrigerator and the high, keening sound inside my head.

22

IT WAS DARK WHEN I REACHED MY HOUSE IN MIDWAY City. Pale and somber amidst towering elm and oak, eighteen hundred square feet of emptiness surrounded by Old English brick walls and chest-high shrubbery, it waited patiently for the lord of the manor to bring light to its blind glassy eyes, sound to its textured walls, life to its cloistered heart.

I went around turning on lights, the stereo, the TV, the kitchen radio. Illumination and sound. I needed both to help battle loneliness that rode me like a bad habit.

Peace. Solace. Solitude. The very things I had gone to Butler Wells to seek had driven me home, cringing like a failed hound. Behold the elusive patterns of malicious fate; old lives converging like ineptly orchestrated opera. Not since Tommy's death had I felt so utterly and starkly alone, so useless and sorry, the flow of normal lives around me as incomprehensible and obscure as the Memphite system of ancient Egyptian theology.

Before I ate I got out an unopened bottle of whiskey and set it in the center of the kitchen table. Tonight the game would be a mockery, a preordained conclusion, a fait accompli. All I could hope to do was tread water, line my stomach with something to buffer the shock, to delay the inevitable. I was damned well going to get drunk and I knew it, the pithy part of the question was how soon.

But there is often a yawning abyss between the stated intentions of man and his accomplishments, and so it was with me. Fateful intervention arrived in the form of Captain Homer Sellers of the Midway City Police Department.

I was reaching for the bottle when the phone rang—jangled—screamed its clarion call at me from less than three feet away. Startled, I reacted as if I had just been caught in some despicable act with a child.

My hand stopped, sprang back, wavered, continued, and struck the curving neck of the bottle with stiffened fingers as if it had intended doing that all along. I watched in horror as the fifth toppled, twirled cunningly on its axis, rolled majestically out of reach and over the edge of the table. It shattered with a cruel splash.

The phone rang again, sedately.

Fumes joyously attacked the room, bringing tears to my eyes, effervescing in my sinus cavities, lodging in my throat.

"Hello! Dammit!"

"That's no way to answer a phone, son," Homer Sellers said, clucking in his most annoying, fatherly fashion.

"Christ, Homer, you just caused me to trash a fifth of Jack Daniel's best."

"That's no reason to get edgy. Anyhow, you drink too much."

I stretched the phone cord around the door frame into

the den, plopped down in my recliner and breathed through my mouth.

"You get my message on that recorder of yours?"

"I just got home a little while ago, Homer. I haven't had a chance to check my calls. I'm on the kitchen extension."

"Well, I'm at home too. I just wanted to tell you I've got that info you wanted on Mr. Boggs. Ain't much to it. He's just your run-of-the-mill average naturalized citizen."

"Run of the mill? A death camp inmate, a French freedom fighter, an English Commando, a Grand Prix winner, a writer—"

His rumbling laugh boomed in my ear. I tilted the receiver and waited until it came to a wheezing halt.

"I don't know about the writer part, but he ain't been any of them other things. Not unless he did it after 1947. That's as far as these records go." He squeezed another chuckle out of it. "Somebody been pulling your leg, son."

"Yeah, and a few other things. Do you know when he came to the States?"

"Yep. 1938. Worked at a library in Los Angeles three years, then after we got into the war, he went to work at Douglas Aircraft. That took him through 1945. He went to work for some museum in San Francisco after that. That's about as far as they go. You already knew he had a little record here in Texas?"

"Sodomy?"

"Yeah. Dallas and Houston. Washington didn't turn up anything else."

"What did he do at Douglas?"

"Blueprint file clerk. One reason we got such good records on him. He handled a lot of classified stuff. They run a pretty tight check on him. Probably because of his German parentage.''

"What? He's supposed to be English and Jew."

"Ain't what it says here. Half German. Father was an Englishman, mother a German. He was born in England all right, but his mother emigrated from Germany."

"What did you find out about WWNF?"

"Nothing."

"Hell, Homer, they're in the phone book."

"So am I. All that signifies is that I have a phone. Anybody can have a phone and use whatever name they want. Nope. We came up empty. Zilch. Same with my cousin Ken at State. There's been several groups since the war engaged in Nazi hunting, but WWNF ain't one of them."

"Well, I'll have to admit the woman I talked to sounded like she hadn't had her eggs candled lately. I wonder how Boggs came across that name?"

"He probably saw it in the phone book same as we did. Maybe he was just curious, wanted to know what it stood for. Who knows? That woman is probably a kook same as he was."

There goes the Nazi connection, I thought, the remote possibility that Boggs had been killed because of his activities in that direction. The subsequent attacks on me by Alex Bremmer and his hirelings had supported that scenario to a degree, lending credence to the theory that I was getting close to something or someone, stirring up waters somebody wanted to stay calm. That could still be true, but for entirely different reasons. All I had done was eliminate a possible motive.

"Hey, you there, little buddy?"

"Yeah, I was thinking." Another thought that chilled my blood: What if Bremmer's attack had nothing to do with Boggs? What if it was some sort of personal vendetta against me?

"About what?"

And what about the black girl? Would she come forward when they found Bremmer and Mingo? Had she known my name? I tried to remember if Bremmer had mentioned it in her presence. For the first time I began to doubt the sagacity of my decision not to report my kidnapping and the deaths of my three captors to Webb and the county sheriff. Not doing so could create untold difficulties should the truth come out. I could see that now in the pristine clarity of sober retrospection.

But, on the other hand, Seth and Mingo had died accidental deaths, albeit with a little choreographing on my part, and I had arranged things to indicate that Bremmer had shot himself to end the obviously excruciating pain of his burns.

That left the black girl. A hooker. She would, I hoped, fade into the shadows at the first whiff of danger, the first hint of revolving lights and guns and badges and clanking jail cells.

"Thinking about what?" His voice had dropped to a low rumble, a sign of impatience.

"About Boggs."

"What?"

"It was all a lie. Every damn bit of it. And not being half Jew really tops it off. His best friend in Butler Wells is a Jew, and he never suspected." I decided it would serve no purpose to tell him about Bremmer, Mingo, and Seth.

"Why do you think he'd do that?"

"Beats me. Same reason he pretended to be a Commando and a French freedom fighter. He wanted to appear

227

to be something other than what he was. I guess when you get down to it we all do a little of that."

"Not me," Homer declared. "What you see, et cetera. Now that we got that out of the way, you gonna be ready to go down to your land Saturday?"

"Hell, Homer, I just got home."

"Don't matter. I've got Swain and Jeffers all primed to go. Only got two more weekends before the big 'un."

"You guys really don't need me, you know."

"Don't matter. You said you'd go and you're gonna go if I have to come over there and haul your ass out of that bed."

"Please don't do that. I might have to whip yours and how'd you explain that to your stalwart minions? Man half your size—"

"Half my size, my butt. I only weigh about thirty pounds mor'n you, and I'm three inches taller. You ever take me on, you better piss on the fire and call in the dogs 'cause you're done." His barking laugh ended with its usual wheeze.

"Okay. But if we're going, we're going early. Six o'clock."

"That's fine with me, but I'll let you tell Jeffers. You know how he hates that early shit."

We settled on eight o'clock, the time we usually left on this kind of excursion. I hung up the receiver with mixed emotions. A part of me looked forward to it, a crisp autumn day in the field with good companions, free-flowing beer, and the easy labor of preseason preparations. Rough humor and persiflage, the comfort of ritual done right, the careless profanities of men away from the restraining influence of society.

I cleaned up the whiskey and glass, feeling a little giddy and wondering if you could get a second-hand high from

23

I WAS AWAKE BEFORE DAWN THE NEXT MORNING, HAVING dragged myself to bed sometime during the early hours of the new day. I ate bacon and eggs in the den in front of the tube, watching the 6:00 A.M. newscast for the first time in recent memory. Nothing new had happened during the night except another PLO terrorist bombing in Jerusalem, killing six and wounding twenty-seven. Israeli retaliation expected momentarily.

I put on a jacket and stepped out onto my front porch for an after-breakfast cigarette and to watch the sunrise over Dallas. Not a particularly inspiring sight at the best of times, that morning's spectacular was further muted by a low-hanging haze, the collective exhaust of a million weary lungs. Like all the rest of the metropolitan giants in the country, Dallas and Fort Worth could no longer boast of smog-free air and uncontaminated water, but, unlike some others, we could still see the sun for days at a time.

Somewhere along the way we had lost the easy measured gait that had once been the hallmark of the South. We had become sophisticated and chic, nervously chomping the bit, the lure of more and bigger urging us on to greater heights of statistical glory. But more and bigger is seldom better, and we were paying the price in congestion and frustration, in quality of life.

Back inside the house, I scraped my breakfast dishes and stacked them among the ones I had abandoned in the dishwasher before taking off for Butler Wells. Since it had been more than two weeks, I decided a double washing would be in order.

I was squatting in front of the controls, working out the right combination of dials and buttons, when the sun peeped over the sill of the dining room window, tentative and diffused, yet strong enough to wink merrily on something caught against the far leg of the kitchen table.

I punched the dishwasher to life, crossed to the table, lifted, and tapped the object with the toe of my boot. It skittered out into the open, an oblong piece of glass from my ill-fated fifth of whiskey. It lay in a patch of sunlight like a jeering sardonic eye, pale gray and slightly curving, the length of an egg but wider, more rectangular.

I squatted and picked it up, feeling a tickling sensation at the base of my throat, a coolness on my neck. I felt my brow wrinkle without conscious stimulation, something shifting in my brain, clicking, sliding, falling into place.

I turned it over and over in my hand and stared, mesmerized . . . and stared . . .

And suddenly remembered.

It took slightly more than two and a half hours to reach Butler Wells. Not a mean achievement even in the old days, it was a minor miracle with the fifty-five mph speed limit. But I made it, and in one piece, my brain electrified with new knowledge, seething with new assumptions, skittering off in a dozen new directions.

I topped the rise behind Pete Dixon's crappie house, let

the pickup coast to a halt in the saddle wash at the foot of the hill.

I got out and stood wiping my sweaty hands on my denim jacket. Now that I was here doubt assailed me, swarmed in to diffuse certainty, to confuse and ridicule the new hypothesis I had carefully constructed during the wild hundred and twenty mile ride.

I shrugged it off as best I could, lit a cigarette, and went about what I had come to do.

The lens was still there, exactly where I had buried it with the shards of glass. I liked it out gingerly, feeling a tingling shock at its translucent clarity, wondering if after all my memory was playing tricks.

I cupped it in my palm and walked out of the thicket into the light. I held it up to the sun and felt a sharp thrill as it began to change, darkening, a man-made chameleon adapting to its new environment.

Feeling a surge of elation, I tucked the smokey-gray lens carefully into my shirt pocket, and continued with the balance of my appointed task. I gathered a half-dozen blood-stained tissues, the balled handkerchief stiff and crusty with blood, the stained toothbrush.

The sanitary napkins and the shriveled condoms draping the bushes like desiccated artifacts of an ancient age, I left for atmosphere.

I drove back to the fork in the road, up Scales Drive to the Boggs residence. I found Mrs. Boggs well on her way to being smashed, lighthearted and gay, not even bothering to ask me why I wanted the manila envelope with Mr. Boggs's effects.

While she went off humming to find them, I called the police station and talked to Webb.

"Where can I get an agglutination test performed?"

"A what?"

"I need to type some bloodstains. You don't have facilities, do you?"

"We use the hospital lab as much as we can. More sophisticated stuff has to go to Waco or Dallas. Why? What do you have?"

"Some bloodstains," I said impatiently. "Give me the name of your contact at the lab."

"What the hell are you doing, Dan? I thought you'd gone—"

"Boggs. Ardell P. Boggs. Remember him? While I've got you I need to know his blood type from the autopsy report. Get it, will you?"

"B-negative," he said slowly. "I remembered because it's the same as mine.

"Who do I see at the hospital?" Mrs. Boggs drifted into the room, the envelope clutched to her stomach, her face sagging, eyes slightly out of focus, a vacant smile on heavily rouged lips. A strand of hair had broken loose and played across her shriveled cheek as she stood watching me benignly.

"Evelyn Pierce," Webb said. "But they don't do this kind of thing free. We have to pay for it."

"So we'll pay for it. Thanks, Webb. I'll have her bill the city." I hung up.

"Here you are," Mrs. Boggs said brightly. "I hope you put them to good use. I was planning to give them to the Goodwill. Those shorts and that shirt are practically brand new." She had trouble with the sibilants, stretching the vowels until they cracked.

"I'll take good care of them," I promised. "You did put the glasses back in here?"

"Oh, yes," she said. "All the large pieces of glass, I put them in there, also."

233

"Fine," I said. "Did Mr. Boggs buy his glasses locally?"

"Yes. Wayne Goddard's Opticals. It's on the square."

"Did he have more than one pair?"

"Yes again. His other pair is on his bureau." She made a fruitless effort to iron the wrinkles in her cheek with a flattened hand, her expression vacuous and coy.

I thanked her and took my leave, revising my estimate of her condition. One more good stiff drink and she'd belly-up in a welter of distilled spirits, her answer to empty days, ennui, and inexorable time.

Thinking somberly about old age and loneliness, I drove back across town to the new hospital. It was a long, rectangular brick building, two stories high, with a modern-functional look, small heavily tinted windows, and a flat roof. The unusually large macadam parking area hinted of future expansion, and two towering pecan trees guarded the sliding glass door entrance.

I found the laboratory and Evelyn Pierce without problem, clumping through beige-colored corridors, following the signs and the explicit instructions given me by the fresh-faced young brunette at the front desk.

Evelyn Pierce was expecting me; a tall, thin-faced young woman in her mid-twenties, she poked at my collection of bloody samples with the tip of a yellow pencil, a faintly disapproving look on her face.

"You want all of these tested?"

"Yes ma'am."

"The toothbrush too?"

"Why not?"

She wrote something on a small white pad, toted up some figures and gave me a cost estimate of fifty dollars.

"Just charge it to the city."

She looked dubious. "Chief Chandler didn't say anything about that. He said it was a private matter, but that he would appreciate our cooperation." She smiled sweetly. "I'm sure you can get reimbursement from the city, if it's city business."

"Uh-huh. I suppose you want it in advance."

"Yes, I'm afraid that's hospital policy."

I handed her two twenties and a ten. "When can I pick up the results? Actually, all I want is blood type."

"That's all you'll get for fifty dollars. You can pick it up tomorrow."

"I need it by three this afternoon."

She bit her lower lip and shook her head. "I'm sorry, there's too much ahead of you. I'd have to shuffle—"

I laid another twenty on the counter. "Four o'clock."

She laid a slim palm over the bill. "Six o'clock would be the earliest possible—"

I added another ten. "Four o'clock."

She glanced at my wallet. I closed it firmly and put it away.

"Four-thirty then, Mr. Roman, we'll have it ready for you."

"Fine," I said. "Will you still be here?"

"Yes, I work until six."

"If I can't come by, I'll give you a call."

She wrote me out a receipt for fifty dollars, annotated the lab extension number, and handed it to me with a Sunday-School-innocent smile. "That'll be fine, Mr. Roman."

I returned her smile and left, my faith in the predictability of human nature completely restored. Actually, I was pleased. I'd expected to pay at least a hundred.

Wayne Goddard's Opticals was on the north side of the square, the affluent side. Nestled between a dentist's office and a flourishing dress shop, it had once housed a dry cleaning establishment, the "Walt's One-hour Cleaners" logo still faintly visible on the high false front of the tan brick building. Some attempt at refurbishment had been made: a modern automatic door and a huge plate-glass window, both heavily tinted.

Wayne Goddard proved to be a tall, thin young man with more hair on his lip and chin than on his head. He smiled amiably at me over an old-fashioned glass showcase crammed with sample frames, long, thin fingers splayed on the counter top as he leaned forward in a motion faintly resembling a bow.

"What can we do for you, sir?"

I returned the smile and laid Boggs's wire frames and the loose lens on the counter. I spilled the broken fragments of the other lens beside them.

Wayne Goddard's hands fluttered in dismay. "My goodness, we did have an accident, didn't we?"

"Maybe," I said. "Maybe not. I understand Ardell Boggs was a customer of yours."

"Oh, yes indeed." His expression snapped to grim. "That was such a terrible—"

"I need to know," I interrupted, "if this lens came out of these frames. Can you tell me that?"

His high forehead wrinkled, radiating subsidiary lines upward into his gleaming scalp. He sucked on the edges of his moustache.

"You mean these are Mr. Boggs's frames?"

"Yes. I know the fragments came from the left lens. I need to know if this is the right lens to these frames."

"Oh, I see. Yes, of course, I can tell you if this is Mr. Boggs's prescription. The frames are terribly twisted. I'm not sure I can fit the lens back again. If you'll look closely you can see the bent edges of the retaining groove—"

"That isn't necessary. All I want to know is if this is Boggs's lens."

"I'll be just a moment." He picked up the lens and the frames and disappeared through a doorway at the end of the counter.

I lit a cigarette and wandered around the room. Open display cases along the walls offered frames of every conceivable configuration: from small round lenses no larger than the eyes of an owl to overblown monstrosities the size of small grapefruit, rhinestone encrusted, gold leaf and silver inlays. Changing times and changing styles. A far cry from the plain black plastic and wire-rimmed spectacles of my childhood; simple and functional giving way to flashy and over-priced.

I ended up in front of the plate-glass window, its darkly tinted eye casting an ominous pall over an otherwise sunny day. People trickled by, glancing at me with the casual indifference they might have given a naked mannequin. One young girl stared, nudged her companion; they both covered their mouths with their hands. When they were out of sight, I checked my fly.

Down at the corner a group of young boys in curving cowboy hats made of straw jostled and shoved, broke out in small domination-oriented flurries of jabbing and punching, healthy restless young animals establishing rank in the pack. I wondered idly why they weren't in school.

From the back room I heard a popping noise, an exclamation, and a moment later Goddard swept into the room, Boggs's glasses held out in front of him like an optician-of-the-month award. He was smiling broadly.

"I got it in after all," he said excitedly. "I don't think it will stay, though."

"That's great," I said. "Was it Boggs's lens?"

237

"Of course," he said, and gave me a pained look. "I sold him these myself."

"You're positive of that? No chance for error?"

The pained expression became indignant, a trace of scorn. "Please give me credit for knowing my own product."

I nodded. "Sorry. I appreciate it. How much do I owe you?" I took out my wallet.

The ladder of grooves climbed his forehead again. "Owe me? Owe me for what?"

"For your time. For your help."

He spread his hands on the counter. "I have a lot of free time. What did it take? Five minutes? I'd be pretty sorry if I charged you for that."

"Well. . . thanks."

I shook his hand and left, feeling a little disgruntled. Just when I had the human race all figured out, this honest jerk had to come along and screw it up for me.

I pulled into a shady slot on the west side of the square. I opened the window to the crisp November breeze and lit a cigarette.

So Ardell Boggs had been killed after all. Murdered. There was no other reason a part of his glasses would be a mile away from where his body had been found. At least none that I could think of, none that made any sense. He had been struck down in the saddle wash behind Pete Dixon's crappie house, transported up the hill to Scales Bluff and shoved or thrown over the edge onto the rocks. Even if he had been killed in the heat of some incomprehensible passion, his disposal had been coldly premeditated, executed flawlessly. Well, almost. The missing lens was a flaw. Maybe a fatal one. Had the killer been working with such frantic haste that he hadn't noticed? Or hadn't he cared?

The blood-stained tissues and handkerchief could be more flaws. Possibly. Or they could be just what I had thought at first: the by-product of insouciant young lovers. They could have also been used to wipe Boggs's blood from the killer's face, hands, arms, the murder weapon, his shoes, his—the possibilities were endless, and if the samples proved to be B-negative, then the logical conclusion would be that the killer had done exactly that.

But why had he been so careless? Or had he been working in a state of shock, his only thought to dispose of the body as quickly as possible? And would that indicate a spontaneous act, a moment of blind panic? Crazed fear?

Questions. Still too many unanswered questions, with the really big one nibbling at the fringes of my mind as persistent as a nagging cough.

''Why?'' It took a moment for me to realize I'd spoken aloud.

I dropped the cigarette out the window and watched a passing boy stare at me curiously, his eyebrows cocked. I grinned at him and took out another cigarette.

I had no clear idea why. On that issue I was back to square one: Who would want to harm an inoffensive little old man like Boggs? A pathological liar, maybe, but an essentially harmless one.

I lit the cigarette and started the engine.

Maybe I had no clear idea why, but, by God, I did have a suspicion.

24

MRS. FLORA DAWSON HAD TO BE FIVE YEARS OLDER THAN
Ethel Boggs, but she looked ten years younger. Short and
thin, as fragile-looking as good pie crust, she had merry
blue eyes and a wide contagious smile. Upswept, meticu-
lously coiffured hair tinted the color of wheat enhanced the
carefully nurtured image of graceful aging. A faint blush
stained the upper reaches of each cheek, gave credence to
a face that had somehow escaped the more corrosive rav-
ages of time.

I had no need to introduce myself. She had been the
county clerk for forty years, had been the one to annotate
to the cumbersome tomes the glad tidings that Daniel Austin Roman, eight pounds and six ounces, had come to save
the world. She had been there to give me my first driving
permit, my birth certificate, had taken the money for my
first fine.

She offered me tea or coffee, and we moved to the
triangular redwood deck behind her house at my suggestion.

We found seats at a white metal table and I let her chatter
about the fine old days, the differences between then and

now, the inexplicable changes that were, alas, not for the better.

We talked about people we had known, the famous and the infamous, and inevitably about football, that grand and glorious year when I had almost won the state championship all by myself. I graciously accepted her blandishments, modestly averting my face as befits a legendary hero.

When she went inside to replenish our coffee, I walked over to the railing at the apex of the triangular deck. The marina spread out below, the crappie house off to my right. I could see a part of the saddle wash where I had found the lens. The rest of the road to Scales Bluff was hidden behind a bulge in the brow of the hill.

"It's a nice view, isn't it?" Mrs. Dawson came up beside me.

"Very nice. You have a good view of the marina. Not that it wouldn't be better without it. I imagine it is a nuisance, the boats coming and going at all hours."

"Oh, I don't mind. I don't hear as well as I used to, so the noise isn't much of a bother. It used to be worse, you know. The marina was almost twice as large as it is now."

"I thought it looked smaller."

"There were two other wings. They were destroyed by a tornado. Clay Garland had them cut up and removed. I think he wanted a place to play more than anything else."

"That sounds like Clay. I understand you had some problems with ricochetting bullets."

She gave me a quick sidewise glance, the blue eyes bright and penetrating. "I expect you must have been talking to Webb Chandler."

"Yes. We were talking about the night Clay killed himself." I turned to face her. "You were sitting out here that night, weren't you?"

She took a deep breath. "Yes. I called Chief Chandler. I've never quite known whether to feel guilty about that or not, the way things turned out."

"Don't," I said. "What you did had nothing to do with it. That would be carrying cause and effect a little too far."

"I hope so," she said unhappily. "I've known Clay all his life, the same as I have you. I'd hate to think I'd caused his death even remotely indirectly."

"Mr. Boggs. He usually walked down that road in the evening. Did you happen to see him that night?"

"You mean the night Clay—yes, as a matter of fact, I did. I believe . . . let me think now . . . yes, he was standing on that little rise just down from the crappie house. I could see him in the glow of light from the marina. Just standing there. He did that sometimes before turning back. Sometimes he would walk on around to the marina. He and that young man seemed to be friendly . . . that young Mr. Trumble."

"Was he there when you heard the shot?"

She pursed her lips and stared out across the lake, her brow knitted. "Yes, I believe—yes, I'm sure of it. It was faint, muffled. I wasn't really sure at the time that it was a pistol shot. But I remember wondering if Clay could be shooting off the other end of the marina. I kept watching to see. The next time I thought of Mr. Boggs, he had disappeared." Her brows knitted again. "And come to think of it, so had the car."

"What car?" Something slithered in my chest, shimmied upward, clogging my throat, drying my mouth. I turned my face toward the lake.

"Oh, one of those little ones, racing cars, sports cars, whatever you call them."

"Where was it?"

"It was parked in that little dip behind the crappie house.

A couple of youngsters smooching, I expect. They go back there all the time. I was sure that was what it was when I saw it drive by down there without its lights." She laughed lightly. "They must think a body can't see."

"How long after you saw it go by did you see Mr. Boggs?"

"Oh, not long, as I remember. Ten minutes, perhaps. Come to think of it, Mr. Boggs probably scared them off."

"Yeah," I said. "Probably."

"Well, they didn't come back out, so they must have driven up over Scales Bluff and on out the back way."

"Around the dead end, you mean?"

"Yes. The road continues on around the hill. It's in bad shape but you can drive it if you're careful. That's what I hear, anyway."

"Could you tell what color the car was?"

"No. A dark color I would say, but that's only a guess."

"You were out here then when Zeke Fairlee and the Chief and Melissa left?"

"Zeke? No, I didn't see Zeke leave. I saw the Chief and Mrs. Garland—Melissa."

"He left a short time before they did."

She shook her head slowly, face puckered in thought. "No, I don't remember—no, wait. I went inside to get a glass of tea and to check the time. I was just getting settled again when the Chief and Melissa went down the gangplank. Zeke must have left while I was gone."

"The timing's right," I said. "And when did you see the car go by, before or after the Chief and Melissa left?"

"It . . . well, it must have been not long afterwards. I'm not really positive about that. I didn't pay a lot of attention to the car. They drive back in there quite often." She paused for a moment, then slowly shook her head again. "It could have been before they left. I can't remember for certain.'' She took a sip of coffee, the blue eyes twinkling over the cup. ''All these questions. I've had a funny feeling for the last few minutes that this isn't altogether a social call, Daniel.''

I apologized for being so nosey and made up for it by listening to a litany of her illnesses from ingrown toenails to her recent gallstone operation. I surreptitiously dumped my coffee over the railing before we wandered back to sit at the table. I lingered for a while over a third cup, eating fresh chocolate chip cookies and laughing at titillating tidbits about people I had known during my formative years. Her eyes sparkled and the stories tumbled out, a rapid-fire staccato delivery that Georgie Jessel would have admired and envied.

I found myself having fun, laughing too much and probably too loud. But for the first time in days I was thinking about something besides other people's problems and my own drifting indecisive life.

I let a pleasant hour slip by before reluctantly saying goodbye, thinking with surprising poignancy that the path of this bright irrepressible lady and my own would probably never intersect again. Not a great tragedy for either of us, but an unpleasant thought all the same. Another signpost of my life, slipping into the past. Gone.

I found Jake Trumble tinkering with a small outboard motor mounted above a rusty barrel filled with water. Trim and fitlooking in tight jeans and a long-sleeved sweater, he glanced up at the sound of my boot heels on the deck, paused in his labor to watch me approach, his ready smile a white slash against the darkness of his beard.

''Howdy.'' He wiped his hands on a towel hanging on the edge of the barrel. ''I heard you'd gone home and left us.''

I nodded and shook his hand. Everybody and his dog seemed to be keeping tabs on me. "The reports of my departure have been greatly exaggerated."

He laughed and leaned a shoulder against the wooden A-frame on which the outboard motor was mounted. "Mark Twain, right?"

I lit a cigarette and got right into it. The afternoon was slipping by like sleep, the growing certainty of what was coming nibbling at my edges like a school of optimistic minnows.

"The night Clay Garland killed himself. You were here. Exactly where were you?"

"Right here," he said promptly. "Mr. Boarman and I were working on his trolling motor. It was mounted right here on this rack."

I turned and looked at the storeroom office. It was no more than fifteen feet away, the door in plain sight.

"You were here when you heard the shot?"

He nodded without speaking, smooth tanned forehead wrinkled.

"You said you came late. How long had you been here?"

He shrugged and spread his hands. "Twenty-five, thirty minutes. Somewhere in there. We got here just as Chief Chandler and Mrs. Garland were leaving. We met them on the gangplank as a matter-of-fact. Chief Chandler warned us that Clay was drunk and in a bad mood and he advised against crossing him." He laughed softly. "Not that I needed the warning. I never went near him if I could help it."

"How about Zeke Fairlee? Did you see him?"

"Only a glimpse. He was driving out of the parking lot when we arrived."

"Did you happen to notice which way he went when he reached the fork?"

He shook his head, frowning. "No, I didn't. We were busy getting the motor out of Mr. Boarman's trunk and I didn't pay any attention. I don't know that I'd have noticed anyhow. The trees are pretty thick along there."

I tossed the cigarette into the still water next to the dock. Something swirled. The butt disappeared, only to appear a second later two feet away. Instant analysis and rejection. Fish were smarter than people.

"How long was it after you heard the shot before you went in?"

His brow furrowed again. "I don't know, not exactly. The Garfields heard it too. We kinda stood around for a few minutes wondering if we should do something. I thought Clay had probably shot down into the fishing hole or something. We talked about it and finally Mr. Boarman said to hell with it and knocked on the door. When nothing happened, we all went in and found him. Maybe three, four minutes at the most." He folded his arms and glanced toward the office, then back at me, eyes squinted warily, a poised cautious expression that said "I don't want to get involved."

"Is this connected to the Boggs thing? Or do you think there was something funny about Clay's death?" His voice was pointedly bland and indifferent, as if we were discussing the deaths of two Yankee tourists out on the Interstate. It's something a drifter learns early: if there's going to be trouble, drift.

"And he was already dead?"

He nodded somberly. "Yeah. I've had some first aid training. Enough to know a dead man when I see one. I couldn't raise a pulse in either his wrist or his neck, but I already knew. He had the color—or lack of it."

"Not much time to lose his color."

He shrugged. "Works that way sometimes."

246

I took out another cigarette, tapped it needlessly on my thumbnail. "What if somebody slipped something thin, a piece of tough cardboard, or plastic, in front of that spring lock shaft on the trapdoor? Wouldn't it be possible to come back later and enter the room that way?"

He thought about it, pursing his lips, tugging his beard, eyes narrowed, finally shaking his head.

"Same thing applies as last time we talked," he said. "Not unless Clay helped him, I don't think. The water's too far away from the trapdoor. First he'd have to get the thing raised and pushed back against the wall. That'd take some doing. You probably noticed I couldn't reach the water lying down and leaning over the other day. Even if he had arms long enough to reach it, he'd have to push it open while treading water. That door weighs about fifty pounds. The resistance would simply push him down in the water. It's at least ten feet deep along in there."

"What if he used something, a broom handle, a two by four, a long stick?"

"That's possible, but the resistance would still be the same, and anything he used would leave marks on the underneath side of the door. I didn't see any marks the other day, did you?"

"No," I said, "I didn't."

"Maybe it could be done. Maybe using something we haven't thought about. But one thing sure it would make noise, a lot of noise. I'm not sure we wouldn't have heard it all the way out here." He stopped, face puckered in thought. After a moment, his features smoothed out, his eyes brightening. "One more thing. Water marks. This lake was muddy as hell back then. That crappy vinyl they have in there marks like a bastard. I oughta know, I've had to swamp it out enough. Somebody come up through that trapdoor, he's gonna leave water all over the place. Can't

247

get away from it. It would evaporate and leave rings of dirt. But that don't really matter, because I'll damn guarantee you if there had been water on that floor I'd have seen it. One of us would have probably slipped and busted our ass.''

I nodded and lit the cigarette. "Except for the water marks—I hadn't thought of that—you've confirmed what I've been thinking: nobody could have come up through the trapdoor and shot Clay without his help. Now, considering the business about the water marks, it looks like nobody came up through there, period." I grinned at his perplexed expression.

"You know what that leaves us with, don't you?"

His head wagged slowly. "No, what?"

"A classic locked room murder mystery. Without the lock, of course."

He looked even more perplexed. "But how, if he committed suicide?"

"Right," I said sagely, and walked off and left him with a stunned look on his face, blue eyes wide and clouded with confusion, a subtle alteration in the way he stood, tense, poised, a roebuck assessing the intentions of a prowling lion.

I found a telephone booth at a Shell station and called Dr. Ragen's number. He was out to lunch, expected back momentarily.

I crossed the Interstate and ate a plastic hamburger and gummy fries, made the illegal pass across the highway again to my telephone booth.

Dr. Ragen was in, but he was busy. I said I'd wait since this was something of an emergency. She wanted to know what. I told her it was personal. Ten minutes later Dr.

Ragen came on the line. I identified myself and smiled a little at the intense silence on the other end.

"I only have one question, Doctor. Clay Garland. Was the gunshot wound definitely a contact wound? You know, powder burns—?"

"I'm quite familiar with the peculiarities of contact gunshot wounds, Mr. Roman. Yes, it most definitely was. I should think you could have obtained that information from Chief Chandler. He had the autopsy report." He paused for a moment. "Clay Garland? Why are you asking about Clay Garland? There is absolutely no doubt in anyone's mind that he killed himself."

"Open and shut? Just like Ardell Boggs?"

"Yes . . . well, no, there was some room for doubt in Boggs's case. Very little, I might add, but a slight possibility of accident or—"

"Or murder." I finished it for him. I took a deep breath. "He was murdered, Dr. Ragen. Ardell Boggs did not jump or fall. He was murdered and thrown or pushed or rolled over Scales Bluff."

This time the silence seemed to hum, to vibrate. I hung up right in the middle of it.

25

I FOUND BEN BOARMAN AT HIS EXXON STATION ON THE east side of the Interstate. Short and stocky in a blue workingman's uniform, he had a round, florid face with brown and grey hair showing beneath a soiled, baseball-style cap that still bore the old Enco logo. Years of weathering had seamed his skin like a soccer ball, stamped his features with futility and cynicism, dredged revealing grooves along each side of his small womanish mouth.

He reared back in his chair as I entered his cubbyhole office, brown eyes cold and speculative, appraising me as if I were just another old wreck he might dismantle for parts.

But when he spoke his voice was mild and friendly. "Yes sir, what can we do for you?"

"My name is Dan Roman, Mr. Boarman. I'm a private investigator. I wonder if I might ask you a couple of questions?"

He looked startled. "About what?"

"The night Clay Garland killed himself."

"Oh." He came forward slowly in the chair. "Oh, I see. Insurance company, huh?"

"Just routine. I understand you were at the marina that night."

"Yeah, that's so, I was." He gestured at a hard-backed chair in the corner. "Have a seat, Mr. Roman." He absently fished a cigarette out of his shirt pocket and smiled amiably. "Don't know that I've ever met a real live private eye before. Something I've always wondered. You guys really carry guns?"

"Only when I plan on shooting somebody." I slid the chair to the corner of his desk and sat down.

He slapped his leg and laughed. "I thought that was probably a bunch of bull."

"Hollywood hype." I lit his cigarette and one of my own. "Jake Trumble tells me you came by to get him to work on a trolling motor for you."

"That's right. Jake's a good man with motors. I was planning on doing a little bass fishing last Sunday and my trolling motor had conked out on me."

"He said you met Mrs. Garland and Chief Chandler on your way up the gangplank."

He frowned. "Yeah, somewhere along in there. The Chief said to watch out for Clay. Said he was on a rampage." He stopped and shrugged thick shoulders. "Didn't make no difference to me. I've seen Clay throw tantrums before. If you ask me that boy just never growed up."

"How long after that would you say it was before you heard the shot?"

"I don't know exactly . . . maybe twenty, thirty minutes. I didn't keep track. I was talking to Ted Garfield and his wife Alice. They were catching crappies right and left right there for a little while. You don't pay much attention to time when that happens."

"I thought you and Trumble were up near the marina office working on the motor."

He grunted and stubbed out his cigarette. "Was. For a while. But it's kinda a one-man job. I wandered off to talk to Ted and Alice. Trumble kept on working."

"Were you there when you heard the shot?"

He gave me another hard appraising look. "Was I with Ted and Alice? Yeah."

"Could you see Trumble working from where you were standing?"

"I was sitting. Alice gave me a deck chair." He fingered his small, round chin. "What're you getting at?" A bell clanged sharply—twice. He stood up and looked out the door, then grunted and sat back down. "Gotta watch these boys every minute."

"I'm just trying to establish the scene. You know, like where was everybody when the lights went out. That kind of thing."

He smiled. "Yeah, I see what you mean. No, as a matter of fact, I couldn't. That rigging where he works on motors is off to the left of the office. Too many boats in between, especially that pocket cruiser of Clay's." He reared back and laced his fingers around one knee. "He was back there, though. When that shot sounded, he walked out where I could see him. Me and the Garfields went right on up there. We talked about it a while, wondering what was going on. Jake wouldn't go in on Clay, so I finally did."

"That fits what he told me, all right. Could you see the marina office door from where you sat?"

"Sure. It's right straight up the deck."

"How about the Garfields? Could they see it also?"

He thought for a moment. "Sure. Alice in particular. She was in the front of the boat."

"Facing you?"

"Well, not exactly. More like facing the lake."

"And you were facing which direction?"

He scratched the end of his nose, fingered his chin again. "Well, kinda facing her, I guess."

"Then you weren't facing the marina office door."

He stirred uneasily. "No, not exactly, but I could see it from the corner of my eye." The bell chattered again, four times, then two more. He stirred, but remained seated.

"But it is possible that someone could have entered the door without you seeing them, particularly if you happened to be distracted by one of the Garfields catching a fish."

"Sure, anything's possible," he said, scowling. Then his face brightened. "Naw, Jake would've seen them. No way anybody could have gone through that door and him not see them." He stared fixedly at me for a moment. "What's the deal? You think something funny went on in there that night?"

"Not at all. Nothing funny. Did you happen to notice if there was a lot of blood, and what condition it was in?"

'Condition it was in? I don't get you. He had fallen out of his wheelchair on the cot, at least his head and shoulders were on the cot. The rest of him was kinda slumped against the wheelchair. All I saw was the place the bullet went in. There wasn't hardly any blood there at all. But I saw the Doc lift his head later and there was a big spot where the blood run out on the other side. It soaked into the sheet and mattress, I guess. Just a big red spot, kinda shiny. I'll tell you I didn't look too close." He scowled. "What's this got to do with anything?"

"Background stuff." I said. "How did the shot sound?"

His eyebrows bunched, came together to form a single quizzical line. "I don't get you. It sounded like a gunshot. A little muffled, maybe." His voice was suddenly furred with impatience. The bells were ringing again, an almost continuous clatter, and he was chomping the bit, visions

253

of sales lost and unhappy customers dancing in avaricious eyes. His fingers drummed the arms of the chair.

I stood up. "I won't keep you any longer, Mr. Boarman. I appreciate your time."

"Sure, you bet, glad to help." He was amiable again, edging me out the door.

A bulky man in a three-piece suit waited with ill-concealed impatience while a young boy filled out his credit card ticket. The man's cold, baleful eyes drilled a hole in the back of the kid's head.

"Everything all right, sir?" A note of servility had crept into Boarman's voice.

I missed the text of a gruff answer walking toward my pickup, pondering Ben Boarman's answers to my questions.

Matching Boarman's statement with Trumble's was somewhat like fitting a round rod into a square hole; it wobbled a little.

I drove back to the courthouse square and parked. I sat smoking and waiting for four o'clock, watching the desultory flow of humanity in and out my side of the courthouse, the slow waltz of housewives in jeans and ponytails around the square, seeing and being seen, killing another uninspired afternoon, something to talk about when Tom or Bob or John came in from the fields.

Old men in quilted windbreakers and overalls had established beachheads along the street-side park benches, wielding pocket knives in long practiced strokes, pausing occasionally to expectorate, to stare into space, seeing better than yesterday the wondrous world of fifty years ago, their time, when the land was as raw and young as they, when old age was just something the oldtimers grouched about, something as far away as walking in space or going to the moon.

Why?

The word intruded like a cockroach sliding through a crack in the floor.

Why kill Boggs?

There had to be a reason.

And that reason had to do with—the car? Clay's death? Or both?

That much was reasonably clear. One or the other, or both. Boggs had seen something he shouldn't have.

Where? That much was also reasonably clear—the marina or in the car.

What? If it had something to do with the marina, then logically it concerned Clay's death. If it had to do with someone in the car, then it would be anyone, or anything.

According to Mrs. Dawson, Boggs had been standing on the rise watching the marina when the gunshot sounded. A few minutes later he was gone. What could he have seen?

Nothing, dammit! What had happened to Clay happened inside the marina office. No windows, no openings at all on that side. So Boggs could not have seen anything inside the marina office. So? So what he saw must have occurred outside the marina office. . . .

A thought struck like a slap to the back of my head.

I got out of the pickup and started up the walk to the courthouse. Halfway there I changed my mind and went instead to a telephone booth on the corner of the square.

I dialed Webb Chandler's number.

A bored female voice answered, then transferred me without a word to the Chief's extension.

"Webb. This is Dan. When you got to the marina the night of Clay's suicide, was Jake Trumble there?"

"Dan? What the hell? I thought you'd gone—are you home?"

"I'm across town. Was Trumble there?"

"Well, hell, let me think . . . yeah, he was around when we removed the body. I remember talking to him. Not that I needed to particularly in view of what the Garfields and Ben Boarman—"

"But did you see him before that?"

"Hmmmm. Well, I don't remember, but he must have—"

"Does he have a car? Do you know?"

"I don't know."

"Find out for me, will you? I'll get back to you."

"Yeah, I can do that, but what the hell—?"

"And Candice Garland. What kind of car does she drive?"

"Corvette. Why?" His voice had changed, become more strident. I was no longer talking about a drifter; I was talking about the daughter of the woman he loved, his own blood.

"Bear with me, Webb. I'll get right back to you. Okay?" I broke the connection, held the bar down while I counted to five, then released it and fed more coins. I dialed the hospital and asked for the lab.

"You're early, Mr. Roman." Evelyn Pierce's voice sounded different on the phone, huskier, sexier.

"I know," I said humbly. "I just thought I'd check. You obviously are a very efficient lady, and I—"

"You're right, I am," she said crisply. "I have your results right here. Are you ready?"

"Shoot," I said, a curious tremor in my voice.

"Six tissue samples. Four were of the same type, B-Negative. Two were O-positive."

"And the handkerchief?" I discovered I was holding my breath.

"Also B-negative. The stains on the toothbrush were rust."

Five out of eight wasn't bad. And B-negative wasn't the most common blood in the bank. Fifteen percent or less of the population had B-negative blood.

"Were there any identifying marks on the handkerchief? Initials? Laundry marks?"

A moment of silence. "You didn't ask me to look for any." She sounded aggrieved. "But I will, if you want, although I'm sure I would have noticed."

"Thanks, I'll check back with you later. Were the tissues all the same, or could you tell?"

Another small silence, a faint sigh. "Tissues are pretty much tissues. It would take a microanalysis or a neutron activation analysis to tell them apart if—"

"That's okay. You've done a great job."

I thanked her and hung up slowly.

Boggs's blood and the lens from Boggs's glasses a mile away from where he had been found under impossible circumstances.

That spelled murder beyond a reasonable doubt.

But I still didn't know why. Or who. Not yet.

The marina was deserted. The small outboard motor still dangled into the barrel of water, the cowling on the deck beside it. But Trumble was nowhere in sight.

My boot heels ringing hollowly on the painted plywood deck, I searched the two wings comprising the marina, checking each boat as I passed. Trumble was gone. An hour and a half before his normal quitting time. I wondered why.

I walked back to the office and turned the doorknob. It was unlocked. I went in.

It was just as we had left it, stale air, the faint odors of oil and fish and tobacco intermingling, overflowing ashtrays and Clay Garland's cluttered desk. Sinister silence.

I pulled the small brass ring and lifted the trapdoor to rest against the wall. Smooth, white, and untrammeled, the bottom side of the trapdoor gleamed dully in the poor illumination from the window. I turned on the overhead light and examined it closely.

No marks. No scuffmarks or lines. No dents or abrasions. Nothing to suggest that it had been forced upward from below. But I hadn't expected there would be. If Clay had truly been murdered and, in turn, became the reason for Boggs's death, then his killer had walked in through the door, gone out the same way. All I had to do was figure out who and how. Why would present an entirely different problem. His life seemed to have been rife with enemies, people who disliked him for what he had, others who despised him for what he was.

Trumble had removed the candy wrappers, but the rest of the debris still rolled restlessly with the faint movement of the water within the coffin-sized rectangle: gum wrappers and cigarette butts; the two ice cream sticks; a well-chewed cigar stub; the broken pencil; a medium-sized, ziploc plastic bag.

I stood staring down at it, wondering why it seemed suddenly important, fluttering fragments of thought ranging the edges of my mind the way hungry wolves circle a campfire. I was still staring down into the murky water, almost mesmerized, when I heard the clatter on the gangplank.

Soft thudding sounds and the rattle of boards. That indicated deck shoes. Trumble wore deck shoes.

I whirled and walked out of the office, across the store-room, stepped through the open doorway into the arms of Zeke Fairlee, huffing and puffing, red-faced, loaded down with fishing rods, a tackle box, a minnow bucket, the small styrofoam cooler from his car, and two aqualungs dangling across his shoulders.

"Ooooh, shit!" He jumped backward, stumbled, his face blanching. "Dammit, Dan, you scared the hell out of me!"

I grinned and steadied him with a hand on the shoulder. "Who'd you think I was? Clay?"

"Shit. That's not funny, man." He made a sour face that slowly worked its way to a reluctant grin, color creeping stealthily back into his face.

"No, I guess it wasn't. Where you going in such a hurry?"

"Crappie fishing. Stub Monahan called me a little while ago. Said the crappie are hitting down at the north end of Mantilla Island. Want to go?"

"I don't think so. Thanks all the same."

He glanced past me into the lighted office, the trapdoor against the wall. "What the heck you doing here, anyway? He paused. "I heard you'd gone back to Dallas."

I shrugged and took out a cigarette. "Just nosing around."

"Nosing around about what?" He glanced at his watch. "Come on over to the boat and tell me about it. I wanna get out there and get set up before dark."

I carried the tackle box and minnow bucket and followed him to his boat. Showing me a flash of his old easy grace, he leaped nimbly into the boat, dropped the tanks onto a seat, stowed the rods, and turned back for the tackle box and bucket.

"You going diving for the crappie?"

He laughed. "I've got a storage locker forward. Running out of room in my car trunk.'' He shook loose a Winston and lit it, leaning around the wheel to tap his fuel gauges.

"Okay, nosing around about what?'' He looked up at me, grinning crookedly, the gray eyes darker in the shadow of the slip. "Surely you're not still cocking around on that Boggs thing. Man, you're busting your balls for nothing.'' He opened one of the live wells, placed the pail of minnows inside, and closed the lid carefully.

"Maybe not,'' I said, a little stung by his derisive tone and casual indifference.

He shrugged and began going through his pockets. "Hope I didn't forget the damn—nope, here they are.'' He fitted a key into the dashboard slot, then turned as the gangplank rattled again, a clatter of resounding footsteps and a medley of excited voices.

A man and a woman and two young boys came into view, crossed in front of the office, and moved into our wing. We watched them come toward us, the two boys, as alike as panda bears, tripped ahead of their parents and passed us with the woman trotting to catch up. She flashed us a wincing smile as she went by.

"Watch it, boys,'' the man called, nodding at me and smiling, stopping as he came abreast of Zeke's boat and caught sight of him.

"Hey, Chute! How you doing? Going out after them, are you?''

"Hello, Curt. Yeah, thought I might give it a try. Hear they're going crazy down near Mantilla Island.''

"Yeah, me too. That's where we're headed.'' He was short and stocky, blond hair and blue eyes, and strangely familiar. He cast another glance in my direction, screwed up one eye in an apologetic grimace. "Seems like I oughta

260

know you from somewhere. But I just can't put a name to your face."

I nodded and took a step forward. "You look familiar. My name's Dan Roman—"

"Oh, hell! Hell, yes. You played ball with my brother. Alex Bremmer? I'm Curt Bremmer. You guys were seniors the year I started high school." He stuck out his hand. "You wouldn't remember me, but I sure remember you. Too bad old Alex got kicked off that team. That was one blue ribbon team, you hear me? You guys were the best we ever had. Old Chute here and Webb Chandler and Clay Garland and you. Man, that was something." He looked at Zeke clambering across the hood to throw off the port bow line. "Alex said he saw you the other day. Said something about you getting a big promotion. Way to go, Chute!"

Zeke lifted the stern line free and spoke without turning. "Yeah. Tell your brother I said hello." He gestured toward the starboard bow line. "Throw off that line, will you?" His voice was awkward and stiff, oddly false.

"You bet," Curt said. He flipped the line free and lifted a hand. "Nice seeing you, Dan. I'll see you later, Chute." He trotted off down the deck, toward the excited jabber of the boys, the admonishing voice of the woman.

Chute!

Shoot!

They sounded the same!

"I'd better take off," Zeke said without looking up. "Sure you don't want to come along?"

"*Sure . . . I'm sure . . . fairly . . . shoot . . . fair . . . be fair . . .*" Garbled words from a dying man trying desperately to form truth. I felt drunk, lightheaded, my skin on fire.

I walked over and placed my foot on the bollard where

261

the starboard stern line was attached, my skin crawling, shrinking, an iron band closing on my chest.

Zeke looked up, his face lugubrious with strain, the freckles cast against the bloodless skin like gold leaf on stone, eyes flicking across mine.

"Chute," I said. "Alex Bremmer always called you Chute, too."

He gave me a fleeting puzzled glance, a smile that didn't come off. "Yeah, so what?"

"Shoot. Dan. Fair . . . be . . . fair . . ." His halting, bumbling words had told me, but I hadn't been listening.

"Chute," I said, my voice as thick as Alex Bremmer's had been. "It sounds like shoot."

"What? You're talking crazy, man. Come on, move your foot, I gotta go."

"Try it," I said doggedly, my mouth as dry as the inside of a dirty sock. "Chute. No matter how you say it, it sounds like shoot." I felt febrile, vindictive, wronged.

He wagged his head in exaggerated exasperation. "You're flipping out. Come on, I ain't got time for this shit right now." He shoved my foot off the bollard and flipped the line. The boat drifted free. He stared up at me, his eyes fevered, incandescent.

"You son of a bitch," I said, a bubble of rage bursting in my head. "It was you Alex was talking about. Chute! And goddamn you, I shot him!"

"Hey, Dan, come on. What the hell's wrong with you?" His voice had changed, become soft, placating, the tone you might use to a raving lunatic. He leaned over and pushed against the dock. The boat drifted out of the slip.

"You, Zeke! Goddamn you, you had him try to kill me! Why?" I was shouting, unmindful of the four startled faces staring at me from the other boat floating out of a slip farther down. "That's why I scared you so much. You thought I'd found out!"

Zeke shook his head and twisted the key. The engine whirred, but didn't catch. He tried again. I raised my voice above it.

"Why, Zeke? Was it Boggs? Was it Boggs, Zeke? Why did you kill him, Zeke?"

Head down, he fought the ignition switch, holding it down, letting up only to twist again, trying to drown out my voice, ignore my presence, my very existence.

Watching him, seeing the desperation in the taut shoulders, the florid, homely face, a tiny breaker flipped somewhere in my brain, switches clicking, and comprehension came smoking in like a clubbed fist to the solar plexus.

"Clay," I said, my voice a ragged whisper rising. "It had something to do with Clay. That was your car in the wash. Boggs saw you—" My eyes skittered, landed on the diving tanks. "In the water. He saw you doing something—coming back from the marina—!"

The motor caught, roared, punctuating my epiphany with an explosion of sound as definitive as Alex Bremmer's pillar of fire had been. The boat lurched, went into a tight controlled drift, sped away.

"You killed Clay," I said, talking as if he could still hear me. "Somehow. Or maybe you just hired Trumble to do it."

I watched as he roared by the port side of the smaller Bremmer boat, almost capsizing them, watched until he was leaving the mouth of the bay.

"You have to come back sometime, buddy," I said aloud. I lit a cigarette and found a seat in a nearby boat. I settled in to wait.

He was near the center of the lake when it blew. A blip of flame that flared like a struck match, a swelling mushroom of smoke, sound that rolled across the water like cannon shot.

For the first time in days I thought of Trumble's warning about the gas leak.

I sighed and flipped my cigarette into the water. "I'm sorry, man, we forgot to tell you."

26

I spent the night in my pickup on the bank of the lake watching them search for Zeke's body. I owed him that much, at least. They never found it, the best guess of the firefighters being that he had been burned so thoroughly that there was nothing left to sink except the bones.

But they did find Seth. Floating belly down in open water. I saw them bring him in, watched the coroner check him for signs of foul play, then curtly attribute his death to drowning, circumstances unknown.

By the time I got around to checking on Trumble near midmorning, he was gone. Bag and baggage, as they say. The drifter drifting on. The tumbleweed blowing with the wind, indifferent and uncaring, looking out for number one.

But it didn't matter. During the long hours of the night I had worked it out, the way it must have happened, gone back and put it together from the bits and pieces I had found, fragments that others had given me, from shadings of truth and circumlocutions, from downright lies.

Zeke had killed Boggs right enough. I'd stake my life on that. Out of fear, as I saw it, fear and blind unreasoning panic. Fear for his life, perhaps, or more likely for his way of life, fear of what Boggs had seen, what he could tell. In one frozen instant of time he must have seen his world crumbling, shattering, and all because a little old man liked to take an evening walk. He had reacted predictably.

And when he had finally decided that I wasn't going to give up on Boggs he had recruited his old friend Bremmer to kill me—or to scare me. I'd give him the benefit of the doubt on that since it didn't matter any more. But in either case it had gotten out of hand with Seth's death, as such things sometimes have a way of doing.

From Trumble's bare squalid room I went directly to the cabin. There was more to come and I needed sustenance. I showered and shaved and ate a half-dozen scrambled eggs and bacon.

I drank a cold glass of milk and later a beer, and felt as if I might survive another day. I hadn't slept for twenty-four hours, but I was curiously alert when I sat down to make the phone call, arrange the meeting that would finally and irrevocably bring it all together, finish it one way or another.

Mrs. Boggs watched me, her expression vague, un-comprehending, blurred eyes slowly rounding as her al-cohol-fuzzed mind absorbed my words. Her hands fluttered, gathered at her throat.

"Then . . . then I was right?" There was more incred-ulity in her tone than satisfaction.

"You were right. Zeke killed Mr. Boggs. He didn't fall and he didn't jump."

"My—my gracious." She swayed, her voice thready, barely above a whisper.

"Zeke drove his car back in there—probably too fast, without lights." I stopped to allow her to catch up. "He hit Mr. Boggs. Then when he saw that he was dead he panicked. He put him in his car and—well, you know the rest of it."

"He shouldn't have—that was not right what Zeke did."

"No, it wasn't," I agreed soberly. "But you knew Zeke. He had a strong sense of self-preservation, and he tended to act rashly, without thinking."

She nodded and drew in a slow deep breath. "Yes, I knew Zeke. And now he's dead." She shook her head. "Poor Valarie."

"Valarie? Zeke's wife?"

"Yes, and those poor little kids. Did you know Valarie is distant kin of mine on my mother's side?"

"No, I never met Zeke's wife."

She sighed, her eyes moist. "To lose her husband like that—and now this." She hesitated, then looked at me and wet her lips. "Do you think . . . have you told anyone about . . . you know, about Mr. Boggs and Zeke?"

"No," I said. "Only you."

"It can only hurt," she said, her expression suddenly anxious. "Can we—do you have to tell anyone?"

"No," I said. "I'm working for you. I'll do what you want."

She took another deep breath, her face brightening. "Then we'll just keep it our little secret. Is that all right?"

"That's fine," I said, ignoring a thready little rill of guilt. "We'll do just that." I pushed to my feet.

She moved to rise out of the scratchy chair, then sank back with a girlish little laugh, a shake of her head. "Just one moment, Daniel, and I'll get my checkbook. I seem to have a tiny bit of vertigo."

I crossed to the door. "No need. Don't worry about it until you get my bill."

"All right, Daniel, and thank you."

"You're welcome, Mrs. Boggs." I gave her a smile that

267

felt fractured, inane; then I walked through the door and out of her life feeling Machiavellian and sorry. I had not lied to her, had not led her to her empirical assumptions. On the other hand, I had not told her the entire truth, either, and that might well take a while to rationalize away.

It was five minutes before three when I made the turn into the trees on Lookout Point. The road wound, rough and rutted, for another hundred yards before breaking out into the open, the gravel surface of the parking area empty except for the Cadillac.

I braked to a stop on the side of the car away from the lake. Because of the slightly sloping grade I set the handbrake. I lit a cigarette and got out of the truck. I walked around and opened the rear door of the Cadillac and climbed in.

They were both watching me, turned around in their seats, expressions serious but not morose, placid but not docile. Quiescent would be the word.

"Well, here we are," I said.

"Hello, Dan," Webb said.

"Hi, Danny," Melissa said.

I opened the ashtray built into the back of the seat and carefully deposited my ashes, calmly delaying the apocalypse—Holmes confronting Moriarity, Hammer at trail's end.

"You know about Zeke."

They nodded in unison."

"You know he killed Ardell Boggs."

They were silent, looking at each other. Finally, Webb said: "I had an idea he might have."

"I find that hard to believe, Webb. In view of everything else."

He nodded. "I know. It's the truth. I suspected he did it. I didn't ask him, and he didn't tell me."

"You're the chief of police and you didn't ask him?"

"That's right. I didn't want to know."

I laughed and pushed back into the soft luxurious seat. "Hear no evil, see no evil."

"There's a third one."

I mashed out a cigarette and automatically reached for another. I waited until I got it going.

"Which one of you killed Clay? If you say Zeke, I'm going to be very disappointed in both of you."

Melissa sighed. I saw their shoulders move, and I knew they were holding hands on the other side of the seat.

"I killed him," she said quietly. "And whatever you're thinking, Dan, it was not a conspiracy. It just happened. I killed him and I'm not sorry." She smiled reassuringly at Webb. "Zeke and Webb had nothing to do with it."

I laughed again, a barking mirthless sound that hurt my throat as much as it startled them. "Zeke commits another murder to cover it up and Webb aids and abets. That's a tad more than nothing." I leaned forward to dust ashes and look at Webb. "I know why you helped her, but I'm a little puzzled about Zeke."

He shrugged. "Zeke did what he's always done. He looked out for Zeke. Clay had fired him ten minutes before. Not that that bothered him too much. Clay's done it before when he was drunk. But until that night Zeke always had an ace in the hole, and Clay would always back down. That ace in the hole was Melissa. She didn't know that she wasn't the driver of that death car eighteen years ago. That was Zeke's leverage with Clay. But that evening Clay went off the deep end. He told Melissa the truth, taunted her with it."

"So that's when he told you?"

269

She nodded without looking at me. "Yes, I lied to you a little."

"Don't feel bad, I've been lied to by the best people." She acknowledged my efforts with a faint parody of a smile.

"That wasn't all he told her—us." His voice was thick, phlegmy, his even features twisted with pain. "The . . . bastard told her he was . . . was—" He stopped, choking, turned his face forward.

Melissa's head dipped. She breathed deeply and looked over the seat at me. "Clay said he was having sex with Candice," she said rapidly, the words falling from her lips like curses. "I was stunned. I couldn't believe it. But then he turned to Webb, told him he knew we had been seeing each other, told him about being sterile, told him that Candice was his, Webb's, and that he had been having sex with her for three years." She was almost panting, the words slurred and tumbling. She stopped and breathed deeply again, shuddering.

"And that's when I picked up the gun, put it against his head and pulled the trigger."

Webb put out a clumsy hand and touched her cheek. "She did it to keep me from doing it," he said. "Another minute—"

She smiled at him gently and shook her head. "I did it for myself, for Candice, for the eighteen years of my life I lived with the belief that I had killed three people. Compared to that, living with Clay's death will almost be easy."

"And then," I said, "you woke up to reality. You had a dead man on your hands. And society frowns on that no matter how much of a scoundrel he may be. What I've been wondering is why you didn't just say he'd shot himself there in front of you. A fit of despondency or Russian roulette. People would believe that of Clay."

"I thought of that," Webb said. "But Zeke said it would

never work. Clay was too rich, too powerful, too many important people asking questions. He said he'd never be able to stand up under tough questioning, that he'd fold under pressure. He said this way there'd be no question about Clay killing himself if he was in the office alone at the time with witnesses just outside on the deck." He sighed. "It made sense, a crazy kind of sense, and we weren't thinking too clearly. He was, of course, trying to get another hold on the new head of Garland Enterprises." He looked at Melissa. "She wanted to tell it the way it happened, but I wouldn't hear of that." He turned to me, lips pulled tight in an uncompromising line.

"There was my—Candice to consider. It would all come out, about me seeing Melissa, about Clay and Candice—the sex—everything."

"Candy is only seventeen, Danny," Melissa said, as if I might not be aware of that. "And I didn't tell you, but she's well, a little . . . slow."

"Not retarded," Webb said quickly. "She's just now catching up to other kids her age."

"How has this affected her?"

Melissa's face softened. "Not too much, thank God. Things don't . . . don't seem to affect her as much as . . . well, some people."

"So you hatched a plan. It wasn't a bad plan, Webb, all things considered."

"It was Zeke's mostly. He was the one who had to do all the work." He grimaced and then smiled faintly. "How were we to know the Answer Man was coming?" He took a pack of cigarettes out of his shirt pocket. "I still don't understand how you knew."

"You know what they say about best laid plans. One thing led to another. Once I knew for sure that Boggs had been killed I had to start looking for a reason. Only one

271

thing made any sense considering where Boggs had been killed: Clay's suicide. But that made even less sense, so I started thinking in terms of murder, Clay's murder. Who would want to kill him? The answer to that was almost anybody.''

"And you picked me and Zeke and Melissa."

"No. That came later. I zeroed in on Trumble after I satisfied myself nobody could have come up through that trapdoor without leaving some evidence of it, scratches on the door, water marks on the floor, noise. But Trumble would work only if the silencer was still in the room after you and Zeke and Melissa left. But then I remembered you said you had confiscated it."

He stared at me blankly.

"I don't follow that. Why Trumble?"

"Opportunity. He was alone near the door to the office. He could possibly have slipped in, shot Clay with the silenced gun, removed the silencer, then slipped out again and a few minutes later fired another gun under the marina to deaden the sound. It was wild, I'll admit that, and I had no motive, but right then it was all I had. It was only after I found out about Zeke that I began to think in the right direction, to put it together, to understand that Zeke must have had help inside the office, someone to prop open the trapdoor for him, or at least someone who saw him prop it open. You were the last one in there.'' I looked him in the eye. "I don't mind telling you that was the hardest part of all to believe.''

His eyes met mine for a moment, then slipped away. "I guess you know it all."

Melissa sat quietly facing forward as if we were strangers making idle conversation on a bus.

I shrugged. "I'm not sure I know it all. I know it involved Zeke leaving the office before you and Melissa, parking his car behind the crappie house, and swimming back to the marina under water. I know it involved someone leaving the trapdoor propped open so he could reach up and fire his starter pistol into the room to attract the people on deck. I'm assuming he used the two ice cream sticks as props and the zip-loc bag to carry the gun in. Zeke should have taken them."

He nodded. "He was supposed to. I guess he forgot. He didn't think he had much time. As it worked out, he had plenty."

"The swimming bothered me for a while. I couldn't figure how he could swim that far in muddy water without losing his sense of direction or taking a chance on getting too near the surface and being seen. I finally figured that one out; he used the trotline."

"That was my contribution," Webb said. "He'd never have made it swimming blind." He dragged furiously on the cigarette.

"Excuse me," Melissa said. She fanned the smoke and smiled ruefully. "I need to get some air." She clicked open the door and stepped out, limned by the sunlight for an instant, the false composure dissolving in the split second before her pale face moved out of sight.

Webb sucked on the cigarette, blowing out the smoke without inhaling, watching Melissa cross to the guard rail, her chestnut hair flying in the breeze. "If only Zeke hadn't gone and killed Mr. Boggs," he said, almost as if he were talking to himself.

"I suppose Boggs saw him come out of the water and approached him. Maybe it frightened him into a reflex action. Striking out before he thought. It's the kind of thing Zeke would do."

"He was supposed to jack up one wheel of the car as if he had a flat and had gone for help. Just in case somebody drove back in there for some reason. But I guess it didn't do him much good with Mr. Boggs since he was walking.''

"He was careless, Webb. He hit Boggs with something. Maybe a tire iron. He got blood on his hands, or some-where, and he wiped it off with his handkerchief and tis-sues from his trunk. And he just left them there. He also left a lens out of Boggs's glasses.''

"He didn't expect an investigation. He knew I couldn't investigate or use anything I found out even if I did. And knowing Zeke, he was probably panic-stricken.''

"He tried to have me killed,'' I said.

Webb's head jerked around, the blood draining out of his face. "My God, no!''

"Yes.''

"My—my God, what happened?''

"They didn't succeed,'' I said, deciding that was as far as it needed to go.

"Jesus Christ, Dan! I swear I didn't know.''

"I never thought you did.''

Webb opened his window and threw out his cigarette. He ran both hands through his disarrayed hair, then turned to face me again, features struggling for composure, leached of color.

"Where do we go from here, Dan?'' His voice was quiet, colorless, gaze drifting back to the window and Me-lissa motionless at the guardrail, her face into the wind, sun-brightened hair riffling over her shoulders, as taut and poised as a watchful doe.

"I didn't know I had a choice, Webb.''

"There's always a choice. Always.''

"Suppose you tell me mine.''

He sat silently for a time, nostrils flaring slightly as he breathed, eyes squinted, lips an austere line across the handsome face. Finally he sighed, reached up, and unpinned the badge from his shirt. He stared down at it, then slid his hand across the top of the seat and dropped the small silver star in my lap.

"You can take this to Stan Monroe and tell him your story. Tell him where we are. Tell him to come and get us." He looked at me and smiled crookedly. "Or you can walk away from it. You've been a cop. You've walked away from things before. We all have. The law is not always justice." He breathed deeply, audibly, the smile gone. "You could do that, Dan, and I'll guarantee it'll be the easiest thing you've ever done."

I turned the badge over in my hand, fastened the clasp. I looked up and met his unsteady gaze. "How about the gun, Webb?"

He shook his head, an ironic tilt to his lips. "I'm a cop. Cops never give up their guns. You know that."

"I have your badge. You're no longer a cop. You don't need a gun."

"I need it."

"Don't be crazy, man. You can't fight your own men, guys you've worked with—"

He looked up, startled. "What makes you think I'd do that?"

"Then why do you need the gun?"

He shook his head, smiling.

I stared at him, comprehension creeping in like floodwater under a door.

"You're nuts," I snarled.

"We've talked it over," he said solemnly, eyes going back outside for reassurance. "We've both been in prison for eighteen years. No more, man."

"Like hell you will!" I yanked the .38 from under my arm and pointed it at his head. "Give me the gun, Webb."

He stared at me blankly for a moment, then pounded the wheel with big corded hands and convulsed with laughter.

I watched him laugh until the absurdity of the situation struck me, my untenable position. Feeling foolish, I slid the gun back into its holster. But bruised dignity demanded retaliation, and I slid across the seat to the lake side door. I opened it and got out, stood looking down at him wiping his eyes, his broad face turbulent with a ludicrous combination of defeat and despair and hilarity.

"You're dumb, Webb," I said harshly. "Just plain, damn dumb." I slammed the door.

Melissa watched me come toward her, back to the rail, holding the blowing hair from her eyes with one hand, the tailored pants suit hugging her lithe frame like static cling.

Her expression reflected humor, violet eyes as calm as the blue waters far below. "I see you left him laughing," she said. "But he doesn't look happy."

I started to speak, but she stopped me with an upraised hand. "I want you to know, Danny, that what I told you out at your cabin the other day is true."

"You said a lot of things," I growled, watching the white flash of wings as the gulls swooped and circled above the water.

"About you," she said softly, earnestly. "About me . . . the way I feel." Her gaze clung to my face, compelling me to look at her, into brimming eyes, glistening spheres of velvet darkness I could feel myself drowning in.

"Dammit, Melissa! You've got a man in that car who's willing to die for you! Don't tell me how you feel. Tell him!"

"I have," she said, her voice low and even. "He knows how I feel about you, how I feel about him. He's satisfied it's enough. So am I."

"I hope so," I said. "Because if it isn't, you'll break his heart. I don't think he can take much more of that."

She nodded earnestly and smiled. "He won't have to. I promise."

I looked away from her again, fingering the badge in my coat pocket, understanding abruptly in the flare of a minor epiphany that I had been showboating, that the decision had already been made, perhaps as long ago as the moment I had discovered Zeke's culpability and realized with a sinking heart that Webb and Melissa must also be involved.

In my usual omniscient fashion I had subconsciously been weighing guilt against justification.

Zeke had killed Boggs and he was dead, the scales were balanced.

Melissa had killed an unregenerate bastard who should not have survived adolescence, a thief who had stolen eighteen years of her life, flayed her with indignity, corrupted her child. Once again the scales were balanced, or should be to any rational man's conception of justice.

And what the hell? Who had appointed me judge of the world? I had done what I set out to do. I had discovered who had killed Ardell P. Boggs and why. I had learned something about the tenuous nature of old friendship, the tenacious quality of first love. If Webb and Melissa could live with what had happened—well, it was their song and they would have to sing it. All I had to do was finger the chords and hum backup.

And besides, I had problems of my own, not the least of which entailed walking away from the lovely creature watching me with moist eyes, a solemn softness in her face that brought a warm sliding in my chest, a fleeting glimpse of the cold, aching loneliness I had known twenty years before.

I reached out and pinned the badge to the lapel of her

coat. "Tell that dummy I said goodbye." I stepped back away from temptation, out of the danger zone.

She moved a pace forward, smiling tremulously, her eyes bright. "You could kiss me goodbye, Danny. Webb wouldn't mind."

I would," I said harshly. "I won't even shake your hand. If I touch you I may not want to let go."

I stared down at her for one more second, trying not to care, fighting the urge to take her at her word, make one final imprint of touch and taste. But it would only make an intolerable situation impossible, and I turned and walked off, firmly, feeling magnanimous and self-righteous and cheated, making a grand exit—Rhett Butler leaving Tara, Shane riding into the sunset.

One foot in front of the other is the way it's done. No looking back, no wavering. Webb had been right when he said I could do it, but he had been wrong as hell about the other thing.

It wasn't easy.

ABOUT THE AUTHOR

Edward Mathis resides in Euless, Texas. This is his first novel.

"Joe," Sally cooed, "welcome to *Kiss the Bride!*"

The reality-TV hostess gestured to Casey. "The show where you marry the woman of your dreams. Doesn't she look gorgeous?"

Joe opened his mouth, but it took him a couple of tries to get any words out. "She does," he managed to say at last.

Relief washed over Casey, restoring her heart to its normal rhythm. *It's going to be all right.*

"Joe, this is your big moment," Sally said. "All you have to do is pop the question and you can marry Casey right here." She beamed encouragement.

Joe hesitated. Casey gave him what she intended to be a loving smile, although she was afraid it might have emerged as pleading. Still he hesitated.

"Joe, aren't you going to ask Casey to marry you?" Sally sounded like a mother addressing a recalcitrant child.

Joe spoke, loud and clear this time. "No, I'm not."

Dear Reader,

In 2009 Harlequin will celebrate sixty years of providing women with pure reading pleasure. To mark this special anniversary, we are pleased to offer you this book written by popular Harlequin Superromance author Abby Gaines.

With the focus on a complex and satisfying romance, Harlequin Superromance has been entertaining readers for many years. Each month you'll find six new Harlequin Superromance books that deliver realistic, heartwarming stories.

If you want to read about real people and their journey to happily ever after, then Harlequin Superromance is the series for you!

Happy anniversary,

The Harlequin Superromance Editors

ABOUT THE AUTHOR

Abby Gaines wrote for five years before she sold her first novel to Harlequin Superromance. During that time she worked as a business journalist and as an editor of a speedway magazine. Little wonder she also ended up contributing to the Harlequin NASCAR series.

Abby lives with her husband and children in a house with a sun-filled office whose sea view provides inspiration for the funny, romantic stories she loves to write. Visit her at www.abbygaines.com for details on upcoming books and more!

Books by Abby Gaines

HARLEQUIN SUPERROMANCE

HARLEQUIN NASCAR

Don't miss any of our special offers. Write to us at the following address for information on our newest releases.

Harlequin Reader Service
U.S.: 3010 Walden Ave., P.O. Box 1325, Buffalo, NY 14269
Canadian: P.O. Box 609, Fort Erie, Ont. L2A 5X3

CHAPTER ONE

THE BRIDE WORE A long white dress and a look of utter despair.

Adam Carmichael saw her through the glass wall of the Memphis Channel Eight boardroom, scurrying down the corridor as fast as the full skirt of her dress would allow, flicking furtive glances over her shoulder.

Damn, a runaway bride. Could this day get any worse?

He stepped out of the boardroom, and she saved him the effort of stopping her when she cannoned into him, preoccupied by one of those over-the-shoulder checks. Soft yet firm breasts pressed hard against Adam's chest; honey-gold hair tickled his chin.

He steadied her with his hands on her upper arms. And saw tears welling in her eyes. Instantly he released her, took a step back.

She brushed at the tears with short, impatient movements. "I'm sorry, I didn't mean to..." She looked behind her again and said distractedly,

"Anyway, it was nice meeting you, but I really must…"

She gathered up her skirt, ready to run, giving Adam a glimpse of slim ankles above a pair of silk shoes.

Overhead, the PA system crackled to life, and Adam recognized the voice of Channel Eight's senior producer, unusually agitated. "Would Casey Greene please return to makeup immediately. Casey Greene to makeup." There was a pause, then the producer said, "Now!" more ferociously than Adam had ever heard her speak before.

There was no mistaking the whimper from the runaway bride, nor the flare of panic in her eyes, which were the gray-green of the Mississippi when a storm was brewing.

Adam clamped a hand over her forearm. "Sounds like they're looking for you."

"I can't go back." She tried to tug her arm free.

Fleetingly, he considered letting her go. But much as he hated this wedding show, he wasn't about to sabotage it.

They were due to go live in an hour, so it was a safe bet people would be scouring the building for the missing bride. In her panic to get away, she'd obviously taken the elevator up instead of down. It might take awhile for the search party to reach the top-floor boardroom, but they'd get here in the end.

"You can't leave like this," he said. "You look

terrible." Oops, that wasn't the most tactful thing to say to a bride. "I mean, you look great...fantastic." He ran a quick eye over her to check if he'd made a fair assessment. She was a little on the short side, around five-four in her shoes, he estimated, but the dress hugged some very attractive curves.

He pushed open the door to the boardroom. "Why don't you take a minute to pull yourself together?" He gave her no chance to refuse, shepherding her in, then steering her to one of the black leather couches arranged along the far wall. He turned a chair from the boardroom table around to face her, and sat down. "I assume you're Casey Greene?"

She nodded. Someone walked past the boardroom, and she shrank down in the couch.

"It's only my secretary," he assured her. But she looked jittery, as if she might spring up at any moment. Adam estimated it had been a minute since that call over the PA, probably several minutes since she'd left her minders. Where *were* those guys? He said chattily, "So you're a guest on *Kiss the Bride?*"

"I was."

Uh-oh. This was just what he needed, after he'd worked through the night to get this show into some semblance of order, tying up the loose ends his cousin Henry, the show's creator, had overlooked. Except Adam hadn't had time to check if Henry had lined up a replacement bridal couple in case someone pulled out. He'd bet money the answer was no.

Any minute now, representatives of the show's sponsor, New Visage Cosmetics, would arrive at the studio to see the debut of "their" show. New Visage was in a different league from Channel Eight's other sponsors; having them on board would bring the station to the attention of the major players. Adam couldn't afford for anything to go wrong.

He wanted to haul this woman back to the production suite—anyone dumb enough to sign up for a surprise wedding show deserved whatever she got. "It's understandable you have cold feet. Just remember, this is the happiest day of your life."

He couldn't have sounded very convincing, for she shot him an unbridelike glare.

"Oh, sure," she said. "I dupe my fiancé into coming to the TV studio, and he won't find out until we're on air that he's here to get married. Happy days."

Adam should never have left Henry in charge while he was in New York. His cousin must have had this crazy idea in mind for months, to have set the show up in just four weeks. Adam had come home two days ago to find the station abuzz with excitement about *Kiss the Bride.*

He could have canned it. But then the family stockholders would accuse him of being high-handed again. Better to let tonight run its course, then convince New Visage to put their money into a higher quality program.

The muted sound of the PA system drifted in from the corridor. "Paging Casey Greene. If anyone has seen Casey Greene could they please notify Production immediately."

Adam eyed the telephone on the boardroom table.

Casey stiffened. "You wouldn't."

He would, if he didn't think it would scare her into resuming her escape. He had an hour of live TV to fill, the viewers had been promised a wedding show and that's what they would get. A show delivered to the highest possible standard. Which meant no empty seats on the set. "How about we let the crew know you're okay?"

Her eyes narrowed. "Who *are* you?"

"Adam Carmichael." There was no flash of recognition—he had to assume she didn't read those magazines that voted him Memphis's Most Eligible Bachelor. "I run this place."

"So you can get me out of here? Off the show?" She stood in a flurry of excitement, a hopeful smile curving her mouth, crinkling the corners of those gray-green eyes, hinting at a dimple in her right cheek.

"Why don't you tell me," he hedged, "exactly what the problem is?"

Her smile faded and she sat down again. "You're not going to help, are you? Don't worry, I'll figure it out myself."

Adam hadn't missed the vulnerability that shadowed her eyes.

The vulnerability that made her not his type.

"Have you changed your mind about the wedding?" Maybe he could find someone—a woman, someone happily married, anyone but him—to talk her around.

"Not exactly. I'm desperate, or I wouldn't have resorted to coming on *Kiss the Bride*."

She didn't look desperate. With her eyes still bright with moisture and her cheeks flushed at the personal nature of the conversation, she looked more than ordinarily attractive, like the kind of woman who would have potential bridegrooms lining up on her doorstep.

"Is your fiancé giving you trouble?"

Casey shook her head. "Joe is pretty well perfect. Kind, good-looking, honest—fun to be with."

"He sounds great," Adam said heartily. "How about we get you to the studio so you can marry him?"

Okay, so that wasn't subtle. She fixed him with a stung, accusatory expression. "But what about love?"

Adam felt the kick of a headache at his left temple. He looked through the glass, out into the empty corridor. How the hell could the production team be doing such a bad job of finding this woman? "I don't know," he said cautiously. "What *about* love?"

Casey eased back into the cushions, as if he'd hit on her favorite subject. "I love Joe, and he loves me." She spread her hands, palms up. "We wouldn't have got engaged otherwise, would we?"

"I suppose not," Adam said.

"But sometimes, people love you for what you can do for them, as much as for who you are, and it's hard to tell the difference. I always wanted a husband who'd adore me just for myself, and someone I adored back. Real love, no strings attached." Her finger traced the piping that edged one of the cushions. "If I'm honest, that's not what Joe and I have."

Adam groaned. Poor Joe, expected to "adore" this woman for the rest of her days, when, if he was anything like most guys, all he wanted was a quiet life.

Her eyes sparked in annoyance. "Don't you think people should hold out for their dreams?"

"I think people should figure out what they *want,* then go for it," Adam said. "But…a guy who adores you? No strings?" He shook his head. "Those are teenage daydreams."

She thought that over. "You mean, you used to dream of marrying a woman who adored you, but you grew out of it?"

Adam cast another longing glance at the phone. "The last thing a teenage boy wants is to be adored by some woman for the rest of his life." *Some of us never grow out of that.* "Boys dream about NASCAR racing."

"Did you?"

If sharing that misguided ambition would get her back on the show, Adam would do it. He nodded.

"Believe me, I never regretted joining the family business instead."

Even if he had run off to Charlotte, the racing capital, he'd probably still be on the receiving end of constant demands from his grasping relatives.

"Are you married?"

Did he *look* like a sucker for punishment?

She rushed on without waiting for him to reply, as if it was a relief to be revealing her doubts. At least someone was enjoying this. "Joe and I started dating in high school. We drifted into our engagement at graduation—that was seven years ago. We said we'd wait until we could afford to buy a house before we got married."

"Good idea," Adam said. He inched his hand toward the phone.

"Every time we set a wedding date, something happens to change our plans," she said. "But now I need to hurry things up. Now, I *have* to get married."

A shock of…surprise surged through Adam, and he forgot about the phone. He stole another quick look at Casey's figure, to see if he'd missed any suspicious bulges. No sign of a baby—but pregnancy would explain her emotional state.

She looked as if she was about to break down again. Adam, inured to tears through years of dealing with weepy female relatives, planned to wait her out. But something about the way Casey's eyes shimmered, then widened as if to say she wasn't about to cry, no, not at all, got to him. He whipped his hand-kerchief out of his pocket and offered it to her.

She took it without a word. He read the Emer-gency Fire Instructions pinned to the wall while he tried to ignore the way her snuffling did funny things to his insides. Eventually he gave up, and glanced sideways long enough to find and pat the creamy shoulder nearest him. At his touch, Casey straight-ened, drew on some inner reserve to blink the tears away, and met Adam's gaze full on.

"I'm sorry." She blew her nose one last time.

"Why don't you tell me more about Joe?" Dwelling on her husband-to-be's good points might cheer her up.

"He's very nice. We have a lot in common," she said. "He's about to join the navy, which means he'll be away a lot, but I can handle that."

For all Casey's dreams of being adored, Adam would bet the marriage she had lined up with Joe would be a lot happier than one based on some infatua-tion.

"Unless," Casey said, "I pull out now, and wait for a man who adores me."

He wished she wouldn't keep saying that. She had stars in her eyes when she talked about love and adoring.

Besides, if Casey was pregnant, she should marry the father of her child. The pretty-well-perfect father of her child.

"You could wait a long time for a man who adores you," Adam said, and was annoyed to find he felt like a heel, telling her to abandon her dreams. More forcefully, he added, "You might never find one. Marry Joe and be happy with what you've got."

"Casey!" A voice from the doorway startled them. Adam recognized one of the production assistants. *About time.* Casey leaped to her feet.

"There you are." The woman's voice was overly bright. She flashed Adam a look of sympathetic exasperation. "They're waiting for you in makeup. We need to hurry."

Casey hesitated. She swallowed, then turned to Adam. "You're right, I'm sure it'll be fine." Her voice held the faintest question, so Adam nodded reassuringly. She smiled, a proper smile this time, which made her eyes glow more green than gray. "It was nice talking to you."

"You, too. And—" he might as well admit he knew what she'd been alluding to "—good luck with the baby."

Her eyes widened. He saw confusion, the dawn of understanding, then amusement chasing through them. She laughed out loud. "I'm not pregnant."

"So why did you say you have to get married?"

She beamed, still amused. "It's complicated. Family stuff." She stuck out a hand and said, "Bye, Adam."

"Goodbye, Casey. And good luck." Whether it

was because he knew what desperate measures family could drive a person to, or because he felt unaccountably relieved she wasn't pregnant, or just because she was dressed in such formal, elaborate style, Adam did the weirdest thing. Instead of shaking her hand, he lifted it to his mouth, pressed a kiss to the back of her fingers.

And found himself sorely tempted to kiss Casey Greene all the way up her arm and keep right on going.

CASEY HAD CONVINCED herself she had her nerves under control. She'd gotten over that crazy bout of crying in front of a complete stranger. She'd gone through makeup, final adjustments to her hair and the fitting of her veil, ninety-five percent certain that following her dream justified this extreme step.

Now, a renewed surge of misgiving tightened her grip on the seat of the high stool center stage in the baking-hot television studio. The show hadn't started; a buzz of conversation drifted from the studio audience toward the stage.

"Remind me why I'm doing this," she muttered to the bride on her right, her best friend, Brodie-Ann Evans. Beyond Brodie-Ann, the third bride overheard the question and tittered. She'd introduced herself as Trisha from Truberg and, in her wedding dress, was alarmingly reminiscent of a giggling meringue.

"Two words," Brodie-Ann said. "Push. Over."

Oh, yeah. I am not a pushover. Not anymore. Casey recalled the way Joe kept postponing the date for their wedding, and how their plans to move out of Parkvale kept getting put on hold. Then she summoned to mind the letter she'd received last month from her sister, Karen. A letter that gave Casey the urge to get as far away as possible from their hometown.

It was time her life started happening, and tonight was the night.

"Thanks, hon," she breathed to Brodie-Ann.

Signing up for the pilot episode of *Kiss the Bride* had been Brodie-Ann's idea—but Casey had instantly recognized its genius. If her best friend could marry the man she loved after dating him just six months, then Casey would darn well marry Joe.

Which was how she'd ended up here, dressed in a silk-and-lace concoction she could never have afforded in real life.

The floor director, who'd introduced himself earlier, stepped up on to the stage in front of Casey. "Two minutes, ladies, so get ready to smile. And remember, don't look at the cameras while you're being interviewed."

Instinctively, Casey's gaze darted to the nearest camera, which appeared to be pointed right at her. The director tsked. "Keep your eyes on Sally, the camera will find you." He paused, pressed his headphones against one ear as he listened, then smiled at the brides. "I'm happy to report that your men are ready and waiting in the green room. No cold feet." He nodded brisk reassurance, then hurried to talk to Sally.

Casey wasn't surprised to hear the men weren't worried.

She'd told Joe they were competing on a game show and were likely to win a lot of money. They'd driven three hours to Memphis this morning. Brodie-Ann's boyfriend, Steve, along with a third unsuspecting man had been taken out for lunch by Channel Eight staff and given bogus details as to what the show was about. They doubtless assumed their female partners were getting the same treatment.

How could it have occurred to Joe that Casey would be selecting a wedding dress, having a makeover and planning on marrying him in front of millions of viewers?

She shuddered. Thank goodness it was only a local show. No one outside of Tennessee would see what she'd had to go through to get married.

"I'm not conning Joe into marrying me," she told Brodie-Ann. "I'm just bringing the date forward a bit."

"You told me that already. Twelve times."

Casey closed her eyes and prayed she wasn't crazy.

What *was* crazy was that her fingers should still

be tingling from the kiss of a stranger. Worse, as she tried to conjure up Joe's face, that same stranger's image kept intruding.

Adam Carmichael was the kind of guy any woman would think about, she consoled herself. Those broad shoulders, those strong hands that had steadied her... At first, Casey had thought his eyes an arctic blue, but when he kissed her, they'd glinted a warmer azure color. Most of the time he'd looked tense, with a furrow in his brow that told her the tension might be habitual.

When Casey opened her eyes, Adam stood in her line of vision, next to the camera she wasn't supposed to be looking at. He was looking right at her, frowning again. She couldn't see that furrow, but she knew it would be there. She guessed he might be worrying about her, and her delusions of romance.

She mustered a reassuring smile—*I'm not going to fall apart*—and waggled her fingers at him. He waved back, but it was a brief, tense movement.

A production assistant clipped a microphone to her dress, obscuring Casey's view of Adam. When the assistant stepped aside, he was gone. A peculiar loneliness made her chest ache.

Then someone was counting down. Sally Summers, the show's host, looked in the mirror one last time and...they were on air. It took all Casey's willpower not to flee the set as Sally began her introduction. The words passed Casey by, but she was jerked back to reality when Sally came over to interview Trisha from Truberg.

"Trisha, how long have you and Martin been dating?"

Five years, Trisha told Sally. They'd been engaged for three, and their families still couldn't agree on a wedding date.

After the interview, a drumroll rounded to a crescendo, then Sally called Martin Blake to the set. He emerged from backstage to the strains of "Here Comes the Bride," and the audience applauded on cue. Martin did a double take, but to Casey's relief—*maybe this won't be so bad*—he got over his initial shock.

Sally explained he could marry Trisha right now. The deputy clerk of Shelby County Court would issue a marriage license and a minister would perform the ceremony. Then Martin and Trisha would head off on a luxury honeymoon.

Martin scratched his head. "Now? Tonight?"

Sally repeated the offer, this time stressing that the honeymoon was all-expenses-paid.

"Just think, baby," Trisha coaxed him, "no more arguing with your mom about the wedding." She giggled as she darted a look at the camera. "Oops, sorry, Mrs. Blake."

Maybe that was the clincher, because Martin said, "You're right, hon, let's do it." Trisha squealed with delight. The marriage license was completed during the commercial break, and when they were back on air, the minister stepped up. Five minutes later, Trisha had her wish.

"That went okay," Casey murmured, as the audience clapped. Brodie-Ann didn't reply. She appeared frozen in her seat, as if she'd only just realized what tonight was all about.

After the next commercial break, Sally introduced Brodie-Ann to the audience and invited her to tell everyone about Steve.

"He's the most wonderful guy I ever met," she said, the quaver in her voice barely discernible. "We haven't been together long, but I adore everything about him. I know he's the one."

The audience oohed appreciatively.

Casey felt a twinge of envy. She couldn't remember ever loving Joe like that.

Then it was Steve's turn to come on stage. He was a smart guy; it took him only half a second to realize what "Here Comes the Bride" and Brodie-Ann in a long white dress meant. A huge grin split his face. He stepped right up to her, went down on one knee and said, "Sweetheart, will you marry me?"

The crowd went wild—and they did again when, at the end of the brief ceremony, Steve and Brodie-Ann shared a kiss that raised the temperature in the studio by several degrees. Then the new Mr. and Mrs. Pemberton joined Trisha and her husband on the studio couch.

"TELL ME THIS ISN'T CRAP," Adam demanded of his good friend Dave Dubois, who was standing next to him at the back of the control room. As a freelance programming consultant, Dave occasionally worked with Channel Eight. He hadn't been involved with this show. But he was keen to see it. In front of them, the show's director focused intently on a wide, multiwindow screen. The footage currently being broadcast played out in the large center window. Smaller windows around it displayed feeds from the other cameras. Adam could see Casey, the last bride, in one of those windows.

"It sure isn't your normal kind of show." Dave's response lacked the contempt Adam would have welcomed.

"It's no one's normal kind of show. It's my cousin Henry's kind of show."

The director said into his headset, "Ready, two, with a close-up on bride three. Standby mics and cue." Camera two obediently zoomed in on Casey, ready for her to take center screen. Her jaw appeared to be clenched so tightly she risked breaking a tooth.

"Look." Dave pointed to the image feed from camera three. The studio audience was apparently enthralled by the whole tacky proceedings. To Adam's irritation, his friend evaded the opportunity to savage Henry, settling for an ambiguous, "You're still the boss around here, right?"

"If you mean does my charming family still see

me as the bad guy, you bet. If you mean does fear of me stop Henry creating idiotic new shows while I'm out of town…"

"Hmm," Dave said. "Any progress on the legal front?"

Just what Adam wanted to think about right now. He sent his friend a withering look.

Dave said hastily, "Y'know, this show's not bad. And the reality market is still booming, no matter what the doomsayers predict."

If he'd intended to distract Adam from thoughts of the lawsuit that Henry and his mother had instigated against Adam, he'd picked the wrong topic. Adam fixed him with a black look.

"Okay, so it's not the last word in good taste," Dave admitted. "But it's got pretty women—that third bride is a real babe. It's got romance and happy endings. Though I do think something's missing."

"A dancing girl bearing Henry's head on a platter?"

Dave gave the suggestion due consideration. "You're on the right track. The whole thing needs more tension. More drama."

ANOTHER COMMERCIAL BREAK, then they were back on air. Casey licked her dry lips, feeling very alone at center stage. She looked around for Adam, but couldn't find him.

"Folks, this is Casey Greene. She's come all the

way from Parkvale for today's show," Sally announced.

The crowd cheered, expecting great things from
another Parkvale girl.

"Casey is twenty-five. She's a journalist and a psychology student, and she wants to be a novelist," Sally
continued. "What do you want to write, Casey?"

"Books," she answered numbly.

"And your fiancé is Joe Elliott," Sally added
brightly. "Tell us about you and Joe."

"We met in high school, and we got engaged at
graduation." If she'd been any more wooden, they'd
call her Pinocchio. *Relax.* Casey exhaled slowly
through her nose.

"How's that, folks? High school sweethearts!"
Sally tried to rally some enthusiasm from the crowd,
but their applause was muted. They must have sensed
this wasn't the love story of the decade. "Casey, tell
us what you love about Joe."

Casey's mind went blank. "Uh, he's, uh…"

Sally's smile froze.

"He's so honest," Casey said at last. "So handsome." Silence. For Pete's sake, they wanted more?
"I've known him forever. And…I can't imagine
being with anyone else."

At least she couldn't until about an hour ago,
when a stranger had left the imprint of his lips on her
hand. She glanced quickly down at her fingers—of
course there was no sign of Adam's kiss. "I really

want to get married," she said, and added, with an emphasis that was too loud and too late, "to Joe."

At last the interview was over. The strains of "Here Comes the Bride" filled the studio. Across the stage, Joe appeared. He stopped dead, looked around, saw the other two couples on the couch, heard the audience chanting, "Joe, Joe, Joe," and, finally, looked at Casey. A dragging inevitability slowed his progress across the stage.

"Joe," Sally cooed. "Welcome to *Kiss the Bride,* the show where you marry the woman of your dreams." She gestured to Casey. "Doesn't she look gorgeous?"

Joe opened his mouth, but it took him a couple of tries to get any words out. "She does," he managed to answer at last.

Relief washed over Casey, restoring her heart to its normal rhythm. *It's going to be all right.*

"Joe, this is your big moment," Sally said. "All you have to do is pop the question, and you can marry Casey right here." Her brilliant smile encouraged him.

Joe hesitated. Casey gave him what she intended to be a loving smile, though she feared it might have emerged as pleading. Still he hesitated.

"Joe, aren't you going to ask Casey to marry you?" Sally sounded like a mother addressing a recalcitrant child.

Joe spoke, loud and clear this time.

"No, I'm not."

CHAPTER TWO

"YES!" DAVE DUBOIS PUNCHED the air with his fist. "You did it, buddy. This is much better than Henry's head on a plate."

Adam cursed as the center screen flipped from one camera feed to the next as the director searched for something other than frozen expressions and hanging jaws. So much for convincing New Visage Cosmetics that Channel Eight could mount a professional, sophisticated production.

With Dave on his heels, he rushed out of the control room and into the studio, where stunned silence had given way to a hubbub of excited chatter.

On the set, Sally Summers's famous smile had evaporated. Joe stepped toward Casey, and the microphone clipped to his shirt picked up what he said, despite his low voice.

"I'm sorry, Casey, but I don't want to marry you— I don't love you that way anymore. I didn't want to hurt your feelings...." He stopped, perhaps aware his words were being broadcast around Tennessee.

Make that the entire U.S.A.

As Adam headed to the front of the studio he noticed Channel Eight's PR manager had pulled out her cell phone and was talking in urgent tones. She'd be instructing her assistants to get this story on the late news. By tomorrow, she'd have sold the program nationwide. Casey's disaster was great TV.

Joe said again, "I'm sorry." Then he turned and—as if he hadn't done enough damage—all but ran offstage. Sally patted Casey's hand in what might have been intended as a gesture of comfort, but looked perfunctory.

Adam headed for his cousin Henry, next to camera three. To reach him, he had to pass the New Visage executives, huddled in anxious consultation in their front-row seats.

"Adam." Henry's round face was flushed with panic. He grabbed Adam's arm. "I had no idea this would happen, I swear."

Damn, that meant there was no contingency plan.

Henry jerked his head toward the stage. "Do you think she's going to faint?"

Adam looked up at Casey, swaying on her stool, blinking rapidly.

Behind him, the chatter of the studio audience swelled to an unruly level. He shut out the sound, focused on what needed to be done. *One, restore order to the studio. Two, salvage the show so New Visage doesn't pull the plug. Three, get Casey out of here before she decides to sue Carmichael Broad-casting for public humiliation.*

"Tell the crew to follow my lead on this," he told Henry. His cousin began issuing hurried instructions to the floor director, who was in radio contact with the director in the control room. To Dave, Adam said, "How good an actor are you?"

"I played a tree in *The Wizard of Oz* in fifth grade."

"I hope you were a damn good one," Adam said. "Wait here until I tell you to come up on stage. Then do as I say."

The security people let Adam through and he stepped up onto the stage. Sally became aware of his presence. She turned and took a few hesitant steps in his direction.

"Mr. Carmichael," she said, then remembered to flash her dazzling smile. "Welcome to *Kiss the Bride,* the show where—"

He stalked up to her and motioned to her to mute her mic. When he was sure no one would hear him, he said, "We need to fix this—*now.*"

"How do you propose we do that?" she hissed.

"That bride—" he nodded toward Casey "—is going to have a wedding." He added grimly, "Even if I have to marry her myself."

"You can't do—"

"You're going to help."

Sally flicked a yearning glance over his shoulder

at her teleprompter. When no script appeared, she
started to shake her head.

"Right now, Sally." Adam dropped his voice to a
menacing murmur. "Your contract negotiations are
due at the end of the quarter."

Sally Summers was nothing if not pragmatic.
Adam could almost see the dollar signs in her eyes
as she turned to the audience wearing a wide smile
that only the two of them knew was false. She
switched her mic back on and stepped forward.

"Well, folks, the course of true love never runs
smooth, and who knows that better than Casey? But
tonight, one man's loss might be another man's gain.
It turns out Casey has another admirer here in the
studio, a man waiting in the wings—literally—for
his chance at love."

Adam winced at the stream of clichés. But Sally
was headed in the right direction, however painful
the route she took to get there.

"Folks—" she was warming to her task and by
now had some real enthusiasm in her voice "—meet
Adam Carmichael, Memphis's most eligible bachelor.
And, if she'll have him, Casey Greene's bridegroom!"

The audience broke into a cheer, which Adam
suspected was more out of confusion than celebra-
tion. He strode over to where Casey clung dazedly
to her stool, and took both her hands in his. She
clutched them as if he'd thrown her a lifeline.

"Casey—" he spoke loudly so his words would

carry to the audience without a mic "—will you marry me?"

He heard a shriek from someone in the crowd. Casey stared at him. He leaned forward, and his lips skimmed the soft skin of her cheek as he whispered in her ear, "We're going to fake a wedding."

He stepped back and said again, for the benefit of the crowd, "Casey, will you marry me? Please?"

He wondered if she'd understood, she sat there, unresponsive, for so long. Then she expelled a slow breath and smiled radiantly, her gray-green eyes full of trust. "Yes, Adam, I will."

For a second, he felt a tightness in his chest, as if he'd just seriously proposed marriage to the woman he loved. Whatever that might feel like. A din exploded around them, the audience cheering, Sally yelling to make herself heard. Someone called for a commercial break.

Five minutes later, the clerk had issued a marriage license. Under Tennessee law there was no waiting period, no blood test. Adam announced he would use his own marriage celebrant, and beckoned to Dave. His friend looked around, then twigged that Adam meant him. He bounded forward, and by the time he reached the set his face was a study in solemnity. If you discounted the gleam in his eyes.

Dave patted his pockets, then turned to the ousted minister. "I seem to have forgotten my vows. Could I borrow yours?"

Just as they went back on air he clipped on a microphone. He began laboring through the "wedding."

"Adam James Carmichael, do you take—" He slanted Casey a questioning look.

"Casey Eleanor Greene," she supplied.

"Casey Eleanor Greene to be your wife? To have and to hold, for—"

"I do," Adam said.

"Right." Dave moved down the page. "Casey Eleanor Greene, do you—"

"I do," Casey said.

"—take Adam James Carmichael to be your husband?"

"She said she does," Adam snapped.

At the same moment, Casey repeated desperately, "I do!"

Dave got the message and started to wrap things up. "Then, uh—" he lost his place and improvised "—it's a deal. You're married, husband and wife. You may—"

"Kiss the bride!" the audience yelled on cue.

Why not? They'd gone through all the other motions of a wedding. Adam turned to Casey and found she'd lifted her face expectantly.

One kiss and this nightmare would be over, Casey told herself. She could escape the scene of her utter humiliation, and barricade herself in the house in Parkvale for the next hundred years.

Going after your dreams was vastly overrated.

She leaned toward Adam, went up on tiptoe to make it easier for him to seal this sham. *Just kiss the guy and we can all go home.*

She wasn't prepared for the same current of electricity that had left her fingers tingling earlier to multiply tenfold as their mouths met.

Shaken, she grasped his upper arms to steady herself, and encountered the steel of masculine strength through the fine wool of his jacket. His hands went to her waist and he pulled her closer. The shock of awareness that somewhere deep within her a flame of desire had been kindled snapped Casey's eyes open. She met Adam's gaze full on, saw mirrored in it her own realization that this was about to get embarrassing. Even more embarrassing.

Slowly, he pulled back.

The audience hooted in appreciation. Casey blushed.

"Folks, none of us expected this when we came on stage an hour ago, but there you have it. Casey Greene married Adam Carmichael, right here on *Kiss the Bride*." Sally ad-libbed with ease, now that time was almost up. "These three lovely couples will head off on their honeymoons, courtesy of Channel Eight. Don't miss next week's show—anything can happen on *Kiss the Bride!*"

Casey and Adam didn't wait around for the inevitable interrogation. By unspoken agreement, they headed offstage and back to the boardroom where they'd met—could it really have been just two hours ago?

Casey sank onto the leather couch, trying to control the shaking that had set in now she was out of the public eye.

Her savior scrutinized her as if she might be dangerous. "Are you okay?"

She heard a wild quality in her laugh—no wonder he looked nervous. She took a deep, calming breath. "I've had better days."

"I'm sorry," he said. "I shouldn't have told you to go ahead with the wedding."

"I probably would have done it anyway." She ran a hand down her face, suddenly exhausted. "I'm the fool for agreeing to go on the program in the first place."

"I should have cancelled that stupid show the minute I heard of it."

A gruff voice said, "When you two have stopped arguing over who's to blame for this mess, you might want to think about how you're going to get out of it."

A middle-aged man, tall and trim, dressed conservatively in a dark suit and tie, had entered the room. Adam introduced him as Sam Magill, Channel Eight's in-house legal counsel and Adam's own attorney. The lawyer's sharp eyes narrowed to a point where Casey thought they might disappear.

"What you do in your private life is your business,

Adam," he said. "But I'm amazed you'd get married without a prenup."

"Hey!" So what if it hadn't been a real wedding? Casey resented the implication she was after Adam's fortune, which presumably, since Sally Summers had described him as Memphis's most eligible bachelor, was considerable. "I'm not that kind of girl."

"Missy, everyone's that kind of girl when there's enough money involved," the lawyer said. "I don't like what happened to you back there, but if you plan on taking advantage of this situation to feather your own nest, I'm warning you—"

"That's enough, Sam," Adam said sharply. "That wasn't a real wedding, and as soon as Casey has a chance to work out where she's going next, I'll make an announcement to that effect."

The lawyer's jaw dropped. Then he broke into the wheezy laugh of a chronic smoker, a laugh that sent a tremor of unease through Casey.

"What's so funny?" Adam demanded.

It took a moment for Sam to regain his sober countenance. "Am I wrong, or was that David Dubois who performed that little ceremony out there?"

Adam nodded.

"The same David Dubois who served as a commissioner in Fayette County a couple of years back?"

Adam nodded again. "I believe he did."

"Then, my friend, I have news for you. The state

of Tennessee allows marriages to be performed by any current or former county executive, as well as ministers, judges and the like." The lawyer cast his eyes to the ceiling as he spoke, as if reciting directly from Tennessee Code. "And unlike most other states, the executive doesn't have to have served in the county where the marriage is performed."

He brought his gaze back to Adam, a smile hovering on his lips. "For the rest of his life, your pal Dubois can legally marry anyone anywhere in Tennessee, as long as they have a marriage license." He paused, then delivered the coup de grâce. "You did get a license, didn't you?"

The wheezy laugh started again, and Casey knew the sound would haunt her for the rest of her days.

LEGALLY MARRIED. To a woman I don't know.

The irony wasn't lost on Adam as he held Casey's hand, waiting for the press conference to start. His reluctance to rush into marriage had opened the door to his relatives' lawsuit against him. If it was possible to laugh from beyond the grave, right now Adam's father would be in stitches.

Sorry, Dad, but this one won't last. The sooner Adam extricated them from this mess, and got his focus back on his real problems, the better. Sam Magill had already left to start working on an annulment.

"Keep Casey with you until you hear back from

me," he had said on his way out the door. He was probably worried she would sneak off and open a joint checking account.

Adam had agreed, mainly because he'd been forced to scrap his plan of smuggling her out of the building, which was surrounded on all sides by media. Fortunately, Dave had slipped out before the press arrived.

Casey hadn't argued with the lawyer. She looked as if she was in shock, Adam thought. Her face, flushed with embarrassment in the studio, had paled to the same shade as her dress.

As many journalists as could fit were crammed into the Channel Eight lobby. Adam cursed the fact it was silly season—midsummer, when there wasn't enough news to fill the papers—which meant their wedding had attracted far more attention than it should have. He'd agreed to the press conference on the condition the journalists would allow them to leave privately afterward.

"I'll do the talking," he told Casey. His plan was to say as little as possible, to be noncommittal about their future until they knew where they stood legally. They would lie low for the weekend, and with any luck the fuss would have died down by Monday. Hopefully, by the end of next week the announcement of their annulment would be absorbed by viewers over morning coffee, and his and Casey's brief alliance would soon be forgotten.

"*Kiss the Bride* is the hottest show in the land," the PR woman crowed to the media. "We're expecting huge demand from networks around the country...."

When she'd finished her spiel, she read out a hastily prepared statement from New Visage, which claimed to be delighted with the show and confident its relationship with Channel Eight would be both long and mutually beneficial.

That succeeded where nothing else could in putting a smile on Adam's face as he and Casey faced the barrage of camera flashes and the questions hurled at them.

"Mr. Carmichael, is this a ratings stunt?"

"Casey, why did you say yes?"

"Adam, how long do you give this marriage?"

"Are you in love?"

"Casey, what will your family think?"

At this last question, he felt the tremor of her fingers in his grasp. She looked imploringly at him. He held up a hand for silence.

"Ladies and gentlemen," he began, "as you've probably realized, tonight didn't go according to plan for either of us." Chuckles from the crowd told him they were on his side. All he had to do was give them enough to satisfy their immediate need for a story, without exposing Casey to further humiliation and without actually lying. "We're asking you to respect our privacy beyond what we tell you now. I can reveal that Casey and I knew each other before this evening's show—" only an hour before, admittedly "—and that for as long as I've known her I've considered her a very special lady."

Any grown woman who could cling to her dream of being adored had to be special.

He looked down at Casey, noting that a few tendrils of honey-colored hair had escaped her veil. Gratitude warmed her eyes, and her lips curved in a tremulous smile. He turned back to the waiting media. "Can you blame me for seizing the chance to marry her?"

Applause broke out among the journalists. Pleased at the success of his speech, Adam grinned at Casey. She smiled back, obviously relieved.

"Hey, Mr. C." It was one of the older hacks. "How about you kiss the bride?"

Photographers readied their cameras in a flurry of motion.

Adam raised his eyebrows in silent question to Casey. She gave a barely perceptible shrug, then a nod.

Once again, their lips met.

Like last time, he intended a brief kiss, one that would allow the cameras to get their shot.

Like last time, he found himself drawn to her.

Despite the crowd around them, he couldn't resist the temptation to test the softness of her lower lip with his tongue. Her indrawn breath told him she was just as intrigued by the exploration.

The catcalls of the journalists pulled them both back to reality.

"Okay, folks, that's all." Mainly with the power of his glare, but using his elbows where necessary, Adam parted the throng and ushered Casey out the front of the building and into a waiting limo. She scrambled across to the far side, gathering her skirts about her to make room for him.

"Where to now?" Casey asked. The last half hour had passed in a blur, and she couldn't imagine what might come next. All she knew was it couldn't be worse than what had happened in the studio.

Adam's half smile held equal measures of cynicism and resignation. "Our honeymoon."

CHAPTER THREE

IT WAS TEN O'CLOCK at night—her wedding night—
by the time they got to the Romeo and Juliet Suite
at Memphis's famous Peabody Hotel.

Casey—or Mrs. Carmichael, as the hotel recep-
tionist had called her—roamed around the room,
while Adam tipped the porter. The original honeymoon Channel Eight offered hadn't included the
suite, which Casey suspected went for several
hundred dollars a night. But a standard hotel room
wasn't going to work for a newly married couple who
had no intention of sharing a bedroom, let alone a bed.

Judging by the crowd of reporters who'd followed
them from the TV station, and were now being held
at bay by the Peabody's doorman—so much for their
promise to respect the newlyweds' privacy—Casey
and Adam wouldn't be leaving the hotel in a hurry,
so the bigger the suite the better. Casey climbed the
curving staircase to the bedroom. The king-size bed
was a sea of snowy-white covers and elaborately
arranged pillows. Surely a real honeymoon couple
would want something cozier?

There was a bathroom off the bedroom, in addition to the one she'd seen adjoining the living room. More white—marble and porcelain—offset by highly polished stainless steel fittings.

"Casey?" Adam called from downstairs.

Dreading having to sit down and hash out the legal implications of what they'd done, she joined him in the living room. How was she going to explain this to her family? How would she respond when they demanded her immediate return to Parkvale?

Right now, she doubted she could resist. The new-found backbone that had empowered her to seize control of her future had crumbled when Joe jilted her. She would get it back; of course she would. But not tonight.

"It's late," Adam said. "You must be exhausted. How about we get some sleep and talk in the morning, when we've heard back from Sam about the annulment?"

"Sounds perfect." At least she'd married a man who didn't expect her to solve all their problems.

"You take the bedroom, this couch will do me."

Considerate, too. Casey wasn't about to argue. She tried but failed to stifle a yawn. "Thanks, Adam." She ran a hand around the back of her neck to ease muscles exhausted from the strain of holding her head high through today's fiasco. "Good night."

A knock at the door interrupted his reply. Adam opened it and a bellboy presented him with an envelope. Casey caught a glimpse of the words *Private and Confidential.*

"From Sam," Adam said.

Thank goodness. Hopefully the lawyer had figured a way out of this predicament.

Adam tore it open. It took him only a second to read the contents. He uttered a half laugh, half groan.

"What is it? Bad news?"

He didn't answer, only gave her a brooding look.

She stretched out a hand. "May I see it?"

He held the note just out of her reach. "I'm not sure you want to."

In answer, she snatched it from him. And read Sam Magill's instruction, etched on the fine paper in bold blue strokes.

DO NOT CONSUMMATE THE MARRIAGE.

"Oh." Casey dropped it on the coffee table, her cheeks burning. "As if we were going to. That's… that's…"

"Ridiculous?"

"Exactly."

"Sam is very thorough. I imagine he wanted to cover all contingencies." Adam grinned, and that furrow of tension disappeared. "Perhaps he was worried by your enthusiasm when you kissed me at the TV studio."

Casey sputtered. "*I* kissed *you?* You're the one who heated things up." The memory of his mouth on hers flooded back, leaving her light-headed. She clutched at the only possible explanation. "It was a rebound thing for me."

That wiped the smile off Adam's face. He looked pointedly toward the couch. "I think it's time we got some sleep. Separately."

In the bedroom, Casey discovered the reason why someone else had buttoned her dress for her at the TV studio. There must have been at least thirty tiny pearl buttons down her back, most of them beyond her reach.

She grappled with the dress for another minute, but it was hopeless. Peeking down into the living room, she was relieved to find Adam hadn't yet gone to bed, he stood by the window, staring out over Union Avenue, deep in thought.

Casey headed down the stairs. "Adam? I can't undo my buttons. Could you help?"

She half turned her back so he could see the problem, and he came to her aid.

Casey had never realized the area between her shoulder blades, where the buttons started, was so sensitive. The brush of Adam's fingers against her bare skin stimulated a whole bunch of nerve endings. She shivered.

"Cold?" he asked, his tone impersonal.

Casey nodded, holding herself rigid to prevent any more of those traitorous shivers. But it didn't lessen the sensation. She felt the release of each little button, aware that more and more of her flesh was showing. Warmth rose within her—was it possible her back was blushing?

This had to be because of that note from the lawyer. They'd been told not to consummate the marriage, and five minutes later she'd had to ask Adam to undress her.

"You can probably manage the rest yourself," he said, his voice clipped.

She stepped away. "Thanks. I hope you won't be too uncomfortable on that thing." She gestured to the couch.

He looked at her for a long moment, then his gaze dropped to her shoulders. He said tightly, "Time you were in bed."

DESPITE HER EXHAUSTION, Casey slept badly. All that subterfuge, her humiliation aired on national TV, the extreme step of marrying a stranger, and she was no better off than when she had left Parkvale on Friday morning. Her family would be frantic to know what was going on. But perhaps the worst thing was that she hadn't even thought about Joe since he'd run out on her, aside from a brief urge as she left the stage to murder him by the most violent means possible.

That compulsion had passed, leaving a curious void.

It took no great psychological insight to realize how little Joe really meant to her. How could she have planned to marry him? She'd convinced herself she could give him the no-strings love she wanted for herself, when really she was using him to get away from her family.

In hindsight, she deserved to be dumped. Perhaps not quite so publicly…but she'd brought that on herself.

Casey allowed the recriminations to chase around in her head as she lay in bed until eight o'clock, when she was sure Adam would have had time to get dressed. She showered, then looked in her suitcase at the clothes she'd packed for her honeymoon. She'd bought a couple of new items, skimpier than she would normally wear, with the idea, she supposed now, of turning Joe on.

She rejected a strappy top in favor of a white, sleeveless T-shirt, which she teamed with a denim skirt. She checked her reflection in the full-length mirror. No way could Adam think she'd dressed to turn him on.

He was standing at the dining table when she got downstairs. Someone must have brought his luggage during the night. He wore jeans and a black polo shirt, open at the neck. Casey's gaze was drawn to his bare forearms, tanned and strong, as he lifted the covers off several dishes on a room- service trolley. He pulled a chair out for her, and Casey wiped her palms against the sturdy fabric of her skirt as she sat down.

"I ordered breakfast," he said. "It's not safe to go

down to the restaurant. The manager tells me a couple of journalists checked into the hotel."

Casey helped herself to fruit and yogurt, shaking her head at Adam's offer of a hot meal. He piled his own plate with scrambled eggs, bacon and toast, raised his glass of orange juice to her in salute, and started on his breakfast.

Casey took a sip of her own juice as she glanced at the newspaper that lay folded by her plate—and promptly choked.

"Oh, no." After all those photos she and Adam had posed for at the press conference, they'd published one taken in the TV studio, obviously at the moment Joe had jilted her. Her face, panic in her eyes, mouth open, gaped back at her from the front page beneath the headline Carmichael Rescues Jilted Bride. She grabbed a napkin, wiped away the rivulet of juice she could feel on her chin, without taking her eyes off the newspaper.

"It's not as bad as it looks." Adam was presumably referring to the article and not to her photo, because that couldn't be any worse. "They speculate that Channel Eight cooked up this scheme to boost the ratings of *Kiss the Bride*. They tried to get a comment out of your fiancé, but he wasn't talking."

Casey unfolded the paper, then clamped a hand to her forehead at the sight of her father, peering around the front door of the house. "They spoke to my dad."

"That's not so good," Adam admitted. "They also

talked to my stepmother. Seems she told them we've been secretly engaged for months."

"Why would she say that?"

Adam shrugged. "My guess is she didn't want to be caught not knowing about something as important as my wedding." Casey gathered from the careful neutrality of his expression that he didn't much like his stepmother. "Still, she's probably helped confuse the press, which can't hurt."

"Any word from the lawyer?" Casey asked.

"I've had a few calls." He gestured to the cell phone on the table between them. "But not from Sam."

His phone trilled again.

"Hello, Eloise," he said with resigned patience. "Did you like the show?"

Who was Eloise? His stepmother? His girlfriend?

Whoever she was, Adam was obviously enjoying her reaction to their wedding. Not his girlfriend, then. He grinned and held the phone away from his ear—Casey heard a spate of words pouring out. "Sorry, Eloise, I have another call coming through. I'll get back to you."

That set the pattern for the next few minutes, with Adam receiving one call after another, mostly, she gathered, from family, all anxious to know how his marriage might affect their interests. His reticence must have infuriated them.

Bored with waiting, Casey turned on her own cell

phone. Almost immediately, it beeped with a text message from the answering service to say she had twenty-one new messages.

She dialed the service and scrolled through the worried communications from her father (five messages), her sister (six) and her brother (one). There was also one from Brodie-Ann, and several from people who were concerned her wedding might make Casey unavailable to help them. People like the church choir director (did the wedding mean she wouldn't be singing her solo this Sunday?) and the head of the Parkvale Children's Trust (Casey was still okay to bake two cakes and a batch of cookies for next week's open day, wasn't she?).

No and no. She couldn't help smiling. She'd figured getting married would give her the perfect out, but not like this. Still, she wouldn't call anyone back just yet. Not until she and Adam had talked. His phone rang again, and she sighed. Whenever that might be. She realized she hadn't touched her food yet, and took a mouthful of yogurt-smothered melon.

Then her own phone rang, chirping "You Are My Sunshine." By the time she'd convinced the Parkvale librarian she wasn't available to fill in during children's story hour that afternoon, Adam was off the phone and regarding her quizzically.

"Did your phone just play 'You Are My Sunshine'?" he asked.

"Uh-huh. It's a personalized ring tone. It's affirming."

He laughed, until the dignified raising of her eyebrows told him she was serious.

"Affirmations are good for your self-esteem," she told him. "Every time my phone tells me I'm its sunshine, it makes me feel good." Though at this precise moment it didn't seem to be working. Still, she gave Adam a sunny smile as she popped another piece of melon into her mouth.

"You really believe that?"

She nodded. "You have to find an affirmation that works for you, of course. 'You Are My Sunshine' gives me confidence." Casey thought about that furrow that had made a permanent home in Adam's brow. "Whereas you might want to look in your mirror each morning and tell yourself you won't get stressed today."

He frowned, and the furrow deepened. "I hope you didn't pay good money to learn that psychobabble."

"That comes direct from my community college lecturer," she protested.

"I'll bet he didn't tell you to get affirmation from your cell phone."

"No, *she* didn't. I'm extrapolating."

Adam tackled his bacon and eggs, which must surely be cold after all those phone calls, with renewed energy. "So why are you studying psychology? To overcome childhood trauma?"

"I'm not in therapy," she said with exaggerated patience. "I study psychology because it helps with characterization in my writing." Her phone warbled again and she looked at the display. "It's my dad."

Her father took a moment to remind her he loved her, then launched into a monologue about how much her family needed her and how she'd better sort out this confusion and get back home as soon as possible. He ended with a plaintive query: "How am I supposed to get to physical therapy on Tuesday?"

Call a cab. Don't you think I have more on my mind right now? But she'd taught her father she would always be there when he needed her, so how could she blame him? She was saved from answering by a beep on the line.

"Just a moment, Dad, I have another call." She switched to the other line.

Her sister. Casey straightened in her seat. "Yes, Karen, I did just get married. No, I'm not crazy—" she hoped that wasn't a lie "—and no, I'm not coming back to Parkvale." She hoped that wasn't a lie, either. "I'd like you and Dad to— Hello?"

When she got back to the other line, her father wasn't there.

"Bad connection," she explained to Adam. She put her phone on the gilded, glass-topped table between them and looked hard at her plate so he wouldn't see the hurt she knew must show in her face. "Now that we're both free—"

"Free being a relative term," he interrupted. "We're still married."

"—let's have that chat you mentioned." Her phone rang again, but after a glance at the display she ignored it.

"You could always turn that thing off," Adam said. His own phone rang, and he answered it. Which at least gave Casey a chance to regain her fighting spirit.

"You were saying?" she asked sweetly, when he'd finished.

He frowned. "I'm expecting a call from Sam. I don't want to miss it."

"And I need to talk to my family," she said. "Even though I don't know what to tell them."

There was a moment's silence. Then Casey's phone chirped "You Are My Sunshine" again.

"Karen, please, honey, don't cry." Casey's voice wobbled. "I'm sorry, I know you wanted me there, but this is for your own good, sweetie."

Adam realized Casey was blinking in an effort to hold back tears. Rising hysteria emanated from her cell phone, audible even to him, several feet away.

He checked his watch. If she was going to spend the whole morning arguing with her family, they'd never get this mess sorted out. From what he could see, her folks were as bad as his own relatives. There was only one way to deal with people like that. Get tough.

One look at Casey told him that wasn't going to happen. In two seconds, Adam had moved around the table and slipped the phone from her grasp—easily done, since she wasn't expecting it.

"Karen? I don't know who you are, but you're not helping Casey right now." He crossed the room, aware of Casey's startled expression. Karen sputtered on the other end of the phone.

"My *wife* and I—" damn, that sounded weird "—need some time alone." He reached the huge vase filled with an elaborate display of flowers, delivered last night compliments of the Peabody management. Casey, following right behind, bumped into him. "So goodbye."

With Karen still squawking, he dropped the phone—right into the vase.

Casey yelped. "Have you gone crazy?"

"You're not prepared to turn that thing off, and it's upsetting you. I'm dealing with the problem." He dusted his hands together. "Doesn't that feel better?"

"No! How could you…" She stopped. "Actually," she said slowly, "it does." She ventured a small smile.

From across the room they heard the sound of his phone.

"Allow me to deal with that." Casey moved toward it.

"It's okay." He followed her. "I'll take it."

She'd picked it up already and was reading the display. "It's Eloise."

"My stepmother again." He rolled his eyes. "Pass it here."

"I said I'd deal with it," Casey reminded him. She stepped back and moved around the other side of the sofa.

Adam wasn't quite sure what happened next. But somehow, he went one way and she went the other, toward the open window.

"Casey, don't—"

Too late.

She dropped the phone just as he reached her.

Adam looked so shocked, Casey wondered if she'd gone too far. She held her breath as he stuck his head out the window. When he turned back into the room, his face was grave. "You just killed an Elvis impersonator."

Casey clapped a hand to her mouth. "No! I looked, there was no one—" Then she caught the grin he was trying to hide.

And they were laughing, clinging to each other in helpless hilarity that for a moment made the whole mess go away.

Adam looked into Casey's eyes, where tears of merriment glistened. On automatic pilot, he wiped the corner of her eye with his thumb. And found himself robbed of all sensation except the pressing desire to feel her mouth beneath his.

CHAPTER FOUR

THAT TOUCH OF HIS THUMB seemed to wipe away Casey's mirth. Her gray eyes widened and her teeth caught her bottom lip. After the tiniest of hesitations she swayed against him.

This time, there was no tentative overture on his part—and no audience to inhibit the eager parting of her lips to admit him.

Kissing her, Adam told himself as he claimed her mouth, was a reaction to the stress of the past twenty-four hours.

Then her tongue met his with a fervor that matched his own, she wound her arms around his neck and he gave up trying to justify his actions. Gave himself up to the sensual pleasure of kissing Casey, to the press of her body against his, to his own undeniable physical reaction. He cupped her firm derriere, pulling her closer. With a murmur of surprise, she arched into him.

If he didn't stop now, they'd be in danger of complicating this disaster beyond repair.

Tearing his mouth from hers took a degree of

willpower he didn't ever recall needing with a woman. When at last they stood apart, Adam ran a hand through his hair as if that might erase the memory of her touch there. He made a conscious effort to slow his breathing. Casey's cheeks were flushed, her lips still parted in what looked to him like invitation.

"Adam." Breathlessness made her breasts rise and fall, her voice husky. "You have *got* to stop doing that."

Okay, maybe not invitation.

She turned away, gazed with studied casualness at a framed photograph on the wall, a shot of downtown Memphis at night. "Not that it wasn't nice," she said. "But…you know."

Yes, he knew it was a dumb idea to get distracted from fixing this catastrophe. But she'd enjoyed that kiss as much as he had, so he was damned if he was going to apologize.

At the sound of rustling, they turned to the door. A piece of paper had been slid underneath.

Adam picked it up and scanned it. "It's a message from Sam. He's at home and ready to take my call." He'd instructed the hotel reception not to put any calls through to their suite. He reached for the phone on the sideboard next to the dining table and started dialing.

Casey took the opportunity to move as far away from him as she could. She plunked herself on the blue-and-gold-striped couch, grabbed up the room service menu from the coffee table and held it open so Adam couldn't see her face. Her red face.

Good grief, she'd acted like a sex-starved wanton, wrapping herself around him that way. She'd be the first to admit that her sex life with Joe had been rather lackluster the past few years—and nonexistent for nearly a year—but that was no excuse to throw herself at the first man she met. Even if he was her *husband.*

From behind the menu, she listened shamelessly to Adam's side of the conversation with Sam. Which didn't tell her much; he was a man of few words. When he'd finished, he dropped the receiver back into its cradle. He muttered something under his breath that Casey didn't quite hear, but it didn't sound like, "Yippee, we got our annulment."

"Is there a problem?" she asked.

He came to the couch, stood over her with his hands jammed into the pockets of his jeans, his eyebrows drawn together. "Getting an annulment will be difficult."

Casey gulped. "How difficult?"

"They're something of a rarity in Tennessee. There's no statutory basis for annulment here. Each case has to be argued on common law principles."

"Meaning?"

"Meaning," he said, "there's no official annulment process. My lawyer will put a case together and argue it before a judge. If the judge agrees, we get our annulment."

"And if the judge doesn't agree?"

"We get a divorce."

"But I don't want to be divorced," Casey protested.

"Right now, I'd rather be divorced than married," he said, with a flat finality that prickled the back of her neck. He sat down on the couch opposite, saving her the strain of looking up at him. "Sam tells me he can make a good case for annulment. Nonconsummation of the marriage is a definite plus. Even stronger is the fact we didn't know it was a real wedding. Still, some of those old judges take marriage pretty seriously." Cynicism twisted his mouth. "Sam wants to make sure he gets a sympathetic judge, and that might take up to a month."

"So we'll be married for a month," Casey said, "and then it'll be as if it never happened."

"Exactly."

"Everything will be just the same as before."

"Uh-huh."

"Nothing will have changed. *Nothing*."

"Yes," Adam said impatiently. Didn't she understand plain English?

"No," she said.

Adam's head hurt. "What's that supposed to mean?"

"I'm not going back to Parkvale. I'm done with that place."

"You can go wherever you like," he said. *The sooner the better.*

"They'll make me go back." Her eyes flickered toward the door.

He'd married a paranoiac.

She stood and paced to the window. There was something hunted about the way she put her palms against the glass. Staring out into the distance, she said desperately, "Can't we—can't we just stay married?"

A *delusional* paranoiac.

Keep her calm, Adam told himself. *Talk up the joys of a future on her own, then get Sam here fast with some kind of agreement for her to sign, relinquishing all claim on me.*

She turned around, perched that derriere he'd enjoyed caressing—*that was before I knew she was nuts*—on the windowsill. "Stop looking like I'm about to jump you." She folded her arms under her breasts. "I didn't mean it about staying married. Even if the past twenty-four hours hadn't totally turned me off wedded bliss, you're not my type."

He didn't believe that for a second, not after the way she'd kissed him. He started in on the keep-her-calm stuff. "No one can make you go anywhere," he soothed. "You have your whole life ahead of you."

"You don't know my family," she said gloomily. Her eyes narrowed as she looked at Adam. "Your in-laws."

His instantaneous recoil made her giggle.

"They're not that bad," she said. "I've just kind of overdosed on them. I've looked after Dad—and Karen and Mike, my sister and brother—since Mom died when I was twelve. I'm the oldest, so I ended up taking care of the house, the cooking, everything."

"Very commendable," Adam said politely.

She looked dubious. "It wasn't like I had a choice. They needed me. Not that I minded," she said hastily. "I love them to bits."

"You don't have to go back just because you didn't marry Joe."

"I'm a pushover," she said with the confessional air of someone about to embark on a twelve-step program. "When I tried to leave home and go to college, Dad convinced me the others needed me while they were still in high school. Then I was all set to leave after Mike graduated, but Dad got injured in an accident at work. He was in the hospital for six months, in a wheelchair for a year. He's better now, but he needed a lot of help, and I was the logical candidate."

"You could have left once he was better."

She leaned her head back against the window. "Like I said, I'm a pushover. Dad's become dependent on me. For his sake, he needs to learn to look after himself again. If I'd married Joe and moved away like we planned, Dad wouldn't have a choice. Now he'll insist I go back, and Karen will be right there with him, putting in her two cents' worth."

"Does she still live at home?"

Casey shook her head. "She was a lawyer in Dallas until she had a baby a few months ago. But she just separated from her husband, and she's moving home to Parkvale. She wants to go back to work and leave Rosie with me. She says she wouldn't trust a nanny."

Casey didn't tell Adam how Karen's letter had filled her with equal parts longing and dread. Dread because once again her plan to leave home would be thwarted. But even greater, and unexpected, had been Casey's longing to lavish all her maternal love on her sister's baby—love that might otherwise go unused.

Adam walked over to the window. He stood so close to her she could have reached out and touched him. "Just tell them no."

"Haven't you ever said yes to someone when you didn't want to?" she demanded.

"I don't do anything I don't want to do," he said starkly.

She blinked. "Well, that's nice for you. But I just can't say no to all that…that—"

"Emotional blackmail?" he suggested.

Casey nodded. Maybe, despite his uncompromising claim, he did understand. Back when Mom died, Casey had been the only one who could do what had to be done. She'd done so without knowing it would become a trap of her own making, a mutual dependence none of them could escape. Because being needed had a seductive appeal all its own. Which made *not* being needed tantamount to a withdrawal of love.

It was screwy, but somehow she'd fallen into that way of thinking.

Even her relationship with Joe had been built on need and dependence. Joe's mom had left him when he was a kid. He needed a woman who would stick with him forever. He didn't mind that Casey might never have a baby of her own, if the doctors were right; Joe would've been happy not to share her with a child. Or so she had thought.

"A couple of months ago, I won a writing contest with part of a young adult novel I'm writing," she told Adam. "The editor who judged it wants to see the whole book. She's speaking at a conference in Dallas in August. I arranged to meet her there and give her my manuscript." She sighed. "If I go home, I'll never finish it. My family sees my writing as a hobby, and every volunteer organization in Parkvale has me down as a soft touch."

To Adam, writing a book sounded like another girlish fantasy. It ranked right up there with being adored. She needed to stop dreaming and start doing something that would halt the emotional blackmail. Like Adam was. Though in his case, the blackmail was as physical as it was emotional.

And in his case, blackmail wouldn't work. He'd meant it when he told Casey he didn't do anything he didn't want to. That was why his dad had gone to such extreme lengths when he'd made his will, a last-ditch attempt to make Adam do what his father wanted.

It was ironic that despite the differences between them, he and Casey were both struggling with pressure from their families. Ironic that if their marriage had been real, it would have solved both their problems....

The idea burst into blazing, clamoring life.

"You're right," he said. "We should stay married."

"What?" She slipped off the windowsill, grabbing for the curtain tieback to steady herself. "I'm sure you're very nice—" she didn't sound at all sure, he noticed "—but I'm not desperate enough to stay married to a stranger."

His eyes narrowed. "You were desperate enough to lie to your fiancé and marry him on a reality-TV show."

"I was bringing the wedding *forward,*" she said. "We were *engaged.*"

"And we—" with a wave of his hand he indicated the two of them "—are married." He paced between the window and the couch as he thought about how they could make this work. "I don't mean we'd be married for real. We'd just stay together until the annulment comes through. For a month, we pretend we're truly husband and wife. In public," he added hastily.

"I can see that might help me," she admitted. "But how does it help you?"

Adam figured he'd have to tell her enough to convince her. "When my father died, he left me his majority share of Carmichael Broadcasting. His will stipulated that if I'm not married—or as he put it, in a marriage of a lasting and committed nature—when I'm thirty, my share passes to my cousin Henry."

"Is that legal, demanding that someone be married in order to inherit?"

Adam shrugged as he leaned against the back of the couch. "No. At least Sam says it's not. But the will stands until we make a case in court to prove it's invalid. Sam and I are working on that now. But Henry and his mother, my aunt Anna May, have their lawyers working to prove the will *is* legal. They're hoping Henry will inherit. They know I'd never get married just to please my father."

"Sounds like your dad was a real romantic," Casey said. She caught a glint of irritation in Adam's eyes.

"Dad had reason to believe I was anti-marriage. I admit that when he died, getting married was the last thing on my mind. But I assumed I'd find someone suitable over the next few years."

Someone suitable? Did he mean someone he loved? "But you didn't," she guessed.

"I was wrong." He shoved his hands into his pockets. "I turn thirty next month. If the will's ruled legal, I'll have until I turn thirty-one to find a wife. My stepmother's not so confident we can have it overturned. She'd like me to get married, so that I win either way. She's spent the past few months arranging *accidental* introductions to the daughters of her friends. She's organizing a party for my birthday, and I know she's planning on inviting practically every woman in Memphis. I don't have time for this crap—I have a business to run and a lawsuit to fight. But with Eloise, my life is turning into one long *bridefest*." He poured loathing into the word.

"Hey," Casey protested. "This sounds just like my family. If you don't do anything you don't want to, how come you don't just tell Eloise to take a hike?"

"I wish I could," Adam said with feeling. "Before Dad died, he asked me to take care of her. I *want* to honor his memory, to keep my promise. But she makes it damn hard."

"Were she and your father close?"

Anger flickered in his eyes, then vanished. "You could say my father died for her." The look he gave Casey said, *Don't ask.*

Briefly, she considered asking anyway. But that might be pushing her luck—and she still didn't understand why Adam wanted to pretend their marriage was genuine. She abandoned her position at the window to return to the couch. "So you want to beat your aunt's lawsuit and you want to escape Eloise's bridefest." She spoke the word with relish, and he glared.

"If I'm married, she'll have to back off. No more introductions, no birthday party. Anna May and Henry will think they've lost the battle because I've already met the will's conditions. By the time the annulment comes through and they realize they were wrong, Sam and I will have built a compelling case against the will."

Adam spread his hands, palms up, as if to say this was unarguable logic. "So what say we buy ourselves some time? A month is long enough for me to deter Eloise and get my legal battle under control. Is it enough for your sister and your father to sort out their problems? You can use the computer at my place to work on your book, since you'll have nothing else to do."

He smiled and Casey's danger sensors went on alert. This man was used to getting what he wanted, and she suspected he might ride roughshod over others to get it.

"It could be just what you dreamed of, a no-strings marriage," he added.

She'd dreamed of no-strings love.

"It sounds selfish," she said, trying to imagine lying to her family just so she could stay away from them.

"Exactly," Adam said with satisfaction. "This is all about being selfish for once in your life." He regarded her doubtfully. "I suspect you're no good at it, but I'll show you how. Then, when our time is up, we'll go our separate ways. No demands on each other, no...*neediness*." He all but shuddered at the word, and in that moment Casey decided to grab with both hands the opportunity he presented.

"You're right." She felt a sudden, blissful lightening of her gloom, and sprang to her feet. "I'm sick of being needed. Let's do it, Adam. Let's be selfish."

"Utterly, totally, one hundred percent selfish." He smiled broadly, and that furrow in his brow turned into a laugh line, making him look younger, almost carefree.

He put out a hand to shake on the deal. By now, the buzz of electricity his touch produced was so familiar, Casey could almost persuade herself to ignore it.

But could she ignore it for a whole month?

CHAPTER FIVE

ELOISE CARMICHAEL DIDN'T let her hesitation show in her walk. Sam Magill had eyes in the back of his head where she was concerned. She wouldn't put it past him to have sensed her arrival and be watching her progress up his front path on this fine Sunday afternoon.

She wouldn't want him to get the wrong idea about her turning up at his house uninvited. She stiffened her spine and took brisk, businesslike steps, which wasn't easy wearing delicate high-heeled pumps in the green silk-linen fabric that matched her suit.

She pressed the brass doorbell near the wide front door and waited, clutching her green kid leather purse in front of her.

Sam opened the door. He blinked twice in astonishment, making his face seem even more owlish than usual. Then a flush crept up his cheeks from somewhere below his chin. Today, that predictable reaction was a relief, not an embarrassment. Because Eloise was here to take advantage of Sam's…interest in her.

He smiled warmly. "Eloise, what an unexpected pleasure."

She had to admit it was nice to know at least one man was always happy to see her. Sam's regard went some small way toward countering all the frosty welcomes she'd endured from her stepson over the years.

"What can I do for you?" That catch phrase prefaced their every conversation.

Eloise wondered if the man had ever heard of "Good afternoon" or "How are you today?" He was still smiling, hopefully now.

She shouldn't have come. She dropped her gaze from the transparent eagerness of his expression. Then blinked. He was wearing bedroom slippers on his feet! Brown-and-cream checked ones that had seen better days, judging by the pilling at the toes. Eloise drew in a breath. It was silly to be shocked, but James would *never* have answered the door in his slippers.

James is gone.

"I need to talk to you about Adam," she said, the wobble in her voice part grief at the reminder of what she'd lost, but mainly anxiety for her stepson. "I should have called first, but I thought you might refuse to see me."

"Refuse... No, of course... Why would I?" Sam stepped back to let her in. He stumbled against an Oriental pot used as an umbrella stand and it toppled over, spilling two neatly furled black umbrellas onto the polished floorboards. "Oh, dear, just let me—" He bent to retrieve the umbrellas, and when he stood up, dislodged a hat hanging on a row of pegs on the wall.

Sam had never looked twice at Eloise during her marriage, nor in those early years after James's death. But for three years now, he'd had this crush on her. He knocked things over, blurted tactless remarks, blushed to the roots of his hair—just like a teenage boy, minus the acne.

Knowing it would take him half a minute to regain his composure, Eloise waited in silence while he stumbled over words and furnishings.

She valued loyalty, so she appreciated that his attachment to her never wavered. But she wished she wasn't too much of a lady to tell him bluntly there was no point. That she didn't need or want anyone if she couldn't have James.

Blast you, James Carmichael, for leaving me a widow. Do you know how lonely I feel every day? Every night?

When Sam was coherent and no longer in immediate danger of destroying anything, she followed him into the living room.

She'd never been to this house before, and now she looked around with curiosity. Leather couches and chunky wooden tables stamped a masculine seal on the high-ceilinged room. A deep-piled rug in chocolate-brown warmed the floor, and bookshelves lined the walls.

The room was comfortable, uncluttered. Expensive. Adam often said Sam had the sharpest legal brain in Memphis. In these surroundings, Eloise could almost believe there was another side to the man, beyond his bumbling adoration.

She moved toward the nearest couch, and a sudden prickling in her throat made her cough. Now she smelled a familiar, spicy aroma, saw the faint blue haze that hung over the coffee table.

Sam caught the direction of her gaze. "Let me get rid of that." He pushed aside the newspaper spread across the table, and reached for his cigar, grinding the lighted tip into the cut-glass ashtray until it looked quite dead.

"Thank you," Eloise said. She waited for him to offer her a seat.

But Sam was looking her up and down, taking in her fitted mint-green suit and ivory silk blouse with an overtness that surprised her. "That's a very nice outfit, Eloise. You look…crisp and, uh, fresh."

Gracious, the man has no idea. Small wonder he'd never found himself a wife. "You make me sound like an apple."

He blushed again. "I'm sorry," he said, "I meant to say you look…you look…" The hunger in his eyes dismayed Eloise.

Mercy. "I can't stay long, I'm on my way out for

dinner," she said. He appeared so alarmed, she had to add, "At a girlfriend's house."

"You look sensational," he blurted, as if he'd just found the right word. "And those shoes are perfect."

Call her vain, but Eloise couldn't help smiling. "You know, Sam," she said, "next time you meet an attractive, unattached lady, you should try paying her a compliment like that. You'll be amazed at the results."

"But you're an—"

"May we talk about Adam now, please?" she said firmly.

At last, he showed her to a seat, and took the leather recliner next to her.

Eloise crossed her legs at the ankles, and strove for the right blend of command and entreaty. "I need to know about this wedding. I spoke to Adam on his cell phone, but he wouldn't talk—you know how he gets. Now he's not answering at all. Tell me what's going on, Sam."

Patently uncomfortable, the lawyer ran a hand through his iron-gray hair. "Adam is…married."

She tightened her grip on her purse. "But who is she? How long has he known her? Does he love her?" Eloise heard the rise in her voice as she asked the questions that had kept her awake the past two nights. She drew a deep breath. "Sam, I'm worried my pressuring him to find a wife might have driven Adam to do something foolish."

Sam shifted in his seat, clearly agitated. Eloise could see he wanted to help her, but his voice was firm when he said, "Adam's my client. You know I can't tell you that."

She flashed her most charming smile. "Now, Sam, we're friends. At least tell me if the woman is nice. Does she love Adam?" Eloise swallowed. "I can't bear the thought of someone else latching on to Adam for what she can get." Not after what the poor boy was going through with his aunt and his cousin. "Tell me at least if you made her sign a prenup."

Still surprisingly unmoved, Sam spread his hands. "I'm not at liberty to say."

"Does his marriage mean Anna May's lawsuit won't get anywhere?" Eloise pressed. If Adam had traded one grasping woman for another, he might at least come out even.

Sam coughed for several long seconds, with the apparent intention of ignoring her question.

"Don't think your smoker's cough lets you off the hook," she said reprovingly. "Maybe you can't talk about Adam, but you can about Anna May."

But Sam remained annoyingly reticent. "Hmm, you know your sister-in-law."

Which Eloise did, only too well. James's sister clung to Henry, her son, in a way that had stopped the boy growing into a man with any decent backbone. Not like Adam—so independent, so strongminded. Of course, sometimes it would be nice if

Adam would allow just a tiny bit of clinging. Eloise's relationship with him was the polar opposite of Anna May's with Henry.

"Just take me to see him. Please, Sam, you're my friend." Oh dear, she hadn't meant to reach out and clasp his hand where it rested on the arm of his recliner. It was the sort of gesture she wouldn't think twice about with one of her girlfriends, but with Sam… The feel of his fingers beneath hers distracted her, and for a moment she tightened her grip. How long had it been since she'd touched roughened male skin? *Oh, James, James.*

Sam's face was brick-red as he extricated his hand. He stood up. "James was one of my closest friends," he said, and for a moment she thought he'd read her thoughts. "I count Adam a good friend, too. But you and I both know you don't see me as a friend, Eloise."

She felt heat in her cheeks and was about to contradict him when he said fiercely, "And we both know I don't think of you as just a friend."

Eloise scrambled off the couch, less elegantly than she'd have liked. She stared at Sam, uncertain.

But the fire left him as suddenly as it had blazed. "If there's anything else I can do…" he said mildly. "Maybe drive you to your dinner tonight? If you plan on drinking wine I could fetch you afterward…."

It was the sort of offer he was always making, implying she was incompetent. "I am perfectly capable of driving myself." Eloise drew herself up to her full five feet seven—which suddenly didn't feel tall enough—and said with all the imperiousness she could summon, "You asked what you could do for me. I told you, and you refused. Don't ever say those hollow words to me again."

As she swept from the room, she said over her shoulder, "You, Sam Magill, are no gentleman."

"ADAM," CASEY SAID on Sunday afternoon. "Are we rich and famous?"

Adam looked up from the newspaper. Casey was sitting on the couch, along with…was that the hotel maid sitting next to her, face blotchy and eyes puffy?

"We?" he said cautiously.

"Mr. and Mrs. Adam Carmichael."

He flinched, and she grinned.

"Why do you ask?" The maid was definitely crying, sniveling into a handkerchief that looked suspiciously like one of Adam's. Casey was clasping the girl's free hand.

Whatever was going on, Adam knew he wasn't going to like it.

"I mean," Casey said, "do people do as you tell them?"

"Usually." Everyone except his family.

"Great." Casey turned to the maid. "Don't worry, Ria, we'll help you."

The girl sobbed something incoherent in Spanish.

"Casey…" Adam murmured. Her eyes met his,

wide with innocent inquiry. He jerked his head meaningfully at the maid. Counting on the girl not understanding, or being too upset to listen, he said, "Emotional blackmail."

Casey bristled. "Poor Ria hasn't seen her fiancé in six months. He doesn't have a U.S. work permit, so he's stuck in Mexico. I'd be crying, too."

"Did she ask you to help?" The girl had a nerve—Adam would complain to the hotel management.

"Of course not," Casey said, affronted on the maid's behalf. "I offered."

That was even worse.

"What happened to being selfish?" he demanded.

"I can't be *that* selfish."

"This—" he meant their plan "—won't work if you don't."

Before he could stop her, Casey phoned the manager and invited him up to the suite. When he arrived, she asked him to apply for a work permit for the maid's boyfriend and give him a job. "My husband and I would be so grateful," she said, with what Adam conceded was an impressively straight face. And when the manager appeared less than willing, she grasped his hands and pleaded with him.

With Casey holding his hands and batting her eyelashes, what else could the guy do but agree?

The maid was ecstatic, the manager thrilled to have earned Casey's glowing smile. Adam found himself tipping the girl what he imagined would be half a week's wages. Which totally went against his policy of giving generously through organized charities. He suspected his sole motivation was to earn the same kind of approval from Casey that the manager had.

Why should I care what Casey thinks of me?

"See how easy that was?" she said, when they had the suite to themselves again. She beamed that wide smile he was coming to associate with her, an open smile that drew people to her with their problems and melted the hearts of hotel managers.

He wondered if it was a form of manipulation, and the thought provoked him. "What I see," he said, "is that you're as good at dealing out emotional blackmail as you are at taking it. You pressured that manager into something that's most likely against his job ethics."

When Casey put a hand to her mouth, stricken, he felt no satisfaction.

ADAM WOKE FROM AN UNEASY sleep on the couch in the middle of the night on Sunday. Make that Monday. The digital display on the clock across the room glowed 1:30 a.m.

He heard it again, the noise that must have woken him. A cry from upstairs.

Casey.

He pushed the sheet aside, rolled off the couch and grabbed his pants from the back of the chair. He hauled them on, then headed upstairs.

"Casey?" he called softly, noting she'd left the door ajar.

He snapped on the landing light and pushed the door open.

She lay sprawled in the center of the king-size bed, the duvet twisted across her lower body. Her top half was bare save for a strappy, satin confection in turquoise, which he guessed she'd chosen for her wedding night.

She didn't stir; whatever dream had disturbed her must have ended. Adam's mouth went dry and he felt like a voyeur. But, hell, how could any red-blooded man not notice Casey was gorgeous, even fully dressed? And Adam was as red-blooded as the next man. He also happened to be married to her.

Don't go there.

His marriage to Casey was strictly business. As they said on the infomercials: No Obligation, For a Limited Time Only. Of course, on those infomercials, they also said Satisfaction Guaranteed....

Damn. Adam pulled the door shut with a click that hopefully hadn't woken her, and went back to his couch.

And didn't sleep.

MONDAY, ADAM'S FAVORITE day of the week, found him overtired, overstressed and even more relieved than normal that the weekend had ended.

If he'd planned to fake a marriage to someone, he

would have chosen someone tougher than Casey. Someone who could plow past other people's feelings in pursuit of her goal.

Not a woman who bought into the sob story of a hotel maid she'd never met before and then didn't hesitate to drag him into it, as well.

He wouldn't let her distract him from what he wanted to achieve in their month together, he told himself as he folded his clothes and packed his bag in preparation for their return to real life. He approached Casey, who had been packed and ready to go for ten minutes—he liked a woman who didn't keep him waiting—and said, "We need to set some ground rules."

"Hmm?" She looked up from her cross-stitching.

She'd taken a cross-stitch on her honeymoon. Adam wasn't sure if he admired her practicality or pitied her. Had she been sleeping with Joe so long that she wasn't anticipating any excitement?

He scowled at the thought of the intimacy she might have shared with her fiancé. "Ground rules," he said. "If we're living together for a month, we need some rules."

"You mean who gets to go first in the bathroom?" She smiled sunnily. "You go first. I don't have to get to work in the—"

"I have more than one bathroom," he interrupted, still trying to erase the idea of Casey in bed with that jerk. "I want to make sure we're in agreement about what's involved in this pretense. And what's not involved."

As if they didn't both know what was *not* involved. Casey kept her face blank, trying to appear undisturbed by what had hung heavy in the air between them all weekend. For goodness sake, they were virtually imprisoned in a honeymoon suite, with congratulatory cards and letters from complete strangers being delivered every half hour. Cards and letters addressed to Mr. and Mrs. Carmichael.

"For example," Adam said, "we're both free to spend our time as we wish. We don't owe each other any company."

"Sure," she agreed. "The last thing we'll want is to spend time together after we've been cooped up here so long." If that was true, how come she'd felt more alive this weekend than she had in years?

"But to convince our families our marriage is genuine, at times we'll have to exchange caresses and endearments." He sounded as if he was proposing some extreme form of torture.

"We seem to do okay on the caresses," she said, trying to be more positive than he was.

His brows drew together. "I like you, Casey, and I think we'll get along fine. But as soon as the annulment comes through, it's over. I wouldn't want you to think there's any chance of a permanent relationship between us."

Good grief, the guy had an ego. Just because she'd

responded to his kisses like a heat-seeking missile locking on its target... Kisses that had sizzled in a way she'd never experienced with Joe...

"Ouch." She'd pierced her thumb with her needle. She sucked at the tiny hole, saw his eyes following her movement. She put down her needlework. "Adam," she said, "you're a good kisser, I'll grant you. But from what I've seen, you're single-minded about your work, you're resistant to change and you're emotionally unavailable. So don't *you* go getting any ideas, either." That was telling him.

"If emotionally unavailable means I don't want to adore anyone," he said, "you're damn right."

She wished she'd never mentioned "adoring" to him. It made her sound like a loser. She picked up her cross-stitching, squinted at the green thread she needed to knot. "I don't know why we're even talking about this," she said. "Sure, we'll be living in the same house for a month, but it's no big deal. You won't even know I'm there."

Adam watched her as she made some complicated maneuver with her needle. Watched his *wife*. Through the glass tabletop he observed that her red skirt had ridden up to bare more thigh than he had any right to see. Her navy T-shirt hugged her curves, and she'd pulled her rich, honey-colored hair back into a loose ponytail that made her look like an eighteen-year-old.

A *hot* eighteen-year-old.

He sighed. He'd know she was there, all right.

THEY TOOK A TAXI from the Peabody to Adam's home in Germantown, an upmarket district about ten miles from downtown Memphis. Casey peered out her window as the cab drove through wrought-iron gates toward a three-story brick house. Make that a mansion. Yet the impressive pillared, Georgian-style structure had a welcoming look to it, enhanced by rolling green lawns and patches of colorful shrubbery.

She noted the high stone wall that edged one side of the property, and the thick hedge of poplars on the other. "I'll bet you never even see your neighbors," she said.

No one would be knocking on her door several times a day to borrow something or to ask if she could "mind the kids for an hour."

Adam looked alarmed. "No, I don't. And if I come home and find you've arranged a getting-to-know-you party or any such thing, this marriage will be over."

The taxi driver's eyes met Casey's in the rear-view mirror.

"No neighbors," she promised, putting a hand on her heart for effect. For the taxi driver's benefit, and to Adam's further alarm, she added, "Sweetheart."

Adam helped her out of the car while the driver retrieved their bags from the trunk. "I'll show you around before I head to the office."

She preceded him through the front door into a

two-story lobby, breathing in the smell of beeswax from the gleaming oak parquet floor. Adam deposited their bags at the foot of the staircase and directed her into the living room.

Casey guessed the lobby and the living room between them were almost the size of her father's whole house in Parkvale. Having just escaped her long-time role of cook and cleaner, she shuddered.

Adam noticed. "Something wrong?"

She made a sweeping gesture that encompassed the Persian rugs, classic furniture and eclectic artwork. "This place is beautiful, but it must be a nightmare to clean. You might want to think about that next time you're looking for a wife. Any woman who took this on would have to be crazy. Or masochistic. Or..."

Too late she recognized the warning in his eyes and the signal in the barely discernible tilt of his head.

Casey turned and realized she'd come face-to-face with his housekeeper. A gray-haired, gray-faced woman in an apron regarded her with pursed lips and open disapproval.

"—or very well paid. Or a saint," Casey concluded, with an apologetic smile she hoped would redeem her. There was no answering smile. How dumb of her, not to have guessed Adam would have a housekeeper. She stuck out a hand to the woman, who took it reluctantly.

"I'm sorry," Casey said. "I didn't mean to insult you. The house looks wonderful. You obviously take pride in your work. I'm Casey Greene—Casey Carmichael."

"Selma Lowe," the woman said. "Pleased to meet you, Mrs. Carmichael."

A barefaced lie, if ever Casey had heard one. "Please, Selma, call me Casey."

Going by her sucking-a-lemon lips, Selma didn't take kindly to the suggestion.

"Thank you, Mrs. Lowe, that will be all," Adam said. "Don't go upsetting her," he warned Casey when the woman had gone. "She's worked here for years and I don't want to lose her. She's the most organized woman in Memphis."

"I've never upset anyone in my life." But it wasn't worth arguing the merits of nice over organized, Casey decided as she followed Adam upstairs.

He showed her to a guest bedroom with a colonial-style king-size bed covered by a hand-stitched gray-and-white quilt. The window shutters had been flung open to let in the morning sunlight. Casey longed to slip out of her shoes and curl her toes into the plush navy-blue carpet.

"I hope you'll be comfortable," Adam said.

"It's lovely," she assured him. "Where's your room?"

He pointed to a door across the landing.

"Won't Selma—Mrs. Lowe—think it odd we're not sharing a room? Will she tell your stepmother?"

"Mrs. Lowe and Eloise despise each other. And Mrs. Lowe is the soul of discretion."

"If only you could have married her," Casey said brightly. More seriously, she added, "If she needs any help, or if you do, I'd be happy to—"

"That's exactly what I *don't* need," he said. "I don't need anything from you at all, beyond helping convince Eloise. My home life is very well organized. I don't want anything to change."

Once he was satisfied Casey knew her way around, he muttered something about going to work, and headed downstairs. Five minutes later, from her window, she saw a red Aston Martin DB9 sports car pass through the gates.

She only knew what sort of car it was because Joe had always held it up as his dream set of wheels. Imagine conservative order-freak Adam Carmichael owning one. If that wasn't sublimation of his teenage desire to race NASCAR, she would eat her Psychology 101 textbook.

Back downstairs, she found a less formal living room, where the morning newspaper lay neatly folded on a side table. She picked it up.

The headline jumped out at her: TV Couple's Peabody Love Nest. She groaned and began to read the article, which was just as sensational as the headline. According to the reporter, "Memphis's hottest couple, Adam and Casey Carmichael, spent the weekend closeted in their Romeo and Juliet Suite at the Peabody Hotel. They ordered in all their meals, including reputed aphrodisiacs champagne and oysters, say hotel staff, and unplugged the telephones. One employee described the Carmichaels as 'obviously very much in love.'"

Casey threw down the newspaper in disgust. "How much do they pay people to tell these lies?"

"Did you say something, Mrs. Carmichael?"

The silent approach of grim-faced Mrs. Lowe startled her, and Casey shrieked. The housekeeper bent to pick up the newspaper, and folded it back into shape with precise, sharp movements that Casey knew were designed to make her feel guilty.

But she didn't. In fact, she felt sorry for Mrs. Lowe. The poor woman must be worried that the new lady of the house would want to bring in her own staff. Casey wished she could tell the older woman to chill out, she'd be gone in a month. But Adam hadn't said anything about dropping their pretense in front of the housekeeper.

"I'm planning country fried steak with gravy for dinner, Mrs. Carmichael."

"Really?" Casey managed to bite back her distaste. She didn't want to start off by disagreeing with Adam's perfect housekeeper, but surely it would be even more offensive when she didn't touch the fatty meal set before her tonight. "I don't know, Selma— Mrs. Lowe. It's such a hot day, do you think we could have something lighter? Maybe a chicken salad?"

"As you wish, Mrs. Carmichael." The woman glided from the room.

Whew, culinary crisis averted.

CHAPTER SIX

"WHERE'S MY COUNTRY FRIED steak? The gravy?" Adam asked as Mrs. Lowe set a plateful of leafy green stuff before him. Mrs. Lowe didn't reply but as she left the room, her gaze flicked toward Casey. He might have guessed.

Pretending he and Casey had a real marriage, which in the confines of their suite at the Peabody had seemed a brilliantly simple solution, now seemed fraught with unexpected complexity. All day at the office, when he should have been immersed in his work, he'd found his thoughts drifting to his honey-haired wife.

"Mrs. Lowe offered to prepare steak, but I asked for a chicken salad instead," Casey said. "I don't like a heavy meal on such a hot evening."

"But I had a light lunch today, knowing it was my favorite for dinner." What hope did he have of keeping her out of his thoughts, if he came home every night to find his life disrupted? "I told you I didn't want changes around here."

"I'm sorry, I won't interfere again."

His point made, Adam tackled the salad. It was delicious, as all Mrs. Lowe's meals were, and he started to feel better. He could always fill up on bread.

Prepared to be conciliatory, he said, "Are you missing out on your psychology classes, staying here?"

She shook her head. "Summer vacation. I start again in September."

"So what did you do today?"

Casey took a sip of her wine. "I read about you and me in the newspaper, saw the highlights of our wedding on the Channel Eight news and checked out which TV stations are showing *Kiss the Bride* this week—which are quite a few."

Adam made a mental note to tell the Channel Eight newsroom not to run any more stories about him and Casey. Then he remembered his strict policy of nonintervention in the news department. He sighed. "Did Eloise call?"

"The phone rang several times, but I wasn't sure if I should answer it. I think Mrs. Lowe took some messages."

"It's okay to answer it," he told her. "Did you do any work on your book?"

"I don't have it here with me," she said. "I have a couple of articles due to the newspaper I freelance for, too. I'll have to go back to Parkvale to fetch my files. Besides, I'll need more clothes. I thought I might take a bus home tomorrow, then I'll drive my car back here."

"A bus?" Adam thought about that as he chewed.

"Why don't you do a one-way car rental? It'll be faster."

She hesitated, her fork halfway to her mouth. "I can't afford that. The bus will be fine."

"I'll pay for the rental."

Casey shook her head. "No thanks. Like you said, you don't want someone needy."

"I didn't mean it like that."

"I know, but I don't want to feel as if I'm taking advantage of you." She grinned. "What would Sam Magill say?"

"Forget Sam." Adam watched her evident enjoyment of her meal. "If my wife is seen taking a bus long distance, people will talk." He drummed his fingers on the table. This marriage was turning into a whole new set of obligations he didn't need. "I'll drive you to Parkvale myself. We'll leave early in the morning."

She opened her mouth, and he said, "Don't even think about offering to pay for the gas."

She closed it again.

He might as well get all his obligations out of the way. "There's one more thing." He reached into his pocket and pulled out a crimson velvet jeweler's box.

Casey bit her lip. Surely he hadn't gone out and bought her a ring?

He opened it and she saw a gold wedding band, engraved with a delicate, swirling pattern.

"This was my mother's," he said. "You'd better wear it while you're here."

"I don't think—"

"We're trying to make this marriage look real," he interrupted. "You have to wear it."

Casey extended her left hand. She could have sworn that, despite his impatience, Adam hesitated before he slid the gold band onto her finger.

His touch was warm as he held her hand for another moment, looking down at the ring. She couldn't help feeling that in wearing it she was joined to Adam by some invisible bond that hadn't been there a few minutes earlier.

"I guess your Mom's not around anymore," Casey said.

His expression became shuttered. "She died when I was ten years old. Just died in her sleep, no one knew why."

"How awful for you and your father."

Adam took his time finishing the last of his salad and she thought he wasn't going to answer. But he pushed his plate aside, looked her in the eye and said, "My father didn't give a damn. My mother loved him, but there was never a day in their life together when he acted as if he might love her back."

The raw pain in Adam's voice shocked Casey. "Did he love you?"

His black look said he resented the question, but maybe because he'd just put a ring on her finger, he answered it. "Dad loved the business."

She examined Adam's mother's ring, saddened

that the woman who'd worn it before her had been unloved, at least by her husband. "You loved your Mom," she said to Adam.

"It wasn't enough," he said flatly. "She needed my dad, but it seemed he just didn't have it in him to love people. Like an illness that wasn't his fault."

Suddenly, Casey had an inkling about something. "What about Eloise?"

Adam scowled. "When he met Eloise he became a different person. He was crazy about her." His mouth tightened.

"You were jealous of Eloise?"

"I wasn't jealous, I was angry," he said calmly, but she could see a glint in his eyes. "Dad was so besotted with her, he lost all sense of balance. He lost focus at work—he'd take days off at a time to go away with her. He spent a fortune and let the business slide. Then I discovered—" He bit off his next words, pressed his lips together.

"But things came out right?" Casey asked.

Adam shrugged one shoulder uneasily. "When he woke up to how much trouble we were in, Dad did what he had to do. He mortgaged his house and poured money from his personal investments in to save the business and settle some of the lawsuits against the company. But he didn't want to tell Eloise. So she kept spending. Dad had a heart attack and died six months later." Adam paused, then delivered his damning judgment. "Because of Eloise, he lost control of the business he loved and paid for it with his life."

"Adam, I'm so sorry." Casey reached across the table and took his hand. Absently, he stroked the back of hers with his thumb, drawing a tingling energy to that spot.

"I've spent nearly seven years paying off the debts, getting back on top. It's been hard work, but they're all cleared. We're profitable, we're poised for major growth and we're finally starting to attract the bigger advertisers."

"You love that business as much as your father did," Casey observed. Suddenly, Adam's single-minded pursuit of what he wanted didn't seem selfish. It seemed like the only way he'd been able to get by.

He pulled his hand away. "I shouldn't have said anything—now your heart is going to bleed all over me. Forget it, Casey, it's all in the past."

"If you say so," she said doubtfully.

"Then stop frowning." He stroked a finger across her forehead.

"Frowning is your thing," she said. "Don't tell me we're already getting into that behave-alike married-couple thing."

Adam smiled reluctantly. "No chance of that."

CASEY FELL IN LOVE with the Aston Martin DB9 the moment Adam started the engine. Its quiet purr, the sensation of controlled power, its smooth acceleration to speeds she'd never traveled at before—it was bliss.

"This is wonderful, Adam. We'll be in Parkvale in an hour at this rate," she said in gross exaggeration as they sped northeast on I-40.

Adam eased off the gas a fraction. "It's a fast car," he agreed modestly.

They drove in silence for a while, but Casey found that when she was left alone with her thoughts, the air seemed to prickle with her awareness of Adam. To relieve the tension, she told him her theory about the Aston Martin as sublimation of his NASCAR ambitions. He snorted, but apparently didn't consider that worthy of comment.

"I don't suppose you want to drive my car back to Memphis and let me take this one?" she ventured some time later.

He started, as if she'd suggested an equal division of assets at the end of their month. "No one drives this car except me."

Casey sighed. "You NASCAR drivers are so selfish." That earned another snort.

Halfway there they stopped for gas. Relief propelled Adam out of the car. At last, a chance to put some distance between them. Didn't Casey realize the navy linen skirt, which looked so prim and proper, rode up her thighs every time she twisted to talk to him? A guy could crash his phenomenally expensive car with that kind of distraction.

Adam got back into the Aston Martin resolving to keep conversation—and thus thigh baring—to a minimum. But five minutes into the second half of the trip, it occurred to him he wasn't sure what to expect in Parkvale.

"Should I be worried about meeting your family?" he asked. "What are we going to say to them?"

Casey twisted in her red leather seat. Adam kept his gaze fixed on the road ahead.

"They won't be there," she said. "Karen's not due home until later in the week. And Tuesday morning is Dad's physical therapy. That's why I wanted to come today," she admitted. "I figured I'd sneak in and sneak out again."

"What about your brother?"

"Mike has a summer job in Dallas. But he's not as demanding as the other two—he's a typical young guy, caught up in his own stuff. It's Dad and Karen who are still calling me several times a day."

"We'll have to deal with them," Adam said. "They're going to want to meet your husband, so we should invite them to visit, maybe for a weekend."

"That's a great idea," she said. He knew without looking she'd be beaming again.

"The sooner you convince them you're truly out of their lives, the sooner I've kept my part of our bargain."

"I'll keep my part, too," she promised.

"I was going to talk to you about inviting Eloise

over for dinner tomorrow night, so we can put on our happy couple act for her."

"That's what I'm here for," Casey agreed.

"Yep," he said. "I'm using you, you're using me. That's what this marriage is all about."

ALTHOUGH CASEY HAD NEVER said anything bad about her family, Adam had built up a mental image of her home as an environment of daily drudgery, enlivened only by her girlish dreams.

So he was surprised when they arrived in Parkvale and she directed him into the driveway of a freshly painted white cottage with a wisteria-draped porch.

Inside, the furnishings were simple, and obviously not expensive, but the place had been cheerfully and imaginatively decorated. Casey was, as he might have guessed, a good homemaker.

"It's nice," he said.

She gave him a knowing grin. "What did you expect?"

"I had no idea," he lied. "Did you do the decorating?"

She nodded. "I had a blitz in the spring. I thought the sight of me working might get Dad out of his armchair."

"Did it?"

"Bad call," she said, with a typical lack of resentment.

Upon closer observation, he realized everything

was coated in a thin layer of dust. In the kitchen, dishes were piled in the sink and flies hovered over a mound of food scraps on the counter.

Casey headed toward the sink. "I might as well wash these."

"No, you won't." Adam moved quickly after her and clamped his hands on her shoulders. He turned her around, resisting the temptation to plant a kiss on the lips she'd parted in surprise. "Your father has to learn to cope without you, remember?"

"Yes, but—"

"Tough love," he reminded her. He released her to look at his watch. "I have a meeting at two o'clock. We need to get out of here." He was already looking forward to two and a half hours of peace and quiet, just him and the Aston Martin.

"You go ahead," Casey said. "I'll do a few things then follow in an hour or so."

"I'm not leaving you here to get sucked back into this family stuff. You've got a job to do back in Memphis." And when she looked blank, he added, "My stepmother, tomorrow night."

"You can't seriously think doing a few dishes is going to keep me here."

"It's not just the dishes," he said. "It's the egg baked onto the stovetop, the crumbs on the floor, the—"

Casey shuddered. "You're right, I can't believe I even thought about it." She walked briskly out of the kitchen. Over her shoulder, she said, "I'll get my things together. How about you back my car out? The key's on the hook in the kitchen."

Adam headed to the garage. "What the—"

Casey's blue Ford Fiesta might have been a peppy little car once, but not in the past twenty years. It was clean, but there were limits to how well rust scrubbed up. And while you could say the matching dents in both fenders lent it an air of symmetry, that was about all you could say.

"I didn't do those." Casey came into the garage with an armload of files. She stepped in front of one of the dents, as if to shield it from view. "They were both hit-and-runs in the hospital parking lot when I was visiting Dad."

"Dangerous places, hospitals," Adam said. He didn't ask why she was driving this heap of junk. He knew the answer. Money. So he wasn't about to wound her pride by suggesting they drop her car at a scrap dealer on the way out of town. "I'm following you back to Memphis."

Casey opened the back door and dumped the files on the seat. "Don't be so Neanderthal. This car is perfectly safe." She shut the door, but it didn't catch, so she opened it again and slammed it, which caused the window to drop to half-mast. She glared when Adam directed a pointed look at it. "You are *not* following me back."

"What are you going to do?" he taunted. "Outrun me?"

Her reply was drowned out by the sound of an engine, louder than a car's, in the driveway outside, followed by a screech of brakes, then a crash and the shattering of glass.

Adam had a horrible feeling he knew what that crash was. By the way Casey's face paled and how she edged away from him, she did, too.

Outside, doors closed with angry thuds.

"You idiot," a male voice yelled. "I drive all night to get you here. All I ask is that you take over for the last half hour so I can sleep, and this is what happens."

"You might have told me this damn truck takes ten minutes to stop after you press the brake," a female voice accused. "What is that…that *thing,* anyway? Who put it there?"

Adam pressed the button next to the light switch and the garage door opened. He stepped forward into the sunlight. "I did. And it's an Aston Martin DB9."

At least, that's what it used to be. Now it was an Aston Martin DB9 with built-in U-Haul. Adam winced at the sight of the truck wrapped around his bumper.

The woman, who turned out to be a younger, not-so-pretty version of Casey, yelped.

Casey ran forward. "Karen, it's me." She hugged her sister, and Karen stuck to her like a prickly bur. Casey shook her, but didn't manage to detach her. "Where's the baby? Karen, is Rosie with you?"

"She's with her father. He's going to bring her down this weekend." Karen hiccupped on a sob. "You came home," she said. "I knew you would. Oh, Casey, thank you, *thank you*." She squeezed her tighter, then said tremulously, "Is this…is this your rental car I smashed? I'm sorry. I didn't expect anything to be in the driveway. But I'll pay for it, I promise." She directed a doubtful look at the Aston Martin—even in its current state, it looked like a million dollars. "Uh, did you take the insurance option on the rental?"

Adam met Casey's eyes over her sister's head, which she was patting reassuringly. She gave him a breezy smile, one that said, *I have this under control.* It didn't fool him. He counted to five, long enough to convince himself the damage to his car wouldn't get any worse if he waited a few minutes to inspect it.

"It's my car," he said, "I'm Adam Carmichael." She lifted her head, looked at him blankly. He didn't want to say it, but it was somehow easier than saying he was Casey's husband. "Your brother-in-law."

She frowned. "What are you doing here?"

"Karen!" Casey turned to Adam. "She's in shock from the accident, she's not usually—"

"Such a pain," interjected the still visibly simmering young man who'd been standing to one side. "Yes, she is, Casey, and you know it."

That set Karen crying again. Casey glared at him.

"Adam, this is Mike. My brother. Who can be equally painful when he chooses."

Mike grinned and maneuvered around Karen to give Casey a belated kiss on the cheek. Then he shook hands with Adam. "Sorry about your car. That's one hot set of wheels. Automatic or stick shift?"

"Stick shift." Adam forced a smile.

"It's great to see you, Mike," Casey said.

Taking her cue from her sister, Karen said, "Mike's been wonderful. He loaded this thing for me—" she indicated the U-Haul "—then he drove through the night. I couldn't have done it without him." She wrapped her arms around her brother.

Adam suppressed a shudder. Karen was a clinging vine.

"Did Dad tell you I was coming today?" Karen asked. "It's so cool you're here to help."

Adam could see alarm in Casey's eyes. They hadn't survived a wedding and a honeymoon for her to give in now.

"My wife and I—" that turned out to be easier to say than he expected "—are due back in Memphis right away."

Karen looked around as if she was trying to figure out who Adam's wife was.

"So Casey and I," Adam clarified, "can't help you."

Casey shifted from one foot to the other. "Adam, that's a little harsh. I can stay a few hours."

He mouthed something at her, and Casey recognized the words *tough love.* She bit her lip. He was right. Postponing by two or three hours what Karen would see as her abandonment wouldn't change anything.

She cleared her throat. "We're not staying, Karen." She stepped closer to Adam. He locked her hand in his, and she sent him a startled glance. That's right, they were pretending this marriage was genuine.

Tears filled Karen's eyes again.

Adam tightened his grip on Casey's hand and eyeballed Mike.

"Casey has to go," Mike told Karen. "I'll help you unload." Adam continued to stare at him, until the younger man said, "I'll stay on a couple of days until you're settled."

Karen nodded, dragged her sleeve across her eyes in a curiously childish gesture. "I—I love you, Casey."

How the hell was Adam supposed to compete with that? Karen must know it was exactly what her sister wanted to hear. He couldn't tighten his grip on Casey any more without hurting her. He settled for caressing the finger that bore his mother's wedding ring.

"I love you, too, sweetie," Casey said. "Too much to stay."

She was shaking as she turned away from Karen. Adam wrapped an arm around her, shepherded her to inspect the damage to his car. It wasn't too bad—drivable despite broken taillights and a dented bumper. At his request, Mike moved the U-Haul onto the lawn to clear the driveway.

"Go pack some clothes," Adam told Casey. "I'll get the Aston Martin out of the way, then I'll move that thing you call a car out of the garage."

The Fiesta started first try, which was something. Adam drove it outside, moved the driver's seat back to where he thought Casey had had it, then got out. When he walked around the back of the Fiesta, he got an eyeful of the sticker fixed to the back bumper.

Honk If You Think I'm Sexy.

He was still trying to convince himself it couldn't really say anything so tacky, when Casey emerged from the house lugging a suitcase and a carry-all that was almost bursting at the seams.

"What is *this?*" He pointed at the offending sticker. "Let me guess, it's affirming?"

Her smile, shaky after the encounter with Karen, told him he'd got it in one.

"It was Brodie-Ann's idea," she said. "And I must admit, it works."

He rolled his eyes. "I'll bet it does. Brodie-Ann has a lot to answer for. Are you ready?"

"Yep. I left a note for Dad to say I'll call him about getting us all together."

Adam stowed Casey's bags in the Fiesta's trunk while she detached herself from a prolonged goodbye hug with Karen. He waited until she was out of the driveway before he headed for his own car.

Casey drove off at a speed that could charitably be called sedate. More like a snail's pace. Adam sighed as he turned his key in the ignition of the Aston Martin. This would be a long trip.

He pulled out his cell phone; he needed to call his secretary and cancel his two-o'clock meeting, then phone his insurance company. At this speed, driving one-handed presented no problems.

Within three blocks, the honking started.

CHAPTER SEVEN

ADAM'S BRIEF HAD BEEN simple. His stepmother would come for dinner. Adam and Casey would act loving, which according to him meant he would call her darling and hold her hand. They'd have an excellent meal, served by the efficient Mrs. Lowe, then Eloise would go home, fully deluded that her stepson had done what she wanted and married a woman he loved. And the logical outcome was that she would stay out of Adam's life. No more party planning, no more introductions to eligible women, no more bride-fest.

"How will she feel when we get an annulment?" Casey had asked.

"She'll get over it."

"Adam!" His callousness shocked Casey.

"What?"

She narrowed her eyes, and he threw up his hands. "All right, she might be disappointed at first. But by then I'll have a plan in place for dealing with Aunt Anna May's lawsuit, the business will be secure and Eloise will see it's all good."

The finality of it silenced Casey. "If you're sure," she said at last.

"Quite sure. I know my stepmother. Don't worry, this plan is perfect."

OH, YEAH?

Adam had reckoned without his wife's ability to disrupt his arrangements, Casey thought grimly, as Mrs. Lowe, back ramrod straight, stalked out the front door and climbed into a waiting taxi.

How had this happened? All Casey had done was offer to make dessert, and the housekeeper had taken off her apron and said with chilly politeness, "Mrs. Carmichael, I am not used to having my work questioned. You may no longer require my services, but many other people do. I will leave now, and I will telephone Mr. Carmichael to send on my wages."

Ten minutes later, she was gone.

The kitchen clock showed quarter to six. Casey's new mother-in-law—or was she a stepmother-in-law?—was due in fifteen minutes, and right now dinner comprised a half-assembled hors d'oeuvres tray, several piles of chopped vegetables and a bowl of marinating meat.

This was all Adam's fault, she thought crossly. He'd promised to be home by five-thirty. If he'd been on time, he could have cajoled Mrs. Lowe into staying.

Reluctantly, Casey decided to phone him and

confess. It would mean facing his anger sooner rather than later, but at least he could call Eloise and ask her to postpone. By tomorrow, Casey could whip up a decent meal.

She dialed his cell phone on the assumption he was on his way home. When he answered, the tension in his voice made her hesitate to give him the bad news.

"I'm glad you called, Casey. I'm afraid I'm going to be late, so you'll have to look after Eloise for a while. I wouldn't ask, but it's an emergency." She heard agitated voices behind him, and Adam lowered his tone to murmur, "I'm in a room full of lawyers, trying to figure out how not to lose several million dollars." He paused. "Did you want something?"

"Uh, no, nothing important. I'll see you later." Casey hung up the phone. She briefly considered ordering pizza, but if Eloise was a stickler for routine like her stepson, that would be a very bad idea.

She looked at the dinner ingredients on the counter. Steak, mushrooms, potatoes, salad, garlic, strawberries… She could do something with these.

CASEY HAD EXPECTED Adam's stepmother to display the same unshakeable love of order as he did, and arrive right on time. But fortunately, the doorbell didn't chime until twenty past six. Casey went to the front door, only remembering as she opened it that she was still wearing Mrs. Lowe's voluminous apron.

The tall, elegant, silk-clad woman on the doorstep had light-blue eyes that right now were coolly assessing.

"Mrs. Carmichael?" Casey said brightly. "I'm Casey."

"Well." Eloise sounded bemused rather than hostile. "You look rather different from when I saw you on television on Friday." Then, as Casey hesitated, she asked, "Are you going to invite me in?"

"I'm working in the kitchen," Casey explained as she followed her mother-in-law across the foyer. When Eloise looked around, bewildered, Casey wondered if she even knew where Adam's kitchen was. She led the way, aware of the silent tread of her bare feet in contrast to the clack of Eloise's heels on the parquet floor.

"Where's Mrs. Lowe?" Eloise surveyed the clutter on the counter, sniffed the baking shortcake. She cast a wary glance around.

"I'm afraid she's gone," Casey said. "I said something to offend her—again—and she walked out."

Eloise broke into a huge smile that stripped away the suspicion, the cool elegance, and left her looking like someone's mother. "Bravo, my dear," she said. "If I'd known it was that easy, I'd have tried it years ago. This calls for a drink."

She got a bottle of champagne from the refrigerator, but clearly had no idea how to open it. Casey did the honors. Eloise raised a glass of the fizzing liquid.

"Good riddance to Mrs. Lowe," she said.

Casey joined her in the toast, feeling rather disloyal to Adam, but sharing the sentiment wholeheartedly.

"So," Eloise said, "have you told Adam yet?" Her eyes gleamed with anticipation.

"I called, but it wasn't a good time. He's running late, by the way, and sends his apologies. Mrs. Carmichael, do you think—"

"My dear Casey, you can't call me Mrs. Carmichael," she said in her soft Southern drawl. "You may call me Mother—" she saw the doubt on Casey's face "—or Eloise, if you prefer."

"Eloise, then." Casey looked around the kitchen, a trifle wildly. "Adam's having a really bad day at work. Yesterday his car got smashed thanks to me—" Eloise drew in a sharp breath that acknowledged the importance of the Aston Martin "—and now I've lost his precious housekeeper. Maybe I should tell him tomorrow, let him think Mrs. Lowe cooked tonight."

Eloise tilted her elegantly coiffed head to one side. "Not a chance. That old dragon never makes strawberry shortcake. She knows it's my favorite. It won't take Adam two minutes to notice something's wrong."

Casey had feared as much. She groaned and got back to her dinner preparations. To her surprise, Eloise pitched in and helped, with a lot of enthusiasm if not much actual skill. Adam's tale about his father had given Casey the impression Eloise might be demanding or selfish, but right now she was neither.

By the time Adam arrived home a half hour later, the steak had been seared and was ready to be finished off in the oven, the mushroom sauce was made, the vegetables were awaiting a final steaming, and the hors d'oeuvres tray was a fully assembled work of art.

When they heard the front door open, Casey and Eloise froze, as if they'd been caught stealing the silver.

"You run upstairs and change," Eloise said. "I'll head Adam off at the pass." She chortled as she snatched up the champagne bottle and headed out to the foyer.

"Adam, darling…" Her voice wafted back to the kitchen.

As Casey raced up the back staircase, she heard her cooing at her stepson, and getting what sounded like a grunt in response. It didn't seem as if Adam's day had improved any. Casey grimaced at her reflection in her bedroom mirror. She was flushed with heat—and, no doubt, with champagne. Grease streaked her face and her hair hung limply. Too bad she didn't have time for a shower.

She splashed cold water over her face and upper body, then twisted her hair and pinned it at the back of her head. Thankful she'd had the forethought to select her clothes earlier, she put on the silky lilac dress, taking pleasure in the way it shimmied over her hips. The slim fit showed her figure off to advantage, and a slit up the side enabled freedom of movement. Quickly, she applied lipstick—no need for blusher. She grimaced as she realized a few tendrils of hair had already escaped their pins.

On her way to join the others, she collected the hors d'oeuvres from the kitchen. The heavy tray forced her to slow her pace, so she had a moment to collect herself.

When Casey entered the living room, Adam moved immediately to relieve her of it. Although she was expecting some kind of embrace, she flinched when his lips touched her forehead.

"Darling," he said, as he set the hors d'oeuvres down on the table, "you should let Mrs. Lowe do this."

Casey looked at Eloise, who frowned and tipped her head toward Adam's untouched champagne glass. Eloise was right. It might be better for him to relax with a drink before Casey gave him the bad news. "It was no problem…honey," she said.

"But Mrs. Lowe—" Adam began.

Casey did the only thing she could think of to forestall the inevitable. She stood on tiptoe and planted a firm kiss on his mouth. Time slowed as she absorbed the sureness of his lips against hers. Her hands went to his chest to brace herself, and she felt the strength of his muscles beneath the crisp cotton of his shirt. The kiss lasted barely two seconds, but when she pulled away, Casey felt herself blushing furiously.

"What was that for?" Adam sounded dazed—and not at all like he was thinking about his housekeeper.

"You had a bad day. I wanted to make it better." She took a step backward. "Did it work?"

He touched a finger to his lips. "Well, it didn't hurt any."

"How did your meeting go with the lawyers?" Casey asked.

"It, uh, wasn't too bad," he said distractedly.

"Adam, I must congratulate you on your wife," Eloise said. "She's lovely." She smiled at Casey.

Adam didn't look at Casey, but took her hand, entwined his fingers loosely with hers. "Yes, she is."

Eloise lifted her glass in a toast. "To true love, the kind that lasts forever."

Casey raised her glass with only the tiniest twinge of guilt. She still believed in true love, even if it didn't have a place in her marriage. Adam muttered something about forever being a very long time, but at last he drank some champagne. By the time they finished the hors d'oeuvres, he'd had two glasses and did seem more relaxed, though Casey could still see that furrow in his brow.

"I'll go check on things in the kitchen," she said. "Why don't you two go through to the dining room?"

She steamed the vegetables and reheated the

sauce while the meat finished cooking in the oven. She served the meal with some pride—she'd done a great job at short notice.

When she carried all three plates into the dining room—a skill she'd acquired waiting tables to help pay her father's medical bills—the atmosphere was like thunder. Adam was glowering at his stepmother, who looked decidedly sheepish.

"What's going on?" Casey asked.

"Eloise has confessed that she annoyed Mrs. Lowe so much tonight, the poor woman quit," Adam said.

Something seized in Casey's chest. She set the plates down carefully. "Eloise, that is the nicest thing you could have done." She blinked and clamped her lips together to stop the prickle behind her eyes from turning into an overflow of emotion. When she was sure she could continue, she said, "Adam, it was my fault." Briefly, she recounted the true sequence of events.

"I figured I can do the cooking and look after the house for the next…while," she finished.

Adam had the same black look he'd worn the night Casey had canceled the country fried steak. Only this situation wouldn't be so easily resolved.

"Darling, don't be silly." He smiled, but he spoke through gritted teeth. His doting husband act required him to stifle his annoyance in front of Eloise. "This house is so big, no self-respecting wife would take it on. I'll call the agency and find a replacement."

"Perhaps Casey should interview the candidates," Eloise suggested, "to make sure she finds someone she likes."

Adam agreed. Even if his acquiescence was just for Eloise's benefit, Casey decided she would contact the agency in the morning. It was the least she could do.

Over dinner, Eloise demanded details of their romance—where they'd met and how long they'd known each other.

"Here in Memphis and long enough." Adam's evasive reply covered both questions.

He stopped just short of being rude to Eloise. He might claim any ill-feeling toward his stepmother was in the past, but obviously he still held a grudge.

"You must be a very special woman, Casey," she said. "I think Adam always believed he couldn't have both the business and a woman he loved, and he was far more comfortable with the business."

Adam scowled. "Eloise knows nothing about it," he said.

His stepmother ignored that. "I'm sure he's figured out by now that a marriage built on true love will strengthen him, rather than weaken him."

Adam clutched his head in his hands. "Spare me two amateur psychologists in the family."

Later, when Eloise rose to leave, she hugged

Casey warmly. "I can't wait to get to know you better, my dear." To Adam, she said, "I know you'll be relieved not to have me foisting young women on you every time I see you."

"You bet," he answered, with more enthusiasm than he'd displayed toward her all night.

TOO EASY.

By Friday, Casey had recruited a new housekeeper, Adam having failed in his attempt to persuade Mrs. Lowe to return. Sue Mason was goodnatured, young enough to be happy about using first names, and keen to start work on Monday. Those were all the qualifications she needed as far as Casey was concerned. She'd asked Adam his opinion, and he'd told her to go ahead and do what she thought best. He probably planned to find a carbon copy of Mrs. Lowe as soon as the annulment came through.

But for now, Casey thought, as she put the phone down after confirming Sue's employment, everything was going just fine. She and Adam had been married for a week, and she'd already made good progress on her book. Karen was still calling several times a day for advice about Rosie, but Casey's ignorance on the subject of babies meant she couldn't be of more than limited help. By the time their one-month marriage was over, Casey and Adam should both have achieved their goals.

Who needs to be adored?

THE SECOND WEEK of their marriage flew by. Everything was running smoothly in the house, thanks to the new housekeeper. Adam was busy at work, and Casey's days involved plenty more writing, punctuated by visits from Eloise, who seemed determined to get to know her daughter-in-law. When Casey mentioned to Adam she felt guilty about deceiving Eloise, he gave her a lecture about focus and selfishness.

The next Sunday, they had lunch at the Peabody Hotel with Eloise and two of her friends, Celeste and Beth. Adam told Casey that whenever his stepmother was home, he took the ladies to Sunday lunch. "It lets me off the hook of having to see her the rest of the week," he explained.

But it seemed to Casey the way her husband treated Eloise and her companions went beyond routine courtesy. He made considerable effort to charm the three women he called the Merry Widows, as they sat at the best table in the house. The Peabody staff had greeted Casey and Adam like long-lost friends.

Casey sipped on her mint julep tea, ordered at Eloise's urging and served in a tall frosted glass. The refreshing combination of bourbon, mint and tea should have helped her relax. But Eloise had introduced her to the other ladies as "my dear daughter-in-law," and Casey found herself the center of the conversation. She felt like a fraud.

When Adam waved at someone, she was ready to

welcome any distraction. Even Sam Magill, the lawyer, who'd arrived with another group. Sam caught Adam's signal and excused himself from his friends.

"What is that man doing here?" Eloise creased the fine linen napkin between her fingers as she watched him approach. How did he do this, turn up wherever she went? She couldn't so much as take Adam a tray of his favorite cornbread at the office without Sam popping up to ask if she'd taken her blood pressure medication, or to remind her it was time to pay her federal taxes, or to warn her a prowler had been sighted in her area. Now he was fiddling with his tie, which was already perfectly knotted, and in his distraction he bumped an elderly woman's chair on his way over.

Sam stopped to check if the old lady was all right, then at last reached their table.

"Eloise." He greeted her with a half bow, just as James used to. When James did it, she'd thought it charming.

"Hello, Sam."

Sam knocked her purse, which she'd hung over the back of her chair. He apologized, red in the face. Feeling sorry for him, Eloise smiled. Hope leaped into his eyes. Oh, dear. Sam could interpret even ordinary courtesy as something more when he wanted to badly enough.

That visit she'd paid to his house had revealed he

cared for her more deeply than she'd suspected. It wasn't fair to let it continue. Somewhere out there was a woman who would return his feelings.

Eloise bit her lip. Though it went against her upbringing, though her mama would have a fainting fit if she were alive to witness it, maybe Eloise should be…less polite to Sam.

For both their sakes.

She turned her back on him to speak to Celeste, making the exclusion deliberate.

Sam's voice was gruff when he said to Adam, "I planned to call you at home this afternoon."

It was rare for Sam to phone on the weekend. Adam figured it couldn't be good news. He reached around to the empty table behind him and pulled a chair over for Sam. "What's the problem?"

The attorney directed an anxious glance at Eloise as he sat down, but she wasn't paying him any attention. "I heard a rumor from the offices of your aunt's lawyer. Your marriage—" he nodded to Casey, sitting next to Adam "—has Anna May worried you've met the conditions of the will and put Henry out of contention."

"That figures," Adam said.

"So she's claiming," the lawyer said, "your father was out of his mind when he wrote that will."

Adam gripped the edge of the table. If Anna May and Henry were here, he'd knock their stupid heads together. This time, they'd gone too far.

"My father was *not* crazy." His anger erupted at the worst possible moment. The waiter had arrived with their food, and the women had stopped talking. Everyone at Adam's table heard his declaration. And judging by the curious glances directed their way, everyone at neighboring tables, too.

"Adam?" Eloise said uncertainly.

This news would hurt his stepmother. He wished he didn't care, but... Casey reached over to prize his fingers from the table edge. She curled her hand around his and squeezed gently.

Adam felt the tension seep out of him. Whatever Anna May was up to, they would get past it.

"It's Anna May's latest tactic," he told his stepmother. "She's claiming Dad wasn't of sound mind when he wrote his will."

He was about to add that his aunt wouldn't get anywhere with such a preposterous claim, when Sam blurted, "She has evidence."

Eloise uttered a word Adam didn't know she knew, not quite under her breath. Sam coughed into his handkerchief.

"Are you still smoking, Mr. Magill?" Eloise gave the lawyer a chilly look that cleared his cough miraculously. "Such a bad habit," she said to no one in particular. "James smoked cigars when I met him, but he stopped eventually. He always felt it bespoke a lack of self-control."

Sam made a choking noise.

Casey blinked. She'd never heard Eloise be anything less than charming.

"But then," her mother-in-law continued, "what would James have known about it? Given he was *insane*." She spoke lightly, but fixed Sam with a gimlet glare.

The lawyer blushed, and Casey felt sorry for him. From the second he'd approached their table, it had been obvious he had a crush on Eloise. His harsh-edged self-assurance evaporated, and it seemed all he could do was open his mouth and insert both feet.

"I didn't say James was insane," Sam mumbled. From somewhere, he dredged up a speck of his usual confidence. "I had a lot of respect for James, Eloise. You know that."

She nodded jerkily. But when she spoke, she still sounded hostile. "Then you won't let Anna May get away with this, will you?"

Sam looked as if he badly wanted to assure her that hell would freeze over before Anna May got to say anything against James in open court. But from the way he squirmed in his seat, Casey guessed the answer wasn't that straightforward.

"I believe Anna May has a sworn statement with regard to your husband's state of mind. That statement is the basis of her case," the lawyer said formally.

Eloise gave a decidedly unladylike snort. "I'll bet she has no such thing."

"Who made the statement?" Casey asked.

The lawyer's eyes widened, as if he hadn't anticipated what was surely an obvious question. Yet more evidence he didn't think straight when Eloise was around. He shot a pleading look at Adam. "We should continue this discussion tomorrow."

"We want to know now," Eloise said.

Adam nodded at Sam to continue. The attorney closed his eyes as if in pain. "The statement is from one of the nonfamily directors of Carmichael Broadcasting. He had a conversation with another director, in which that director expressed a firm opinion that James Carmichael had lost his mind."

"Which other director?" Adam and Eloise demanded simultaneously.

Sam slumped in his seat and raised his hands, conceding defeat to the forces ranged against him.

"It was you, Adam."

CHAPTER EIGHT

As Casey and Eloise stared at Adam, a flash of white light blinded them.

"Thanks, folks." A photographer, a man Casey recognized from the crowd who'd gathered at the TV studio after their wedding, slipped his camera back into its case. "Enjoy your meal."

Lunch pretty much fell apart after that.

Adam began to deny the accusation, then he went beet-red and clammed up.

Eloise's eyes filled with hurt. She stood up. "I can ignore Anna May's poison—that woman's always been a fool. But, Adam, for you to say such a thing about your father, a man who, whatever you may think, loved you. The finest, most intelligent man I've known…" She stopped, and Casey saw her throat working with emotion. "*That* is a betrayal." She slipped her purse off the back of her chair, then asked a passing waiter to bring her coat. "Thank you for lunch," she said with her usual good manners, "but I plan to take a taxi home."

The other two Merry Widows glared at Adam—

extending their hostility to encompass Casey by association—with a ferocity that made Casey hope neither of them was packing a weapon.

Sam sprang to his feet. "Eloise, how can I help you? You shouldn't be alone if you're upset. I can take you—"

Eloise gave him a look that said he'd done enough, and stalked out of the restaurant.

Celeste and Beth left with her, while Adam settled the bill. Casey followed him outside, where the valet reluctantly relinquished the newly repaired Aston Martin.

Adam pulled out into the traffic with a screech of tires. From the passenger seat, Casey cast him a sidelong glance. A frown darkened his face, and his chin jutted forward.

"What?" he demanded.

She spread her hands. "I didn't say anything."

"You didn't have to," he grumbled. "I can see you think I'm a prize jerk."

"You're certainly a contender," she agreed. "But right now I'm giving you the benefit of the doubt."

He managed a half smile. "Thanks, but it's more than I deserve. I did tell John Hanson I thought Dad had lost his marbles. Years ago, a few months before the heart attack."

The self-recrimination in his eyes gave Casey the urge to comfort her husband, to wrap her arms around him and tell him it would be all right. Instead, she said, "Did you mean it?"

Adam shook his head, then nodded. "In a heat-of-the-moment way. I'd just found out Carmichael Broadcasting's accountant had been embezzling funds. It seemed Dad had lost touch with reality when he married Eloise. The business was on the brink of disaster, and I vented to John Hanson. Big mistake."

"No judge will accept a one-off remark as evidence your father was insane," Casey said.

Adam grimaced. "There was one other occasion. At the reading of Dad's will, when I heard about that marriage clause, I did say something along the lines of, 'He must have been nuts.' Eloise didn't take it well at the time. Anna May was there, too. I'm sure she'll remember."

"But still," Casey persisted, "it's not exactly expert psychiatric testimony."

"Which we can't get, now that Dad's dead," he pointed out. "Maybe what I said isn't enough. But maybe we'll get a judge who agrees that what Dad did was crazy, and he'll order a full hearing."

Adam stopped at a red light. To think his own careless remark had fueled Anna May's case. His foot tapped the brake.

"You made a mistake," Casey said. "But you'll get past it."

He turned to face her, found her expression full of sympathy. Casey was on his side, without reserva-tion. She reached across to squeeze his hand on the steering wheel—only it felt more as if she'd squeezed all the air out of his lungs. She snatched her hand back, but not before Adam had seen the flare of desire in her eyes—one that matched his own.

"It might hurt Eloise less if you call to apologize," she said.

Damn if she hadn't tapped into the vein of guilt he tried to pretend didn't exist. Adam didn't need this. "What are you, my wife?"

She snickered, her cheek dimpling, and Adam found himself saying, "I'll think about it."

IT WAS UNUSUAL for Brodie-Ann to take a day off work just so she could drive up to Memphis and have lunch with Casey.

When Casey got to the downtown bistro where they'd agreed to meet on Tuesday, the woman who would spill the contents of her soul at the slightest urging shied away from Casey's questions, deflecting the conversation at their courtyard table to news of what was going on in Parkvale.

"I saw your sister out with the baby last week," Brodie-Ann said.

"How were they?" Casey asked over a lump in her throat. She missed her family, even if she didn't want to be back with them.

"We chatted for a few minutes, then Karen got teary."

Casey chewed her lip. "Maybe I should call her tonight."

"She didn't seem too bad," Brodie-Ann assured her. "It might have just been new-mom hormones."

It wasn't until the waiter had set their chicken Caesars in front of them that Brodie-Ann got to what might have been the point of this get-together.

"Is marriage what you expected?" she asked.

Casey took a sip of her ice water. "I can't say I ever thought about what it might be like to be married to a complete stranger who happens to be the cutest guy I ever met, even if he is a little set in his ways." She put her glass down and turned the question back on Brodie-Ann. "Is marriage what *you* expected?"

Her friend ducked the issue. "So you think Adam's cute, huh?"

Was Brodie-Ann blind? Could she not see he was *gorgeous?* Casey bit back the suggestion that her friend have her eyes tested. "Sure I do. He's a great guy, too." No point denying it.

"Does he have you ironing his shirts yet? Taking meals to his dying grandmother? Hosting soirees for important clients?"

Casey shook her head. "None of the above. He doesn't need me at all." Somehow that came out sounding pathetic.

"That's great," Brodie-Ann said uncertainly. "I'll bet you're enjoying the break."

"Absolutely." Then why did Casey suddenly feel lost?

Brodie-Ann glanced at her watch, then said with a strange urgency, "Casey, sweetie, does Adam like you back?"

"I don't think so." Why would he want a woman who had nothing to offer him? *This is stupid. For years I've wanted to get away from people who only want me for what I can do for them.* What was she, a dependence junkie? "Like I told you," she said, "we're sticking together until the annulment comes through, that's all."

When the waiter appeared suddenly to top up their water glasses, her friend jumped a mile high.

"What's the matter with you?" Casey demanded. "I've never seen you so on edge."

Brodie-Ann flicked a glance over her shoulder across the crowded courtyard. "Nothing. I thought it was…" She stopped, nibbled on a thumbnail.

"You're scaring me," Casey said. "I know you didn't come here for a chat, so tell me what's going on with you and Steve. Right now."

To her shock, Brodie-Ann put her hands over her face, and her shoulders started to shake. Casey dropped her fork and moved around the table to hug her friend. "Honey, what's wrong?"

Brodie-Ann pulled herself together and wriggled out of Casey's embrace. "I'm sorry, I'm being silly." She waved Casey back to her seat and managed a watery smile. "It's just…it's not how I thought it would be. I mean, I still adore Steve, but it's not…" She gulped, on the verge of crying again.

"What's he done? Is he mean to you?" Casey half rose from her chair again.

Brodie-Ann laughed. "Can you imagine Steve being mean to anyone? He's wonderful. I'm lucky to have him."

"But?" Casey prompted.

"You'll think I'm so selfish." Brodie-Ann's gaze slid away from hers. "Before we were married, Steve was so romantic, he'd do anything for me. Once, he even laid his coat down in a puddle so I could step across, just like that guy did for Queen Elizabeth."

Casey looked suitably impressed, though she wouldn't dream of stepping on a man's coat, even if he did lay it down for her—she'd only have to launder it afterward. That kind of romantic gesture was all very well, but the kind of guy Casey could love would be one who…

Who drops my cell phone into a vase when he sees the caller is upsetting me.

Who listens when I suggest he apologize to his step-mother, then goes and does it. And thanks me after-ward.

Who from the very start of our marriage has made my goals as much a priority as his.

Casey clapped a hand over her mouth, as if her thoughts might escape.

I am not falling for Adam Carmichael.

"Did you even hear what I said?" Brodie-Ann demanded.

Casey shook her head in mute apology.

Her friend tutted. "Steve still does those things sometimes, but often as not, I'm the one who's making sacrifices. And it's all bigger stuff than walking on coats. It's giving up my time, my priorities."

"Does he give up those things, too?"

Brodie-Ann nodded glumly. "But he was always good like that. I'm not. I've always been about, well, about *me*," she said with such honesty that Casey laughed. "I'm horrible, aren't I?" she said plaintively. "As soon as Steve figures that out, he'll leave me."

"Steve fell in love with the real you," Casey reminded her. "Yes, you can be demanding. But he loves that. You can also be sweet and generous. He loves that, too. I'm right, aren't I?"

Brodie-Ann didn't reply. But though her lips curved in only the smallest of smiles, her eyes gleamed. Casey fought a twinge of envy.

"Honey, these things take time," she said. "You and Steve are made for each other, but that doesn't mean you don't have to work at your marriage. That's a good thing."

"I guess." Her tone wasn't enthusiastic, but Brodie-Ann looked happier. Then she started chewing her thumbnail again. "Casey, I have a confession."

Casey realized the flush on her friend's face was guilt. "What have you done?"

"While I was worrying about whether I was right to marry Steve, I started to think about you and Joe. And although the wedding didn't work out, I wondered if maybe *you* were right that you should marry someone you know really well." Brodie-Ann babbled on, getting pinker by the second. "Obviously, I didn't know that you, uh, liked Adam, so when Joe came to see me last night and asked if he thought he had any chance of getting back with you, and I was having lunch with you today, I, um…"

A shadow fell across the table, and she stopped.

"Hello, Casey," Joe said.

Her ex-fiancé stood there, handsome in his navy uniform, twisting his cap in his hands.

"Sorry," Brodie-Ann murmured. She pushed her chair back. "I'll let you guys talk." Before Casey could grab her, she was gone, crossing the courtyard at a pace just short of a run.

"May I?" Joe sat in Brodie-Ann's chair without waiting for an answer.

A clammy heat dampened Casey's palms, gave her itchy feet. She'd been fine talking to Brodie-Ann about Parkvale, but now, seeing Joe, she felt her old life reaching out to her with long, bony fingers. She wanted to shrink away from him and sprint after her friend.

"I should have called you." Joe read the reluctance

in her face. "But after what I did, I wasn't sure you'd talk to me. I had to tell you how sorry I am."

An apology? That's why he was here? Not to get back together with her? The threat receded, and Casey's relief came out as a shaky laugh. "Don't worry about it," she said. "I shouldn't have tricked you into going to the TV studio. It was humiliating for both of us." She smiled wryly. "Although you might have told me sooner that you didn't love me."

Joe grabbed her hand across the table, leaning forward so his eyes gazed directly into hers.

"It wasn't true. You've always been my girl, Casey, since we were eighteen years old." Urgency raised the pitch of his voice. "I panicked, I made a mistake. But you and I are perfect together. Come back to me, Casey."

She tried to tug her hand away, but he wouldn't let go, and it felt as if all of Parkvale was pulling on her in a tug-of-war. "Joe, it's over between us. It's too late."

He came around the table and hunkered down in front of her, grasping her knees. "How can it be too late?" he demanded. "A couple of weeks ago you were all set to marry me—so you can't tell me your marriage to this Carmichael guy is the real deal. In your heart, where it matters, nothing's changed at all." He gave her knees a shake to emphasize his point.

Mindful of the curious onlookers at nearby tables, Casey lowered her voice. "Joe, what you did in that

TV studio was the exact opposite of chickening out. Until then, you and I were both prepared to settle for something comfortable, a marriage we knew we could live with, rather than risk not finding someone we truly love. You were the one who was brave enough to say that wasn't right."

"It's not like that." Confusion clouded Joe's face. "I do love you, Casey, and I need you. You're the only woman for me. Wherever you want to go, whatever I have to do to make this work, I'll do it."

Coming on the heels of her realization that Adam didn't need her, Joe's words soothed her spirit like a comforting, even tempting, balm. Casey didn't doubt Joe loved her. She shut her eyes, imagined Adam was here. He'd be mouthing, *Tough love,* holding her hand tight, pulling her away.

But Adam wasn't here. She had to do this on her own.

She opened her eyes.

"I'm not coming back, Joe. What you and I had isn't enough for me, and it shouldn't be enough for you."

It took another few minutes to convince him, but at last he left Casey alone with the remains of her lunch. Exhausted, she gulped down her water, patted some of the cool droplets from the rim of the glass on her temples.

She'd actively severed her ties to her family and to Joe.

She was the temporary houseguest of a man who didn't need her.

She felt as if she'd cast herself adrift.

CASEY COULDN'T SETTLE back into her work that afternoon, so she headed out into the garden and busied herself dead-heading the flowering shrubs that grew against the wall between Adam's house and his neighbor's. The work was calming and satisfying, though what Adam's gardener would make of it on his next monthly visit she couldn't be sure.

"Hello there." A voice from above startled her out of her absorption in a camellia bush.

An elderly gentleman peered over the wall, his wrinkled face and blue eyes visible beneath the peak of his orange baseball cap. He had to be standing on a ladder—the wall was about seven feet high. "I'm Bob Harvey," he said.

Casey straightened and pushed her hair back off her perspiring forehead. "Casey Gr-Carmichael," she replied.

"You must be one of the newlyweds. I saw you on TV."

She nodded.

"I don't think I've met your husband."

"He's very busy with work."

He nodded. "Thought that might be it. What about you, do you work?"

Casey ended up spending a pleasant half hour in

conversation with Bob. She was still in the garden when Adam came home, late, around eight.

The first clue she had of his arrival was the appearance of his polished black shoes in front of her as she weeded around the base of the sundial.

"You know you don't have to work in the yard." He sounded annoyed.

She looked up. With the sun low in the sky behind him, his face was in shadow. "I'm doing this for relaxation. Sue left a crab salad for dinner if you're hungry."

"Maybe later." His tone more friendly, he said, "If you're ready to stop relaxing, how about a drink?"

She smiled. "Sure, I'll just finish up here."

By the time she'd stowed her tools in the shed and washed her hands, Adam had surprised her by setting up drinks on the back porch. He stood waiting for her, two glasses of chilled white wine on the wrought-iron table. He looked tired, his eyes shadowed, lines visible at the corners of his mouth. He'd been putting in long hours with Sam, working on their legal case, as well as running Carmichael Broadcasting.

Casey sat on the swing seat and patted the space next to her. "If we sit here we'll see the sunset."

He smiled faintly as he settled beside her. "I wouldn't want to miss that."

Casey leaned back and took a sip of her wine. With her foot, she pushed off the ground and set the swing gently rocking. "I met one of your neighbors today. Bob Harvey."

Adam put one foot down. The swing stopped. "I thought I said no neighbors."

"He stuck his head over the wall while I was gardening. I couldn't ignore him."

Adam looked skeptical. "And when are he and Mrs. Harvey coming for dinner?"

She chuckled. "I wouldn't do that to you."

"Good," he said with feeling.

Casey set the swing in motion again. Then Adam said, "How was your lunch with Brodie-Ann?"

"Interesting." She took a long swallow of wine. "She brought Joe along."

Adam stiffened. "The Joe who dumped you on TV?"

"Ouch," she said in mild protest. "Yes, that Joe."

Adam stopped the swing once more and put his glass on the table. He'd figured this would happen, just not so soon. A guy wouldn't let Casey go and not regret it. "I suppose he asked you to go back to him." Adam kept his voice controlled, though he wanted to shout. Dammit, he never shouted.

"How did you know?" Casey ran a finger down the condensation on the outside of her wineglass. She wouldn't meet his eyes; she must have decided to go back to Joe.

"It's obvious," he said contemptuously. "It was

only a matter of time before Joe finally realized life was a lot harder without you to look after him."

"You think he can't love me for who I am?" She'd taken his words as an insult, but Adam was too riled to pander to her hurt feelings.

"You mean, he loves you so much he was happy to humiliate you in front of millions of people?"

Casey put her glass down. She made a face, as if her wine suddenly tasted sour. "Don't be horrible."

Since that abortive lunch at the Peabody, Adam had worked late at the office to stay out of Casey's way. He'd felt closer to her that Sunday than he was comfortable with, and it made sense to put some space between them. But even knowing she was at home and that he would see her in the evening made a difference to his days. That he would lose that before he was ready to, and that Joe would have her back, sent a surge of fury through him.

"I'll bet he knew just the right words to have you running back into his arms," Adam sneered. "Did he tell you he *adores* you?"

"More or less," Casey admitted. "He was very sweet."

"I don't believe this." The swing rocked violently as he stood up. "I shouldn't have let you see Brodie-Ann on your own. I knew something like this would—"

Casey was on her feet now, too. "You don't get to *let* me or not let me do anything, you jerk. I'll decide who I see, I'll decide who my friends are, and I'll decide if I should go back to Joe or not." She was pale with anger, and it made her lips look redder, softer. Had she kissed Joe when she told him she was going back to him?

"You don't make decisions!" Adam roared. So much for never shouting. "You're a pushover, remember? You let people manipulate you with their neediness and their sweet-talking and their adoring. Just don't blame me when you're back in that rut you used to call a life."

Her cheeks flamed with anger, and she clenched her fists at her sides. "I told Joe it was over!" she shouted back. "I told him I wanted more than he could offer. I told him no."

She took the wind out of Adam's sails. He gripped the railing, breathing hard. "Why the hell didn't you say so?"

"You didn't ask, you just assumed." She flounced past him, and he reached out and grabbed her by the elbow.

"What else would I think when you're such a pushover? You'd still be in Parkvale with your sister if I hadn't dragged you out of there the other week."

"I learned something that day," she said. "You showed me how to say no, and today I did it for myself."

He grinned at the pride in her voice—and deliberately shut out the relief that made him almost lightheaded. "That's my girl."

"I did it for me, not for you," she said, annoyed.

"Of course." His grin widened. "Sorry I yelled."

She smiled back. "One good thing about you, there's no chance of you manipulating me with sweet talk and neediness and adoring." She sat back down on the swing, and Adam did the same.

"Do you realize we just had our first fight?" Casey turned to look at him and found him closer than she'd thought, his face just inches from hers.

"Do you realize," he parroted, "that your new friend next door probably heard every word of it?"

Casey clapped a hand over her mouth.

"You see," Adam said in a superior tone, "if you'd never met him, it wouldn't bother you. Now you've opened a can of worms, and it's your problem, *darling*."

"Likening Bob Harvey to a can of worms is very rude."

Adam slung an arm over her shoulders. It was casual but nice. "So how do you feel about Joe? It can't have been easy."

She leaned into him, just the tiniest bit. "It was pretty awful. But now I feel…free."

"You're a married woman," he teased. His hand tightened on her shoulder, and a tingling warmth spread down her arm. She looked away from him.

"Joe's the only guy I've ever dated," she said, partly to explain to herself why she reacted so strongly to the unfamiliar excitement of Adam's touch. "I need to learn how to build healthy relationships without getting sucked into that need thing. I guess I should start dating. After our annulment, of course." She patted his knee in reassurance, and left her hand there a moment longer than she should just because it felt good.

Adam's heart stopped. He'd only just gotten over the shock of believing she was going back to Joe, and now she was talking about dating other men.

His reaction to that news, on top of his over-reaction to her lunch with Joe, confirmed that his attraction to Casey was more than physical. He didn't want her thinking about dating other men while she was still living with him. Which meant he had to decide what he did want.

Keep her close...but not too close.

He twirled a strand of her hair around his finger. "You don't have to wait for the annulment."

Her eyes widened. "Our fake marriage won't be very convincing if I start dating other guys."

"You could date me."

Casey's stomach flipped. "Date...you?"

"I was Memphis's most eligible bachelor," he pointed out. "I'm considered quite a catch."

She looked at him, at his tall, graceful physique, the strong planes of his face, his intense blue eyes. "I don't doubt it. So how come you don't have a girlfriend?"

He shrugged. "I haven't met anyone suitable in a while."

There was that word again. "Suitable?"

"Someone who wants to make the most of it when we're together, but doesn't demand a lot in between times. And who's happy to say goodbye when it's over."

It sounded as if he dated the way he did everything else. Logically, with decisive intent.

He smiled, a flash of white teeth. "Like you said, I'm not about to manipulate you or need you."

"When we were staying at the Peabody, you warned me there was no chance of a relationship between us."

"I said a *permanent* relationship," he corrected. "We still have a time limit."

"I want to learn how to date," she said. "What do you want?"

He ran a finger along her jaw. "Do you need to ask? You're a beautiful, sexy—" his voice turned husky "—desirable woman."

Adam wanted her.

"What exactly would dating you involve?"

Her practical question made him smile. "We go out together," he said. "Out for meals. Sometimes, we stay in together. It's not much different from what we do already, except there'll be more of this." He moved closer, so his lips were an inch from hers. "It won't hurt a bit," he promised.

This kiss was more tender than the others. He started at one corner of her mouth, worked his way to the center, then his tongue teased her lips until she parted them. At his slow, stroking entry she found her whole body clenching, and it didn't relax until he hauled her against him and deepened the kiss.

By the time he released her, Casey was shaking. He didn't look a hundred percent steady himself. He raked a hand through his hair, gave her a smile that was part triumphant, part perplexed.

But his voice was calm when he said, "There's one other great thing about dating me."

She raised an eyebrow and, despite the roiling of her insides, said equally calmly, "Only one?"

"If we're trying to convince people we're happily married, this might just do it."

Casey stared straight ahead. As she watched, the sun slipped below the horizon, leaving a glowing pink swath across the sky.

"So, are we dating?" he asked impatiently. "I like you, you like me. And I don't believe you would have kissed just anyone like that."

"Well, maybe not a guy with bad breath and warts on his nose."

"I'm flattered," Adam said dryly. "I had no idea you were so picky."

"I guess," she said, striving for a casual tone though her stomach tied in knots, "we're dating."

CHAPTER NINE

ADAM LOOKED ACROSS his desk at the cluster of people filling his office at ten o'clock on a Wednesday morning. They'd arranged themselves in battle lines—Anna May and Henry to his right, Sam and Eloise to the left.

A faint curl of steam rose from a dish on Adam's desk. Eloise had brought him some of what she called her famous, fresh-baked cornbread. Famous for its ability to drown any man stupid enough to swim after eating it. The stuff weighed a ton. But it was Eloise's mama's secret recipe, and although she had a cook to prepare her meals, Eloise insisted cornbread was her domain. Years ago, Adam had set himself a personal challenge of never eating a bite of the stuff.

He didn't plan to deviate from that this morning, despite being warmly disposed to the world in general, thanks to his newly elevated status as Casey's date.

Anna May glared at Sam as they waited for Adam to speak. She'd said no lawyers for the meeting, a stipulation that suited Adam. But as always, the minute his stepmother entered the building, Sam found a reason to visit Adam's office.

"Well?" Anna May snapped, losing patience.

"Let me get this straight," Adam said. "You're saying that if I promote Henry to joint CEO, give him a bonus equivalent to his first year's salary and agree to pay out a regular dividend to stockholders, back-dated for the past three years, you'll drop your legal action to prove Dad was mentally incompetent when he made that will."

From the encouraging nods Sam was sending his way, Adam gathered he was supposed to see Anna May's offer as a good sign. An indication that she feared she might lose and was therefore willing to negotiate. But how good could it be, when his aunt's demands would undermine the financial stability of the business?

Anna May made a dipping, birdlike movement of her head. Vulture-like, Adam thought. He quashed the uncharitable impulse. Somewhere in his aunt's psyche lay the key to her attitude, but he was damned if he knew what it was. It was the sort of thing Casey liked to ponder. The sort of thing Adam didn't have time for.

Maybe he should try doing it Casey's way.

"What made you decide on those particular terms?" he asked Henry.

"We don't want to be unreasonable, Adam," his

cousin said apologetically, "but Mom feels—*we feel*—"

"It's the least Henry's entitled to, according to your father's original will," Anna May interrupted.

Adam and Sam hadn't known about the earlier will before this morning—Adam's father hadn't used Sam for his personal legal work. Anna May had made the most of that, flourishing a copy of the document under their noses. But there was no denying its contents: it divided James Carmichael's stock holdings in Carmichael Broadcasting equally between Adam and Henry.

"But is it what you want?" Adam asked Henry. He'd never seen any sign that his cousin had the same kind of passion for the business that he did. He rephrased the question in Casey-speak. "What are your dreams?"

Henry swallowed nervously. "Actually, I always thought I'd like to—"

"I don't know what this new tactic of yours is, Adam, but it won't work," Anna May said. "We'll be asking the court to overturn your father's will on the grounds that he was mentally unstable when he signed it."

So much for the friendly approach. Adam slipped back into his more familiar, driven mode. "The court will find my father was in his right mind when he wrote his last will," he said, aware of the absurdity of defending a document that he himself planned to challenge, on the basis that his dad couldn't legally insist Adam get married in order to inherit.

He saw Eloise watching him, biting her lip, blinking. He wished she wasn't here, so he could tell Anna May to do her worst. But he figured his aunt had invited Eloise for that very reason. Emotional blackmail. His family was so good at it. Even Dad... When Anna May revealed the contents of the earlier will, Eloise had suggested James had changed it because he'd realized how important his son was to him. Adam would have liked to believe it. But more likely, Dad had seen how much effort Adam was putting into the company, and he'd wanted to be sure that continued.

Adam wished, as he often did, that his dad hadn't asked him to take care of Eloise. It meant he couldn't ignore that his stepmother would be heartbroken to hear her beloved husband labeled crazy in public. But Adam was damned if he was going to cave in a moment before he had to. He turned to his stepmother. "What do you think, Eloise?"

She swallowed, looked over at Anna May, then back at him. "I never give in to blackmail, Adam dear, and nor should you."

What? Adam stared at her, and she inclined her head. He didn't give her a chance to change her mind. "You heard Eloise."

Not the least bit flustered, Anna May got to her feet, and Henry did the same. "We'll see you in court," she said over her shoulder as she stalked out.

Eloise left a minute later. Sam watched her go with a kind of hopeless despair. "Such a brave woman," he murmured.

For once, Adam had no argument. He pushed the dish of cornbread toward Sam. "Why don't you take this?"

"She made it for you." But the lawyer looked at it hungrily.

"Take it," Adam insisted, and Sam didn't need any further encouragement to drag the dish to his side of the desk.

"How do you rate Anna May's chances with the insanity thing?" Adam asked.

"Less than fifty percent."

Not as low as Adam would have liked. "Surely she can't win on the basis of a couple of stupid remarks I made?"

"I'm betting she'll make a big deal out of your father's failure to notice his accountant stealing money from under his nose," Sam said. "She'll try to link that to a loss of mental competence."

Which would be even more upsetting for Eloise. Adam rubbed his temples.

"This marriage of yours…" Sam said thoughtfully.

"What about it?"

"Is it going well?"

"You tell me. You're the one working on the annulment."

Sam waved that away. "I'm asking if you and Casey get along. It seems to me that you do."

Adam shifted in his seat. If burning up every time he touched his wife, if craving the feel of her lips under his and being aware of every movement of her legs, her hips, counted as getting along, then Sam was right. Adam suspected dating her definitely counted as getting along.

"I'm thinking," Sam said, "that once we beat this insanity thing, the simplest way to deal with Anna May and Henry might be to remove the grounds for their complaint, and drop your challenge to the will."

"How do I do that?" Adam asked.

"You make this marriage for real."

He dropped his pen. "You can't be serious."

Sam nodded, every bit as somber as he always was. "I'm saying this as your friend, not as your lawyer. In the strictly legal sense, I think we'll probably win the battle to have that clause struck out of your father's will. But if you want to do this the easy way…the fact is, you *are* married, and as the will stands you need to be married to inherit. There's a certain synergy."

"There's a certain craziness," Adam retorted. He winced. He'd sworn never to use the words *crazy* or *insane* lightly again.

"Think about it," Sam advised. "If there's any way you and Casey can make a go of it…"

"Not a chance." Adam had to quash the thought

before it could take root. So what if he and Casey were dating? He'd dated dozens of women without ever wanting to marry them. He and Casey were poles apart on the things that mattered, with the exception of their mutual exasperation with demanding families. Even if he was interested in making this marriage real—which he wasn't—there was one major obstacle. Casey wanted a man who adored her.

He realized Sam was still talking. "Sorry, what was that?"

"I asked how Eloise is after that fiasco at the Peabody on Sunday. She seemed jumpy this morning."

"I think she's forgiven me," Adam said. He'd phoned his stepmother that night, as Casey suggested. Eloise had still sounded hurt, but also grateful for Adam's call. By the time he hung up, she'd managed a couple of attempts at the lighthearted interference that usually bugged him. This time, he was surprised how relieved he was to know she'd forgiven his indiscretion.

"She's a fine woman." It was a variation on a theme Sam played often.

Adam made a noncommittal sound and added, "She's very loyal to my father's memory."

He didn't intend to warn Sam off. But the attorney had to stop pining for Eloise. He was getting nowhere.

Sam was either in too deep to get the message, or he ignored it. "Time I got going." He stood. "Think about what I said, Adam. Think about how you might convince Casey to stick around."

THE PHONE RANG at eleven o'clock, interrupting Casey just as she neared the end of a chapter.

"Come and join me for lunch." There was no question as to whether she had the time or the inclination. Just a command, delivered in Adam's deep, sexy voice.

"Today?"

"We're dating," he reminded her. "This is what people who date do."

It wasn't something she'd ever done with Joe. Spontaneous lunch dates had never featured in their relationship.

"Be here at twelve."

"Did I ever tell you I prefer new-age guys?" she said. "The kind of guys who ask a woman what she'd like to do?"

"You might suggest something I don't want to do, and then I'd have to refuse," he said. "Just be here at twelve."

Adam hung up before she could argue. If she said too much more, he'd have second thoughts himself. When he'd suggested last night that they date, he'd planned to take her out for dinner Saturday. The housekeeper had the day off, and they had to eat.

He'd had no plans of lunching with Casey until Sam had said his piece about keeping this marriage going. Then a crazy impulse had made him pick up the phone.

Doesn't matter, he told himself. Whether he was just dating her for fun or they were going to make this marriage real, it made sense to start right away.

THEY SAT CLOSE to the riverbank in a secluded area of Ashburn Coppack Park that afforded a spectacular view of the downtown skyline.

"I can't believe you thought of this," Casey said. She grinned, then noticed his hesitation before he smiled back.

"I may be practical, but I'm not totally lacking imagination," he said.

She crossed one leg over the other. The movement drew Adam's gaze, as she knew it would, to the shortness of the light green linen skirt she'd chosen for just that reason, and which she'd teamed with an off-the-shoulder white cotton top. She'd spent half an hour trying on and discarding different outfits, and wanted to be sure he appreciated her final choice. "This is the perfect place for a picnic."

"Perfect," he agreed, his gaze still on her legs.

Casey couldn't quite believe how wholeheartedly Adam had thrown himself into this dating thing. Barely twelve hours after she'd consented to the idea, he'd conjured up a picnic—at least, his secretary had—and driven them to the park, insisting Casey should leave her car at his office.

Adam threw a piece of bread to a passing duck, then helped himself to more potato salad out of one of the deli containers. He could get used to this.

The food was delicious, the chilled bottle of white wine relaxing, and as for the company…

If there was one thing he would take from this month with Casey, Adam reflected, it was renewed pleasure in the simple things in life. Like picnics, sunsets and conversation. Over lunch, he and Casey had talked about everything and nothing, from the new family drama series about to debut on Channel Eight, to a plotting problem she was having in her book. They'd even digressed to a game that involved naming as many towns as they could think of on the Mississippi. He won. At least, he thought he had.

He looked at the potato salad on his plate and realized he wasn't the least bit hungry. He'd already had dessert, a slice of key lime pie. Going back for a second helping of potato salad was, as Casey would say in her quack psychoanalytic way, substitution.

He slid a sideways glance at her, lying on the blanket, eyes closed, face raised to the sun. Her hands were clasped behind her head, a pose that lifted her breasts against the thin cotton of her blouse and shortened that skirt even farther. Strands of silky hair fell over her arms and grazed the blanket. A smile hovered on her mouth.

As if sensing his scrutiny, Casey moistened her lips with her tongue. Adam swung his gaze back to the potato salad. Yep, right now, he was substituting potato salad for a taste of his wife's lips.

Think about how you might convince Casey to stick around, Sam had said.

The most obvious way to do that, Adam had decided, was to take their relationship to the next level. Sex. And, dammit, he hadn't been able to think about anything else since. Not that the idea hadn't occurred to him before Sam started dispensing his advice so freely. But back then, Adam had been able to slap it away as totally inappropriate. Now, it was as if Sam had given him permission to think about having Casey in his bed, about all the things he'd like to do to her there.

Not that he'd even decided he wanted her to stick around. He should probably discuss Sam's suggestion with her.

Trouble was, talking was the last thing on his mind now. The memory of the sweetness of her mouth was driving him crazy.

"Adam?" Casey propped herself up on her elbows, and the movement lifted her breasts even more. There was a languidness in her voice that he found infinitely seductive. "It's sweltering. Can you please pass the water bottle?"

He did as she asked, then stifled a groan as she tipped her head back and, eyes shut, drank greedily, so that a trickle of water escaped the side of her mouth to run down her chin and throat. He touched a finger there to stem the flow, and found her pulse beating.

Casey's eyes opened and he saw heat in their depths, which the water had done nothing to cool. Without looking away, she put the bottle down beside her. Adam slipped his hand around the back of her neck and pulled her up toward him, so their mouths were an inch apart.

He didn't rush into the kiss. He'd been here before and he knew how right it felt. Now that he had her so close, he wanted to savor every second. Her eyes fluttered shut again as his lips drifted against hers.

But the instant their mouths met he could think of nothing but how much he wanted her, and his intended gentleness evaporated. Casey's lips parted to welcome his tongue. She moaned as he deepened the kiss, and she struggled to pull herself upright so she could press herself closer to him.

The hunger in Adam had its epicenter in one obvious place. He moved a hand to cup a full, rounded breast. He felt the tensing of her body, and his mouth absorbed her sigh.

Her arms wound around his neck, and Adam slipped his other hand beneath her shirt to caress her back. He wanted nothing more than to tear every stitch of clothing off her and make love to her. Now.

Then some small corner of his mind remembered they were in a public place.

Home. If he could somehow convince his mouth to move away from hers, he would tell her to get in the car, so they could go home right away and continue this in private. Her protest when he finally managed to pull away almost destroyed the last shreds of his restraint.

"Let's go home," he croaked.

CHAPTER TEN

WORDLESSLY, THEY THREW the take-out containers, plates and food scraps into the picnic basket. The blanket was bundled in as well, then they were racing for the Aston Martin.

Adam kissed Casey again as they fumbled to do up their seat belts, a searing kiss intended to remind them both why were they were in such a hurry—not that he'd forgotten.

He hit the road for home, driving as fast as he dared.

Casey turned up the fan on her side. "If we go home now, we'll go to bed, right?"

Bed, floor, kitchen table… Adam realized with a shock he didn't mind where they did it. "Yep," he said. Had he ever wanted someone this badly?

"Which would mean we'd be sleeping together on our first date." She squirmed in her seat.

"Nope."

"No?"

"No sleeping," he said. "Definitely no sleeping."

She sucked in a breath. "The thing is," she said, "I don't do that on a first date."

Adam slowed for a red light ahead. He turned to her, saw her anxiously gnawing her lip. "You don't have a first-date routine," he reminded her.

"If I did, this wouldn't be in it," she insisted.

The light turned green and Adam accelerated the car, but without the same urgency.

"Would *you* normally do that on a first date?" she asked.

"We're married," he said. "I see you every day. Hell, I've probably seen more of you than I did the last six women I dated combined."

Casey stared out the window. "Joe is the only man I've slept with."

Yeah, and didn't Adam want to punch the guy.

"You're scared," he said.

"I need some time to get used to the idea."

"How much time?"

"How much time will you give me?"

He waited until he'd passed an old lady whose Toyota was weaving down the center of the road before he answered. "It's not about what I'll give you. It's about when you think you can decide what you want."

"Why don't you come over to my place for dinner tonight?"

Suddenly everything looked brighter again. "Second date," he said. "Great idea."

CASEY STARED UNSEEING at her computer keyboard, unable to connect with the words on the screen in front of her, the chapter she'd aimed to finish today.

The heat of that kiss in the park had seared through her, destroying her focus.

In her seven years with Joe, Casey had never known the overwhelming desire Adam had ignited in her today. She'd spent three weeks with him, and was ready to make love. To Casey that had to mean she was in danger of losing her heart to him.

Which wouldn't be a problem, if he lost his to her in return.

She tried to evaluate the odds of that happening. Adam wasn't a lose-his-heart kind of guy. But she knew she hadn't imagined the deeper connection between them. Maybe if they got closer, if they made love, they could move ahead emotionally.

Casey looked at her watch. Four o'clock. She'd promised to visit Eloise this afternoon. She would make it quick, then come home to prepare for an evening with Adam—when they would pick up where they'd left off at lunchtime. Her stomach fluttered.

AN UNFAMILIAR CAR was parked outside Eloise's front door when Casey arrived.

Eloise welcomed her inside. "Sam Magill is visiting," she said in a low, vexed voice. "He's just gone to the bathroom." She led Casey into a spacious living room, sunlit through a double set of French doors and dominated by a huge fireplace, above which hung an enormous gilded mirror. "He came to see if I need any help dead-heading my roses—though what he thinks I employ a gardener for, I don't know." She shook her head. "That man thinks I'm incapable of looking after myself. It's insulting."

Casey felt a surge of sympathy for the lovelorn lawyer. And a rush of resentment for the emotional independence that Eloise and Adam were so determined, each in their own way, to cling to.

"Most men as good-looking as Sam are too selfish to worry about other people," she told Eloise. "I'll bet he has a whole bunch of women after him."

Casey had noticed Eloise's friends eyeing him at lunch last weekend. Sam was tall, in good shape, with rugged features. And he was single, in an age group where men were in increasingly short supply.

Eloise stopped short. "Is Sam good-looking?" she asked, astounded.

"I'm told I am," Sam said from behind them.

Eloise gave a little scream. "Sam Magill, what are you doing, sneaking up like that? You should know better than…"

She trailed off as she looked at Sam—really looked at him—as if for the first time. She blinked, then blinked again. Color stole up her neck and over her face, and her hand fluttered at her chest.

It was obvious Sam didn't know how to react to the scrutiny of the woman he'd admired so long. He stood there in the middle of the living room, saying nothing, with all the eloquence of a sack of potatoes. Casey longed to give him a nudge, to tell him to jump in and ask Eloise on a date.

"Well." Her mother-in-law regained her senses and spoke briskly. "I daresay you're passably handsome. But that's neither here nor there." She turned toward the door in an unmistakable signal that the lawyer should leave. "I surely do appreciate your dropping in, Sam, but I'm fine and so are my roses."

He looked so downcast, Eloise gave him a reprieve. "Just one moment while I fetch you a jar of my pear preserves. I still do them myself every year."

That she hurried out of the room was interesting in itself, Casey reflected. Eloise considered hurrying unladylike.

Casey decided she didn't have time to pull any punches. "You're going about it the wrong way," she told Sam. "Eloise thinks you're interfering."

"I only want to help," he protested, once he got over his initial shock at her direct approach. "She's on her own and must need the occasional piece of advice. But every time I open my mouth…"

"You mess up because you're trying too hard," Casey said.

He moved over to the mantelpiece, stared down at the empty grate. "I just want to do something for her. To earn her…respect."

They both knew he wanted a whole lot more than

respect. Casey recognized the problem. Sam figured Eloise had to need him before she would fall for him.

"What Eloise *needs* is company, someone to share the ups and downs with," she said. "Then maybe, eventually, someone to love."

Sam looked doubtful.

"It's worth a try," Casey said awkwardly.

He harrumphed in a way that might have meant he would give it some thought, or that he didn't want to talk about it. His eyes met Casey's in the mirror above the fireplace. "While we're on the subject of who likes whom," he said, "you and Adam appear to be getting along."

She nodded.

"If you want to do something for him—" Sam turned to face her "—stay married to him."

Her heart raced. "Why do you say that?"

"If you two stay together, Adam won't need to challenge his father's will."

Casey licked her suddenly dry lips. "I don't think Adam wants to stay married to me." But that didn't stop her pulse from jumping, her breath going shallow. She heard the click of Eloise's heels out in the foyer and exhaled slowly.

Sam had heard Eloise, too, and he added in a rush, "He didn't sound opposed to it."

"You...you suggested this to Adam?"

Sam nodded.

"When was that?" *Please, let it be after lunch today.*

"This morning, right after we met with Anna May."

Eloise arrived with a large jar of pears, which Sam accepted with effusive thanks. He clutched it to his chest as if it were the key to Fort Knox. Eloise escorted him to the front door, giving Casey precious seconds to pull herself together.

Giving her time to face the cold, hard truth.

When Adam had started his seduction today, it had been with Sam's suggestion in mind.

She closed her eyes, sick to her stomach. Whatever that kiss had been about, it hadn't been as simple as him wanting her.

It never was.

ADAM LEFT THE OFFICE at five o'clock for the first time in years. Combined with his extended lunch hour, that made it the shortest working day he could remember.

Not short enough.

All afternoon he'd been able to think of nothing except Casey. He'd never been so preoccupied by a woman that his chief accountant had had to ask him a question three times.

It was worryingly reminiscent of his father and Eloise. But Adam figured he'd take the edge off his distraction as soon as he went to bed with Casey.

She wasn't home when he got there, and the place felt empty. He called Eloise, who told him Casey had just left. That meant another ten minutes. He busied himself setting the table for dinner, pouring wine, serving the meal the housekeeper had left.

When Casey finally arrived, he wanted to haul her into his arms and get started right then.

But this was supposed to be a date, and she'd made it clear she didn't want to be rushed. So instead, he kissed her briefly and said, "Dinner's ready."

At first, when she didn't say much through the meal, he figured it was because she was as distracted as he was. But gradually he noticed little details—the dip at the corners of her mouth, the shadow in her eyes.

Adam got a sinking feeling.

He didn't want to get into one of those emotional discussions. For what felt like the umpteenth time recently, he did something he didn't want to do. He ignored the warning bell in his head. "Is something wrong?" he asked.

She dropped her gaze, apparently intensely interested in her baked fish and scalloped potatoes. "I've been thinking about what we said this afternoon, and I don't think we should…you know."

"If you're worried this will affect our annulment, Sam found out the nonconsummation thing is mainly used in church annulments. Our case is based on the fact we didn't know it was a real marriage."

"Adam," she said, "Sam told me he talked to you about us staying married for real."

He put down his knife and fork. "I was going to talk to you about that."

"Before we made love, or after?"

"After I'd figured out whether I thought it was a good idea," he said. "It had nothing to do with you and me going to bed."

When she glared at him, he said, "Okay, maybe it did…speed things up a bit. But you know I wanted you before that. I wanted you the day I met you, though maybe I didn't acknowledge it then. I want you now."

Casey didn't know what to believe. What had he said to her the day they'd met? That people should know what they want and go after it. *He could at least pretend he cares.* She pulled herself up short. She'd said she didn't want to be loved just for what she could do for a man—the implied corollary being that she wanted to be loved for herself. But wasn't it equally true that if Adam wanted to ask something of her, he should do it honestly, without pretending it involved love?

"What did you decide…about Sam's suggestion?"

Adam shifted in his chair. "It has its pros and cons."

"Would you like to share those with me?"

"No," he said. "I'd like to go to bed with you."

He hadn't said *make love.*

"Very much," he added. When she didn't respond, he said, "More than I've ever wanted to before." He sounded surprised, yet about as excited as if he was discussing the scheduling of this week's TV movies. Maybe even less excited. Then he added, "I know you want the same thing."

"On…" Casey's voice came out raspy, so she cleared her throat and tried again, striving for the same detachment. "On one level, that's true." She saw the flare of triumph in his eyes. "But wanting it doesn't mean it's a good idea."

He pushed his chair back and stood, then walked around to her side of the table, his tread deliberate, intent. Casey was forced to lean back in her seat to meet his gaze. He loomed over her, searching her face with smoldering eyes, and the masculine heat that emanated from him scorched Casey's nerve endings. He hadn't touched her yet.

He rectified that by pulling her from her seat. Leaning against the edge of the table, he stationed her between his legs, facing him, his hard thighs around hers to keep her in place. His hands clasped her waist, not tightly, but with enough possessiveness to tell her he wouldn't readily let her go.

"I don't know if it's a good idea for us to stay married," he said, "but I do know this is a good idea."

He dipped his head, took her mouth with certitude. Beguiled by his tongue's provocative exploration, Casey lost the thread of her argument. She opened to his moist caress, felt a thick warmth spread through her, deadening any senses that weren't employed in touching and tasting Adam.

He flicked the buttons of her shirt undone, parted it to reveal her breasts, full and aching in her lacy bra. His eyes darkened, and when he lowered his mouth there, she thought her legs might collapse from under her. She leaned into him, felt his unmistakable hardness, and clutched at his hair.

"Sweetheart," he breathed, as his hands moved to the zipper of her skirt.

For the briefest instant, she reveled in the endearment. Then the voice of reason whispered, *He doesn't mean it.*

Casey wanted to scream, to drown out the thought. But she couldn't ignore it. She tugged on Adam's hair, lifting his head so she could see his eyes. "Stop," she said.

To her surprise, the word came out with sufficient authority that Adam did stop. He straightened, put some space between them as Casey did up the buttons of her blouse, trying to ignore the scrape of her fingers against the oversensitized skin of her breasts.

"I'm not going to make love to you," she said. "It'll complicate everything and I won't be able to decide what I want. You know that, and you're using sex to manipulate me."

His eyes darkened again, this time with anger.

"I'm not like your family or your boyfriend. I want you, you want me—it can be that simple, if you'll let it."

She folded her arms. "I'm not a pushover anymore."

For a long moment, he stared at her. Then he grasped her by the shoulders, planted a swift, hard kiss on her mouth. "I'll wait."

CHAPTER ELEVEN

"You know, my dear, I had quite given up on Adam marrying until you came along." Eloise stirred sugar into her coffee, then tossed the spoon with practiced ease across the kitchen to land in the sink.

When she'd first tried that maneuver a couple of weeks earlier, the spoon had hit the window behind the sink and cracked it. Since then, she'd taken to calling in on Casey most days, and now, by the start of the fourth week of their friendship, her aim had improved remarkably.

Casey smiled, managing not to cringe at the reference to marriage, and continued preparing the seafood salad. It was the housekeeper's day off. Adam had suggested they dine out, but Casey had declined. He hadn't called it a date, but she suspected it was part of his campaign to get her into bed. As far as she was concerned, all dates were off. As extra insurance against temptation, she'd invited Eloise for dinner on several occasions, tonight included.

"Now, Eloise," she chided the older woman. "You

hadn't given up at all. I know all about your bride-fest."

Eloise chortled. "Adam used that awful word just to annoy me."

"Are you saying you weren't trying to find him a wife?"

Eloise almost succeeded in looking insulted. "Not at all." At Casey's snort she added, "All right, I introduced him to various young women I thought I could tolerate as a daughter-in-law. I just wanted him to know the happiness I once did. But I knew it would take a miracle." Her eyes misted. "And then you came along."

Uncomfortable, Casey turned the conversation back to Eloise. "Were you very much in love with Adam's father?"

The older woman's face lit up. "Oh, yes. I miss James every day, but I thank God for the time we had. We'd only been married six years when he had that heart attack, and then a stroke right after." She shuddered. "We were in bed—just reading, my dear," she assured Casey, who really didn't want to know.

"Next minute, I was dialing 911, and the ambulance crew was saying I was lucky I hadn't lost him already."

"So he died that night?" Casey asked.

Eloise shook her head. "He recovered, quite well. The stroke slowed his speech, and he couldn't move his right side much, but they ran all kinds of scans and tests, which showed no damage to anything that mattered. I thought I'd be taking him home with me in a few days' time."

"Then what?" Casey asked, though the weight of grief in Eloise's voice gave her the answer.

"A week later, he had another heart attack." Eloise dabbed a handkerchief to her eyes. "We only had those few years together, but, my, they were wonderful. Every one of them was worth a decade with an ordinary man."

"Do you think you'll ever marry again?" Casey asked. If Sam could only stop making a fool of himself every time he got near Eloise, he might be a good match for her, with his old-world manners and his obvious desire to cherish her.

Eloise shook her head. "I was forty-two when I married James, a spinster and perfectly happy that way. I don't believe the man exists who could measure up to him, and I'm not prepared to settle for less."

"Good for you." Casey meant it. She could learn something from Eloise about not settling. Still, she decided to have one last try at advancing Sam's cause. "Eloise, I know you have lots of friends and you're busy. But sometimes I catch something in your face…. You look lonely."

Eloise read Casey's concern, and it warmed her. Her daughter-in-law was such a sweet thing—Eloise hoped Adam knew how lucky he was. She suspected he didn't. Not yet. Whatever the truth behind Casey's and Adam's marriage, it wasn't what the world saw. But a boy as smart as Adam would eventually realize he'd chosen the right bride, and would do what he needed to make the marriage work.

"I won't say I don't get lonely," she told Casey. "Of course I do. But what I had with James… I can't replace that."

"Was he the possessive type?"

Eloise shook her head. "He didn't need to be. I never had eyes for anyone else."

"I wondered," Casey said, "if you thought maybe he wouldn't want you to find someone else."

"My dear, it's not him, it's me," Eloise said, hastening to quash any implication that James might have been less than the generous, loving man he was. "I'm just…better on my own."

Though if that was so, why on earth had that stuffy Sam been occupying her thoughts to such an alarming extent, ever since she'd taken a look at him last week and realized Casey was right? The man was handsome. Very handsome. She should have noticed that before. Then it wouldn't be bothering her the way it did now.

Eloise fanned her face against a sudden heat that had nothing to do with the late afternoon sun streaming into the kitchen. She was behaving like a silly girl whose head had been turned by a dash of male attention. So what if Sam liked her, in a way that was annoyingly, yet quite endearingly, inept? He wasn't James.

James isn't here.

Eloise tamped down the traitorous thought. She loved James and always would.

"The thing about Sam," she said to Casey, "is he acts as if I do everything wrong. If I ever wanted another man, which I don't, I'd want someone who wants to love me, not to improve me or organize me. Someone who wants what I have to offer. Which is love. Only love." She smiled at her daughter-in-law. "Really, what could be better than that?"

Casey didn't know how to answer. In her experience, few people wanted only love. They wanted love plus housekeeping. Love plus babysitting.

Never just love.

Sometimes not even love.

Eloise's face softened. "I do wish we'd had longer, so James and Adam could have reconciled. Adam blamed James for his mother's death, you know."

Casey tipped the tomato she'd just chopped into the salad bowl. "He says his father changed when he met you."

Eloise nodded. "After I met him, James was ashamed of the way he'd behaved toward his family. His own parents were cold and distant, and he married Adam's mother for the worst of reasons— her family's money—and made no secret of it. By his own admission, he was a lousy husband, and a poor father to Adam."

"It must have been hard for Adam, to see his father so loving toward you."

"So you've noticed I'm not Adam's favorite person?" Eloise laughed at Casey's stricken expression. "My dear, you can understand where he's coming from. I didn't find out about the financial mess James was in until he died, so Adam must have thought me utterly profligate. He was probably right. He wouldn't touch a penny of his father's life insurance to rebuild the business. He said I'd need that for myself. There I was, living the life I'd always lived, while that boy worked like a dog to rescue Carmichael Broadcasting from a disaster he blames me for."

"It wasn't your fault." Casey whisked balsamic vinegar in a jug, together with some olive oil.

"Adam felt betrayed," Eloise said gently. She slid the salt and pepper across the island to Casey. "James taught him that the business came first, that family was a distant second. Then, just as Adam finally had the chance to get close to his father at work, James changed the rules on him.

"Then he made that foolish will, which meant Adam ended up more annoyed than grieved when his dad died. I tried to convince James to change the will after his stroke, but he refused.

"But then you came along," Eloise said briskly. She drank the last of her coffee. "And dear Adam will have the happiness he deserves."

"Adam and I… It's early days. We're still getting to know each other." Maybe Casey could prepare

Eloise for the blow she would suffer when the annulment came through.

"Of course you are, my dear. It must be so exciting. But one only has to look at the two of you together to see how right you are." Tears glistened in her eyes, and she blew her nose delicately. "I'll just wash my hands, dear."

When Casey heard the kitchen door open a minute later, she assumed Eloise had returned. Without turning around, she said, "How do you know when two people are right together?"

"When wanting the other person keeps you awake at night," Adam said.

Casey squawked and spun around. "When did you come in?"

"Just now." He walked up to her, so close he could kiss her, but he didn't. "How long have you been talking to yourself? You know that's a sign you're not getting enough sleep."

"Wanting you does not keep me awake at night," she said, as crushingly as she could.

"You mean you've been stockpiling sleep?" he asked. "In that case, why not spend tonight with me? We can stay awake all night long."

He put his hands on her waist, closed the gap between them. His eyes blazed down at her.

"I won't be in your bed," she said. "Other than in your dreams."

"Hmm, let me show you how my dreams start."

He kissed her, long and hard, until she opened her mouth to him. He walked her to the counter, deepening the kiss so that her head dropped back, revealing her throat. With a murmur of appreciation he left her mouth and started kissing her neck.

"Ahem," Eloise said from the doorway.

Adam cursed and sprang away from Casey. "What's she doing here?" He obviously realized that sounded rude even for him, and said, "Sorry, Eloise, you startled me."

"Evidently," she told him serenely. "Casey invited me to stay for dinner. But if you two would rather be alone…"

"No," Casey said quickly. "We want you to stay. I thought after dinner we could…play Monopoly."

"If that's what you'd like, dear," Eloise said. "Though Monopoly does take rather a long time."

"Does it?" Casey asked.

"Enthralling though that sounds," Adam said, "I need to go back to the office after dinner."

"I'll stay and keep you company then," Eloise offered happily. She reached for Casey's hand, squeezed it. "Truly, dear, getting to know you has been a wonderful treat. It seems odd to say this when I've known you such a short time, but already I love you like a daughter."

Casey returned Eloise's impulsive hug, because she couldn't look her in the eye.

Eloise was offering the no-strings love Casey had

always wanted. A gift she couldn't accept, because she was an impostor.

Behind Eloise, Casey saw Adam's startled recognition of what his stepmother was offering…and something that looked very much like envy.

ADAM COULDN'T EXPLAIN his somber mood next morning. All he knew was that touching scene between Casey and Eloise had left him feeling as if he was missing out on something. He didn't want to think about what that was.

"Is anything wrong?" he asked Casey, in an attempt to get out of his own head. She looked about as cheerful as he felt.

She put down her cup of tea. "Adam, I don't know how to tell you this."

For one awful moment he feared something might have happened to Eloise. "What is it?"

"Sue—the housekeeper. She called last night after you went back to work. She quit."

Relief washed over him. He looked at Casey, rubbed his chin.

"Say something," she demanded.

"You must be doing something right."

"Right? How do you mean?"

"As I recall, Mrs. Lowe lasted approximately forty-eight hours after you moved in. Sue lasted, what—two weeks? That's a huge improvement."

Casey smiled reluctantly. "It's not funny, Adam.

I have no idea why she left. I'm starting to thin
it's me."

"No way, darling," he teased her. "I distinctly
recall you telling me you've never upset anyone in
your life. Right before Mrs. Lowe left, I think it was."

She huffed in protest, and suddenly he was
smiling again. It felt good to have a problem as trivial
as who would take care of the house.

THURSDAY HAD A RED CIRCLE around it on the
calendar in Adam's kitchen. It was the first round of
the court battle with Anna May and Henry. Today,
Anna May hoped to convince a judge that enough
evidence of James Carmichael's mental incompe-
tence existed that the case deserved a full hearing.

Casey cooked eggs and bacon for Adam's breakfast, wishing there was something she could do to
ensure that Anna May's farcical motion never got
beyond today's preliminary hearing. Eloise was
dreading the media coverage, and Adam didn't need
this on top of everything else.

He ate his breakfast in silence, then gathered up
his briefcase and cell phone. "I'll call and let you
know how it goes."

Casey stood. "Good luck." And before she could
question the wisdom of it—before Adam could back
away—she grabbed hold of his lapels and leaned in
to kiss him.

It was meant to be a brief peck. But she ought to

know by now that a quick taste of Adam's mouth was never enough. She moved closer, all but plastered herself to the length of him, and parted her lips.

Adam got the hint. His tongue claimed hers and he dragged her close, and Casey relished the weight of him pressing against her.

When he broke away, he kept ahold of her shoulders. "Thanks. I feel a lot better."

The intense heat in his eyes unnerved her. "That was for luck," she joked. "They call me Lucky Lips."

With his thumb, he traced the outline of her mouth, sending an erotic message straight to her core.

"Whoever 'they' are," he said, "I hope they know I'm the only man entitled to these lips."

For now.

He didn't say those words and neither did Casey. But they hung between them like neon lights, illuminating the tenderness of the moment and revealing it to be false.

Casey stepped out of his embrace. "I'll go see Eloise while you're in court." Adam had asked his stepmother not to attend the hearing, and she'd gladly agreed. Casey wouldn't go either, since, as Adam's bride, she was a sore reminder to Anna May that Adam had fulfilled the will's conditions.

As she drove to Eloise's, Casey fretted over how the older woman must feel. She'd been through so much. To finally meet her soul mate, then to have him suffer a heart attack and a stroke just a few years later... And just when Eloise had thought James might recover, he'd—

"That's it!" Casey thumped her car's ancient steering wheel in excitement. Eloise had mentioned all those tests James had undergone after his stroke. *They must have included tests on his brain.*

Casey pulled out her cell phone and called her stepmother-in-law. A car honked behind her—not because the driver thought she was sexy, but because she'd strayed into the next lane. Casey got the Fiesta under control while she waited for Eloise to answer.

Eloise caught on fast to her garbled questioning. She promised to have the information Casey needed by the time she arrived. Next, Casey phoned Adam. But his cell phone was switched off. So was Sam's. She would have to go to the courthouse.

Fifteen minutes later, Eloise had made two calls to the hospital that had treated James, and one to her late husband's lawyer. The news was all good. She insisted on coming with Casey to the courthouse. "I'll park the car, dear, while you run in."

The hearing was scheduled for ten o'clock. Technically, it wouldn't matter if they were late, but Casey wanted to stop it before it even started. She wanted there to be no public mention of James Carmichael being unhinged.

They made it with ten minutes to spare. Eloise gamely took over the controls of the Fiesta, while

Casey raced inside. She found Adam with Sam Magill outside courtroom number one. Across the hall, Anna May and Henry waited with all three of their lawyers.

Adam's eyebrows shot up when he saw her. "I thought we said…"

Casey was tempted to shout out that she had evidence Adam's dad wasn't crazy. But it occurred to her that some of the people milling around the hallway were likely journalists who'd enjoy provoking a discussion about the sanity of one of Memphis's benefactors. So she pulled Adam and a bemused Sam into a huddle.

She told them how Eloise had called the psychiatrist who'd tested James after his stroke, and how the man was certain James was fully competent.

"We knew that," Sam said. "What matters is James's state of mind when he wrote his will."

Casey delivered her pièce de résistance. "Eloise told me that after the stroke, she asked James to change his will. He had his lawyer bring it in so he could review it. In the end, he decided he was happy with it as it was. Thanks to the psychiatric tests he'd just had, we know the will reflects the thinking of a sane man."

"We do," Sam agreed, surprised but pleased. "But surely if we knew this…"

"Eloise forgot about James reviewing the will until she mentioned it to me on Monday," Casey said, "and even then she didn't make the link between that and the psych tests."

Adam grabbed Casey by the upper arms. "You," he said, "are incredible." Then he kissed her, right there. Not quite the bone-shaking kiss they'd shared this morning, but with enough heat to cause Henry to clear his throat across the hall.

By the time they surfaced for air, Sam was in close discussions with the other side's legal team and Eloise was strolling through the courthouse doors with a spring in her step more suited to a garden party.

Five minutes later, a triumphant Sam announced that Anna May had conceded Casey's evidence out-weighed anything she could present to the judge today. The hearing would be cancelled. Even Anna May's threat that they hadn't heard the last of this couldn't dampen their triumph.

"That's marvelous, Sam," Eloise said, laying a palm on his arm. When she realized what she'd done, her eyes widened. But before she could whip her hand away, Sam covered it with his own.

"How about we adjourn to the café next door for a celebratory coffee?" he said. "Maybe even one with caffeine, Eloise, if your blood pressure is up to it."

She stiffened, and Casey braced herself for the usual retort that would singe Sam's ego. But for once, he appeared to have realized exactly how he sounded, for he darted a look of apology at Eloise.

"On second thought, I bow to your superior knowl-edge in these matters. You choose."

It was obvious Eloise liked that. A smile played at the corners of her mouth.

"Coffee, my foot," she said. "It's gone ten o'clock. This calls for champagne."

To his credit, Sam refrained from expressing any concern about the state of Eloise's liver, or about the wisdom of buying champagne when an American sparkling wine would be better value for money. Instead he bowed, a gesture made awkward by the fact that he wouldn't relinquish his grip on Eloise's hand, and escorted her out the door.

Adam tucked Casey's hand through his own arm as they left the building. "Thanks," he said. "What you did today went way beyond our agreement. I owe you."

CHAPTER TWELVE

WHEN THE PHONE RANG at some unearthly hour on Saturday morning, Casey pulled her pillow over her head to block out the noise.

But Adam's shout pierced her feather-and-cotton shelter. He thumped on the door of her bedroom, and before she could tell him to wait, in he stormed.

He was brandishing the morning newspaper. "Eloise called to say we should take a look at this."

Casey sat up in bed and tried to ignore the fact that his white terry-cloth robe hung open to reveal his bare chest—a frankly yummy chest, its muscled firmness accentuated by just the right amount of dark, curling hair—and black boxers sitting snugly on his hips.

She wasn't doing a very good job of ignoring it— he had to clear his throat to get her attention. The appreciation wasn't all one-sided, Casey realized as she followed the direction of his gaze and looked down at her nightdress. The thin straps had slipped off her shoulders, and the way she was leaning forward didn't leave anything to the imagination.

Casey grimaced and tugged her nightie back into place before she took the paper and read the headline: TV Couple's Wedding a Sham.

"Oh no!" A wedding photo—of her and Adam kissing—had pride of place on the front page. Around it were smaller photos of the two of them, taken, if she wasn't wrong, right here in this house. "How did they—?" The photo at the bottom answered the question. It was their erstwhile house-keeper, Sue Mason. Only the picture was captioned, "Sue O'Connor, undercover journalist."

"How bad is it?" Casey couldn't bear to read the words that laid open their private lives—their private *lies*—to the world.

"About what you'd expect." Adam scanned the article for what he presumably considered a choice extract, and read aloud. "'Adam and Casey Carmichael, a doting couple in the public eye, sleep in separate bedrooms and seldom exchange more than the merest courtesies.'"

"That's not true," Casey protested. "I mean, the bedroom part is, but how dare she say you're courteous?"

"Do you think this is funny?" he said.

She shook her head. "If I don't laugh, I'll cry." Her voice cracked on the last word. She squeezed her eyes shut, picturing her family reading this stuff and knowing the truth.

"It's not all bad," Adam soothed her. "Listen to this. 'Casey Carmichael is a kind and considerate employer, who always has a smile on her face. But one senses that beneath the vibrant facade—'" He stopped.

"What does it say?"

"Uh, nothing, it's just—"

Casey snatched the newspaper from him and quickly found where he'd left off. "'One senses that beneath the vibrant facade is a woman hurt by her husband's indifference.'" She stared at Adam. "I don't know if that's worse for me or for you."

"For you," he said immediately. "It makes you sound pathetic."

"It makes you sound nasty," she pointed out. "I'd rather be pathetic than nasty."

"But any self-respecting man would rather be nasty than pathetic."

"That explains a lot," she muttered. She pushed her quilt aside and climbed out of bed. On the way to fetch her robe, she detoured to the window to open the shutters.

"Casey, don't." Adam rushed to stop her, but it was too late.

She froze. Adam must have left the gates open last night because the front garden was a seething mass of journalists. When the crowd saw her and Adam at the window, the photographers raised their cameras and began snapping away.

BY BREAKFAST TIME Sunday, Adam was starting to feel as if they were on a rerun of their honeymoon. Only this time around, even though they had a whole house to share, being shut in with Casey was even greater torment.

He sighed. Was it too much to hope that something more newsworthy had happened in Memphis overnight to drag the media away from his front yard?

He turned from the toaster to ask, "How are the headlines today?"

Casey read from the front page of the Sunday paper. "'Love or Lies? Carmichaels in hiding.'" She showed him the picture—of her in her nightgown, openmouthed at the bedroom window, with Adam behind her, his expression dark. "This paper claims the other guys got it wrong, judging by the fact that we appeared at the same window together, half-clothed."

"They just wish they'd thought of coming in undercover themselves." Adam took the opportunity to inhale Casey's fresh, morning fragrance as he stepped closer to scan the article. He grimaced at the rampant speculations it contained. "I wish these people had something better to do. We need a real disaster the press can focus on, something else to fill the front pages."

"Earthquake? Political assassination?" Casey suggested helpfully.

"I didn't say I wanted anyone to die. Some fraudster conning old ladies out of their fortunes would do. He could start with Eloise."

"Adam! You don't want that to happen. You know you'd feel obliged to come to her rescue."

"Very funny." Not only would he feel obliged to help Eloise, these days he'd actually want to. Adam turned back to the toaster. "How do you like your toast?"

"Toasted," Casey said.

"What does that mean?"

"It means however it comes. How many ways are there to have toast?"

"There's well done, medium and light," he said. "But pardon me for asking."

He gathered from her humph that she'd never heard such a dumb question. That's what a guy got when he tried to be considerate. Life was so much easier before he'd started...liking Casey.

"We need a strategy," he said.

"Are you still talking about toast?" she asked ominously.

"I'm talking about proving our marriage is genuine."

"You can't prove something that's not true," she objected.

"If you think I'm going to let all of Memphis believe I'm not capable of making my wife happy—"

"Didn't you say it's cool to be nasty?"

"I said it's better than being pathetic. But if they're going to imply it's my fault you and I aren't sleeping together…"

She laughed out loud. "This all comes down to your masculine pride. Memphis's most eligible bachelor, unable to please his wife."

Show Adam the man who wouldn't take that as a challenge, and he'd show you someone truly pathetic. And they'd already established that wasn't him.

He advanced on her.

"Adam, put that knife down," Casey warned him, a wicked look in her eyes. He realized he was still carrying the butter-smeared implement, and tossed it onto the counter. She stepped backward, but soon came up against the fridge.

Adam put a hand on either side of her, effectively pinning her in position.

"I'll scream," she said. "The journalists outside will hear."

"I locked the gates last night," he reminded her. "There's no one here but you and your nasty husband."

He cut off her next words by pressing his mouth to hers. There was a moment of muffled protest, then the familiar heat rose between them and Casey was returning his kisses as fast as he could supply them. The tautness of her breasts through the thin cotton of her sundress, pressing against his chest, reminded

Adam of that first day they'd met, when she'd run right into him.

She pulled away, but not before he'd completed a thorough exploration of her mouth. "Okay," she gasped. "I'll put out a statement to the media saying you're quite capable of satisfying me."

"But you don't know that," he said. "In fact, this whole thing with the housekeeper is your fault. If we'd been sleeping together—as I suggested," he pointed out virtuously, "she wouldn't have had any ammunition for her article."

"I'm not going to sleep with you just in case every housekeeper we hire turns out to be a spy."

"So much for your dedication to our cause," he said. "Let's get back to my strategy, since I at least am willing to prevent our good work so far from being ruined. I think Eloise is okay about these stories. I told her we were in separate bedrooms while the journalist was here because you moved out of our room in a fit of paranoid jealousy over one of my past relationships."

Casey squealed in outrage. "You and your ego. Why couldn't you be the one who was jealous about me?"

"Eloise knows I'm not the jealous type," he said smugly. "Let's not split hairs. We need to ramp up our marriage for everyone else to see."

"Ramp it up," she echoed.

"There's a charity gala on Thursday night," he

said. "I'm one of the patrons, so I'll be conspicuous. If you go with me, we'll both be conspicuous." She looked puzzled. "We'll be conspicuously happy."

"Okay…" she said doubtfully.

"And we'll invite your family to stay next weekend."

Casey groaned, knowing he was right. "I guess we should. Dad sounded suspicious about that article when he called yesterday, and I think he and Karen are making progress on getting their lives together. I wouldn't want to derail that."

She was struck with a brain wave. "How about we invite your family—all the stockholders in Carmichael Broadcasting—for lunch next Sunday?"

Adam looked less than enthusiastic about having to see his relatives on a weekend, but Casey persisted. "It can't hurt to mend some fences, Adam. Whatever the outcome of this court battle, you'll still have to work with Henry and Anna May. And if I introduce your family to mine, my folks will be even more convinced."

"That's not a bad idea," he conceded. "Maybe a barbecue. We can keep it casual."

"Sounds good."

"There's one more thing," Adam said. "We'll be sharing a room when your family is here. Don't you think it's time you and I made love?"

It was the first time he'd referred to it as "love," instead of sex or sleeping together. Casey sagged into her seat, put a hand to her stomach as if she could push down the heat that had pooled there. "Absolutely not," she managed to reply.

"It's going to happen, Casey," he said. "Start counting down."

ADAM HAD FLAT-OUT IGNORED Casey when she insisted she would buy her own clothes for the charity gala, and had sent Eloise to shepherd her around the best Memphis boutiques in search of the perfect dress. And what a dress it was.

The halter neckline of the lime-green satin gown flattered her bosom, the ankle-length slim skirt hugged her hips, and high-heeled black sandals gave her a seductive sway when she walked.

Not that Casey would be seducing anyone tonight, she told her reflection. But she wanted to look as if she was at least capable of seducing her husband. Adam's wasn't the only ego to have taken a hit with Saturday's newspaper article.

"You look great," Adam said when she met him downstairs. "How about you wear that on Saturday night?"

"Why on Saturday?"

"When we make love," he said, "I want to take that dress off you."

Her face flamed. "I told you, we are not going to make love."

He tsked. "Are you sure you're a pushover?" he said. "Because I'm not seeing it."

Casey beamed. He couldn't have paid her a nicer compliment.

Determined to defeat the gossipmongers, she held her head high and her husband's arm tight as she and Adam entered the restaurant for the gala.

There were probably a hundred and fifty people there, and Adam had to talk with many of them. Casey looked around for Eloise and found her in the middle of a group of elegantly dressed women.

"Casey, my dear." Eloise kissed her cheek, then introduced her to the others. It seemed Casey had interrupted a discussion about a controversial painting by Memphis artist Kevin Mallory, which had won a national award.

"It's gobbledygook," one woman said. "A mish-mash of colors, lines that go nowhere…what's it supposed to be?"

"It *is* mystifying," Eloise agreed. "But I find it not so much gobbledygook as—"

"Intriguing," said Sam Magill from behind her, once again startling Eloise. The women willingly widened their circle to include this unattached male. "I can't say I get what Mallory's trying to do, but you look at those colors—the depth—and it takes your breath away."

Sam had the women's rapt attention. He did look rather dashing, Eloise conceded, in a tuxedo that emphasized that he'd kept his shape. Really, some of those ladies were too silly, fluttering their eyelashes, flashing coy smiles that would have been more appropriate at a high school prom.

Eloise inched closer to him, in case the women were making him uncomfortable. But Sam didn't seem to mind the attention. He gave his views politely, allowed others to express theirs uninterrupted. That look of intelligent interest in his gray eyes was rather appealing....

Sam turned and caught her staring at him. His eyebrows rose a fraction. Eloise stepped away, and the movement drew his gaze to her new, high-heeled black sandals, which she knew flattered her ankles.

Sam's eyes lingered there a moment, then he said, "As always, you have excellent taste in shoes, Eloise."

She put her hands to her cheeks to cool the heat she could feel there, then turned to Casey. "My dear, you must let me introduce you to one of my dearest friends. Just over there..."

Casey managed to suppress a smile, but couldn't help shooting a look of encouragement at Sam as she was led away.

They hadn't gone far when Eloise stopped and gazed around the room.

"One of your dearest friends?" Casey prompted her.

Eloise blushed. "Perhaps I was mistaken. I don't see her now."

"We could go back to the others," Casey teased her.

"There's Adam's friend Dave Dubois, let's go and chat with him."

It was the first time Casey had seen Dave since he'd officiated at her wedding. She knew Adam had confided in him about the true state of their marriage, but he greeted her like an old friend, with an enthusiastic kiss on the cheek. Eloise got the same treatment. The older woman laughed, patted his hand, then had to excuse herself when someone summoned her.

"You look radiant," Dave told Casey, all extravagant charm.

"That sounded almost as convincing as your marriage celebrant impersonation."

He wagged a finger at her. "That was no impersonation, Mrs. Carmichael, and you have the husband to prove it."

"Thanks," she said dryly.

Dave inclined his head toward Adam, talking with the mayor of Memphis on the other side of the room. "He's more relaxed than I've seen him in a long time. I'd say marriage agrees with him."

Casey assessed Adam as objectively as she could. Dave was right. He smiled more these days, and he seemed less unyielding. "Maybe," she said.

"Does it suit you equally well?"

She laughed at his blatant nosiness. "It suits both of us for a time."

"I don't know that you should be too hasty about

ending it," he said. "Marrying you two…I couldn't have done better if I'd planned the whole thing."

"You didn't know that ceremony was for real, did you?" she demanded.

"No idea," he said. "But I've looked into it since—turns out, as an ex-commissioner, I can do all kinds of weird things."

Casey sipped her wine. "Can you issue annulments?"

"Uh, no." He shrugged in apology. "But if you want a permit to keep an alligator in your backyard…"

"Really?" She shuddered.

"Maybe I read that one wrong." Dave grinned. "It's mainly pretty boring stuff."

"Are you talking about a conversation with you?" Adam found the small of Casey's back, applied a pressure with his hand that moved her closer to him.

"I'm talking about what it must be like being married to you." Dave punched him lightly on the shoulder.

"Is marriage to me boring stuff?" Adam asked Casey.

The heat of his palm branded her back through the thin fabric of her dress. Somehow she'd moved even closer to him. If she stood on tiptoe her lips would brush his chin.

"Actually," she said, "it's kind of interesting."

For a moment, everything seemed suspended…

her breathing, the chatter around them, the music…
everything except the deepening intensity in Adam's
eyes.

"If you guys don't quit ogling each other, I'm
going to think there's more to this marriage than you
both claim," Dave said.

Adam let go of Casey. "You'd be wrong." He
glanced at his watch. "They'll be starting the
speeches soon, I need to find out when I'm on."

He left, and Casey excused herself a minute later.

As the evening wore on, she found most people
were interested to meet the woman who'd married
Adam Carmichael on TV, but they were polite
enough to keep a rein on their curiosity. Except for
one man around her own age she could have sworn
was flirting with her. He looked vaguely familiar….
Where had she seen him before?

She'd been fending off his advances for nearly ten
minutes when he said, "I guess congratulations are
in order. Maybe a Happy Anniversary?"

"Excuse me?"

"You've been married over a month now,
haven't you?"

It was true. She and Adam had been married for
a month. Which meant any day now, the annulment
would come through.

The stranger's words triggered the memory of
where she'd seen him—below her bedroom window
at seven o'clock on Saturday morning. This slug was

a journalist. Casey struggled to keep her dawning realization from showing on her face. How could she use the knowledge to her advantage?

As it turned out, he handed her the opportunity on a plate. With what looked like deep concern, he expressed sympathy about the press coverage she and Adam had been subjected to.

She nodded gravely. "It was awful." She let a tremor enter her voice. "And all of it lies."

"Really?" He could barely contain his eagerness. "So you and Adam are, uh, a proper couple?"

With a naughty smile she said, "I don't know about proper." She leaned forward confidingly, and he did the same. "You've heard of spontaneous combustion?"

He nodded.

"Adam and I—we're like that." She winked, just to be sure he couldn't mistake her implication.

CHAPTER THIRTEEN

ADAM BROUGHT THE MAIL in with the newspaper at breakfast next morning.

He opened a lilac envelope without a stamp, hand-addressed to "Mr. and Mrs. A. Carmichael," and scanned the contents.

"Casey," he said silkily.

She looked up from her cereal. "Uh-huh?"

"This note is from Mr. and Mrs. Bob Harvey, saying they'll be delighted to attend lunch here on Tuesday…. Tell me it's come to the wrong address."

"Uh, not exactly," she said around a mouthful of cornflakes.

He scowled. "I distinctly remember telling you our marriage would be over if you invited the neighbors here."

"They brought flowers after those awful newspaper reports," she said. "This lunch is to thank them for their support. You'll be at work. You don't have to get involved."

"And it's just Mr. and Mrs. Harvey?" he asked suspiciously.

"Uh, I invited Alison Dare on the other side as well, with her three preschoolers. She and the Harveys don't know each other, but her kids don't have any grandparents, so I thought…"

With a snort of disbelief, he opened the newspaper and held it in front of his face. It was a milder response than Casey had expected. Relieved, she returned to her breakfast.

"What the—" He lowered the paper to gape at her. "Have you seen the headline on page five?"

"How could I when you're the one with the paper?" she demanded reasonably.

He turned it around for her to read, Casey Carmichael: My Husband's Hot. "Did you really say that?"

"Of course not. I told him *I* was hot." How could that idiot journalist have got the angle so wrong? And since when did she and Adam only rate as page five news? "Typical man, giving you the credit for any heat that's going."

"Entirely justified," he assured her. "As you'll find out very, very soon."

"I will not." Had he heard the waver in her voice?

On Saturday morning, Adam proudly surveyed the Aston Martin's dazzling red bodywork. It was time consuming, but he still preferred to polish the car himself.

He just hoped he could do as good a job of convincing Casey's family to relinquish their demands on her. She owed it to herself to finish her book.

The other night, he'd asked if he could read some of her work.

"Writers don't let people read their stuff," she said. Then she handed him her almost completed manuscript.

Although Adam's teenage years were a distant blur, he was pretty sure he hadn't read anything this good back then. Casey had managed to capture teenage angst and put a comic spin on it. Adam figured her book might achieve the near impossible—getting young people not to take themselves so seriously.

He'd considered her novel-writing a silly dream. But Casey seemed to have a knack for making dreams come true.

When he heard the crunching of tires on gravel around the front of the house, Adam went inside and joined Casey at the front door to greet her relatives.

"Let's lay it on thick," he murmured in her ear—and got a jolt of pleasure at the wicked look in her eyes.

But they were only briefly arm in arm, presenting a united front. Then Casey rushed forward to take the baby, car seat and all, from Karen.

"Let me," she said.

Adam rolled his eyes and stepped forward. "Darling, that looks far too heavy for you," he said solicitously. He took the car seat from her and gazed down at Casey's niece.

"Isn't she gorgeous?" Casey demanded.

A far as Adam could tell, this was a pretty ordinary baby—red in the face, with a trail of drool at one corner of its mouth. He'd bet any daughter of Casey's would be far prettier. *Not that I care what Casey's babies might look like.*

"Gorgeous," he agreed with complete equanimity. He juggled the baby seat to shake hands with Casey's father, Ed, who in turn had to juggle the cane he was using to walk. Next, Adam kissed Karen on her cheek. Mike hadn't come, but since he wasn't the target of this campaign, that didn't matter.

When they got everyone inside, Adam had to forcibly restrain Casey from trying to simultaneously carry all the bags upstairs, make coffee and feed the baby its bottle. No wonder her family never did anything for themselves. He sent Casey and the others to the living room, put the kettle on the stove and took the suitcases himself.

He stowed Ed's in a downstairs bedroom, since the older man might have a problem climbing stairs. Karen's bag, along with the portable crib and a mini-Everest of baby gear, went in what was normally Casey's room. Leaving it there reminded Adam that he and Casey would be sharing a bed tonight. Not that he'd forgotten.

Tonight, he wouldn't take no for an answer.

Actually, he knew damn well that he would. Somehow Casey had ended up calling the shots on this sex thing. She was in control, and Adam hated it.

Yet somehow, he couldn't get mad about it.

Back in the living room, he walked right up to Casey and leaned over the sofa from behind to drop a kiss on the top of her head. "How are you, my love?" he asked tenderly. "Feeling better?"

"Is she ill?" Ed asked, confused. Casey looked equally puzzled.

"She's been working too hard," Adam said. "I'm always trying to get her to slow down."

"What work?" Karen said curiously. "The newspaper said you had a housekeeper."

"I'd never expect my wife to do housework, Karen." The guilt in her eyes suggested he'd hit the target. "Casey's been working hard on her writing," he elaborated.

It was plain from Karen's bewilderment that she'd never thought of her sister's writing as work.

"And you, Karen," he said. "You're not working at the moment, are you? You're taking maternity leave?"

"I—well, yes, but it's not easy looking after a baby on my own," she said, a tremor in her voice.

"That's right," Adam said innocently. "You wanted Casey to work as nanny for you, didn't you, so you could go back to your law job?"

If looks could kill, the daggers coming from Casey would have slain Adam on the spot.

Karen's lip quivered. "Casey always knows what to do. She'd be better with Rosie than I am."

"That's not true, honey," Casey assured her warmly. "Rosie's obviously very content—she's been asleep in her car seat ever since you arrived."

It was clear to Adam that Karen actually believed what she'd just said. So while she was being selfish in her expectations of Casey, that selfishness stemmed from fear, a lack of self-confidence. He figured that attacking her would only encourage Casey to take pity on her sister, which wouldn't be good for anyone.

So he said, "Of course it's not true. Babies take some getting used to, that's all. You'll be fine."

Smoothly, he steered the conversation to safer topics. He was still standing behind Casey, so he took the opportunity to give her a neck massage, as a loving husband might. Of course, it involved burying his fingers in that thick, lush hair to reach the tender skin of her nape. Barely discernibly, she arched against him.

He managed to keep his hands on Casey one way or another pretty much the whole afternoon.

"You're overdoing it," she said in a near whisper at one stage, when they were on the back veranda having predinner drinks. Casey had been sitting on the swing, cuddling the baby, her legs stretched out along the cushion. Adam sat on the end, and when she started to put her feet on the ground, he held on to them and played "This little piggy" with her toes—not saying the words, of course, but she knew what he was doing.

Did *he* know what he was doing? Other than having the time of his life? Of course he did. Play acting, that was all. Just enough to convince his in-laws he adored Casey.

Ugh. He was even thinking the word now. *It's only a word. Just because I'm thinking it doesn't mean it's for real.*

Still, Adam cooled it for a while, just stuck to the endearments and kept his hands off her. Which left him feeling as if his hands weren't doing what they'd been made for.

They had dinner late, after Rosie had been put to bed upstairs. During the meal, Karen revealed that she and her husband had now initiated divorce proceedings, so she was back in Parkvale for good. Adam learned that Ed had been doing poorly since Casey left. Both were feeling sorry for themselves, he surmised uncharitably.

At last Karen raised the hot topic of the week. "What about the article in last week's paper? It said you sleep in separate bedrooms."

"The woman was only with us a few days," Casey said. "Adam and I had an argument, so I slept in the guest room a couple of nights. It just happened to be while she was here."

"It was my paranoid jealousy," Adam said help-fully. Casey choked on her water. "Are you all right, darling?"

"Why were you jealous?" Karen asked.

"I found Casey flirting with the gardener," he improvised, and earned a hard kick under the table. "I mean, I *thought* she was flirting," he amended. "She wasn't, of course, and she moved out of our room until I saw sense."

Before he could get himself into more trouble, Adam raised his glass in a toast. "To the Greene family," he said, "who raised me the best wife a guy could have."

The others lifted their glasses, but when Adam sought Casey's eyes to share this moment of triumph, they were clouded with tears. Soon after dinner, she excused herself, saying she was tired and would go to bed. Had he done something wrong?

Adam was torn between wanting to go with her and the need to be courteous to their guests, to make amends for his earlier rudeness to Karen. He decided Casey would appreciate it more if he stayed with her family.

It was another hour before he made his own way upstairs.

The light was off, and he couldn't hear a sound. Could Casey have fallen asleep? When he knew he wouldn't sleep a wink with her beside him? Damn, she was annoying. In the darkness, he stepped carefully in the direction of the bathroom.

Casey closed her eyes when Adam switched on the light in the bathroom. She lay motionless until he'd closed the door. She'd never been good at hiding her feelings. What if Adam had already guessed the awful realization that had hit her this evening, after she'd endured a whole day of his caresses, his loving attention?

The realization that, for better or for worse, she was in love with her husband.

The knowledge weighed on her, holding her there.

Today's tantalizing glimpse of what it might be like to be truly married to Adam, if he loved her, had illuminated the truth she'd been denying for days. *This* was the meaning of the pleasure that curled in the pit of her stomach when he smiled at her. *This* was the cause of the physical ache his slightest touch induced. *This* was why, with him, she felt fully alive, one hundred percent herself.

All week, his assertion that tonight they would make love had caused excitement to thrum through her veins, heightening every sensation, invoking an unbearable tension, even as she'd told him it wasn't going to happen—and meant it. But now she knew she didn't have it in her to deny him.

Casey fidgeted under the crisp cotton sheets. Just knowing that his body normally occupied the space where she now lay was enough to set her on edge. She should have dressed, or rather undressed, for the occasion. Would Adam want her looking like this?

Would he want her if she told him she loved him?

The bathroom door opened, and Adam's deep voice called softly, "Here I come, *wife*."

"You're being Neanderthal again." Her attempt at a casual comment came out a squeak.

He chuckled, then the bathroom light clicked off, and she sensed rather than heard Adam making his way across the room in the dark. Casey froze, wondering where he would touch her first, the suspense tearing her apart. Where was he, dammit?

His hands brushed her collarbone as he reached for the duvet she'd pulled up to her neck despite the hot night. He tugged the cover away, and she felt the play of air over her body. Still he didn't touch her, yet she prickled all over. She heard the soft swish of the comforter hitting the floor, felt a sudden depression on the other side of the mattress. He was in bed with her, no more than a dark shape. She shouldn't have closed the shutters, not when she needed to see exactly where he was.

She felt his touch, featherlight on her forehead, smoothing her hair aside. He ran a finger down her nose, then traced the outline of her lips. Casey took his finger into her mouth, nipped the pad between her teeth, heard his ragged breath as she soothed it with her tongue.

He moved his hand to her nape, buried his fingers there the way he had earlier. Casey arched her neck, felt him shifting closer. When she lifted a tentative palm, she met the firm wall of his chest, felt the coarseness of the hair there. She wondered if he was already naked. Then she registered the brush of a silky fabric against her thigh. Boxers, she concluded.

His hands moved over her shoulders. Then he pulled away. "What on earth are you wearing?" The lamp on the nightstand snapped on, making her blink.

Adam stared down at her T-shirt and jogging shorts. Heat mingled with laughter in his gaze.

"You look fantastic," he breathed, and she giggled at the outright lie. The giggle turned into an indrawn breath as his hand caressed the bare skin of her abdomen where her T-shirt had ridden up.

"I guess your outfit means you're still not planning to let me make love to you," he said regretfully.

"Actually…" She licked her lips and saw his gaze follow the movement of her tongue. Her heart began thudding so strongly she thought Adam must surely hear. "It doesn't mean that at all."

He stared at her for a long moment. She nodded. A smile curved slowly across his lips and ended up in his eyes.

Then his mouth was on hers, and she was matching him, kiss for searing kiss. Whatever she'd said to that journalist about spontaneous combustion had been an understatement, Casey thought, as Adam's lips trailed fire over her face, her neck and, nuzzling her T-shirt aside, her shoulders.

His hands roamed beneath the shirt, exploring the sensitized column of her spine, then moving around to cup her breasts. At that touch, Casey couldn't stifle a cry. Adam pulled away, breathing heavily. The need in his eyes was exhilarating…and terrifying.

"First," he said unevenly, "I need to get rid of your incredibly sexy nightwear."

He helped her tug the T-shirt off. For a moment, he held her hands over her head, snagged in the T-shirt, while he dipped his head to her breasts. She moaned and a low growl sounded in his throat. The T-shirt flew across the room. He reached for the waistband of her shorts and slid them down.

He paused, scanned her body with a heavy-lidded gaze that set her quivering.

"Your turn," she murmured, her hand fluttering toward his shorts in sudden nervousness. He peeled them off in one swift movement, and his glorious nakedness sent a charge of desire through Casey.

Adam touched a hand to her hip, then trailed a caress over her stomach, her breast, up her neck to her mouth.

She reached for him, and he shuddered, the guttural sound he made almost pained. He lowered himself over her so she could feel his hardness, feel how much he wanted her.

"My darling, you're so beautiful," he said.

She was ready for him right then. But the seduction he performed with his mouth, with his hands, was tantalizingly, achingly slow. He found every inch of her, bringing her to a level of desire she hadn't dreamed existed. And just when Casey thought she might die of it, he claimed her as his own.

CASEY AWOKE from the soundest sleep of her life to find herself alone in bed. She jolted upright, then relaxed again when she heard the shower running in the bathroom.

She lay there, hands splayed on the quilt, and let memories of the night before wash over her. The intimacy, the passion that she and Adam had shared had been beyond all her expectations. And despite her limited basis for comparison, it had been clear Adam found it equally sublime. Enough to want to repeat the experience twice during the night.

What next? Her body, which she'd believed to be sated, tingled in readiness. Not *that* kind of next, she told herself; what next as far as their marriage was concerned? She didn't expect Adam to have fallen in love with her overnight. But surely they'd moved onto a different plane.

The shower stopped, and Casey waited for him to appear.

To her disappointment, he emerged from the bathroom fully dressed. Her cheerful greeting died on her lips, sent to its grave by the chill in his eyes.

"We need to talk," he said, and he sat on the very edge of the bed, leaving an expanse of quilt between them.

Casey waited, suddenly not trusting her voice.

Adam seemed to have trouble finding the words he wanted, and for a few moments there was only a strained silence.

"Last night was a mistake. I know it was my idea, and I'd been pressuring you, but I was wrong."

"Why?" she managed to ask in a thin voice.

"I should have realized that because you were… less experienced, it would mean more to you."

"While it meant nothing to you?" she asked, stung.

His eyes darkened to indigo. "You know that's not true."

Maybe he was just worried for her, and she could reassure him. She reached across the coverlet and laid her hand on his.

He snatched it away as if burned. "Casey," he said, "last night was incredible. But it doesn't change anything between us. You and I still want very different things. You want a man who'll adore you. It's your dream, and it's what you deserve. But…I'm not the one who can do that. Making love—having sex—just confuses things."

Tears pricked her eyes, but she refused to cry. "You don't sound confused, and neither am I," she said over the lump in her throat. She steeled herself to lie to him, prayed she would be convincing. "I don't adore you, Adam, and I never thought you would be the man to adore me."

Was it relief that chased across his face?

"I didn't even take precautions that first time," he said. "You could get pregnant."

"It's most unlikely." Casey didn't bother to tell him why. There was hardly any point explaining her probable infertility when he'd just told her they had no future together.

Again he had the nerve to look relieved.

A surge of anger flowed through her, forcing back the heartbreak she knew would return later.

"Leave me alone, Adam," she said. "You were great in bed, but when it comes to relationships, you're a washout."

If she'd hoped he would protest, she was disappointed. He nodded, then left the room.

Casey heard him whistling on his way downstairs.

She eased back against the pillows, let out a slow breath, as if by making only the gentlest of movements she could somehow keep her heart from shattering. Just as carefully, she spread her fingers on the quilt again, forced herself to take another breath in and out. The dull gleam of the wedding ring on her left hand caught her eye.

She had more than this piece of jewelry in common with Adam's mother. Like the woman who'd worn it before her, she had fallen in love with a husband who could never love her.

CHAPTER FOURTEEN

THE LAST THING Casey wanted was to face Anna May and Henry, along with the rest of Adam's extended family, for the lunch they'd planned. Why not just call an end to this charade now?

Because then Dad and Karen would know the truth. Because it would hurt Eloise, and Casey couldn't help wanting to postpone that moment. Because Adam needed more time to build his case against his father's will.

So they would go through with their performance.

Fortunately, both she and Adam were too busy getting ready for their guests to have any awkward moments together. Adam planned to barbecue, and Casey had a half-dozen salads to assemble, plus Eloise's favorite strawberry shortcake to bake.

By one o'clock, all the guests had arrived, and the beef fillet was grilling. Casey moved between the clusters of guests, introducing her family to Adam's, making sure everyone had someone to talk to and all glasses were filled.

Eloise watched her, proud of her gracious yet unaffected daughter-in-law. She knew something wasn't right between Casey and Adam, but she prayed that he would recognize Casey was nothing like his own family. That while she needed him, he needed her so much more.

Today, with the sun shining, and the sweet scent of magnolias mingling with grilling beef, it was easy to be optimistic. Eloise smiled as she turned back to her friends' conversation. But she had trouble focusing. Her mind was restless with thoughts of love and marriage. Unconditional love…

For some reason—probably because he was standing not twenty yards from her—Sam kept capturing her attention.

Adam should never have invited him to this lunch—he wasn't family. Of course, neither were Beth and Cecile. Adam had included them because he thought Eloise would prefer their company to some of his relatives'. It didn't help that Cecile kept giving Sam looks that could only be called flirtatious.

Somewhat acerbically, Eloise said to her friend, "You're rather obvious in your attentions toward Sam Magill, Cecile. It never pays to look too eager."

"It's called admiring the view," Cecile said promptly. "He's a handsome man."

"Tall, too," said Beth, who at five foot one said that about everyone. This time, Eloise happened to agree with her. "He keeps looking this way," her friend continued. "I think he's interested in you, Cecile."

Cecile straightened in her chair and sent a glance over her shoulder that Eloise considered far too sultry for a woman who'd turned sixty last birthday.

Eloise bit back the retort that it was *her* Sam couldn't keep his eyes off. Tears stung her eyes at the thought of how mean she was feeling toward her friend. What was wrong with her? With a huff of frustration that almost turned into a sob, she turned her back on Sam, trying for a joke. "You girls have been widows too long if you think Sam is anything other than a…a tedious, pathetic little man."

Oh dear, that hadn't come out funny in the least. She was met by horrified silence. Which was arguably an overreaction. She'd said no worse than the others had a dozen times about men who—

"Eloise." Sam's gravelly voice spoke behind her.

Eloise gasped. Her heart in her mouth, she turned. He seemed bigger than she remembered. Only a few inches taller than her five-seven, but just…bigger all over. Not overweight, just…big. Male.

She closed her eyes, mortified. Once, when she was a child, her mama had tanned her behind for being rude to one of their maids. And she'd been far less offensive then than she'd been to Sam now.

"Sam, I'm so very sorry. That was inexcusable." For the first time his gray eyes—gunmetal gray, she realized—didn't soften. This must be what he looked like in a courtroom.

He didn't blush or stammer or do any of the inept

Sam Magill things. "Eloise Carmichael," he said in the stentorian tone of a judge pronouncing sentence, "you are a spoiled brat."

Eloise heard Cecile titter, saw Beth's mouth round into an *O* of shock.

"When you decide to keep a civil tongue in your head like the lady you were raised to be…"

Oh, this was too much; now he was channeling her own thoughts back at her.

"…we'll talk about what you think of me. Until then, I'll leave you with this."

Strong hands grasped her shoulders, and Eloise looked up at him in bewilderment. A moment's stupidity prevented her from realizing what he was about to do. Then his lips met hers in a hard kiss.

She gasped and twisted away. "How dare—"

But his hands framed her face, forcing her back to him. Again he kissed her, smothering her protest with the hunger of a man too long denied.

Eloise pushed against his chest, but then— *gracious*—she seemed to be melting into the man. Her fingers curled into the fine linen of his shirt and she heard a noise that sounded very much like herself…*moaning*.

Finally, Sam released her, his face red, but not with embarrassment.

He cleared his throat and said stiffly, "I am not James. I will never be James." The words were a slap in the face. He took a step closer and Eloise shrank

back even as a traitorous corner of her wanted to feel
that mouth on hers again.

"You know what?" Sam said. "I don't *want* to be
James."

He gave her that half bow, so much more awkward than James's had ever been, yet in its own
way…endearing. Then he turned and strode across
the lawn toward the drive.

On the way, he bumped into the sundial.

Eloise watched him until he disappeared from
view. Cecile and Beth watched, too. Then Beth said,
"You see, Eloise? I told you he likes you."

TO HER SURPRISE, Casey enjoyed the family lunch.
Enjoyed being Adam's hostess, making his family
welcome. Even Anna May and Henry. She especially enjoyed seeing Sam stake his claim to Eloise,
who left soon after Sam did, pleading a headache.

Through the afternoon, Casey watched for an opportunity to speak to Adam's aunt alone. Casey hadn't
discussed her plan with Adam. Now, she wondered
if it was a dumb idea. Adam's family problems were
none of her business, he'd made it clear this morning
she was nothing more than a one-month wife.

But she loved him.

Her chance came when everyone had finished
eating. Most people sat around on the porch, nursing
cups of coffee.

Adam, bless his orderly heart, was scraping

down the barbecue and generally getting things straightened out.

Casey plunked herself down next to Anna May, who was watching Henry play tennis with some of his cousins on Adam's grass court.

"That boy is such an athlete," Anna May said fondly, before she realized who it was sitting next to her. She scowled.

"He's good," Casey agreed. To look at Henry's stocky figure, you'd never guess he was a sportsman. But he was wiping the floor with the admittedly limited competition.

"He's always been talented out on the court," Anna May said.

"As opposed to *in* court." Casey figured she might as well get right down to it.

Anna May glared. "I'm not talking to you without my lawyer."

"Anna May," Casey said. "Won't you consider dropping your legal action against James's will?"

Anna May sniffed. "Certainly. All Adam has to do is promote Henry and pay us a dividend. He owes us."

Casey drew a breath. This was where she either screwed up big time or pulled a rabbit out of the hat.

"I know you love Henry, and that's why you're fighting so hard on his behalf."

"Of course I love him."

"But Adam had the impression at one of your recent meetings that Henry's heart isn't in this battle."

The older woman blushed. "You don't know the first thing about what my son wants."

"I know what it is to do things for people out of love." She didn't say, *as a means of tying them to you.* "But in the end, it's not enough, for you or for them." She paused. "Have you asked Henry what he really wants?"

Anna May gaped. "Don't be impertinent. I know what my son wants. I know what I can do for him. Stay out of our business." She turned away to applaud, as Henry lobbed a killer serve that had his opponent scurrying for the ball.

Casey eyed the firm set of the other woman's shoulders with helpless frustration. She had been no help at all.

ADAM'S RELATIVES LEFT around four o'clock. With fewer people to act as a buffer, the strain between Casey and Adam became more apparent. They were wooden and stilted with each other, and despite Adam's best efforts, Casey found herself drifting into brooding silence.

She could barely hide her relief when her father and sister announced their imminent departure.

Before they left, Karen cornered Casey in the living room. "Have you and Adam had an argument? He puts on a polite front, but I can see you're both in a terrible mood."

Casey wasn't up to pretending any longer. "Yes, we have," she said simply.

"Are you certain you've done the right thing, Casey? I don't know how long you and Adam have known each other, but it can't be all that long a time. If this doesn't work out you can always come home to us." For once, Karen's concern sounded genuine.

"I don't know if my marriage will work out or not," Casey said. "Thanks for the offer, but I won't be coming back to Parkvale. I'm proud of you guys and how you're doing."

Despite this morning's disappointment, Casey knew an unfamiliar lightness of spirit. Finally, she'd said she wouldn't go back, and meant it. All those other times she'd talked about leaving home, she realized now, she hadn't been committed to building her own future. In getting away from Parkvale and writing her book, she'd discovered a kind of self-belief that all the affirmations in the world couldn't deliver.

Karen must have recognized the strength of her sister's resolve. "I'm sure we'll fix something up," she said meekly. She hugged Casey. "Good luck. Thanks for everything. And I do mean everything."

And that was it. Mission accomplished.

"YOUR WIFE WAS TELLING ME—" Sam's gaze slid away from Adam's "—I should show Eloise the real me."

"Casey said that?" Adam drummed his fingers on his desk. It was only Tuesday, but already he wanted this week to be over so he could spend two days with

Casey. Which made no sense after what he'd said on Sunday.

"She's the only wife you have, isn't she? Or is this about to get more complicated?" The lawyer grinned. All through the meeting he'd been as chipper as Adam was sour.

Adam ignored Sam's joke. "If the way you groped Eloise in front of everyone was the real you, I'm not sure the world's ready for it."

Sam frowned and cleared his throat. "You may not have realized, but I am, er, very fond of Eloise."

"For Pete's sake, Sam, you all but ate her for lunch on Sunday," Adam snapped, not interested in hearing about other people's love lives when his own was such a mess.

Sam huffed. "I just want to warn you I intend to pursue Eloise with romantic intentions."

"Isn't she the one you should be warning? Assuming she hasn't figured it out already?"

"I intend to do that, too," Sam said.

"Okay, I consider myself warned." Adam let out a breath, and abandoned his churlish attitude. "Good luck with that."

The lawyer nodded, then switched the subject smoothly. "Judge Skelton is back from vacation. I presented our annulment petition to him this morning."

Adam stilled. "Good." His voice sounded thin.

"If you're at all interested in making this marriage

a permanent thing, I can ask him to hold off on his decision," Sam offered.

A rushing in Adam's ears left him dizzy. "There's no point," he said. "Even if Casey stays, Anna May told me she's going to argue in court that our marriage is fake, based on the TV wedding and the media coverage."

"I still think we can win our original argument that the will's not legal," Sam said. "What I'm saying is, if you and Casey do want to stay married, now's the time to say so. Then if Anna May gets somewhere with her new complaint, we can ask the court to allow a couple of years to demonstrate that your marriage is lasting and committed. If you and Casey stay married, we win no matter what."

"How do we prove our marriage is genuine, without inviting Anna May into our bedroom?"

Sam gnawed on his lip. "You have a baby."

A baby! Adam felt as if he'd been socked in the chest. He'd never thought about having children, but he did know he wasn't about to have a kid just to prove a point in court.

"It might be your best bet," Sam said. "We'll still challenge the will, saying your father can't force you to get married. But a lot of judges don't take kindly to that kind of thing. Most of them are within a decade or two of dying themselves. They don't like the idea of someone tampering with a man's final wishes."

"Casey and I aren't going to stay married." Adam was suddenly adamant on that point.

The decision weighed on him like a ton of that stodgy cornbread Eloise was so certain he liked. He looked at his watch. "It's nearly lunchtime. You must need a cigar by now."

The lawyer stood. "I've given them up."

Adam clamped his mouth shut to keep his jaw from dropping. "You love those things." Sam didn't smoke during working hours, but at the end of most evenings there were four or five cigar stubs in his ashtray.

Sam shrugged. "Eloise doesn't like it."

"Did she ask you to quit?"

"She's a lady, she'd never ask that. I wanted to do something for her."

Sam took his leave. Adam scowled at the door as it closed behind the lawyer. How did Eloise do that? Have men falling over themselves to do things for her without her having to ask? As far as Adam knew, she'd never asked anything of Sam. Adam realized now she'd probably never asked anything of his father, either. James had wanted to do things for his wife. Because he loved her.

"Love, schmove," Adam said.

He yielded to the irritation that had been pricking at him all morning. Instead of enjoying his work, all he could think about was his wife.

When had staying home with Casey started to outweigh the appeal of Carmichael Broadcasting?

Staring unseeing at his computer, Adam realized it was before Casey had spent last Saturday night in his arms. The tenderness, the passion of that night were symptoms of his current malaise, not the cause.

Which brought him to the real question: what exactly *was* this malady? There was only one diagnosis that didn't give Adam the urge to lock himself in his office and never come out again.

Lust.

That Casey occupied his thoughts to an alarming extent, not just with the memory of her exquisite body, but with her smile, her eyes, her laugh, her kindness, her mind. It all came down to lust.

He'd hurt her with his coldness the morning after they made love, he knew. But the generosity of her lovemaking had scared him. She'd given him everything, and that intimacy had been more precious than he'd known it could be.

Was she in love with him? Or did she at least think she was?

Adam told himself he hoped she meant what she'd said. That if on Saturday night she'd for some foolish reason thought she loved him, his coldness on Sunday morning had changed her mind.

Because Adam didn't do love. And he especially didn't do adoring.

He glanced at his desk calendar. If Sam's petition to Judge Skelton was successful, the annulment would be through very soon. Life would go back to normal. Adam forced himself to smile.

Hopefully, he and Casey could part as friends. Although, since Sunday morning, there hadn't been anything more than chilly politeness between them.

He should fix that before it was too late. Explain himself better, make sure she understood. And let her know he appreciated just how great her gift had been.

The clock on his wall clicked over to noon. That's right; she had the neighbors Adam had never met coming for lunch. At his house. With his wife.

"Cancel my afternoon appointments," Adam told his startled secretary. "I'm going home."

THE DOORBELL RANG at noon, just as Casey typed "The End" at the bottom of her manuscript. She'd written the book, she'd revised it to her satisfaction, and now those two little words gave her a deep feeling of accomplishment.

They also gave her a sense of foreboding. As if they might refer to more than her book.

She pushed her uneasiness aside as she went downstairs, reminding herself to enjoy the release that came from not having an incomplete manuscript hanging over her head. *I feel great, really I do.* There was an almost genuine smile on her face as she pulled the heavy front door open to welcome the Harveys, and, coming up the walk behind them, Alison Dare and her children. "Come in," Casey said.

She'd just served the soup when Adam walked into the dining room.

What was he doing here? Surely he wouldn't throw the neighbors out, just because he'd told her not to invite them?

He walked up to her, kissed her lightly on the lips. "Hi."

"Hi," she said nervously.

Adam scanned the room. "Are you going to introduce me to your friends?"

Casey performed the introductions, then sat speechless through most of lunch as Adam chatted to Mr. and Mrs. Harvey about the changes in the neighborhood, and took an apparently genuine interest in Alison's three not-very-well-behaved children.

When Bob Harvey made mention of a street party as he left, Adam didn't even flinch.

"WHAT WAS THAT ABOUT?" she demanded, as he shut the door behind the departing guests.

He headed for his den, Casey on his heels. "What do you mean?"

"You didn't want them here. Why were you so nice?"

He leaned against the oak roll-top desk. "I know you could have coped on your own. But you shouldn't have to." When she didn't say anything, he added reluctantly, "That neighborly stuff matters to you. I thought you'd like it if I was here."

Casey caught her breath. "What do you care if I'd like it? You don't want me."

CHAPTER FIFTEEN

THE PAIN BEHIND HER WORDS seared Adam's conscience. "You can't seriously believe I don't want you."

"It's what you said."

And he'd been planning on saying the same thing to her again now.

They stood facing each other, a few feet apart, the tension almost a physical barrier between them.

Adam drew a calming breath, loosened the fists he'd clenched at his sides. "I care about you, Casey. That's why I came home. And I care about your future. You're a wonderful person—I hope you find a man who deserves you."

She took a step closer to him, then another, until she stood only inches away. She swallowed. "What if I find him and he doesn't want me?"

How, despite his best intentions, could Adam not reach out and pull her to him, kiss her hard on the mouth?

It took only a second of body-to-body contact for him to be on full alert and ready for a rerun of the other night. Casey's arms were around his neck, and she was kissing him with a fervor that left him in no doubt as to her wants. He ran his hands down her back to cup her derriere, pulling her against him, and she whimpered with need.

Clumsy with desire, he fumbled at the buttons of her shirt, at last managing to push the fabric aside to cup her breasts through the ivory satin of her bra. She arched against him, and he lowered his mouth to the swell of flesh. At the same time, he tugged the bottom of her shirt out of her shorts, slipped his hands inside her waistband. Suddenly, his progress eased considerably, and he realized she'd unsnapped her shorts. He slid them down and she stepped out of them. She began to tug at his belt.

Dimly, Adam registered that the phone on the desk was ringing.

He ignored it, concentrating instead on the incredible sensation of Casey's fingers undoing his trousers, then pushing them down. He kicked off his pants, then backed her toward the couch, not lifting his mouth from the tender hollow he'd discovered where her neck met her shoulder.

The room was silent, apart from muffled sounds of their need. So when Sam's voice boomed out from the answering machine, it was as if a bucket of cold Mississippi water landed on them.

"Adam, it's Sam. Good news, my friend. I had a call from Judge Skelton's office. He's granted your annulment. I'll send the paperwork out to you, but congratulations, you're Memphis's most eligible bachelor once again."

Adam would never have believed that *not* being married to Casey would be a complete passion killer. But it was. He no more wanted to make love to her now than she did to him—and he could see in her eyes that she'd gone right off the idea.

"We can't…" Casey choked on the words. She twisted from his embrace—he didn't try to stop her—and stumbled over to pick up her shorts, dragging them back on. Adam found his pants and dressed in silence, not trusting himself to speak for a moment.

"So that's it." Somehow he managed to sound calm, even casual, as he ran a hand through his hair to smooth it. "We got our annulment."

"I heard," she said shortly.

Already, there was a distance between them that was more than just the abrupt end to their lovemaking. Frustration and disappointment gnawed at Adam, and suddenly the room wasn't big enough for both of them. "I'm going for a run," he said.

AFTER HE'D RUN NEARLY three miles, Adam turned around and headed for home. Each thud of his shoes on the sidewalk hammered in the reminder that Casey would leave soon.

He didn't want her to go. She added an extra dimension to his life that he would miss. He could make her stay, of course. He sensed that if he wooed her, she could love him. She might even love him already. And marriage was in his long-term plan. So why not?

Because of the kind of marriage Casey wanted.

She wanted to be the most important thing in her husband's life. She'd never put it in those terms, but what else did being adored mean?

Adam breathed more heavily as he ran uphill. Only half a mile to go. *Think faster.*

He cared for Casey. He even loved her, in his own way. Though he wouldn't risk telling her that, in case she assumed he meant her kind of love. He wanted to be with her, he wanted to make love to her with a fierceness that scared him. He wanted to have children with her.

Never mind that until Sam mentioned it, he'd never thought about kids. Right now, something inside Adam went mushy at the prospect of a child of his own.

A son.

A chance for Adam to be the kind of dad his own father had never been.

A chance to heal some of the hurt of his youth, to set a new pattern for the Carmichael family. Adam snorted. Healing! He was starting to sound like Casey.

He rounded the corner onto his street. Home was just a couple of hundred yards away.

He forced himself to focus on the practicalities. As Sam said, having a child would prove their marriage was genuine. It could be the key to securing their future.

Adam wasn't prepared to trade his independence for the emotional ties he'd convinced himself Casey would demand. But maybe he was wrong about her. She'd changed in the past month, as he had. Her willingness to make love to him this evening, when she knew their relationship was nearing its end, when he'd reiterated they had no future, suggested a more practical attitude toward love.

Maybe he should lay his cards on the table, find out if his kind of love was enough to make a marriage work.

IT TOOK CASEY a few seconds to identify the source of the dread that enveloped her the moment she awoke the next day. She looked around her bedroom, with its luxurious furnishings, the wooden shutters at the window. This place had become home remarkably fast.

But no longer. There was nothing to keep her here.

She was thankful Sam's call had come before she and Adam made love again yesterday. How much harder today would have been! With the annulment, they'd tied up the last of the loose ends. The only remaining problem—Casey's broken heart—wasn't going to be fixed in a hurry. And it wasn't going to be fixed here.

She arrived downstairs for breakfast later than normal and was surprised to find Adam still at the table, lost in contemplation.

He looked up at her and smiled, a movement of the mouth belied by the strain in his eyes. "Won't you join me?" he said, almost as if she were a stranger.

Casey tipped cereal into her bowl and nodded her thanks as Adam poured her a cup of hot tea. She ate in silence, aware of his somber scrutiny the whole time.

It was off-putting, and she pushed her bowl away when she was barely half-finished. The movement seemed to act as a cue.

"Can we talk?" he said.

"Of course." Were there more legalities to deal with?

Adam cleared his throat, and she realized he was nervous.

"This might sound odd," he said, "but now that we're no longer married…will you marry me?"

A bubble of hope, joy and laughter rose from deep within her, splitting her face in a grin. "Are you serious?"

Even as Casey asked, she realized Adam was extremely serious. In fact, he looked more as if he was about to have a tooth pulled rather than get married. And nothing like a man who had just realized he was in love. "Tell me more," she said with careful neutrality.

"It makes good sense," he said, and she had the impression he was launching into a prepared argument. "We get along well, I enjoy spending time with you, we're physically compatible. You're a great wife, and I think you'd make a wonderful mother. We could remarry without anyone knowing we'd had our first marriage annulled."

"So it's convenient," she said. "And it fits nicely with your father's will."

He shook his head, seeming annoyed at her logical summation, even though it was just the sort of thing he would say himself. "I still believe I'll win in court, if that's all there is to it. But I'm very fond of you, Casey. We could make a good life together. *Very* fond."

Fond. That was how she'd felt about Joe. Five weeks ago, Casey had been prepared to give up on the idea of a man who adored her. Could what Adam offered be enough? Could she be satisfied with fondness on his part, and desperate, all-consuming love on hers?

"And Eloise loves you," he said.

Which only served to remind her that Adam didn't. And that Eloise had never given up on finding true love.

Casey added sugar to her tea, even though she preferred it unsweetened, and concentrated on stirring the gold liquid.

"We could have a baby," Adam said. "I know you'd like that."

Casey froze.

"Sam was saying a baby would help with our legal battle," he said. "He'll ask the court to delay its decision. He says the best way to prove our relationship is lasting and committed is to have a child." He paused, then a smile—a boyish grin—creased his face. He reached across the table, grabbed her hands. "A baby, Casey. Let's get married and have a baby."

Casey removed her hands from his. "Adam." Her voice shook. "I can't have children." And though she'd known it for a long time, telling him now brought a stab of pain so fresh it took her breath away.

It seemed a full minute before Adam spoke. "What do you mean—can't?" he asked, dazed.

Somehow she strung the words together. "When I had a perforated appendix as a teenager, I got an infection in my pelvis that damaged my reproductive system. The doctors tell me I'll never conceive." She pressed her lips together. "Does that answer your question?"

"Sweetheart, I'm so sorry." His tenderness was unexpected, and tears smarted in Casey's eyes. Adam came around the table and dropped down beside her. Gently, he pushed a strand of hair behind her ear, then ran a finger down her cheek. "My poor darling," he said, and her heart leaped. "I don't know what to say…."

Tell me you love me, that you want me for myself.

But she might as well wish for the problem with her fertility to magically disappear. Adam was being kind, but in his eyes she could still see shock and, worse, distance.

She looked at him steadily, made absolutely sure he understood what she was saying, and put the final nail in the coffin. "So if you want a child, it won't be with me."

She saw, in the sudden blankness of his expression, that he was letting her go. That although he wanted to marry her—and she knew, even if he didn't, that his offer included some degree of emotional commitment—he wanted to secure the business more. And she accepted that. He would never love her as much as she loved him, no matter how fond he was of her now.

He had made his choice; now she must make hers. So though it hurt beyond measure, she pushed her chair back and stood. "I'll leave tomorrow."

"Casey, there's no rush. Can't we—?"

"My writing conference starts tomorrow night," she reminded him. "It'll take all day to drive to Dallas." She paused. "I won't come back afterward."

Adam looked at her, stone-faced, and said nothing.

CASEY COULDN'T HAVE children!

Adam was still struggling to absorb it as he lay in bed, trying to sleep.

He felt betrayed, as if she had lied to him. He shouldn't, of course he shouldn't, but she'd allowed him to come to this momentous decision that he wanted to marry her, which went against all good sense, without telling him the one thing that would never have allowed him to get to this point.

He was being totally unreasonable, he knew. Hadn't he reiterated over and over to Casey that their marriage would have no future beyond the time it took to get an annulment? Until now, her fertility had been none of his business.

And yet he felt cheated of the babies he'd pictured them making together, robbed of the family life he'd imagined.

But however painful this was for him, it was worse for her. A part of him wanted to take her in his arms, comfort her, murmur to her that it didn't matter, they'd be all right.

But it did matter. And they wouldn't be all right.

CASEY DIDN'T SEE ADAM again until the next morning. She breakfasted early, alone, then went to pack her bags. She'd half hoped, half dreaded that he would go to work without saying goodbye, but when she came downstairs at nine o'clock, he was waiting.

"I'll take those." He picked up her bags and carried them outside, where he loaded them into the trunk of the Fiesta. It took only a minute, then she was ready to leave.

She cleared her throat. "Goodbye, Adam. It's been a memorable month. Thanks for your help." She stuck out a hand, but he ignored it.

Instead, he cupped her face in his palms and kissed her fiercely. "Goodbye, Casey."

She clambered into the car, holding herself rigid so she wouldn't cry. She turned the key in the ignition and—nothing happened. She tried again, several times. Still nothing.

"Aargh!" Casey thumped the steering wheel in frustration, and the movement released the tears she'd held in check for so long. She was weeping floods by the time Adam opened the door and helped her from the car.

He held her against him, arms wrapped around her, shushing her gently, one hand stroking her head.

"Don't cry, sweetheart," he said. "It's probably the battery."

"I got a new battery back in May."

"It'll be the starter motor then. We can have it fixed by tomorrow."

"But I have to be in Dallas tonight," she wailed, knowing she never would have cried about such a thing if she hadn't been at the end of her tether.

"Take my car."

She hiccupped. "I can't take the Aston Martin."

"Of course you can," he said calmly. He pulled his keys from his pocket and pressed the remote control. The vehicle beeped obediently as the doors unlocked. "You have to get to Dallas and sell that book."

While Casey wiped her tears and blew her nose, Adam unloaded the bags from her trunk and put them in his. He handed her the keys. "Come back after the conference and we'll do a swap," he said. With sudden urgency he added, "Casey, I don't want us to part like this."

She summoned a faint smile as she thanked him for the keys and climbed into the car. But about their relationship, there was nothing left to say.

She drove off with a crunching of the unfamiliar stick shift that would have made a lesser man wince.

CHAPTER SIXTEEN

EVER SINCE CASEY HAD COME into his life, nothing had gone according to plan. Things hadn't gone wrong, exactly, Adam acknowledged, but if right meant "as planned," then they hadn't gone right, either.

It certainly wasn't right that he should be sitting in Casey's non-air-conditioned car in rush hour traffic on a stinking hot evening a week after she'd left. Why was he still driving this heap of scrap iron, of which the most valuable part was the new starter motor he'd bought earlier this week?

He could have taken a cab to the office each day. Instead, however unwillingly, he squeezed into the Fiesta and suffered the ignominy of being seen in a car sporting a Honk If You Think I'm Sexy bumper sticker, which had proven impossible to remove— and boy, had he tried. And all this because the car smelled, somehow, of Casey.

He scowled at the attractive woman in the BMW alongside, who had honked several times. That was another thing. There was no such thing as simple enjoyment of the opposite sex anymore. Adam used to admire the scenery as much as the next man, but these days, it seemed the sole purpose of the female species was to remind him of Casey.

If she and her pop psychology were right—that he was sublimating his wild side by driving an Aston Martin—what did it mean that he'd given her his precious car to drive? And that he hadn't worried about it while it was gone? Did that mean he was emasculated?

Don't go there.

Adam was only too aware that he teetered on the brink of something he'd assiduously avoided his whole life. At least, he hoped he was still on the brink—that he hadn't yet fallen in the kind of love that turned a guy's world upside down and clouded his logic. The kind that made him believe in preposterous happy endings that in reality just didn't happen. Or if they did they didn't last and you ended up like Eloise, fixated on the past. Surely it wasn't too late to get back to his orderly and—he was proud to admit it—predictable life?

Only it wasn't proving that easy. He'd been distracted in the office, impatient with his staff and less than polite to his stepmother. What really bugged him was that Eloise didn't even take offense, just smirked every time he grunted or snapped.

But what irked him most of all was Casey's parting gift. She'd phoned Mrs. Lowe and begged the housekeeper to come back to work for Adam. And the grumpy old bat was driving him nuts. How could he ever have thought she was a treasure?

Casey's writing conference would be finished by now, and she should have returned his Aston Martin. But he didn't want to call her cell phone, for fear that, hearing her voice, he might give in to the seductive urge to stop obsessing about the business, remarry Casey and just enjoy life. Because what kind of sense did that make?

And Eloise had rolled her eyes when he'd asked her to help get his car back, even though he knew she was still in contact with Casey.

He needed a distraction from his distraction. There was probably a psychological term for it; he must ask—

Cancel that.

By the time he got home, Adam was hot, uncomfortable and sick of being honked at. Did the women of Memphis have nothing better to do? In a fit of pique, he hurled Casey's car keys into the garden, where they sank out of sight into a yew hedge. Ha! Temptation removed. Now he'd have no choice but to take a cab to work.

Pleased that he'd taken the first step toward banishing Casey from his head, Adam checked the answering machine. Instead of deleting all the messages from women who'd called to tell him how sorry they were to read of his annulment in the newspaper this week, he called a couple back and arranged to meet for a drink over the next few evenings. No more sitting around the empty house.

And he'd better sort out his costume for Eloise's birthday party, which was a masked ball in the traditional style of her youth. The party wasn't for a couple of months, but it didn't hurt to be prepared.

Adam whistled cheerfully as he signed on to the Internet and began surfing the Web sites of costume shops. It was a good five minutes before he realized he was whistling "You Are My Sunshine."

Two months later

"YOU MUST HAVE SOMETHING more affirming," Casey pleaded down the line to the help desk at the phone company. "You Are My Sunshine" simply wasn't powerful enough to counteract the funk she'd slid into since the annulment.

"How about 'Blue Eyes' by Elton John?" the girl on the other end suggested.

"No!" Casey took a deep breath. "Do you have that old Split Enz tune 'I Hope I Never Have to See You Again'?"

"It doesn't sound very affirming," she said doubtfully, "but I'll check."

They didn't have it, and Casey ended up settling for "Love Is a Battlefield." She gave her credit card number and got the code to download the new ring tone. She'd barely finished the process when her phone rang.

"Eloise." She greeted the older woman with genuine pleasure. "How are you?"

Eloise had called to remind her Casey had agreed to dine with her tonight. "I can't wait to see you, dear," she said. "It seems so long since we had a good chat."

Guilt pricked at Casey. She'd been so busy working on her new book that she frequently lost track of time, shut away in the studio apartment she'd leased near the center of Memphis. In the evenings and on weekends, she was tutoring several kids in English. She hadn't had much time for Eloise.

"I'm looking forward to it," she said. She ended the call, pleased she'd stuck to her resolution of not asking Eloise about Adam.

Not that she needed to ask. She'd never heard of Adam Carmichael before she married him, but now she couldn't escape him. In the first few weeks after their annulment, which had been front-page news for only one day, his name had appeared regularly in the business section, or in support of some charity. She shuddered as she recalled the photo she'd seen of him with a gorgeous, dark-haired woman on his arm.

Casey didn't want to know how Adam was getting along without her. It was easier to quit reading the newspaper. Besides, she was too busy to keep up with the Memphis gossip. She had sold her first book—an editor from the conference had picked it up—and Casey was making progress on her second.

She went back to Parkvale most Sundays to visit Karen and the baby. She didn't usually see her dad, because he'd started dating a woman in the next town and had taken up driving again.

On the subject of driving... Casey peered over her computer screen to a window of her apartment, and checked that Adam's car was still parked in the street below. She was terrified it would be stolen, yet couldn't bring herself to return it to him. She'd hoped it would bring him back to her, however briefly. But it seemed Adam was willing to relinquish his beloved car rather than speak to Casey again.

She sighed. What was the point of postponing the inevitable? She would leave the Aston Martin at Eloise's tonight and take the bus home. Adam could get the Fiesta back to her however he chose. She would take the car for one last spin, to lunch with Brodie-Ann, who'd taken a day off work and should arrive in Memphis any minute.

When Brodie-Ann arrived, they drove to the park.

"You sure get a lot of attention in this car," her friend commented, as yet another man honked his horn at Casey, then gave her a thumbs-up when she looked in her rearview mirror.

"I don't miss my Honk If You Think I'm Sexy bumper sticker," Casey agreed as she gunned the engine and took off from the lights, leaving the car's latest admirer to eat her dust. She'd attracted more male attention in the past two months than she had in the previous twenty-five years. She would miss roaring around town in this beast.

Not that she needed the car as an ego boost. She'd had plenty of offers of dates, from men who hadn't even seen the Aston Martin. No, these days her confidence ran deeper than affirmations, deeper than how many men asked her out, deeper than the dubious satisfaction that came with believing others couldn't cope without her.

Thanks to Adam.

In the time she'd spent with him—and, ironically, through the inept marriage proposal that had ended their relationship—he'd taught her she could survive, and thrive, without being someone else's crutch. That life's rewards were about taking as well as about giving. That settling for what she could get wouldn't make her happy, but following her passion would. Things she'd suspected before, but never had the courage to test.

When they arrived at the park, Casey and Brodie-Ann sprawled on the grass with their picnic lunch. It was a bittersweet reminder of that picnic Casey and Adam had enjoyed. And it was only a hop, skip and a jump from there to thinking about the one night they'd spent together. Casey had half hoped that, against all odds, she might have conceived Adam's child that night.

She hadn't.

So here she was, oozing misery, while Brodie-Ann couldn't stop chirping about how wonderful

Steve was, how incredible married life was. Her friend tapped her soda bottle against Casey's in a toast. "Here's to three months of wedded bliss."

"Happy anniversary," Casey said gloomily.

"You were right. Steve and I are made for each other." Brodie-Ann grinned. "Things have been great since I figured out how that give-and-take stuff works."

She scrutinized Casey. "Speaking of give and take, have you seen Adam lately? As in, he gave you his Aston Martin and you took it?"

Casey shook her head. "I keep thinking he'll come and demand it back."

She didn't state the obvious. That Adam was so anxious to avoid her, not even his precious car would bring him to her.

Brodie-Ann patted her shoulder. "You're doing great, Casey. Hang in there."

Casey nodded. Things *were* good. She told herself that every day. She had a book contract; she was getting by. And she no longer depended on people being unable to cope without her.

The only goal she'd failed to achieve was the no-strings love. Because Adam had come with as many strings as every other person Casey loved.

AT SIX O'CLOCK, Casey drove to Eloise's house. She climbed out of the Aston Martin and locked it for the last time, then mounted the steps to the porch.

Eloise opened the front door.

"Come in, dear." She tugged Casey inside, then quickly shut the door behind her.

"Is something wrong?" Casey looked around. "Eloise, what's going on?"

The foyer was festooned with streamers and flowers. A uniformed waiter hurried past her carrying a silver tray stacked with wineglasses. Down the wide corridor to the back of the house, Casey could see doors flung wide to the garden and—was that a marquee?

"Eloise, tell me."

The older woman's eyes danced above her guilty smile. "Just a little party, dearest. For my birthday."

"A *little* party?"

"Fewer than three hundred guests, I promise you. Much smaller than last year." She took her hand. "I'm sorry, Casey. I so wanted you to be here, and thought you wouldn't come if I told you."

"I suppose Adam's coming?" Casey grumbled.

"Of course. He hasn't been happy lately, and I thought a party might cheer him up." Eloise's eyes didn't meet Casey's as she added, "I don't recall if I told him you'd be here."

Casey shook her head, indicating any attempt to match her and Adam up again would be futile, but didn't comment. Eloise knew as well as she did that a party was the last thing Adam would want if he was under stress. Casey told herself that why he wasn't looking happy wasn't her business. He probably missed his car.

She glanced down at her slightly rumpled cotton shift. It had seemed all right for a casual dinner with Eloise. "I'm not dressed for a party."

Eloise accepted that as agreement that Casey would stay. She smiled as she squeezed Casey's fingers. "I know, dear, and I hope you won't mind that I took the liberty of buying you something. A birthday present from me to you."

Casey couldn't help laughing. "Shouldn't it be the other way around?" She allowed Eloise to lead her upstairs to a guest bedroom.

"Oh." She was left almost speechless by the dress she found there—a strapless, midnight-blue silk creation that she knew just by looking would fit perfectly. And it did, hugging her curves as if made for her.

"My hairdresser is waiting to do your hair," Eloise said. "And I bought you this." From a box on the bed she lifted out a mask, elaborately decorated with gold feathers and blue ribbons.

"It's a masked ball, darling," she said, seeing Casey's confusion.

A sinking sensation hit Casey. Surely Eloise wouldn't… "Tell me this isn't a bridefest," she demanded.

Eloise snickered. "That's a one-sided way of looking at it. There are several very eligible men coming tonight. Think of it as a groomfest."

"YOU WIN, CASEY."

Alone in the silence of his office, Adam found the words easier to say than he'd expected. Instead of feeling as if he'd lost control, anticipation thrummed through his veins. Anything might be possible when he had Casey by his side....

Except she wasn't by his side. Because he had let her go.

Smart, Adam. Very smart.

He tucked the phone between shoulder and chin so he could lift a sleeve and look at his watch. Seven o'clock. His stepmother's party would be starting right about now. He didn't want to go—he didn't want to go anywhere ever again—without Casey.

"Did you say something?" Sam had been hemming and hawing on the other end of the line as he shuffled through his papers, searching for the relevant section to read to him.

Adam shook his head, though of course Sam couldn't see that. "Just thinking aloud," he said. He could picture the lawyer pursing his lips.

"Strikes me you've done too much thinking lately," Sam muttered. "This was one crazy idea. I'm amazed the judge even agreed to it. Wouldn't you be better just to move on?"

Adam grinned, ridiculously light-headed. "That's your professional opinion, is it?"

"For what it's worth." Sam clearly doubted his advice would be followed. "Still, what's done is done. Just don't expect to be able to undo it so easily."

"I won't be undoing it," Adam said confidently. He leaned back in his chair, propping his feet up on his desk in a way he never did. "Are you going to Eloise's party?"

There was a pause at the other end. "She didn't invite me. Which in itself is significant, don't you think?"

"Uh, maybe," Adam said.

"I'm going anyway."

"You're gate crashing?" Sam never did things like that. No one did things like that to Eloise.

"I believe that is the vernacular term for it," Sam said stuffily.

"Wow." Adam was impressed. "I guess I'll see you there."

He ended the call and changed into the tuxedo he planned to wear. But instead of heading to Eloise's house, he drove the company car he was using, while he figured out what to do about the Aston Martin, toward the leafy suburb where Casey had her studio apartment.

Repeatedly pressing her doorbell brought no response. Adam cursed. He'd been so buoyed up by the thought of seeing her, by what he had to tell her, he could hardly believe she wasn't at home. No sign of her car—his car—either.

He would wait.

CHAPTER SEVENTEEN

SAM CLAMBERED OUT OF the taxi at Eloise's house, then took a moment to adjust his costume. Damned uncomfortable getup. The breeches were tight enough to pose a permanent risk to a man's ability to demonstrate his passion, the coat sleeves ended in a froth of lace around his wrists, and as for the color... Sam had never worn peacock-blue in his life and, after tonight, he never would again. He'd drawn the line at the wig. He was Prince Charming, not Prince Ridiculous.

He looked at his watch through the slits in his mask. Eight-thirty. The party would be in full swing. He would make a dramatic entrance, say his piece, claim his prize. Then endure a few more hours in this costume.

He picked up the cushion he'd placed on the step while he straightened his outfit. It took two hands to carry the blasted thing; the glass slipper was attached by discreet threads, but wobbled unromantically if he didn't grip it right.

Sam blew out a calming breath. Wearing this silly

costume was a small price to pay if he got what he
wanted. He reminded himself how Eloise had responded to his kiss at that barbecue lunch—she'd
been even more shocked than he was at her passion.
He didn't doubt that was why she hadn't invited him
tonight. She was running scared, though she might
not know it.

In his younger days, Sam had worked as a pros-
ecutor of white-collar criminals. Some of his most
satisfying moments had come from cases where a
key witness hadn't been able to see what had been
right there all along. When awareness dawned, the
witness's credibility was even greater than that of
one who'd told the same story right through. That
was when Sam knew he had the case in the bag.

He paused at Eloise's front door. He wouldn't go
so far as to say he had Eloise in the bag. But she was
in that dawning realization phase. And because Sam
was several steps ahead of her, he had the upper hand.

He lifted the heavy brass knocker, and let it fall
with a thud. Instantly, the door was opened by a man
in uniform, whose eyebrows shot up.

Sam stepped inside.

And realized immediately the advantage an invitation would have given him.

"So," he said to the doorman, as he surveyed the
sea of women dressed in bright evening gowns and
tuxedo-clad men, "it's not a fancy-dress ball, then?"

"No," the man agreed. "Just masked."

Sam sent up a brief prayer of thanks that he'd resisted the suggestion of the girl in the costume shop that he paint an authentic eighteenth-century beauty spot on his cheek.

"Sir, do you have an invitation?" the doorman asked.

Sam decided he'd had enough of chatting to the hired help. He'd screwed up on the costume front, but he still had his mission. Clutching his cushion and glass slipper, he stepped forward and paused in the entryway, scanning the crowd for Eloise.

"Hey!" the doorman called from behind him, but Sam ignored him.

There she was, stunning in dark green velvet, a dress that molded her slim waist and showed she had enough curves to satisfy any man. Her gold-and-green mask rendered her mysterious, exotic, but still the Eloise he…loved. Yes, loved, dammit.

He'd behaved like an idiotic schoolboy the past three years. But over that time, his feelings for Eloise had grown into an unshakeable love. If she wouldn't have him…

Her eyes met his across the room. He imagined them widening with shock beneath her mask, as much that he'd dared to arrive uninvited as with surprise at his costume. She raised her hand to her lips, but Sam saw the corners of her mouth quirk. She was laughing at him.

Declaring his love for her now would doubtless send her into hysterics.

Sam tasted bitter disappointment, and swallowed. So the witness hadn't yet reached the stage of enlightenment that he'd hoped. It was his job to fix that.

He nodded curtly to Eloise, shook off the restraining hand of the doorman, then strode into the crowd, away from her.

ADAM WAITED OUTSIDE Casey's apartment until eleven o'clock, growing increasingly despondent, then annoyed.

She'd better not be out on a date.

He pushed away the unreasonable jealousy that thought provoked. He wanted to see Casey tonight, but had to accept that might not happen. The evening might be a disaster for him, but he'd better not disappoint Eloise by missing her birthday party.

When Adam pulled into Eloise's driveway, things started to look a whole lot better. In the glow of the fairy lights threaded around the pillars on the porch, he saw his Aston Martin sitting right by the front door.

Elated, he ran up the steps and into the house. People thronged the foyer, the staircase, every available space to the marquee out the back. Adam made his way toward the ballroom.

He saw her immediately. Casey, in the arms of a man he didn't recognize. But he did recognize the sappy smile the guy was giving her.

As Adam watched, the man leaned close and

whispered something in Casey's ear. Adam stiffened, his hands clenched at his sides.

At a light touch on his arm, he turned. It was Eloise, resplendent in dark green velvet and a green-and-gold mask.

"Adam, darling." She patted his cheek below the blue domino mask that didn't hide his identity one bit. "You made it."

"I'm sorry I'm late," he said formally, his gaze back on Casey, who appeared to be smiling at something that jerk had said.

"You've been unbearably slow these past months, but you're not too late, and that's all that matters."

"Huh?" Adam turned back to Eloise, who was also looking at Casey. Of course, his stepmother had known she would be here tonight, but had chosen not to mention it to Adam. No doubt part of some elaborate scheme to bring them together.

Typical. Didn't she know he had this all mapped out?

But gratitude for her good intentions welled in his heart, constricting his chest. "Thanks," he said gruffly.

Eloise smiled at him, tears in her eyes. "Go," she ordered. "Claim your bride, before Richard Lovington III nibbles her ear off."

Further realization dawned, halting Adam in his steps. "Your birthday's not till November," he accused her. "This party isn't for you. It's for me—and Casey."

Eloise sighed, but the look in her eyes was far from penitent. "It's the bridefest, darling. I know I shouldn't have, but I—"

Adam hushed her with a kiss on the cheek. "Thank you," he said again. "Thank you, Eloise."

She hugged him, then pushed him away, brushing impatiently at her eyes. "I don't think I'll ever understand men," she said. Half indignant, half amused, she added, "Sam came to my party without an invitation. Look at him!"

Adam choked on a laugh. The preposterous elegance of Sam's Prince Charming costume couldn't hide his distinctive shuffling step, even as he danced with a woman in a low-cut red dress. "Has Sam danced with you?" he asked.

"He hasn't even spoken to me," Eloise huffed. "What does the man think he's playing at?"

The dance ended, and as if he'd guessed the subject of their conversation, Sam made his way over to Adam and Eloise.

The two men nodded to each other. Adam swallowed his comment about Sam's outfit.

"Good evening, Eloise," Sam said. He stood close to her, and Adam saw that she didn't move away, but swayed toward him slightly.

"Sam." Her voice was cool.

"It seems my invitation to your party went astray," he said.

"I didn't send you one."

"Then I apologize if my presence here embarrasses you."

Eloise inclined her head. "Not at all."

"I had to come," Sam said.

"To check how I'm spending my money?" Eloise asked. "To see if I've briefed the catering staff correctly? To nag me about keeping my insurance paid up?"

"To dance with you," Sam said.

"Oh." Eloise was clearly flustered.

Adam enjoyed the spectacle.

But she had no trouble seizing the upper hand again. "Then why haven't you asked me to dance?" she demanded acerbically.

"I've been waiting for the band to play the tune I requested." Sam paused, alert. "It should be about now."

Sam had done it again, Adam realized. Knocked Eloise off balance. For the first time, it occurred to him the lawyer might be good for his stepmother.

The band struck up "All the Things You Are."

Eloise caught her breath, glanced uncertainly at Adam. He nodded encouragement. She turned to Sam. He gave her his hand. "Dance with me."

CASEY HAD LOST COUNT OF the men she had chatted with over dinner in the marquee, and danced with in Eloise's ballroom. But despite the masks that concealed their faces, she knew none of them was Adam.

Had he heard she was coming and decided to stay away? Eloise was at a loss to explain his absence, and Casey sensed the older woman's disappointment. Damn the man.

Then, as if her anger had conjured him up, he appeared over the shoulder of her current dance partner, masked but instantly recognizable.

Adam tapped the other man on the shoulder. "May I?"

Her partner, who had been in the middle of asking her out to dinner, hesitated. To Casey's shock, the infallibly polite Adam Carmichael elbowed him out of the way. The other man started to say something along the lines of "See you later," but the glitter in Adam's eyes, behind his blue domino mask, deterred him from finishing.

Casey fitted her hand into Adam's, trying to calm the sudden racing of her pulse. How had he recognized her in a dress he'd never seen, with a mask obscuring most of her face and hair?

But she said nothing, just relished the sensation of his hand at her waist. For a few moments they danced in silence.

"I knew you by your shoulders," he said at last, sounding almost angry.

"I...what?"

He lifted his hand and ran a finger along her shoulder, from her neck to the top of her arm. Casey shivered.

"Isn't that curious?" he said, his tone conversational now. "I walked into the room and I knew you."

"Curious," she agreed, hardly daring to breathe.

He pulled her closer, both hands on her waist as they danced. Casey was faint with desire.

"I've been reading about you in the newspaper," she said.

"That photo. That woman?" he asked, and she nodded.

"There's a psychological term for it," he said. "Sublimation, or substitution—something like that."

"Substitution for what?"

"You're the psychologist, you figure it out. But know this—I haven't so much as touched another woman since you left. Not beyond a kiss on the cheek."

"Thank you…." But it wasn't enough. "It's been two months."

"Some people are slow learners." He rested his chin lightly on the top of her head. "I have some bad news for you."

"What's that?"

"I had your car towed away."

"You what?" Casey pulled back in alarm, but he wouldn't let her move more than a couple of inches.

"I lost the keys," he said. "What else could I do?" He'd maneuvered her to the doorway that led to the back porch, and they stepped out into the cool evening air. He guided her to a seat on the edge of the porch, where he pulled off his mask and, without speaking, helped Casey remove hers.

"So I want you to keep the Aston Martin," he continued.

She gaped. "But you love that car."

"It's not a car, it's the sublimation of my boyhood dreams." He smiled, took both her hands loosely in his own. "I have different dreams now."

"Which are?"

"I'll get to those in a moment. Besides, I wasn't happy at the thought of my wife driving around in that heap of rust you call a car."

"I'm not your wife."

"Ah, yes. That's the other piece of bad news. We're still married."

Her heart stopped for a moment. "What? How?"

"All my fault, I'm afraid." He didn't look the least bit apologetic. In fact, she'd bet he was enjoying her outrage. "I couldn't live a lie any longer."

"What lie? Adam, what is this?"

"Sam gave me a copy of the judgment from our annulment hearing. Turns out the judge considered two key factors in deciding to grant it. First, we hadn't intended to get married. And second, we hadn't—"

"Consummated the marriage," she finished for him. "Oh, no."

"That's not a particularly flattering reference to our consummation," he said.

"So this is about your ego? You didn't want it on public record that you hadn't slept with your wife?"

He tightened his grip on her hands. "It wasn't public record," he said. "The judgment was sealed. I petitioned the court to revoke the annulment because I couldn't bring myself to deny the best night of my life."

"The best?" Casey swallowed.

He nodded. "Sam argued the case at the county court, and he called me earlier tonight to say the judge revoked the annulment."

"So now what? We get divorced?"

"Now, I tell you my new dream. Which is to spend the rest of my life being distracted, provoked and seduced by you."

"You asked me to marry you once before, Adam, and I told you no."

"But this time I'm laying down some strict conditions," he said.

"Oh, are you?" Indignation colored her tone.

"You might think it's okay to be fond of your husband, but I'm settling for nothing less than mutual adoration." He lifted her fingers to his lips and kissed them.

The reminder of the day they'd first met, when he'd told her she might never find a man who adored her, brought a lump to her throat. Casey gazed into his eyes, and saw all she needed to know about how he felt toward her.

"Adoration? That's a lot to ask," she said thought-fully. "You could wait a long time for a woman who adores you, Adam. You might never find one."

"I'll wait," he said.

"But what about your father's will? What about that baby you want to have, to secure the business?"

"That's all over," he said. "Soon after you left, Anna May backed down from her lawsuit. Turned out Henry didn't really want to run the company. He wants to coach high school tennis and still pick up a fat dividend from the business every so often. I said that can be arranged."

"That's great."

"Anna May figured all this out after you gave her a lecture about wanting what's best for the people you love," Adam told her. "She asked Henry and he finally got up the guts to tell her what he *did* want."

He broke off as another couple stepped out on the porch. A loaded stare from Adam soon had them re-treating back into the ballroom. "Once Anna May dropped her opposition, Sam was able to get the marriage clause struck from Dad's will."

"So you don't need a wife," Casey said. "Or a baby."

Adam squeezed her fingers. "But I do need *you*. I need your company, your love, your faith in me, the way you inspire me to be a better person."

"What about a baby?" Casey asked. "Because if you need one of those…"

"We'll figure something out," he said carelessly.

"No!" She stood and stepped back.

He rose to join her, his face pale. "No, you won't stay with me?"

"Adam, I love you—I adore you—and I want to us to be married. But I can't promise you a baby."

"We'll figure something out," he told her again. "Maybe, if you want a child as much as I do, we could look at adopting. I know you'll be a great mom, whether it's our natural child or not. Or if you want, we can try for our own baby and decide that whatever will be, will be."

He leaned forward and kissed her gently. "I adore you, my precious, darling wife. Stay with me forever, and we'll take everything else as it comes."

Had there ever been as sweet a sensation as this? Casey almost laughed out loud with sheer joy.

"If I say no, do I still get to keep the Aston Martin?"

He chuckled. "Of course."

"Mrs. Lowe's not going to like it if I come back," she warned him. "You'd better think hard about this, Adam, because it's her or me."

"I've already sent her off into retirement with a healthy bonus," he said. "I couldn't take another day of those frosty grimaces she seems to think are smiles."

Casey giggled, then snuggled into his embrace. "I was wrong about something," she said against his chest.

Adam kissed her hair. "You, darling? Never."

She pulled away just a little. "I agreed when you said we should be selfish. I said I wanted no-strings love. But it's not true. I want to be tied to you, Adam. And I want you tied to me."

His eyes, brilliant with emotion, met hers. "Real love," he said, "comes with strings you tie yourself."

Casey's heart swelled. The man was the perfect soul mate for her. It seemed too wonderful to be true. Reluctantly, she came back to the stumbling block she couldn't believe might not prove impassable. "You're sure you don't mind if we never have our own baby? I wouldn't blame you if you did."

He paused. "Of course I want you to have my child. But Casey, you are the only woman for me, baby or no baby."

She planted a kiss on his chin. "And what about—?"

"Enough," he ordered. "You can make as many objections as you like, but I'm not going to change my mind. I adore you, you're my wife and we have the rest of our lives to argue over the details. Now, are you coming back to me or not?"

"Of course I am."

The kiss that followed lasted a very long time. When they parted, Adam's eyes were dark with desire.

"You're quite sure we're still married?" Casey asked.

"Positive."

She held out her hand to him. "Then I know just what I want to do next."

They pushed through the throng, hand in hand, single-minded in their determination to reach one of Eloise's many bedrooms. But Casey stopped dead when she heard "All You Need Is Love" playing tinnily from the vicinity of Adam's pocket.

She turned to grab him by the lapels. "What," she demanded, "is that?"

Sheepishly, Adam pulled out his cell phone. "Personalized ring tone," he said. "It's affirming."

Casey took it from him, pressed the off button, then slipped the phone back into his pocket. On tiptoe, she pressed her lips to her husband's. "Stick with me," she said, "and I'll give you all the affirmation you'll ever need."

EPILOGUE

"SHE LOOKS NOTHING LIKE her cousin." Casey placed their beautiful daughter back in her crib and tucked the blankets around her tiny body.

"She's way more beautiful." Adam leaned forward to get another good look at his second-best girl. "This one takes after her mom."

"She's very noisy," Casey agreed with a grin. "And she likes fast cars."

"And she's worth any amount of effort," Adam said, conscious that most of the effort had been Casey's. She'd had to have the surgery to repair her damaged fallopian tubes twice before it worked. But for the rest of their lives, Adam would do whatever it took to cherish his family. Casey nodded, tears glistening in her eyes. She always insisted her out-of-kilter hormones were responsible for her easy tears, but Adam knew his sensitive wife better than that.

He continued to list the similarities between his daughter and his wife. "And she's gorgeous, sweet-natured, intelligent—"

"She's six weeks old! You have no idea how intelligent she is. And she was three weeks late," Casey grumbled. "She's going to have to improve her timing."

"Takes after her grandmother," Adam said, and dodged the swat Casey aimed at him. "Speaking of her, what time are Eloise and Sam due?"

Casey looked at her watch. "Right about now."

"Good, that gives us at least half an hour. Ever since they got married, Sam's been as hopeless as Eloise at getting anywhere on time."

"Half an hour for what? Oh!" Casey squealed as Adam swung her up into his arms and carried her along the hallway to their bedroom. He staggered slightly and she said, "I still weigh a ton from having your baby, don't I? Admit it."

"Never," he said through gritted teeth. He deposited her on the bed, then pulled off his T-shirt and lay down beside her, propped up on one elbow. With his free hand, he began to unbutton her shirt.

Casey felt the heat between them, so familiar yet still untamed. She tugged Adam's head down to hers.

"Are you sure you're ready for this?" he said, an inch from her lips. "Because if I kiss you now, there'll be no stopping me."

Thrilled at the thought, she brushed the briefest, teasing kiss across his mouth, so that he groaned when she pulled away. "The Adam Carmichael I married prided himself on always staying in control." She ran a tantalizing hand down his bare chest.

In a movement so swift it startled Casey, he straddled her. His strong hands pinned hers to the pillow and he covered her mouth with a kiss so hungry, so tender, so loving, that she seriously considered never leaving this bed again.

"In that case," he said, "I must apologize for the total loss of control you're about to experience."

With a sigh of satisfaction Casey gave herself up to his demanding caress. "Apology accepted," she murmured.

* * * * *

*Harlequin Superromance is emotional,
exciting and unexpected!*

*Enjoy a sneak preview of
PICTURE-PERFECT MOM by Debra Salonen
on sale from Harlequin Superromance in
May 2009!*

Welcome to Sentinel Pass! This town hasn't been the same since Hollywood descended. Overnight it's gone from a sleepy, quiet village to a bustling place filled with, well, interesting characters, as actors and producers mingle with the residents.

The changes are almost more than single father Mac McGannon can take. He has his hands full learning how to be both mom and dad to his little girl, Megan. The last thing he needs right now is to meet someone who could make him want to fall in love....

"DADDY," a small, sweet voice chirped.

Mac McGannon turned at the sound and opened his arms to the four-year-old—almost five—racing toward him through the crowds of people at this barbecue celebrating the rebirth of Sentinel Pass as a TV show. "Hey, sweetness, I was just looking for you. Where have you been?" He swept her up in his arms.

"Over there with my friends." Megan pointed to the group of kids playing on the other side of the cordoned-off street. She hugged him, then pulled away slightly to whisper, "Can we go meet the beautiful princess, Daddy? I think she might be Snow White."

Mac froze. Without turning around, he knew exactly who Megan meant. The dark-haired woman he'd been staring at earlier. *Pretty as a princess* didn't do her justice. Spectacular. Cover-model material. Hell, she'd probably graced every major magazine in the country. He wouldn't know. He was a miner who usually had his head underground.

Still, who was he to turn down an opportunity to meet someone so gorgeous?

"Okay, girlie-girl, we can be social." He put Megan on her feet. "Do you know her name?"

"She's Aunt Libby, Daddy."

"Huh?" Was Megan missing her mother so much she imagined every woman was a relative? Was this yet another thing he needed to worry about on top of learning to cook meals and tie hair bows?

"In the TV show," Megan explained patiently. "She's going to be playing Aunt Libby."

Mac looked at the stunning woman wearing the wide-brim hat and fashionable sundress. A mix of Jackie O and J. Lo. And yes, now that he looked closely, he realized she did resemble the publicity shots he'd seen of the actors signed on to play fictional versions of the real people in Sentinel Pass.

Mac wasn't all that thrilled to have Hollywood in his town. But they wanted to be here badly. Apparently a TV series about small-town intrigues and larger-than-life characters had "hit" written all over it.

So did he really want to make nice with an actress?

Before he could decide whether or not to intrude on her, his daughter tugged on his hand. "Come on, Daddy. Let's go before she disappears."

He was pretty sure the actress wasn't going anywhere. Not when she had adoring fans surrounding her. Didn't those actor types thrive on the attention? "Okay, honey, lead the way."

Despite his cynical thoughts, he couldn't help smiling as he followed his beautiful, brilliant, delightful daughter through the crowd. He acknowledged several familiar faces with a nod and a wave. Without much effort, Megan slipped out of his grasp and raced ahead through the crowd.

"Meggie...hold up," he called as she plowed through the outer ring of bodies grouped around the woman who seemed out of place on Sentinel Pass's Main Street. Mac didn't know why his heart rate started to speed up as he neared the crowd. He knew most of these people. Nothing to be nervous about.

"Hi. Hi," Megan chirped, hopping up and down with her hand in the air just as Mac caught up with her.

The woman turned toward them, her head tilting slightly so the brim of her hat dipped down, blocking Mac's line of sight to her face. "Hello, there. My name's Morgana. What's yours?"

Morgana. Another M name. His life was littered with them.

Megan stepped closer. "I'm Megan. You're my auntie. Sorta."

The woman's chin popped up and suddenly she was looking straight into Mac's eyes. His heart, which wasn't acting normal to begin with, lurched sideways in his chest, making his throat close up. His explanation was lost as he stared into her rich golden-brown eyes—color he'd mine forever if he ran across it in a vein of rock.

"She's Libby's niece," one of Mac's neighbors explained to the actress. "Isn't she a beauty? And this is her daddy, Mac McGannon."

Mac was so confused by his reaction to Morgana he couldn't acknowledge the introduction.

"Libby's brother? The miner?" Morgana's face lit up with what Mac would have sworn was honest delight. "I love your character in the show. Dark and tortured. It's wonderful to finally get to meet you."

Even if Mac had been able to speak, he had no idea how to reply to something like that. Was dark and tortured a good thing? Somehow he didn't think it was. So he did what he usually did when faced with awkward situations. He kept his mouth closed.

But if he'd ever wished for the ability to charm with a few simple words, now was the time.

* * * * *

What's coming next in the script for
Mac and Morgana?

Be sure to look for PICTURE-PERFECT MOM
by Debra Salonen,
on sale May 2009
only from Harlequin Superromance.

Six new heartwarming romances are available
every month wherever books are sold, including
most bookstores, supermarkets, discount stores
and drugstores.

Share the joy
of love and romance!

Married by Mistake is a heartwarming love story, suitable for sharing with friends, family, book club members or anyone you think would enjoy a romantic read!

Here are some ideas
for sharing books:

◆ Give to your sister, daughter, granddaughter, mother, friends or coworkers.

◆ Host your own book club.

◆ Share the books with members of your church group, community group or PTA.

◆ Bring them to your community center, retirement home or hospital and brighten someone's day.

OR

◆ Leave them for others to enjoy on an airplane, in a coffee shop, at the Laundromat, doctor's/dentist's office, hairdresser, spa or vacation spot.

Please tell us about your experience reading and sharing these books at

www.tellharlequin.com.

Choose the romance that suits your reading mood

Inspirational Romance

Love Inspired®
Contemporary inspirational romances with Christian characters facing the challenges of life and love in today's world.

Love Inspired® Suspense
Heart-pounding tales of suspense, romance, hope and faith.

Love Inspired® Historical
Travel back in time and experience powerful and engaging stories of romance, adventure and faith.

Choose the romance that suits your reading mood

Suspense and Paranormal

Harlequin Intrigue®
Breathtaking romantic suspense.
Crime stories that will keep you
on the edge of your seat.

Silhouette® Romantic Suspense
Heart-racing sensuality and the
promise of a sweeping romance
set against the backdrop of
suspense.

Silhouette® Nocturne™
Dark and sensual paranormal
romance reads that stretch
the boundaries of conflict and
desire, life and death.

Choose the romance that suits your reading mood

Passion

Harlequin Presents®
Intense and provocatively passionate love affairs set in glamorous international settings.

Silhouette Desire®
Rich, powerful heroes and scandalous family sagas.

Harlequin® Blaze™
Fun, flirtatious and steamy books that tell it like it is, inside and outside the bedroom.

IN STORE COUPON

HARLEQUIN®

Super Romance®

Where lives and loves are woven together to tell emotional and unforgettable stories.

On sale May 2009.

Available wherever books are sold, including most bookstores, supermarkets, drugstores and discount stores.

Save $1.00

on the purchase of
Picture-Perfect Mom
by Debra Salonen
or any other Harlequin®
Superromance® title.

Coupon expires September 30, 2009. Redeemable at participating retail outlets in the U.S. only. Limit one coupon per customer.

5 65373 00076 2 (8100)0 11604

HSRBAPCOUP

REQUEST YOUR FREE BOOKS!
2 FREE NOVELS PLUS 2 FREE GIFTS!

HARLEQUIN®

Super Romance®

Exciting, emotional, unexpected!

YES! Please send me 2 FREE Harlequin® Superromance® novels and my 2 FREE gifts (gifts are worth about $10). After receiving them, if I don't wish to receive any more books, I can return the shipping statement marked "cancel." If I don't cancel, I will receive 6 brand-new novels every month and be billed just $4.69 per book in the U.S. or $5.24 per book in Canada. That's a savings of close to 15% off the cover price! It's quite a bargain! Shipping and handling is just 50¢ per book*. I understand that accepting the 2 free books and gifts places me under no obligation to buy anything. I can always return a shipment and cancel at any time. Even if I never buy another book from Harlequin, the two free books and gifts are mine to keep forever.

135 HDN EYLG   336 HDN EYLS

Name	(PLEASE PRINT)
Address	Apt. #
City	State/Prov.	Zip/Postal Code

Signature (if under 18, a parent or guardian must sign)

Mail to the Harlequin Reader Service:
IN U.S.A.: P.O. Box 1867, Buffalo, NY 14240-1867
IN CANADA: P.O. Box 609, Fort Erie, Ontario L2A 5X3

Not valid to current subscribers of Harlequin Superromance books.

**Are you a current subscriber of Harlequin Superromance books
and want to receive the larger-print edition?
Call 1-800-873-8635 today!**

* Terms and prices subject to change without notice. Prices do not include applicable taxes. Sales tax applicable in N.Y. Canadian residents will be charged applicable provincial taxes and GST. Offer not valid in Quebec. This offer is limited to one order per household. All orders subject to approval. Credit or debit balances in a customer's account(s) may be offset by any other outstanding balance owed by or to the customer. Please allow 4 to 6 weeks for delivery. Offer available while quantities last.

Your Privacy: Harlequin is committed to protecting your privacy. Our Privacy Policy is available online at www.eHarlequin.com or upon request from the Reader Service. From time to time we make our lists of customers available to reputable third parties who may have a product or service of interest to you. If you would prefer we not share your name and address, please check here. ☐

HSR09R

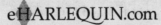

You're invited to join our Tell Harlequin Reader Panel!

By joining our new reader panel you will:

- Receive Harlequin® books—they are FREE and yours to keep with no obligation to purchase anything!
- Participate in fun online surveys
- Exchange opinions and ideas with women just like you
- Have a say in our new book ideas and help us publish the best in women's fiction

In addition, you will have a chance to win great prizes and receive special gifts! See Web site for details. Some conditions apply. Space is limited.

To join, visit us at
www.TellHarlequin.com.